James Allen

THE BUNKER

AUSTIN MACAULEY
PUBLISHERS LTD.

A CIP catalogue record for this title is available from the British Library.

ISBN 9781785545504 (Paperback)
ISBN 9781785545511 (Hardback)
ISBN 9781785545528 (E-Book)

www.austinmacauley.com

First Published (2016)
Austin Macauley Publishers Ltd.
25 Canada Square
Canary Wharf
London
E14 5LQ

CHAPTER ONE

From the moment he wakes up to find himself alone in the room, it is a shock. It is a nightly occurrence which has been going on for years, but he still has not got used to it. Then the shaking starts and it is as uncontrollable as ever. He continues to stare around the room until he gets his bearings back. 'Why do they leave me here alone? Especially her? She should know better.' Eventually his heartbeat starts to slow, as does his erratic breathing. He quickly reaches for the opened can of beer on the miniature table beside him. As he drains it, he looks over at the clock on the mantelpiece and then squints, but it is no good. He gets up and walks the three or so feet to it to find that it is 01:13. He goes to the kitchen and, after checking the locks on the back door and windows a few times, gets a fresh can of beer and opens it on his way to the front door. He stands staring at each lock for seconds before opening it and locking it again. This he does six times before going back into the sitting room. Only after making sure that the window was locked, and scanning the front garden, then the wet road outside, does he sit back in his chair and take a sip from the can while looking at the TV. 'What the hell is this?' He resists the urge to switch to the sports news channel and sits and watches the programme. When it is over, and he has returned with another can, he presses the play button on the remote control and sits back and watches the next one. Another one follows that and when that is over, he looks down at the side of his chair at the three empty beer cans. He picks up the latest one from the table and swirls the end of it a few times before finishing it off and placing it beside the other three. There should be a lot more there, but he knows that Rita had removed them quietly before going to bed. He is tempted to switch over to the sports news but knows if he did, he'd probably end up getting another can, then another, before falling asleep again. Being woken up to her frowning face and knife-edged voice first thing in the morning would not be worth it. She had warned him not to sleep in the chair again because of the kids. Finding their dad like that every morning couldn't be good for them, and they would always remember it. Not that they are kids, as such, but that doesn't matter. He reaches down and while picking them up, knocks two over and grimaces. After a few seconds, he picks the four up and goes to the kitchen and places them beside the others on the worktop. He does not even want to count how many there are so he turns, goes back, presses the standby button on the remote control and the screen flashes and goes dark. He turns off the lamp on the little table beside his chair and begins the climb upstairs. Minutes later, he is snoring. He is back in his chair at 07:42, according to the clock in the corner of the TV screen, after having his breakfast of two cups of tea in the kitchen. He opens a can and takes a good double gulp as always, just to get him started. While he is watching the scrolling line at the bottom of the screen, he remembers the programmes hours before. He searches the planner and finds them. Somehow they had been recorded but he didn't remember doing that. He is just about to put them on again when he hears Rita's phone alarm go off upstairs. He decides to wait until she is gone before watching them again, even though he can only recall snippets. She would be leaving for work within the hour. He hopes that they are as good today as they had seemed to be during the night. He watches them over and over, each show twice, before switching to the sports news for some normality. It is some hours later when he has the urge to put them back on again.

Before he does, he rummages in the kitchen drawer for something to write on and finds an A4 pad with only a few pages used. He also grabs a pen from the drawer, then begins watching them while taking notes. It is now just under twenty minutes since Pauli has walked in the door from college. Fran decides that he will need to get a second opinion, as what he is planning will most likely involve some help from his son and maybe even Matt. He takes a gulp from his can and places it back beside the lamp on the miniature imitation mahogany table beside his chair. "Pauli!" he shouts. Seconds pass, but he hears no movement. "Pauli, for fuck's sake, come 'ere, lad!" The ceiling bangs and he hears footsteps leaving the room. The stairs get taken two by two and Pauli appears at the sitting room door with his jeans fuller than normal at the front, not that Fran notices.

"Now listen, Da, I hope you have a good reason for..." he gasps, "...making me come all the way down them flippin' stairs."

"If you're gonna curse, do it properly! Don't fanny about with that cartoon talk!" Pauli inhales deeply a few times while rubbing his eyes and Fran stares at him. "Are ya alright, son?! Ya look a bit... well, out of breath. Jesus boy, if walkin' down a few poxy stairs does that to ya, then you'll have to stop halfway up for a break," he goes to pick up his can again but stops. "Why don't ya join the football team or something, get ya fit?" he glances down at the pad, puts the pen behind his ear and looks back at the TV.

"Dad!" Fran jumps and looks at him. "Dad, ya called… let me rephrase that. You shouted me name, and when I come down, you tell me how unfit I am, which I'm not! But then ya just sit back and watch the telly. I was doing something and ya interrupted me. I'm going back."

"Hold your horses there, Sundance!" Fran says, interrupting him again as he adjusts himself in the chair. "Ahh, that's better! Now look, whatever ya were doing up there, ya can do it later. Because this, and I mean, THIS, is much, much bigger than whatever ya have planned up in that room."

Pauli waits, but nothing is happening from Fran's side except a smug smile.

"What's it this time, Da?" he puts up his hands. "Don't tell me… the house is not secure enough and we need even more locks?" A smirk begins to appear on Fran's face as he looks up at him while twirling his index finger a few times, before placing it tip down on the A4 pad.

"We're gonna survive, son. I have a plan."

"Survive what?!"

"It's a really bloody good plan."

Pauli closes his eyes with a pained expression on his face. After a few seconds, he opens them.

"Dad… I don't know what you're up to this time, but we're doing fine. Considering the amount of smokes and drink that you and me mam go through, and that's not to mention," he nods at him, "'the other little table that your copy's resting on." Fran looks at the pad.

"What other little table?"

"That belly of yours!"

Fran inhales as he tries to pull it in but it only gets bigger.

"Stop doing that!"

"Doin' what?" Fran asks, holding his breath. Pauli exhales.

"Ah, I give up! Look, I'll get ya a tin and then I'm outta here."

When he leaves the room, Fran stares at the door, waiting for him to come back in. He watches the crack where the hinges are for movement, and the bottom of it for Pauli's shadow. Only when he hears the sound of water coming from the kitchen does he release his breath. Pauli comes back with a can and waits as Fran drains the end of his old one, before taking the fresh one. He opens it and takes a good swig before placing it on the table beside him. Seconds pass.

"Okay then, tell me about… surviving," he says, trying not to sound too sarcastic.

Fran picks up the A4 and slowly waves it in the air.

"This, my boy… this is the answer to everything."

"Everything?!" he snorts. "What answer? Or should I ask… the answer to what?"

"Survival, boy, survival! Us being around when everyone else is dust."

Pauli stares at him while he slowly looks around the room with a smile on his face. He can only assume that Fran is looking at imaginary dust in the air.

"So... you are going off the smokes and drink then?" Fran quickly looks back at him.

"Are you bleedin' mad?!... No!" he shakes his head while laughing falsely. "No bloody way!"

"A heavy bit of Brit came out that time, do ya know that?"

"Well, I was brought up in England, ya pillock!"

"Charming. Okay, back to this survival lark. Tell me, I'm all a quiver."

Fran raises his eyebrows.

"Don't try to be funny, son, it doesn't suit ya."

"Right then. I'll cut back on the attempt at humour, if ya tell me what's going on," he changes his voice and rubs the side of his head. "Dad, dad, daddio." On hearing and seeing this, Fran starts laughing. Pauli stands there straight-faced and when Fran opens his eyes and looks at him, it only makes him laugh more. Eventually, he laughs himself down to some chuckles.

"Ya bollox! Ya bloody know that's one of my favourite films, and you've got that off to a tee."

"Thanks, Paw," he says, before reverting back to himself. "But ya didn't shout me down the stairs to fetch ya a tin or do impressions... so go on, tell."

Fran points the remote control at the TV. "Have a look at this." Pauli watches it until Fran pauses it. "So, boy... what do ya think of that?"

"Honest opinion?"

"Of course."

"I think that there's something wrong with that chap. Who in their right mind would do press ups dressed in that much clothes with a fire extinguisher on their back? And why even bother?!"

"It's not a fire extinguisher, it's a bleedin' oxygen tank!"

"Well that's handy, because that idiot looks like he needs some."

"Hold on, hold on. I'll go to a different part."

Pauli stands there, bored stiff, while watching this programme whizz by at top speed, but it's still not fast enough for him and he yawns.

"Look, I'll be there soon!"

"Dad, that wasn't a pretend yawn just to annoy you, it was a real one."

"Oh... right then, sorry. Here we go... now!" He watches this one and it's just as weird as the last one. Fran sits back and takes a sup of beer. "So... what do ya think of that one?"

"Let me get this straight. That bloke has a big house and loads of land, and he expects people, or marauders as he calls them, to knock on his door and tell him to leave? So he's just going to say... yeah, grand, good luck, and don't forget to feed me dog? Then walk away and pretend to leave, but instead he'll sneak off and get into one of dozens of graves that he has hidden on his land, and stay in there for a few days? Then a few nights later, come back out and shoot them one by one and walk back into his house as if nothing ever happened?"

"Yeah," Fran answers, while smiling at him. "And they're called spider holes."

"If that's supposed to make the idea sound any saner, it doesn't. Believe me, it makes it sound a lot worse."

"That's what they're called in the military, son. Back in the Vietnam days."

"What happened to the good old fox's hole?"

"That's something completely different."

"Ok, whatever," he looks at the paused face on the screen for a few seconds. "He's an imbecile! Instead of living in a grave for a few days, why doesn't… Spider Dude just shoot them when he sees them coming to his house?" Fran sits up and looks at the screen for a few seconds before looking at Pauli.

"Yeah son… why doesn't he? That would be the obvious thing to do alright."

"And another thing. Did he say he was in the army for years?"

"Eh… yeah, he did." Fran replies, with no smile this time, and realising that showing that part of the programme was not a good example either.

"I'm glad it wasn't our army."

"Actually son, me too. For both our Armed Forces' sake."

"I don't know who would want to invade this shitty country. But the idea that if someone did, and all our soldiers were trained to hide in graves for days around the country before doing anything about it," he shakes his head. "Well, now that would be real Irish, wouldn't it?" he looks back at the paused face. "Where's that dope from anyway? I can't make out his accent."

"He's American, I think. He does speak a bit strange alright."

"Good, they can bleedin' keep him!" Fran nods in agreement. "Right so, I'm gonna split back up… Later, Pater!" he says, beginning to turn.

"Pauli?"

"Look, Dad, if you wanna watch that stuff, ya have me blessing. But I've got an appointment with me… game."

"Fair enough, lad. Well, here's what I'm going to do, just so as ya know. I'm going to build a doomsday shelter in the back garden."

Pauli stares at him blankly before walking backwards and sitting on the couch.

"Because of this crap?" he asks, looking at the TV. "What is this crap anyway?!"

"I'll admit that it's a bit—"

"Crap!" Pauli finishes.

"Okay, son, they weren't the best. And yeah, that one was complete crap. Live in a grave for a few days?"

he starts laughing and Pauli joins in. Seconds later, the doorbell rings. "Ignore it." Fran says, reaching for his can. Pauli is already up and walks to the window.

"Ma's car is in the garden."

"Shit!" Fran says, switching to the sports channel. "She must have freewheeled down the bloody road again. Don't say anything about this, okay?"

He looks down at Fran.

"I'm not a complete idiot, Da," he leaves the room and opens the door to find his mam standing there, struggling with five plastic shopping bags. "Mam, this early?!" he turns his head. "Dad, Mam's home!"

"Is she?! She couldn't be home. Bejasus, you're right, son! Her car's in the garden!" Her eyes dart from Pauli, then towards the sitting room and back at him as she mumbles something while holding her car key in her mouth.

"I don't know what you're saying, Mam?" She tilts her head slightly while still biting on the key.

"I said. Heya Shon, I couldn't get ee keyjjs," her head gestures to the bags. "Sho I hadtch chiring the vehh," she finishes, as she brushes passed him. He thinks of offering to help. but she's already in the kitchen. He closes the door and follows her in. "Me bleeding mouth is killing me after that. Do ye even know what I said?"

"Yeah! You couldn't get your keys so ya had to ring the bell," he looks at the floor. "Eh... lots of bags, can't get keys, yet ring the bell. How, Mother?"

She picks up the kettle and walks to the sink.

"Used the oul chin of course." she replies, while filling it and moving her mouth from side to side. "Oh yeah... of course!" he says, as he starts to put the shopping away.

CHAPTER TWO

A few hours later, and the five family members are in the sitting room eating spaghetti bolognese, the ritual Tuesday night dinner, while watching a soap.

"Jasus, Rita, this bolognese is lovely!" Fran says, while chewing loudly.

"Well, Franner, there's loads more out there if ye want it. Is there enough garlic in it for ye?" she says, without taking her eyes off the TV screen.

"Perfect amount, love! And I'll have whatever's left over for me supper, once the kids are finished with it."

Emma and Pauli glance at each other as he takes a slice of batch loaf from a plate, balancing on the arm of his chair and starts putting fork loads onto it. After the fifth load, he takes another slice and places it above, gently pressing down on it as the mince sauce streams onto his fingers. He gives them a quick lick and winks at the sandwich.

"Oh… you are so bloody eaten!" he says, before going for the bite. Pauli looks away, as he's seen this many times before and it's not a pretty sight.

"Mam, I like garlic as well, but do ya not think that there's a little bit too much in this tonight?" he asks, holding up two full cloves impaled on the end of his fork. Rita looks at Fran, then back at him.

"No!"

"I think it's lovely, Ma."

"Thanks, Em."

He puts the cloves on the side of his plate, next to another three, then goes back to eating and wonders how potent he will smell in the morning. As Fran takes another bite, some pasta and sauce splatter onto his lap.

"One hundred and eighty!" Pauli says, and laughs. Fran looks down at the food, then at the three staring at him.

"How long have ye been wearing them feckin' bottoms?" Rita asks. He thinks for a moment.

"About a week or two, love."

"Put clean ones on tomorrow and I'll wash them before they walk off ye."

Pauli is laughing quietly as he winks at Fran, who is still holding his sandwich inches from his mouth. He puts it on his plate, gets a fresh slice of bread and scrapes the food from his lap onto it. After putting that on his plate as well, he takes the original sandwich and takes a bite.

"Emmet, ya little shit! Ma, look what he's fuckin' doin'!"

"Emma, don't call him that, he's only a babby."

"But Ma, the bleedin' food's all over the camp!" she puts her plate on the couch, gets up and goes to Emmet, who is sitting in his high chair wearing only a nappy.

She starts picking food up off the floor, then goes to the kitchen. When she returns, she has a plate and some kitchen towels.

"Who done that?!" The three look at each other in turn and confusion, but Rita is the first to ask.

"Done what?"

"That!" she says, pointing at Emmet. "That piece of spaghetti hanging off his ear." Pauli sniggers and she stares at him. "YOU, wasn't it?!"

"Here, don't blame me for everything that YOUR son does. I suppose if he has a crap, it's my fault, is it?"

"He wasn't wearing that a few seconds ago." Pauli picks up a piece of spaghetti, drapes it across his little finger and begins admiring it.

"I know, spaghetti these days, it's all the fashion. I wouldn't be seen dead without it," he looks up at the ceiling. "Oh, if only I had some spare cash, I'd invest in a penne or two. Maybe even some tagliatelle. That's stylish!"

"Pauli, stop trying to annoy her!" Rita says, as she looks from him to her. "Em, nobody moved. We're all sitting here watching telly."

"Eh, hello?! I'm not watching this drivel! It just happens to be on while I'm here eating," he puts his hand to his mouth and sucks the spaghetti into it. "Only pure sad types watch this form of... stuff. All they do in it is moan and complain, then get angry and moan again. I bet that most of them are just going on as normal, they don't even have to act. Sure, I can act better than that when I'm asleep! And as for you, Dad..." he snorts. "Not impressed, for flip sake!"

Fran waits until Pauli puts a forkful into his mouth before talking.

"Oh... well, maybe me and your mother were just sitting here watching the show, and a piece fell off YOUR fork and landed on Emmet's ear. Or maybe ya just threw it at him!" he says, and goes for another bite.

"Stop it, Fran." Rita says, giggling. Emma stares hard at him this time.

"I wouldn't throw food at Emmet! Jesus, what do ya think I am?"

"Well, ya put chicken bones and skin from a snack box in me schoolbag when I was in the Loreto, didn't ya? And there was me like a dope, walking around with that weird smell following me for days."

"That was just a joke! It's not my fault that it took you nearly a week to notice that they were there. You should've cleaned out your schoo..." he thinks for a moment. "Hold on, hold on! How could I have thrown spaghetti onto Emmet's ear, considering it's on the far side of his head?" he asks, looking at Fran, whose mouth betrays a slight grin but vanishes before Rita or Emma look at him.

"Now that's low, son, that's real low... even for you." he mumbles between chews.

"Even for me? What's that supposed to mean?!"

"Stop it, ye two!" Rita says, getting up. She takes the pasta from Emmet's ear and puts it in his hand. He closes his eyes, shakes his head from side to side and flings it away from him, only for it to land on the TV screen.

"I don't think he likes that piece of spaghetti." Pauli remarks, while glancing at Fran, who is trying not to laugh and pretending to watch the telly.

"Give me one of them towels, Em," Rita says, and takes the pasta off the screen. After giving it a wipe, which smudges it instead of cleaning it, she drops the towel onto the floor and sits back down. "Rewind that Fran, will ye? I missed that part. Can't even sit and watch the fuckin' show without food getting' thrown around the bleeding room!" Emma sits down as well and picks up her plate.

"I'll clean him later," she says, just as he drops a handful of pasta on the floor. "Ma, did ya see what that little bollox just did?! And he has the cheek to smile."

"Em, I'm not even looking. Leave it till the show's over."

As Emma lifts her fork to her mouth, she stops.

"Ah Pauli, there's your moth."

"I wish! She's a fu… lippin' nice looking chick."

"That she is boy, that she is." Fran adds, still tucking into his food. Rita looks at him.

"Checkin' out the youngsters now, are ye, Fran?" she looks back at the telly. "Just your style, isn't it?" He waits until he swallows.

"Excuse me! What are ya trying to say? That I'm a pervert or something?"

"No Francis, ye just said it!"

"Don't call me that!" he sits forward in the chair. "And here, speaking of liking people. Who likes the tiny baldy lad from that dancing programme?"

"He's gay!"

"So?! If I fancy that actor girl, the lesbian one… whatever her name is," he looks at Pauli. "Ya know your one with the blonde hair that's in that new film where she shows a boob, what's her name?"

"Some new film with a blonde lesbian showing a boob? Hmm… let me think. Is it the right one or the left one?"

Fran shakes his head.

"No, it's the bleedin' middle one!" he looks back at Rita. "Well then, is that okay is it?"

She looks at him.

"Oh, you're still talking about a three boobed lesbian that only shows one in some film? Most likely in your imagination. Or maybe ye had it last night in your… dream chair?!"

"It's a real film!" he looks back at Pauli. "Your man's in it. Ya know your man that was in that other film?"

Emma starts laughing.

"Sorry, Dad… don't know who ya mean."

Fran sits back in his chair and scratches his chin for a few seconds while he tries to remember, before looking back at Rita.

"Well, if I did fancy a lesbian, what would ya think of that then?"

She looks at Emma and Pauli.

"Ye can't win with him… he never gives up." Pauli decides to step in and save Fran from any more embarrassment.

"Mam, I'm the one who likes her. Dad just agreed that she is a nice looking bird. Do ya know that she's twenty-eight? She's not as young as she looks." Rita stays silent but continues to eat.

Emma gets up and wipes Emmet's face. When she sits down, she picks up her fork and stops.

"But, Ma, ya do like that little gay fella, don't ya?" Just as she opens her mouth to answer, Emmet drops his nappy onto the floor, stands up and farts. Fran has just taken a bite from his sandwich and starts laughing. He spits food onto the carpet, the coffee table, one of Pauli's runners, and the right leg of his jeans. As Pauli moves suddenly to avoid been hit by the food, his plate slides off his lap and lands face down on the carpet. Emmet sits down and laughs like a maniac as he drops his remaining pasta on the floor.

CHAPTER THREE

"Do ye want another can, Franner?!" Rita shouts from the kitchen.

"Yes, thanks, my lovely!" he replies, in an over the top Somerset accent. Seconds later, she enters the room and kisses him as she places it on his table.

"Sorry for callin' ye a perve, Hammer."

Pauli and Emma look at each other and wince.

"Ugh! Yous dirtbirds!"

She looks at Pauli. "Excuse me?!"

"What ya called Da."

"What about it? Your dad got that name when he was in the army, because he... loved a good ham sandwich. Isn't that right, love?" she asks, while biting her lip and looking back at Fran. "Ye couldn't get enough back then."

"Oh, I'd do serious damage to them... and on a regular basis." he replies, winking.

"Stop!" Emma exclaims, with a hand on each cheek. "No more, or else I'm gonna puke! I know what ya's mean... and it's even worse than what I was thinking."

Pauli looks down at his second plate of pasta for a moment and suddenly doesn't feel that hungry, then at Emma.

"Firstly, I really don't wanna know what ya were thinking," he looks at Rita, then Fran. "And if you think I'm goin' to fall for that one, you have another think coming. Do I look like I slid off the last banana boat that slid up the feckin' Liffey? Or the Thames in your case, Dad?"

As Fran was brought up in England and has only been living in Ireland about sixteen years, he still has the odd problem trying to understand certain things that he hears. He looks at Rita.

"What did he just… what does that mean?" She looks at Fran and looks just as confused as him. Considering that she's from County Monaghan and came to Dublin with Fran, she has not got a clue what Pauli is talking about.

"A banana boat?!" Rita asks.

"Don't play dumb! You know what I mean."

"Is that a speedo or something?" Emma asks.

"It sounds familiar."

"It wouldn't be a boat that carries… bananas, by any chance, would it?" Fran asks.

"Ah, forget it! All I'm saying is… if Dad's called Hammer because he supposedly used to eat a lot of ham sandwiches, then I should be known as… the Baguette!"

Rita's eyes widen. "Pauli, that's disgusting!"

"You wish!" Emma says, laughing. "Bread roll, more like!"

"I… I don't mean it like that!" he says, as his face changes colour. "I mean…" he abandons trying to explain and goes back to Rita's supposed reason for Fran's name. "Dad, that's not something I'd be going out of me way to bring up very often, if ya know what I mean?"

"I don't, son."

Rita sits down on the arm of Fran's chair, "And why not?"

"Because if I was to believe you about that reason you gave, then can you imagine it?" He puts his fork on his plate. "Ok, here's the scenario. Me Dad and two soldier buddies are out in a pub in good old Blighty back in the olden' days, when they spot three chicks. Dad decides that he'll go over and do the introductions before asking them if they want a drink," he clears his throat and changes to a not very good or well-practiced English accent. "Awight laydeeez?! Dis is Bommah, an' eez kold dat koz ekan weely fhrow a grenade! An' dis gent 'ere, iz naym'z Bulleht! An' eez kold dat koz eez a bloody weely good shottt!" Rita and Fran are trying to keep straight faces, whereas Emma is just trying to keep her laughing down so as she can hear the rest. "An' iym 'Ammar! An ya now woy iym kold dit? Dats wight, lav! Koz oy lav a guud 'am sennndwich!" Emma is gone at this stage, lying on the couch with her face squashed into a cushion. Rita and Fran are laughing away and Emmet is behind the couch.

"I'm not Australian, or a bloody Cockney, ya bollox ya!"

25

"Don't all British soldiers speak like that?" Pauli asks, feigning surprise.

"No, they bloody don't!" Fran says, through a chuckle. "At least they didn't when I was a squaddie." Rita wipes her eyes with one hand while fixing her hair with the other as she stands up.

"Pauli. I needed that laugh."

"Fair enough and glad to oblige. But alas…" he slowly looks towards the door, then bends his head downwards. "I must be going now." After a few seconds, he looks up and smiles. "Right, I'm heading to me room now so goodnight, one and all," he takes a few steps towards the door and stops. "Oh yeah, there's one more thing… I wish NOT to be disturbed, if that's not TOO much trouble." He looks around the room.

"Where's Emmet?" Emma goes to the end of the couch and after a few seconds, drags him out by his foot. His face and body are clean after a baby-wipe session and he's wearing a nappy safely locked away under a baby grow. She carries him to Pauli. After giving him a hug and a kiss, he looks at Emma.

"That's not a great smell, Em." She lifts him a bit and smells the nappy.

"It's clean. What smell?"

"It's like a mixture of… bolognese and baby wipes or something."

"Because that's what it is!"

"Well, I think he smells a bit… gone off."

"That's his normal smell!" she says, placing him back on the carpet. He scurries away on all fours and disappears behind the couch again.

"Right, well, adios folks, and remember... NO interruptions! I'm goin' up to play with me game."

"Yeah Pauli, you go up and play with your... stuff, Senor Baguette!" Emma says, with a grin.

"You're a dope!"

"Takes one to know one, breadstick!" Rita giggles and Pauli looks at Fran, who's facing the telly, but looking down at his A4 pad. He sees his belly and shoulders moving, but there's no sound.

"Yeah, whatever! Goodnight, Popeye."

"Gnnng!" Emmet mutters from behind the couch.

"Well, goodnight all." he says, and starts dancing his way to the door. Rita looks at Emma who haunches her shoulders.

"Do ye want tea before ye go?"

"No, I'm grand." he replies, running up the stairs.

"So I'll just take out your plate for ye then?!" she calls, but gets no answer. After picking it up, she walks towards the door.

"Okay, *Celebrity* is starting in a few minutes, so who wants tea?" she asks, leaving the room.

"Me, Ma, and will ya bring in a packet of salt and vinegar?"

"I will. Oh, and I got some choco biscuits."

"I'll have some as well."

"What about ye Franner?!" she calls from the kitchen. He looks towards the door.

"Well love, I know ya just got me one, but will ya bring in another just in case, and a biscuit or two? Ya did say they were chocos, didn't ya?!" he shouts back.

"I sure did! Freshly nicked from the caff today!" she yells. Minutes later, she is back with the tea, biscuits, Fran's can and Emma's crisps. Emmet is in his highchair and is destroying the immediate vicinity around it as he gnaws his way through his biscuit. Pauli comes halfway down the stairs.

"Oh yeah, before I go. I just want to let you all know that there's no need to worry anymore because… we are SAFE now!"

Fran looks at the door and seems a bit nervous. Rita glances at him, then Emma, before looking towards the door as well.

"What do ye mean, Pauli?"

"I mean, we can all sleep soundly now because Dad's building a bomb shelter or something. Night!"

"Pauli, ya bollox, ya!" Fran yells at the door.

"Payback for the spaghetti, big daddio." he says, trotting up the stairs and closing his door. Rita and Emma look at each other, then at Fran.

"What's he on about, Fran?" Rita asks. As he's looking at her and thinking of something to say, the *Celebrity* music starts and he just looks at the telly. Emmet starts rocking his chair from side to side to the beat.

CHAPTER FOUR

The sound of a donkey braying breaks the silence. Seconds later, Pauli starts to rouse and touches his phone and the braying stops. He lies there for seconds, yawning and stretching and then his belly goes weird. He quickly reaches for his phone and puts on the stopwatch just as he releases a fart. It's loud and low even though it's muffled by his quilt, and has a two tone sound to it, much like that of a ship. He clocked it at just over six seconds but he rounds it off as a solid sixer. Quarters or halves don't count. They are exempt according to the rules he and Matt made up. He wonders if he will ever beat Matt's nine seconds. Now... that was a really good one. A smelly one, but a good one. He sniggers as he recalls that day on the train a few months ago. He, Matt, and the four other passengers had to go into a different carriage because it was that bad. He smiles. 'That was a totally swee...' his eyes widen and he throws back the quilt and jumps from the bed while holding his breath.

"Too much garlic, Ma! I flippin' knew it! Too much..." he accidently inhales, "Phwoohh! Holy Jasus!" he says, running to the door. A while later, he walks into the kitchen talking on his phone. Emma is sitting at the table feeding Emmet, who is in his chair facing her.

"Nah, we're not in till eleven. One class and then lunch… I know, they could've done it so as we'd be in for ten and out for twelve and home. But no, we'll have to hang around like two limp dicks for an extra hour. On the plus side, we'll get a good long look at Becka's ti…" he notices Emma looking at him. "Today!" He puts his finger in his ear. "You're breaking up," seconds pass and he holds the phone in front of him and stares at it. "I really, REALLY hate technology," he puts it back to his ear. "Matt, go over to a window or something. Can ya hear me? Window! Matt, go to a… ah, you're back. What happened there? You're where? On the pot?! Piss off, Matt, I'm gonna have me brek."

"Oooh, a lover's tiff." Emma whispers, as she pulls a face at Emmet. He does one as well and starts blowing his breakfast out of the side of his mouth and it is going everywhere. Pauli walks towards the kitchen window.

"Look, I'll see ya at the station in thirty, okay? … Roger that, out!" He puts his phone on the counter. After checking the kettle, he places it back on the dock, then takes two slices of brown bread and puts them in the toaster. He yawns as he turns around to find Emma looking at him while holding a spoonful of cereal inches from Emmet's mouth. He is rocking his chair back and forth, and on the forth part, he's chomping at the spoon and missing it, but not by much. This boy is determined and getting closer.

"You're a dirtbird and Matt's a muckbird! Ringing ya on the jax? Phreppph!" she says, placing the spoon into Emmet's mouth. Pauli exhales, closes his eyes and his shoulders drop to a submissive slouch.

"What did I do now, Em?"

"Whatever ya did upstairs woke me up, and I don't sleep very well these days. Especially with buttocks features here," she nods at Emmet. "Waking me up in what seems like every bleedin' second minute of sleep."

"I'm sorry, Em."

"Hey, it's not your problem, so forget about it. Sure I would've been up soon anyway as... THIS," she nods at Emmet again, "was piling up the blankets so as he could climb out of the cot."

"Em..."

"I just hope ya changed your Y-fronts... or backs!" she interrupts.

"Emma, listen..."

"At least you'll be able to see Becka's ti... DAY, won't ya?!" she interrupts again, while going back to feeding Emmet. "You must think I'm thick!"

Pauli changes tact and goes on the offensive.

"Here, don't start! I suppose every time you fart it comes out as..." he clears his throat and starts humming random notes for a few seconds with his eyes shut and shoulders rocking. He ends with, "...his nappies be clean and white!" This changes her completely and she starts laughing.

"You're mad, Paul. And... not really."

"Ah, ah, the name?"

"Okay, Pauli then. But think of the highlight of your day in college, and remember where I am," she gestures to herself and then to Emmet with the spoon. "So make the most of it. Because if I had another chance, I would.

31

But if it is the highlight of your day, checking out Becka's rack, well, at least keep it out of my ear sight, okay? That's like me talkin' about Ryan's wi–"

"–Okay, okay!" he cuts in with his hands up. "Point made." The kettle knocks off and as he turns to it, the toast pops up. "Perfect." he smiles. When the tea is made and the toast buttered, he turns and stares at Emmet, who stares back. He walks over to him, unnaturally slow. Emmet keeps looking at him without blinking. When he reaches him, he bends down so as their eyes are level and stares even harder. The beginning of a grin appears on Emmet's face. Pauli then breaks into another made up song, using kitchen utensils as random lyrics while blinking rapidly as his neck and shoulders go to the beat. Emmet splits into laughter and Emma also starts, but more at Emmet's reaction. Pauli kisses him on the forehead, then turns and gets his tea and toast. "My work here is done. Where's the old man?"

"At the office." He goes to the sitting room and sits on the couch. He places a slice of toast carefully on his lap, as he doesn't want food on these jeans as well, and takes a bite from the other. After a good slurp of tea, he looks at the telly.

"Alright, Dad, no talk shows this morning?"

"I had it on, but it was the usual. Ugly people, left, centre and right. The audience weren't that great either." he replies, without looking up while writing in the pad.

"Are ya designing your bomb shelter?" He stops writing and looks at Pauli.

"Why did ya tell them, son?"

Pauli's toast stops inches from his mouth.

"Dad, it was a matter of honour! I had to get ya back for trying to frame me with the pasta." Fran starts chuckling. He leans forward. "It was you that put it there, wasn't it?" he asks, in a whisper.

After a bit of laughing, Fran looks at him. "Okay, it's a fair cop."

"Why?"

"I was bored."

"It was a good shot."

"That was the fourth attempt, the rest landed on the carpet." Pauli giggles. "Anyway, don't worry about ratting me out, son. At least now it won't be as much of a shock. I just didn't want your mother to find out until the time was right. She'll probably laugh, then say I'm mad and do that lip thing," he says, returning his eyes to the pad on his belly.

"Ah, Da, ratting is a bit strong, isn't it?"

"Ok... mimi then, is that alright for ya?"

"That'll do nicely! And I hate that lip thing as well," he takes another bite and a sup of tea. "Da, are ya watching this?" Fran looks up again.

"It's a radio station, how can I watch it?"

"I mean..."

"Just joshing with ya, son. I've entered me two competitions so work away." He gets the remote and changes to the sports news channel. A few minutes pass before he looks back at Fran, who still has his head down and is writing away.

"Dad, have you done a plan of your shelter yet?" Fran slowly raises his head with a big grin.

CHAPTER FIVE

Pauli and Matt are on the train to college. Matt watches him as he stares out the window and he seems to be in his own world. He decides to bring him back to the now and break the silence.

"Thinking of a couple of boobs, mate?" He slowly turns to face Matt.

"Actually... I forgot all about Becka."

"So, what has ya in a daze, me ould pal?" Pauli rolls his eyes slightly. Mostly in annoyance at Matt's habit of ending every sentence with, pal, mate, chum, amigo and all the rest which he can't remember right now. But suddenly curiosity takes over and he straightens up.

"Did you ever hear of a show called *Prepping for D-day*?"

"Oh, I think I may have," he sits back and cracks the knuckles on his right hand, then the left. "Would it happen to be about weirdos buying shipping containers, loads of food, stockpiling weapons and ammunition and teaching their kids how to kill squirrels, birds and plants? Then going on to show them how to skin them? Because for some reason, in their warped minds, they seem to think that they'll be able to use said items, to trade with?"

"Kill and skin a plant?" Pauli looks at Matt and wonders if he's making this part up. Then he remembers about 'Push Up Boy' and 'Spider Dude' and has second thoughts. He'll look for that episode when he gets back today, just for the laugh. But at the moment, he wants to hear whatever Matt knows, as he has definitely watched, if not the same show, a similar one.

"Plus, not to forget the ones that regularly make dinner using insects as the main ingredient," he puts his hands together over his heart, bats his eyelids and does one of his sick smiles. "For the reason of getting their loved ones, as in their partner, kids, or BOTH, used to the idea of eating them in case there is a food shortage. Do ya know that they're supposed to have loads of protein?" Pauli shakes his head negatively. "I'd rather try and eat a tyre than an insect. What about you?" He is just about to answer when Matt holds up his halt hand and he complies. "I have to say, P, mate, that I'm not entirely sure that we're on about the same programme," he adds, with a major dose of sarcasm. Pauli decides to just sit back and watch the show. Matt continues with his narrative of what Pauli now knows to be the exact same show, but ones that he hasn't seen yet. Matt starts off with a Polar Shift.

This is when, for some unknown reason, the North Pole will spin around to become the South Pole, or vice versa. And everything will go pear shaped. Next is a nuclear war, which he doesn't bother explaining because as he puts it, "even the animals know what would happen by now." His third finger gets extended and with it comes an economy collapse. Again, he doesn't know how this would happen around the whole world, but as it's pretty self-explanatory, he leaves it there. The ring finger is out now and here comes a solar flare. As Pauli has that blank look on his face, he presumes that maybe he doesn't know or has never heard of one, so he clears his throat. He begins by telling him that the sun emits solar flares regularly, and if a big one or maybe more made it to earth, that the result would be either one or many, E.M.P's, or Electro Magnetic Pulses. Pauli doesn't look too happy with the explanation of what the letters mean, as he thinks it was unnecessary. They both watched *Goldeneye* and played it on the game console many times. He would know that Pauli already knows what it means. Matt gives a "sorry, bud" and decides to push on. The pinkie finger is extended and with it comes, as he puts it, the most used reason for 'the end' with the most appearances on the programme with what must be their favourite word: pandemic. He waits before beginning, but again that blank look. Pauli is in the dark with this one as well. So he starts by telling him of the ones that he saw and how they are always about the same old thing – people with no imagination concerning their demise just wanting to walk around in hospital scrubs while wearing masks, and disinfecting everybody and everything.

As he's talking, Pauli seems to be losing interest and eventually yawns, as he is finding it that boring. Matt yawns as well. He changes hands here for number six, a super volcano. Pauli mentions that there are no volcanos in Ireland so they have nothing to worry about. Matt would normally laugh at something like that, but after the E.M.P thing, decides not to and tries to supress it. He comes at this explanation from a different angle and agrees with Pauli. But goes on to recount a couple of programmes that he saw explaining that if a volcano on the other side of the world had a massive eruption, the smoke and dust would be thrown upwards and could spread around the world blocking out the sun and would be similar to a fallout from a nuclear weapon. "According to these weirdos," he finishes. Pauli stares at him.

"Really?!"

"Well, remember the one that went off in Iceland?"

"Shit!" Matt waits for a few seconds before extending his seventh digit and decides to bring a laugh to the end of this crap. This one comes in the form of an alien invasion. As Pauli believes that we are not alone in the universe, he doesn't find it that far-fetched. When Matt is finished, Pauli continues to stare at him.

"Do ya think any of them could happen?" he realises what he has just asked.

"I mean... except the alien invasion one, of course." Double Phew! Salvaged that nicely, he thinks to himself. Matt glances at the passing countryside for a few seconds before looking back at him.

"If any were to happen, I'd be more worried about the alien invasion."

"Me, too!" He wonders if he has just thought it or said those two words out loud, but remembers that Matt was the one who said it first. "Why?"

"Why?! I'll tell ya, sonny Jim. Because if they do to us what they've supposedly been doing to cows and so forth over the years, then we'd be fucked, hombre. It would be just like Abe's World." 'Hombre, of course. How could I have forgotten that one?' Pauli thinks.

38

"Like what, Matt?"

"Ya know, animals found inside out in fields and others hanging from trees."

"Really?"

"Supposedly. But I'll tell ya this, brah… I'd hate to end up as a big Matt!" Pauli laughs and Matt joins in. Mission accomplished.

"Why did ya ask? I didn't take ya for watching stuff like that," he changes his voice to a clipped British Officer's accent. "Not your cup of tea and all that, old bean, what what?!"

"Well, I never heard of the thing until yesterday. Me Dad was watching it and called me down."

"Were ya choking the bishop?" Pauli stares in amazement.

"Is that even one of those sayings, choking the bishop? No, really, is it?! Because I thought it was choking the chicken and spanking the monkey."

"Tomayto, tomatoe, potayto, potahto."

"Right stop it, stop it right now! You ask a simple question and it ends up with poultry, plants AND the clergy. Forget I said anything, I didn't say a thing!" he folds his arms and looks out the window.

"Take a chill pill, bro." Matt watches him, then catches his eyes in the glass reflection and they quickly move elsewhere.

"Okay, dreary caks! Hurry up and twist your panties the right way round. Forget about bishops and plants and go back to prepping. Hold on… when did I mention plants?" Pauli continues to stare out the window.

"Remember… birds, squirrels and plants get skinned to trade with?"

"Fair comment. Obviously I got a bit carried away there. Ya won't get a Pfennig for a plant pelt these days, least not last time I heard." Matt sees him trying not to laugh. "Anyway, about your prepper question. Some or maybe all of that stuff could happen, but… hopefully not all around the same time." Pauli turns and he's back in the room listening.

"Go on."

"Remember what happened to the jets in *Goldeneye* with the E.M.P?"

"Yeah, they lost all power and comms and crashed."

"Exactly! If that happened, we'd go back at least… a hundred years or so. Straight back into the dark ages."

"Shite!"

"Shite indeed, my young apprentice. You'd be right at home, back in the days of yore with the pimpernel and all that stuff. But the reality of it all is this! Nearly all, if not all, vehicles would be useless. We'd either have to buy a donkey or a pushbike and I'd say they would be mad prices. If we couldn't afford to buy any of them, then we'd have to walk around everywhere like all the rest of them," he pats his stomach. "And as ya know yourself, I ain't too fond of physical exertion. Unless it's with a nice looking chick… which I don't have!"

"What about a horse?"

"Nah, P, I'll stick with our own species."

"I mean to get around on, like the donkey or a bike."

"P, I can barely afford a new pair of jocks unless me ma buys them for me or I nick Lothar's. I didn't forget about horses because that's what the rich people would have. We'd be traipsing around on the olde runners, us poor people."

"Yeah, I suppose... how much is a donkey?"

"Hold on, comrade. We're not dead yet!" Suddenly he doesn't look right.

"Matt, what's wrong?"

"I just thought... there'd be no more internet, electricity, cars or trucks, they'd be all gone or useless. And if there's no trucks, there's no more shops or," he closes his eyes for some seconds. When he opens them, he looks at Pauli. "Takeaways!" he finishes, while starting to breathe deeply.

"Matt... are you alright?"

"Why did ya bring this up, Pauli? I'm starting to get freaked out!" he says, as his face begins to turn pinkish and starts to darken. Pauli is getting worried.

"Matt... Matt, are ya okay? Your face looks... a bit weird, I mean REALLY weird!"

"Ya mean..." he inhales deeply. "It's goin' really... reddish, as in dark red?" he asks, as the corners of his mouth droop.

"Yeah! What's wrong with ya? Will I call an ambulance or something?" Matt puts his hands over his face.

"Aw yeah... yeah! Call something... call..."

"Matt… MATT!" Pauli stands up. "Matt, answer me! What's wrong with ya?!" A few of the passengers are looking their way and some stand up to get a better view. Nothing like someone needing an ambulance while on a train.

"Ke… ke." A voice comes over the speakers announcing the next station and it is their stop. The train starts to slow. Pauli looks around, then back at a sickly looking Matt.

"Ke… ke, what, Matt?"

"Ke… BAB!" he says, looking Pauli in the eye. "Ya owe me a kebab… and chips!" Pauli is dumbfounded as he looks at him, and then it sinks in.

"You dirty bastard! I thought you were…" he trails off in disbelief.

"Ya put me through that, P mate. I'd never have thought of something like that and wouldn't have got upset. That means that I'd have to go out and get me own takeout about two or three days before I'd order it, and I'd be the one delivering it… to meself!"

"But YOU watched the show and told me about it!"

"That's different. I didn't really pay any attention to it."

"Well for someone that didn't really pay any attention to it, it sounded like ya were reading it off a bleedin' page!"

"I feel better now," Matt says, in his random way of going on and starts to stretch while he stands up. "I'm okay, okay, I say! No need to worry anymore folks," he looks towards the seven standing passengers. "Just as well that wasn't a real one. Yous would've been no help! And thanks for the sympathy cards. Oh yeah, there's just one thing I want to say before I finish," he smiles at them. "Go back about your business!" he shouts and they quickly sit down.

"I can't believe ya did that, I was shitting. I thought it was for real."

"Of course ya did," he says matter of factly, while sitting down. He watches as Pauli goes into his well-known freaked out face and waits until his left eyelid starts to quiver, then explains. "Pauli... chill, dude. Let me put it this way. Both of us want to be actors, yeah?" He doesn't say a thing and looks even more freaked out as he has told Matt on more than one occasion that he doesn't like being called dude. "Look, let's say there's a part in a film for a bloke to have a heart attack. Who do ya think would get it, you or me? ... Me, of course! Because believe it or not... I practice that a lot!"

"You're an arsehole! Who in their right mind would practice... I was feeling alright until ya pulled that stunt, ya dope, ya."

"Well, here's something that will cheer ya right back up again and put some colour in your cheeks, boyo, and big style."

"And what's that, ya ponce?!"

"Becka... and her tits! The three will cheer us both up, me auld pal," he says, with a big smile and a wink.

"She has an arse as well."

"Good one, I forgot about that. Now there's four reasons to be happy." Pauli is looking at him thinking, 'you horny bastard.' Then realises that he's right. Two

43

horny bastards. Matt stands up. "Now come on man, this is our stop. Becka's boobs and arse, we're comin', girls!" The two snigger as the doors beep and open.

CHAPTER SIX

Mister Murphy must have been lurking about on the train somewhere listening to the boys and paying close attention to what Matt had been saying, because what could go wrong, did. When they got into class, there was no sign of Becka, or her boobs. They were hoping that she was just running late, but when the end of first class came, they realised that their eye candy, and boob candy, were not going to happen that day.

The class was weird and had that feeling to it that they couldn't quite put their fingers on, especially with Miss McCabe doing a Paul Daniels every few minutes. They made their way over to the garage with glum faces and pulled up joint eighth in the queue. Through the months since they started college, they had seen many a sight of people racing from it at lunchtime in the direction of the garage, and literally as the crow, or any other bird, flies. Not bothering to use the proper entrances or footpaths like normal humans, but instead, running across the grass. Then on reaching the small gap in the hedge, pushing and shoving each other out of the way, so as to be the first to get through it and then to the garage. One particular fellow did attempt to vault the hedge and... sort of made it, as he did land on the footpath on the far side. It was as he was sailing over it, with his arms spread like a bird and a big smile on his face, that his lace caught a twig. The foot he should have put on the pavement was a little slow in arriving after being pulled from his runner, and never made it on time. So while his runner dangled from the top of the hedge, he lay on the pavement with two broken toes and a broken elbow. Pauli had nearly been turned off his baguette after seeing the contorted, crying mess lying there. But after entering the garage, the smell of spicy chicken soon gave him back his appetite and he soldiered on and ate it. When they were passing him on the way back, they could hear the ambulance in the distance and the poor guy was crying like a baby. They sat at their spot and while having their lunch, had a discussion over what they had witnessed. They came to the conclusion that either he was a complete idiot or just another starving bastard. Matt laughingly added that, "He won't be pullin' any stunts like that in the near future." Some spicy chicken fell out of Pauli's mouth as he laughed as well.

Then there was the latest incident a few weeks before, when the charge of the baguette brigade saw the usual simpletons running hell for leather across the grass towards the garage. It was a lovely sunny day, but a rain shower had just stopped minutes before, and some people must have forgotten how good a grip you get on wet grass. This time it was three girls racing each other to the hedge, all screaming and laughing as they ran that got the boys attention. The one in the lead must have thought she was in the Olympics. As her style of running was the open hands up to the face routine with her chin out, back straight, while taking long strides and leaving the other two for dust. But she must have forgotten or mislaid her spiked shoes that day. The boys looked at each other and grinned because they knew the exact spot where it was going to happen. She had to slow down just before the hedge, as the ground rose, and her slipper type shoes or whatever they were, just could not get any traction. So her feet slipped this way and spun that way as she twirled in mid-air before hitting the grass hard, and sliding downwards on her back towards her oncoming friends. The back of her was streaked in mud from the slide and the lads thought that she had got off very lightly. If she had landed face down, she probably would have broken her nose or lost some teeth, or both. With the two agreeing that she was not in the model department concerning her looks, it would have been a horrible price to pay, just to be the first of the three to order a chicken baguette.

They had another laugh that day over lunch. Today, the two pull up at their spot beside a tree across from the garage. No matter how many students are sitting on the grass, they always have it to themselves. Some of the students, after getting their lunch, would normally go back inside the college to eat it with others in the canteen. The rest would take to the campus's grass, especially on the nice days. But no one ever sat at this tree anymore, and here's why. A few weeks after they had started college, the boys were at Matt's one night for a drink. It was supposed to have been, "Just a few nightcaps while playing the game and then off to bed like good citizens" as Matt had put it, but it didn't quite happen like that. Lothar, Matt's older brother, who goes to a college for the deaf and dumb, arrived home in a taxi just after half ten. He came up to the room, signed Matt, who jumped off the bed and ran out the door and down the stairs after him. Since not a word had been said, Pauli decided to just stay where he was and get the rundown from Matt when he came back. When he did come back, he was carrying two slabs of booze and Lothar was carrying another two.

They put them on the floor and signed for a bit before Matt turned to Pauli.

"Ok, here's the skinny. Loth won a raffle today in college and had his pick of five slabs of booze. He shared one with the lads, the stout is for me Da, the beer is for me Ma, and the lager is for yours truly. What a brother!" he said, with his arm outstretched towards Lothar, who laughed at what Matt had just said.

"That's some college where you can win booze."

"That's what Loth said. Well, ya know what I mean. The last slab is for him and his bird, when he goes to Kilbeggan to see her at the weekend for a bit of the old… how's yer father." Lothar laughed again, signed Matt and then came over to Pauli, patted him on the shoulder, then gave him the thumbs up while grinning. Pauli gave the thumbs up as well and as quick as he came in the door, he was gone.

"Is he not coming back for a few?"

"Nah. He had a few with the lads, so he's gonna have some dinner and then split to bed. He's bolloxed tired. So… what do ya think of having a few more, P?"

"Well, I have to say, that sniper's really getting on my nerves. I would like one of us to take him out soon so as we can get past that building. And…" he looked at the unopened slab on the floor. "Them honeys wouldn't hurt in the least… not one little bit!" Matt ripped open a hole in the plastic and took out two six packs.

"There ya go, buddy! Now let's go get that fuckin' sniper!"

The two fell asleep just before four thirty. When Pauli woke up to have a wee, he was lying on Matt's bed. Matt's feet were on the bed but the rest of him was on the floor. He looked at his watch but no matter what he tried, all he could see was a blur. So he decided to go down to the kitchen, as there was a huge clock on the wall. When he staggered in, Maria, Matt's mother, nearly jumped out of her pyjamas.

"I thought you two were long gone!"

Pauli was just about to say hello, when the clock caught his eye and he ran out of the kitchen and fell up the stairs, twice.

The two had not got time for a wee, never mind a cup of tea, so they ran, and that's being generous, to the station and barely got the train. They built up a nice sweat on the run and were still wearing the previous day's clothes, with not a wash in sight. Pauli had commented that Matt smelt like floor, and he responded that he was just happy that he didn't smell like poo. Pauli still needed to have a wee, so he went up to the toilet and came straight back out. The state of it would haunt him for days.

At the break after first class, they made their way towards the garage. Pauli sat Matt against a tree in the campus grounds, across from the garage, and told him to stay there. He was worrying about trying to get himself across the road in one piece, never mind the two of them. So he left him there and made his way to the garage. He ordered two spicy chicken baguettes, four teas and two bottles of Cola. That should sober them up.

After walking out the door with the food and drink, the first thing he heard was shouting. He looked across the road to see some students standing looking at something, and it just happened to be Matt. He was walking around the tree, waving his schlong about as he pissed on the grass, while shouting.

"I've maked... marked this, thisk... spot! And don't forget that its mind... mine! Do ya's hear me?! Ya's pack of fuckers!"

Pauli got over there double time, and in the process nearly got hit by a scooter. He eventually persuaded Matt to holster it and then realised that he didn't have any food or drink. He sat Matt well away from the tree, and after making him promise not to do anything weirder, went back to the garage. He found the stuff on the ground. Some students who had seen everything were laughing and just waited there for him to come back. It seems on that day, it was their turn for the curse of the garage. He picked up the bottles, then kicked one of the baguettes against a petrol pump and stood on what was left of the other one on his way back to Matt. Then he remembered putting the tray of tea and the rest of the stuff on the boot of a car. The fucking thing must have driven off and then everything hit the floor. After that day, the tree was always free.

They are sitting there as normal today, when Matt rips apart the wrapper on his baguette, takes a horse's bite from it and then decides to try and speak.

"Matt," Pauli says, as he looks away "Would you not have said something before ya started to eat?"

Matt mumbles while trying to chew.

"First, I can't make out what you're trying to say. And second, I'm not looking back at ya if ya keep eating like a savage." When he swallows, he begins again.

"Okay P, back to normal. I just had to get that out of the way." Pauli turns back and faces him.

"What? A quarter of your roll you just had to get out of the way in one bite?"

"Starving, man. Look… do ya not think that it's a bit weird today?"

"Yeah, I do actually. There's no Becka, and McCabe's in and out of the room like she's doing it for a bet."

"Don't mind McCabe, she's probably training for something."

Pauli stops mid-bite.

"By walking in and out of a door?! Oh, hold on, you're right. I heard that they're going to add that as an Olympic sport." Matt goes to take another horse's bite but sees Pauli still looking at him, so takes a nibble instead. "Jesus Matt, from one extreme to another. Will ya just eat the fuckin' thing like a normal person, will ya?" When the rolls are gone and the two are sloshing around the end of their drinks in the bottles, Matt clicks his fingers.

"I have it! She probably went out on the piss last night." Pauli looks at him. "Becka, not McCabe. Something like this happened a few weeks ago, do ya remember?"

"Eh… no, I don't! How can you remember when Becka missed a day?"

Matt's eyes look to the side for a moment, then back at Pauli. "I don't wanna know," he says, raising his hand.

"Jesus, Matt… okay, I sort of do want to know. Every day?"

"And the rest! It's all I get at the moment so I have to make the most of it. A feel is a feel, buddy."

"Yeah, and I think that she might be getting a bit suspicious with you bumping into her all the time and touching her arse."

"Nah, that's fair game… and I just say I was pushed."

"Matt, you're always on your own when it happens."

"Well, I don't think she minds. Because when I say I'm sorry, she always says that it's okay, but just to watch where I'm going. And she says it with a smile."

"Really?!"

"Yeah, but that's my trick. If ya want a feel, you'll have to think up something different, sorry, pal."

"Yeah, I'll walk up to her tomorrow and ask, is it alright if I put me hand on her arse, as there's no one to push me into her."

Matt would normally find something like that funny. Not laugh yourself to death funny, but at least a giggle, maybe even a falsey, but there is nothing. Pauli is thinking that either he's up to something, or he just sharted himself, again. "What is it, Matt? What's wrong?"

"Nothin'… I'm grand," he counts to eleven and casually looks at Pauli while pretending to stretch. "So… what do ya think of your one, eh, Lucy?"

"Who?!"

"Lucy, Becka's mate."

"Ahh, the little one, Weaver? Hairstyle of the century." Matt sits forward with a grin.

"Ya know her last name!"

"Yeah, like I know everybody's name that's in our class. We've been here for months. I think I even know where some of them live, why?"

"Nothing."

"Don't tell me you're into her as well?"

"No, no, I was just asking. So… what do ya think of her?"

"Okay, Matt, I'll play along. Firstly, not much. You can't even see her face with all that hair, except for a bit of nose and some chin."

"Yeah… I know what ya mean," he looks around for a few seconds before standing up.

"Okay, I think we should head back for the second half. What do ya say, bro?"

Pauli doesn't reply and stays where he is. He looks up at Matt, who for some reason, keeps looking around and won't make eye contact. Whatever has just been said is not normal speak, and he never keeps an eye on the time. There is something strange going on, and whatever he was thinking before lunch, Matt has just confirmed it right now. This is a weird day.

CHAPTER SEVEN

Rita opens the front door just after four thirty and walks straight into the kitchen. After throwing the food, her jacket, keys and handbag onto the worktop, she puts the kettle on and preps a cup for tea. She goes into the sitting room to find the TV muted and Fran in his chair, pen in hand and pad on belly.

"Hello love, you're home…" he looks at the clock on the TV screen. "Early."

"Ah, it was mental most of the day but then it just died. So Nuala let me and Sophie go," she says, walking back towards the door, stopping to give him a peck on the cheek and continuing out to the kitchen. "Can, Sarge?!" she calls.

"Yes please, love." When she comes back, she places it on the little table beside his chair and continues over to the couch and takes out a smoke.

"Do ye want one?"

"No thanks, love."

After lighting and taking a pull from it, then a sip of tea, she looks at the TV. He bends his head slightly, but watches her from under his eyebrows, waiting. He knows that it won't be long now. Rita has known about this trick of Fran's for a long time now, and even though he thinks she can't see him looking at her, she can. She sits in silence with her tea and smoke while watching the muted sports news. After noticing him blink a few times, she turns to look at him.

"Why is the telly muted?"

"Well... I was doin' some calculations."

"Say that again."

"Calculations."

"Where did ye find that word... Em's dictionary?"

"I've plenty more where that came from."

She breaks eye contact and picks up the remote, unmutes the TV and changes the station. Fran goes back to his pad and minutes pass.

"That shitebag settled on 4,535 and had 75,000 in his box. I'm delighted! I didn't like the look of him... too feckin' smug," she drinks the end of her cold tea and looks back at him. "Calculations for what?" He looks up. Honesty is the best policy, and it will be over quicker, touch wood.

"Well love... I was thinking of building a bit of a shelter." As he knew she would, she does that thing with her lips when she's trying not to laugh. But he's prepared and is not having any of it. There is going to be no lip biting nonsense in this house today, no sir! Every time she does it, he knows that she thinks she is the cheese. Plus, it makes him feel like an idiot.

"Ohh, is this what Pauli was on about last night?" He sits up and puts his pen behind his ear but it falls off, hits his shoulder and disappears past the arm of the chair on its way to the floor. He looks over at her and she almost looks happy. He reaches down for it and while his hand searches the carpet, he feels his face redden. Real smooth Fran… real fucking smooth.

"A shelter for what?" He keeps searching for the pen. "Fran, stop doing that. A shelter for what?"

"A shelter… just in case something were to happen." he replies, while sitting back in his chair and looking out the window, trying to think of how he can explain to her what…

"Fran!" she yells.

He jumps.

"Sorry, love. I was just eh… thinking."

"What are ye on?" He stares at her with a blank look on his face. "Fran, I feel like a fuckin' parrot because I've never said your name this much before. Did ye take extra meds?"

"No… why?"

"Because ye keep goin' into these dazes when I ask ye something and you're acting weird. Maybe ye should go off the drink for a bit." He clears his throat.

"I'm going to build a survival shelter. Or as I like to call it… a bunker!"

"That's it! I'm getting those stations chopped. We'll go back to the basic package and save a few bob." He glances over the side and spots the end of his pen sticking out from under the table. He picks it up and firmly places it behind his ear.

"Well, excuse me for worrying about the safety of this family, and our future survival from anything Mother Nature or anything else has to throw at us."

She looks at him in silence which gets too much for him, so he checks his cans, and finding the one she gave him nearly empty, decides to take it with him. She purposely waits until she hears him in the kitchen.

"Fran, love?!"

Seconds later, he pops his head around the door. "Now don't tell me... ya want another brew?"

"Okay, I won't... but I do, my hunk of a man. And take your empties out, there's a good chap. Oh, and I'll have two biscuits, please." He picks up the cans and her cup and goes back to the kitchen. When he returns, he hands her the tea and a side plate with three chocolate biscuits, two covered with cheese and onion crisps and the rest spread around the side of it. This is his idea of fine dining. He removes a can from a pocket in his wine flannel tracksuit bottoms and sits back into his chair, picks up his pad and retrieves the pen from his ear. He watches her dunk a biscuit into her tea without taking her eyes off the telly and is convinced that she can see through her ears as well. He decides to leave it until the show is over before talking to her, but can only wait for a few minutes before enthusiasm gets the better of him.

"Love?" he says sheepishly.

"Hmm?" she murmers, still watching the telly.

"I need ya to start bringing home more food." Up until that moment, he had never seen a human head turn as quick as hers did from the TV to him.

"More food?! I'm fuckin' fleecing the place as it is! Steaks, chops, sausages, goujons. Then the bleedin' duck breasts a few weeks ago, even though they were like rubber. I'm taking bleedin' loads of food, not to mention a few bob here and there, and ye want more?! I'm lucky that the boss works up in the restaurant in Cavan, or there'd be nothing to bring home. I... actually, hold on. Why more food?"

"To store it up," he thinks for a moment. "In case there's a... food drought." She closes her eyes, shakes her head and a sound comes from her mouth.

"A food drought? Ah," she shakes her head again. "I've heard it all now. Is your real name Fran Laurel?" she raises her voice. "Really, is it? A food drought... a fuckin' food drought?!" she yells, as she gets up and leaves the room. In the kitchen, he hears her growl loudly. When he hears more tea being made and the lighter click, only then does he start to relax. Well, at least things are not getting thrown through the windows again. He hates it when she is like this because it makes him feel nervous. Dumb move, Francis... but it had to be done. She remains in the kitchen for the duration of her tea and smoke before coming back into the room and placing a can on his table.

"There ye go, love," she says, as if nothing happened. After sitting back down, she looks at him and she has that mad look in her eyes, but he doesn't feel nervous anymore. While looking at her, he wonders why he finds her even more attractive when she is like this. Maybe thirteen years in the army will do that to you. But whatever the reason, he knows that what happened a few minutes ago was only a warm up. The real onslaught is just about to begin. "Fran… why do ye want me to bring home more food, really?"

"I'll be honest with ya, Re. In case of the… In case… the end of the world." She looks at the TV for a few seconds, then back at him.

"Fran, if the world ends, and I don't know when or how that would happen, but if it did… I don't think that a load of fried food is gonna make that much of a difference."

"But if something happens, I want us to be prepared. And that's why I want… I mean, I would like ya to bring home, now only if ya can without getting caught, a little bit more food… please."

She gets up and walks over to him, then places her hand on his forehead while looking down at him.

"Good news is, ye don't have a temperature. I need another cup of tea. Be back in a minute." When she returns and is sitting comfortably, she begins. "Right. I'll bring home more food, or I'll try. Then what?" He looks at the pad for a moment, then back at her.

"We preserve it so as it lasts for years because ya don't know how long it will last."

"What? How long the end of the world will last?"

"No, I mean if something else happens. Like… another catastrophe."

"Two big words in one day, I am impressed. So tell me, how is a few sausages and rashers going to last for years? Oh yeah, the freezer, because we'll still have electricity, won't we? But, Fran, just in case the postman doesn't make it, remind me to change to direct debit, won't ye? Because if we got cut off… now that would be a real bummer."

"Well, Re, I just happened up to that German shop today and…"

"Ye went there today?! Ye mean ye actually walked out the front door?! That's a twelve minute walk, what did ye buy?"

"Ah nothin. I went because I remembered when I went with ya a few times that they had glass jars of food."

"Fran, all shops have glass jars of food! What did ye buy?"

"As I said… nothing. I just went for a recce."

"I NEED stuff from there! Ye wouldn't even bother to ring me, would ye?" He nods slowly. "Ye just walked your skinny arse around there to stare at some jars of food? And then walk out without buying anything?! They probably think you're some sort of simpleton. You're not coming back there with me."

"Why not?"

"Ye've got some cheek, boy!" she stares at him and that mad look is gone from her eyes. It has been replaced with anger. "Here's why! Because every time I go there, it's mostly after work and there's always a smell of food off me, and when I walk past people, their heads turn."

"What's that got to do with me?"

"Here's what it has to do with ye, ye feckin' moron! If we go back there together, the staff will be saying… ahh, there's that poor simpleton who comes into stare at the food and goes off without buying anything. And there's the bleedin' cow that doesn't feed him, even though SHE always smells like food," she stares and she is far from happy. "That would've saved me a trip."

He reaches behind the chair and pulls out a jar of gherkins.

"I got these."

"I thought ye didn't buy anything."

"I didn't… except these little beauties." Her stare softens and she starts giggling.

"Fran… ye don't eat gherkins."

"I'm not a dope, I know that. But Pauli does."

"So ye walked all the way there just to pick up a jar of gherkins for Pauli?" What will ye get next time, a tray of kidney beans for Em? Tooth floss for Emmet? Now ye better not forget me, Franner. Hmmm, let me think. Oh, I know! I'll get a welding helmet and a fishing rod from ye, won't I? Just what I need."

"You have to look at the bigger picture, Re. Ya can store stuff in these for years."

"So if you're buying jars of gherkins for Pauli to eat, and I'm pretty sure you'll turn him off the feckin' things… what are ye going to put in these empty jars?"

He takes a good long swig from his can before looking her in the eye.

"Sausages!"

Her face freezes in a cross of shock and disbelief.

"And yes you've guessed it; he's made a pig's ear out of that as well. Oh I am surprised. Taxis!" She mutes the TV. "Fran, honey, I know that ye like your sausages… but is this not taking it a wee bit to the obsessive?"

"It's not just sausages, Re, it's anything! Rashers as well, can't forget them. Eh… chicken, too, once it's cooked."

"Now let me get this right? Ye want me to take home more sausages and ra…"

"No, Rita! I mean ANY food that ya can get," he blurts. "Especially canned food."

"Okay, any food, right then. But when I bring it home, you're gonna put it in empty gherkin jars… to make it last longer?"

"Yeah, but we'll put them in salty or vinegary water so as to preserve them for years… and that's the plan."

She exhales almost wearily. "Do ye want a cup of tea, love?" He picks up his can and takes two long gulps while pointing at it with the finger of his other hand. He looks excited at the idea of all this and she wonders why?

"Fran, now listen to me, won't ye? Do ye not think that going to all the trouble of me risking me arse robbing even more food, and then wasting money buying jars of unwanted food to make Pauli eat it so as we can… YE can, use the jars to preserve sausages in salty or vinegary water… well, is it not a waste of money and a load of crap?"

"But it makes perfect sense, and it makes the food last," he sits forward with his can and looks out the window. "Them poor saps out there don't know what's coming. We'll be eating the best of grub," he laughs.

"And they'll be chasing each other around hunting for cats and dogs," he sits back and looks at her. "And that reminds me… we'll have to stray that poxy cat as well."

"What?! That cat's going nowhere! And if it does go on the missing list, you're brown bread, pal!"

"Right love, your pussy's safe," he says, with a wink.

This conversation is draining Rita and she is going on the beer in a few minutes, as she needs it after this. She wonders if maybe his meds need to be changed again? But he seems happy so that can't be it. The midlife? Whatever it is she can find out a different time. As it stands now, she's going to put a finish to this rubbish for today and get a beer.

"Look, if ye want sausages in a jar, then the next time you're up there ye should open your eyes, because they sell them. In jars!"

"Really?" he asks in amazement, while sitting up.

"Yeah yeah, real sausages in jars. Ready made for the end of the world. They're called hot dogs, Fran!" He opens his pad and after searching a page, crosses something out. He looks back at her.

"Right then, love. That's what we'll do then. We'll get plenty of them and other tinned stuff. Ya don't have to nick any more food than ya do at the moment. At least that way you'll be safe and you're arse won't be getting risked."

"Thanks, love, you're very considerate," she says, rolling her eyes. After a few seconds she gets up and walks out of the room. "Do ye fancy a sandwich?" she calls, from the kitchen.

"Ya know what, love? I feel like skin and bone. What are ya having?"

"Crumbed ham, cheese, coleslaw and cucumber!"

"I'll have ham, cheese and some potato salad!"

"I don't have any potato salad!"

"Ya just said ya did!"

"No I didn't! I said coleslaw!"

"Aw, potato salad would've been a bit of alright!"

"Fran, I don't have potato salad... I said bleedin' coleslaw!"

"Fair enough then, I'll have everything but the cucumber!" She goes to the fridge and takes out three bottles of beer and opens one. She drains it in two goes and smiles. She makes the sandwiches but does hers last. When she gets to the cucumber, she stares at it, glances at her bag and decides not today. She brings in his sandwich, fine dining style of course. With prawn cocktail crisps, his favourite, around the edge of the plate, plus two cans.

"There ya go, love." she says, before kissing him on the cheek and leaving.

"Ah thanks, Re. You're one in a billion!" he calls after her. When she gets back to the counter, she looks at the cucumber again and quickly puts it in her bag. She feels a smidgen of guilt but then tells herself that it's not like she's with another man. At the thought, her stomach turns. When, or if, Fran ever gets it back together, that is what she'll wait for. Suddenly the bag doesn't seem that bad. After picking it, the beers and the sandwich up, she leaves the kitchen and stops outside the sitting room door.

"Fran, just going up for a wee bit of a lie down. Won't ye call me before the soaps start?"

"I will, love. Go up and relax and I'll shout ya before they begin." She takes the stairs.

CHAPTER EIGHT

The next morning, Rita enters the kitchen to find Fran sitting at the table with his pad, pen, and a calculator. There are also two cups of tea, one of which he moves across the table as he looks at her and smiles.

"There ya go, love."

After glancing at the clock, she looks back at his still smiling face, then down at the pad which he immediately covers with both hands. After a few seconds, he slowly withdraws them to reveal a page. She cocks her head slightly and squints while trying to read it but gives up after a few seconds. It is way too early for this and her eyes are not fully awake yet, so she sits down on the chair opposite him. She removes a cigarette box from a pocket on her housecoat, takes one out and slides the box across the table to him. He clears his throat. "Eh... no thanks love, just had one." After lighting her own, she takes a sup of tea and places the cup slowly back on the table. She is watching him and that smile is still on his face.

"Okay... well, thanks for the tea. Second, I haven't got a clue what's on that pad and third, it's 5:07. Why or even how are ye up this early?" He is just about to speak but she raises her hand. "There's a four, but I'll get to that in a minute." she gestures for him to start.

"Well, firstly I heard ya mouching around upstairs, so I made ya a brew and you're welcome. Four, I couldn't sleep. Two, I got a few ideas so I came down to put them on paper," he clears his throat. "So... what's your four?"

"Ye forgot your three." she says, before taking a sip of tea.

"I don't really have a three, I just thought it sounded good. Your turn."

"My turn is... what is all this? What's going on, Fran? I think at 49, you're a wee bit old for a midlife crisis. But if that's the case," she rests her chin on her hand and looks at the ceiling for a few seconds before resuming eye contact. "Well, the usual is what... a motorbike? Sports car? Or even... the younger woman? Now I suppose they're the first things that someone normal would think of. But no... not my fella. When he's going through the change, he decides to buy unwanted jars of food and make someone else eat it, and then," she rolls her eyes. "I don't believe I'm goin' to say this," she takes a quick pull of her smoke. "Fill them with sausages to preserve them in case... In case, there's a fuckin' food drought?" Fran sits there looking at her and stays quiet. Suddenly, she grabs each side of her head and stares as if remembering something. "Lamb of Jasus! I thought this part was a dream."

"What part, love?" She smiles, giggles and slowly starts to laugh. Just then, Pauli walks in and looks at her for a few seconds, then at Fran and nods his head back at her.

"Must've been some joke, Dad."

"She's still laughing at that squaddie thing ya done," he lies, as he hunches his shoulders and pulls a confused face. He doesn't know what she finds so funny.

She comes back down to a giggle and eventually stops while wiping her eyes and looks at the two faces staring at her.

"What's so funny, Mam?"

"There's the bomb shelter or whatever, isn't there? Ye said yesterday that ye are going to build a bomb shelter or something, didn't ye?" Pauli looks at Fran, then back at Rita.

"So you're in?!"

"Aw no, Pauli! Not ye as well?!" He starts to say something but stops. Just then, a thud comes from upstairs and the three look at the ceiling.

"I guess Emmet's awake." he says wryly. Muffled screams can be heard.

"Emmet, ya little bollox ya! I'll fuckin'… no ya don't. Ya little fu… Aarrgh! Biting now, are ya?! Well ya can't stay under there forever! Ouch! Ma… MA!"

"What, love?!" Rita shouts back.

"Will ya bring up the brush?!" She takes a sup of tea and shakes her head slowly as she puts the cup down.

"Ye know what? I'm the only sane person in this house. Excuse me while I bring up the sweeping brush so that your daughter can get her son out from under her bed," she stands and looks at the clock. "It's not even half five yet. This is gonna be some day," she goes and

68

gets the brush. While leaving the kitchen with her lips distorted in a weird smile, she looks up at the ceiling. "I'm coming, love!"

CHAPTER NINE

Shortly after, Rita walks into the sitting room with two teas and places one on Fran's table and sits herself down on the couch. She looks at the sports news, then at Fran who is engrossed in it.

"Well, did they win or what?"

"Don't know yet, nothing's come up."

"There is such a thing called the text, Fran. Ye could chec…" His palm shoots up facing her.

"Hold!" he reads the scrolling line at the bottom of the telly. "Yes! My beauties, get in!" After closing his eyes, he slowly lays his head back against the chair with a huge grin. She decides to let him enjoy the moment and wait until he's ready to return to normal in his own time.

He eventually looks at her. "Heh… welcome back. Right, what's going on with ye? Are ye having a midlife crisis? And before ye put on your little boy lost face, ye know what I'm on about and don't lie to me." He opens his mouth to speak but she's not finished. "For Jasus sake! Ye even got Pauli on board."

He squints.

"On board? I like that."

"Fran!" He jumps.

"Okay… okay, relax!" he takes a deep breath and looks at the tea, wishing now that it was a nice cold can of beer. "It all started with some Chinese characters from back in the day. A good long time ago. I mean a few hundred years or so, maybe even a couple of thousand."

She is looking at him, waiting. "Anyw… anyway, they seemed to do this sort of calendar thing. No, maybe not a calendar. Eh… I don't really. Well, I think that the stuff they wrote about has come through so far."

"Like what?"

"Well, wars and stuff." She exhales and looks out the window. Seconds later, she looks back at him.

"Well Fran, I don't mean to burst your bubble, especially after all the extensive research ye went and done and all. But with the wars that are happening now around the world, and ye have to keep in mind that I'm no Chinese person from a hundred, to a couple of thousand years old. When going out and having a war was most likely as common as going to watch a football match today. But I can predict that there will be some sort of military conflict between some countries or individuals in… the next two years." He stares at her.

"What's wrong with ye now?"

"I forgot ya done your GCSE's. That was really good."

"It's called the Leaving Cert and… sorry, Fran. Go ahead, carry on."

"Thanks Re," he takes another deep breath. "Okay, well they said that the world will end on the 21 December 2012. So there, that's it!" His shoulders drop as if point proven. She looks at him for a few seconds and smiles.

"Do ye believe this crap?"

"Re, it's getting close… too close."

"Fran, listen love. This is 2014. 2012 was two years ago."

As she is looking at him, his eyes seem to go blank. He slowly looks away from her and stares at the window. This would be the perfect time to get him back for buying those gherkins. But she knows that if she were to laugh now, which she is trying harder than any time in her life not to, that it could probably send his recovery back years. She decides to take a different approach. The blame game. She has been with him long enough to know him inside out. If she is too easy on him, he will know it and feel even more stupid than he already feels. This will have to be a finely balanced operation, and it won't be the first time that she has used her amateur psychology skills on him.

"I don't know what you're watching… but Jasus, I thought you'd have more cop than to fall for any of that shite!" He keeps staring at the window. "Fran!"

He slowly turns to face her. While he is looking at her, his head starts to shake slightly from side to side. His mouth opens, but no sound comes from it so he swallows. He looks like he's about to try speak again, but she gets in there first.

"Hold on, hold on. Firstly, they weren't Chinese, they were Mayans. And for fuck's sake, from a few hundred years to suddenly thousands of years ago in the same sentence? Ye don't even have your facts right. From what I know, they disappeared about a thousand years ago and they were a pack of evil bastards! They done human sacrifices as often as they took a piss, and I mean with their own people, even the kids got it. Then they'd fling their bodies into some lake, but this lake was their water to survive. So with all these dead bodies rotting away in it, it got contaminated and the story says that they had to move on. Then they just disappeared… poof!" she says, looking at her hand and opening it as if releasing something. She stares at its invisible ascent for a moment before looking back at him. "So much for predicting the future? Ye would think that they would've seen that one coming, wouldn't ye?" she says, folding her arms.

"How do ya know all this?" he asks, finding his voice again. Nothing like a frontal assault to get someone's attention.

"I work in a cafe and I'm surrounded by people most of the day, and most of the time they're talking complete shite! And the same shite does the rounds again and again. Then there's the radio. That's the reason why we play CD's instead of having it on, because all they do is talk shite as well. The Mayans and the end of the world. It's scaremongering, that's all it is. Back in them days, those people used to walk around bollock naked. And you're worrying about them saying that the world will end a thousand years later… to the day?! BOLLOX is what I say!"

Fran has a good think about what he's just been told and she does seem to know what she's talking about. Jesus, that was a good goal, he thinks while glancing at the muted telly. He looks back at her and he is impressed. No wonder they don't have stupid kids with her as their mother. Emmet on the other hand, now he must take after his dad.

"But, love... what if something does happen? Maybe they were a little late? We won't be prepared."

"Francis, listen, do..."

"Fran!" he interrupts, while picking up his tea. She mentally pats herself on the back and decides not to bother mentioning that they are definitely a little late, by two years.

"Okay... Fran. Did they happen to know how we're all supposed to meet our end? Any old time? I mean... if they picked the exact day, surely there would be a precise time and a cause, don't ye think... anything?"

He's trying to think of something sensible to say, but it's not going to happen, he can see that from a mile off. Say something to her, don't sit there like a cabbage. Damn her and her GCSE's or whatever it was that she done. And damn that poxy programme as well. He has an idea and it has never failed yet. He will just play the good old reliable forgetfulness card.

"Well, the thing is... that there's so many ways on the D-day show, that I forget which one says what."

On hearing this, her face begins to change colour and her nostrils start to flare. Oh yeah, those mad eyes are back and they look even madder as they start to widen. This is not going to be good, this he could tell from even ten miles away. She, on the other hand, is wondering where her laugh went? Because if it was still here, she would laugh in his face this second.

"So, ye don't even know what the fuck you're watching, never mind what you're talking about?! 2012 my arse!"

Just then, Emma enters the room carrying Emmet.

"What's all the shouting about? I could hear yiz loud and clear when I was in the head."

"Don't say that word." they say in unison.

"I just said… head." Rita stands up.

"Emma, I told ye before, I don't like it. It sounds vulgar."

"I agree." Fran adds, as he stands, relieved that the flak is going away from him.

"You're on about givin' head, Ma." she tries to clarify but not very well.

"Emma, don't bleedin' start me! I don't want to hear that word again. I'm putting up with enough from… Ray bleedin' Mears here." He smiles at the comparison as Rita thinks for a moment.

"Look Em, I know the programmes that ye watch. All the lads say… I'm going the head this or where's the head that?" she tries in an American accent. "They're all marines or sailors or whatever they are. But you're a young mother. And the last thing I want is for ye to be in a pub or club or some place, and to come out with that. Because… well people, especially blokes with a few drinks on them, might mishear or misinterpret what ye mean and think that…"

"Okay, Mam, I get where you're coming from. I won't say it anymore. I'll just say the john, okay?" Rita smiles. "Well I'm going to feed menace out in the kitchen. Do ya's want tea or coffee or anything?"

"No thanks," the two answer; again at the same time. As she walks out of the room, they hear her talking to Emmet.

"You're gonna have a boiled egg with some tea and toast for your brekkie, Popeye. You'll like that, won't ya? Mmm, lovely." Fran starts to sit down and Rita looks at him.

"And as for ye! With your sausages in jars, Mayans, Chinese and… D-day or whatever it's bleedin' called! We're not finished yet," she starts towards the door. "Not by a long shot, pal."

"Love, would ya get me a can?" She stops and looks at him.

"I'll give ye this, ye have some neck! Do ye want a breakfast roll with your can?"

"Ya have rolls?"

"Sure do, Sarge. Perks of the job."

"Oh yeah! A roll and another brew will be perfect."

"I'll get your roll and your tea for ye, but remember," she leaves the room while pointing her finger at him. He waits in case she reappears as she has a habit of sneaking back in after a few seconds, but nothing. When he hears her in the kitchen, he unmutes the TV and stretches.

"Ah… safe at last."

"I heard that!" she shouts from the kitchen.

"Damn it." he whispers. Seconds later, Pauli runs down the stairs into the sitting room.

"How did we do last night, Dad?"

"We won! 4-2, son."

"Yes!" he says, running into the kitchen. "Mam, have ya any blueberry bars left?"

"What's wrong?"

"Fell back asleep. I'm gonna miss the flippin' train."

"They're my bars." Emma says, looking around.

"Can I have one for me brek?"

"Go ahead, and take one for Matt. There's strawberry, too."

"Sweet!" he says, running to the press and taking one of each. He puts both under his chin and goes to Emmet and gives him an egg, which makes him shiver and laugh wildly. He takes the bars and pecks Rita on the cheek, then Emma and runs back into the room where Fran is watching the telly. He has his left hand over his shoulder, palm up. Pauli slaps it and runs to the door.

"Later folks!" The door slams. Rita looks towards the door, then back at the near ready breakfast roll. Seconds later, it's up with the tea and brought into Fran. She returns and goes to Emmet's chair and starts arranging the food on his tray into a small pile in front of him.

"Pauli seems pretty happy."

"Yeah, he does, too. Must be those two new friends he met in college." Emma says, with a grin while rinsing a cup.

CHAPTER TEN

Matt is standing on the footbridge and spots Pauli skidding around the corner and going on his toes.

"C'mon, ya dil, run!" he shouts. The station tannoy warns people of an approaching train. "Run faster!" he shouts. "I'll hold it up, chop chop!" He turns and jogs to the end of the bridge and descends the steps three by three. He stares at the ticket office on the opposite side of the tracks and sees Pauli pull up behind a person having difficulty getting through the barrier. The train comes under the road bridge and within seconds, it breaks Matt's view of the ticket office. He moves to the door of the last carriage, presses the button and the doors slide open. He watches the footbridge for any sign of Pauli. Seconds later, beeps sound and the doors start to close.

"Come on, P, man," he whispers, while still staring at the bridge and presses the button and the doors open again. He moves and stands between them while he looks through the window of the train and sees Pauli running for the steps. "Good lad!" The beeping starts again and the doors begin to close, but he stands firm and after they touch him, they slide back open.

"Excuse me... but I have to get to work."

Matt looks at where the voice came from to find a man sitting in a seat across from him and smiles.

"He's nearly here. It'll be alright, pal," he says, and looks back out the window and spots Pauli taking the steps two by two. The beeping starts again. "Any second now." The man looks at his watch, then picks up his coffee cup, realises it's empty and puts it back and stares out the window. "Pauli, come on for fuck's sake!" Matt screams. The man begins to look around, but decides not to and stares out his window. Pauli makes it on just as the beeping starts again. The two sit across the aisle from the man and Pauli is trying to catch his breath. After about a minute, he holds out the two bars.

"Pick what ya want." he says, still breathing heavily.

"I'll have the blueberry," Matt says, after swiping it from his hand and holds it up to find it squashed in places. "What the hell happened to this?!"

"Have this one then." Matt scans it.

"That one's as bad, both of them are mangled. Where did ya get them, off the road?" Pauli coughs.

"Did ya ever sprint with a bar in each hand, then run up and down two sets of steps?"

"Ah, so your hands did that?"

"Not intentionally. Shit, me legs are numb." Matt checks the wrapper.

"It's still sealed so, to me it's fair game. Ah… breakfast!" He unwraps it and shoves it in his mouth. When he swallows it, he gets up and crosses to the man with the empty coffee cup who needs to get to work. "Sorry about that, man. But he has a test today, and if he misses it…" he exhales dramatically. "Phttt! Out the door! No more college."

"And what about yourself?"

"What about meself?"

"Have you got tests as well?"

"Yeah… that's right. Both of us have tests today."

"So the two of you are going to college?"

"Eh, yeah… tests!" Matt starts to turn away.

"College on this route? … Where?"

"Ah, it's miles away. Dundalk cod. Cash on delivery." he sniggers. The man stares at him.

"Dundalk cod?"

"No, college of Dundalk. It's a stupid name really. Dundalk, college of Dundalk. Maybe they just like the word Dundalk. Eh… wait there." He comes back to Pauli. "Brah, are ya eating your mangled bar?" He looks at it on the table.

"I don't really feel like it after that run."

"Give us it then."

"Take it."

"Be back in a sec," he says, grabbing it off the table and turning back to the man. "Look, here's a peace offering for stalling the train on ya," The man looks at the bar in Matt's hand. "Yeah, I know. It doesn't look all that hot but mine was cool. Once the wrapper's not broke, you're sound," Matt checks it. "It's intact so… it's good to go, and these are really beautiful, enjoy!" he says, putting it on the table and turning.

"Thanks for the bar," he says, picking it up and examining it carefully. "So what are you studying in Dundalk… cod?" Matt slowly turns back and can only think of one thing to say.

"Architecture. We're both training to be architects."

"Training… that's good. Well good luck with your tests to you and your bleeding greyhound friend." he says, as he continues to check the bar. Matt double takes before returning to sit facing Pauli.

"Do ya know him?" Matt looks at him and seems confused.

"'Eh… no."

"So… what was all that about?" Matt thinks for a few seconds and whispers.

"Ya know what? I think he's gay."

"Well, I bet he loved that."

"What do ya mean?"

"Well, you're nineteen, and for no reason you went over to some old lad, gave him my strawberry bar and… here hold on, that was my breakfast! Why didn't ya give… hold on! Why did ya give him my bar?" he asks, with a raised eyebrow.

"I had to keep pressing the button and stand in between the doors to hold the train for YOU," he glances at the man, then back at Pauli. "He started moaning, saying that he had to be in work and all that. So, I thought if I said sorry and gave him the bar as a peace offering, that it would even out the Karma."

"You and your bleeding Karma stuff," he thinks for a moment. "I suppose, just to be on the safe side."

"Exactly!" Matt looks over at the man who does a cheers with the bar, then takes a bite and smiles at the two, eventually turning to look out his window at the sea. He looks back at Pauli. "I shouldn't have done that, should I?"

"Nah... wasn't your best move. I wonder what he's thinking of right now."

"Do ya want to move seats, P?"

"What?! And deprive your new friend of his eye candy? Hmm hmm, no way!"

"Stop it." Matt whispers, turning to look out his window.

CHAPTER ELEVEN

Fran and Rita are watching a morning talk show. Occasionally, he messes with his calculator and writes stuff down. Every time he does it, it catches Rita's eye but she continues to try and watch the telly. After the fourth time, she is just about to ask him what he is calculating, as the last time she checked, he wasn't an accountant, when she hears Emma coming down the stairs. She pushes the buggy into the room while carrying Emmet.

"Ahh, my little bloody devil incarnate." she says, as she stands up with her arms outstretched towards him.

"Ah, Ma, don't get all mushy. We'll only be gone a few hours." Rita takes him and checks his head.

"I checked. Nothing! Head like a coconut."

"That's my boy," she continues checking.

"Are ye sure, Em?"

"Yeah Ma. Mutton head has a... mutton head, he's grand. The bang woke me up, and the first thing I did after gettin' him out from underneath me bed was to check his head." she says, while picking bits of food out of his buggy.

"I know, darling, it's just that bruises sometimes take a while to show."

"Ma, that child has a head like a boulder, and I'm not just talkin' about his looks. It's all clear." Rita starts laughing and when Emma realises what she said, she laughs as well. Emmet sees this and joins in and Fran chuckles quietly to himself. "Alright, so we're goin' around to Jessie's. Mikey and Jade will be there and we'll have a quick coffee, hit the P.O, then the bus into Swords. There's this lovely little top in the Pavilions that I wanna get. So basically, me and handsome here will be home around teatime."

"Franner, she's going to the post office." He looks up.

"And?"

"Your weekly charity thing?"

"Ohh! Good one, Re! Em, will ya get a postal order for £5 and an envelope?"

"You're still sending them money, Da?!"

"And I will continue to! This is for soldiers that are less fortunate than meself. Some have lost limbs, sight... or have what I have. A £5 donation to one of them every week is nothing!"

"Right, Da, keep your knickers on!" He searches his pockets and pulls a creased folded page from a back one, then skips through a few pages in the A4 pad and starts writing. Rita looks at Emma and nods her head slowly. Emma mimes, 'sorry,' and looks back at him. When he finishes, he rips the page out and hands it to her with a ten-euro note.

"The charity and its address are on that, okay, love?"

"I'm sorry, Da. I forgot how much this means to ya."

"You're grand, love." After putting both in her bag, she takes Emmet from Rita and brings him over to Fran.

"Give your Grandad a kiss," he stares out the window and Fran kisses him. She then turns to Rita.

"And don't forget your Granny."

A sound between a low cough and a sneeze comes from Fran and the two look at him. He does his pretend to watch the telly routine as if nothing happened.

"Something on your mind, O'Neill?" He looks at Rita.

"No! Why do ya ask, love?"

"Because ye made that sound again. Ye know the one ye always make when Granny is mentioned?"

"No... I can't say that I do, love," he says, turning back to the telly. Rita takes Emmet and gives him a big hug and a plethora of kisses, then he is strapped into the buggy, nice and tight. She walks them to the door and watches as they walk away. The minute they are out of sight, she goes to the kitchen.

"How are ye for a drink?!"

"Grand, love!" Minutes later, she walks in and sits down.

"Re, I know you're gonna go mad because ya didn't look happy earlier and ya done your finger thing. So go ahead. Do it." he says, knowing that it's going to be another third degree or a torrent of abuse, or both. She lights a smoke, takes a pull and sits watching him. She would like to get him back for the 'snough sound' as she calls it, which he makes every time the word granny is mentioned. He knows that she doesn't like being referred to as that. But she decides to let it slide for today. It goes to over a minute of her watching him without saying anything and he is holding it together pretty well. She is impressed.

"Franner... let's go to that German shop." His eyes widen.

"You're messin' with me?"

"No. We'll go and get some provisions for the end of mankind."

When they get there, she stops at the door, but he walks on in and after the door shuts, turns to find her on the opposite side of it. He comes back but it won't open from the inside, and for something so simple, he starts to panic. She walks a few feet to it and it slides open and he runs out and takes a couple of breaths. She is looking at him and wonders what all the fuss is about.

"I thought ya were going to leave me in there."

"Fran... are ye for feckin' real?!"

"I was trapped."

"Fran, all ye have to do is walk out the other bleedin' door!"

He looks around at a trolley getting pushed through the exit door. "Oh, I forgot about that." he turns to face her. "So why did ya stop?"

"I was going to ask ye if ye wanted to get a trolley."

"Really?!"

She nods her head. "Go on, it'll be eaten one way or the other. But you're goin' half on everything, pal."

"Copy that!"

After a shopping experience that she knows only Fran can give her, with him checking and rechecking prices, then comparing the weight of jars and tins with other jars and tins. When all of this was done, he started checking the furthest best before dates that he could find before being happy with what he put in the trolley. She went out for a smoke, only to return to find him gone from where she had left him and found him checking out the night vision scopes. She turned and went straight back out for another. When she came back, he was holding a scope after getting a store assistant to open the cabinet for him so as he could have a better look. They have been there just over forty minutes for what should have taken no longer than ten, and she can take no more. Plus, she needs to have a wee.

"Are ye going to buy that yoke?!"

"Oh, hello love. Where did ya go?"

"Francis... I need to go to the toilet." On the mention of Francis, accompanied by her facial expression, he gets the message. After the scope is handed back to the assistant, post haste, he turns and walks away with the trolley with her following him. Luckily the queue is short and once in the car, the drive home is swift. They enter the garden and after skidding to a stop, she sprints to the front door, rings the bell and crosses her legs. Now she remembers that nobody is in and that the keys are still in the ignition. Because she left it in gear with the engine running, it jumped forward a few times before cutting out. She runs back, snatches them from the ignition and runs to the front door and up the stairs. The first thing he does is to look at her seat but it is dry. He gets the keys from the front door and reverses the car off the grass and straightens it up. It takes him thirteen trips from the car to the kitchen until all of the stuff is in. The normal food is placed on the worktop, and the end of the world items on the floor beside the back door. He is looking from one pile to the other and is admiring his with a content smile.

"Are ye happy now?" she asks from behind, with her face at his shoulder. He jumps.

"Jesus love! Ya nearly frightened the shit out of me. I didn't hear ya come down."

"Fran, I had me wee and went into the sitting room, and ye just walked in and out while I sat there. So, will I get ye a tin?" she says, walking to the fridge.

"'No, I'll have a brew please." She stops and looks at the clock, then back at him.

"Tea?!"

"Tea." She goes to the kettle.

"So be it."

He is sitting at the table when she places the tea in front of him and sits down. She takes a cigarette and pushes the box towards him and he makes a face.

"What's wrong?"

"I… eh… I'm not smoking anymore."

She is stunned.

"Are ya ok, Re?"

"You're joking, right?"

"No, two days it is now. Off them two days and I don't feel as bad as … Ya know, the way they say you're supposed to feel." She glances at his display of cans on the worktop, then back at him.

"You're not drinking as much either."

He feels uneasy, but doesn't know why.

"I'm down from sixteen the day before yesterday to fifteen. Today I'm going for fourteen." She has the most intense stare that he has seen from her in a long time. Maybe he should not have told her about the smokes and the drink on the same day.

"'You're really serious?"

"Yes, love… I am."

He looks towards the kitchen window and stands up. He walks to the backdoor and goes outside. After he takes his runners and socks off, he steps onto the grass and walks around slowly in a circle for about a minute or so before sitting down. He rubs the grass with both hands while his eyes are shut. She stands at the door and watches him for a few seconds before taking off her socks as well and walks quietly across the patio.

"I really love grass, Re. I know it sounds simple… but I do. There's something peaceful about it." he says, as his fingers glide across the top of it. She steps onto it and stands there looking down at him. He looks up, but squints and has to close one eye. "Baby… I can't look up, the sun's way too strong. I'll go blind, my dear girl."

These words are said in his original accent. Before he had been exposed to near sixteen years of living in

Ireland, and they give her a shiver. She sits facing him, cross-legged.

"So… you still do yoga?"

"Ye have forgotten so so much about me, my dear boy," she says, reaching out and holding his hand. "Hey," she looks up at a white trail in the sky. "Em has just missed one. That is one, isn't it?"

"It is! And there's another one behind." They watch the jets until they are nearly out of sight. He looks down at their hands, then at her. "Ya know… it's been so long since…"

She gets up on her knees and moves her face close to him.

"Empty house, kids gone… what do ye think?"

"Go for it, my little beauty."

"Give me five for a shower, Hammer."

"Leave it on for me as well."

"Will do, Sarge!" she says, and gives him a kiss on the lips before jumping up. As she is running to the door, he watches her little bum a-wiggling, then looks down.

"Okay, lads, contact! We're goin' back into action," he looks from his lap to the vapour trails in the sky and smiles. "And about bloody time!"

CHAPTER TWELVE

Matt and Pauli got into college a few minutes late, because Matt had decided that he needed a breakfast roll to keep him going for all of an hour until lunch. They walk up the corridor until they come to room 9 and Pauli pushes open the door. A male teacher stops mid-sentence and looks at them, followed by the rest of the class. Matt and Pauli look at each other, then at the room number, back at each other and eventually at the teacher.

"Do you both practice that a lot?" he asks. They look at each other again, then back at the teacher.

"Practice what?" they ask at the same time. The class laugh.

"Can I help you boys?"

"We thought Miss McCabe had this class today." Pauli says.

"Performing Arts…" the teacher says with a smirk, while looking around the class before looking back at them. "Was moved to the hall today." More laughs resound around the classroom.

"Eh… well, thanks. Sorry for disturbing you." Pauli says, closing the door quickly. Matt waits until they are a few feet away from the door before looking back at it.

"Fucking pack of shitbags." he whispers.

"Yeah, I know. Let's get to the hall and pronto like." When they get there, the other students are running around in a large circle, shaking their arms from side to side in the air, while moving their heads back and forth and kicking out with their legs.

"What the fuck?" Pauli whispers, confused.

"Now THAT looks really difficult." Matt says, before belching. Pauli quickly moves away from him.

"Jesus, Matt! I told ya about doing that next to me. It smells like egg!" he says, as he waves his hand vigorously.

"Well, it WAS a breakfast roll!"

"But three eggs?! I knew that was a bad idea, even your one was left looking at ya. Whatever you do, don't fart unless ya give me a five second sketch, ok?"

"Okay, five seconds. That's if I can hold it that long, homey." Pauli has to back up a few more feet as the smell seems to be getting stronger, then he looks over at the students.

"What the hell are they up to?"

"There's Becka! Whoa… look at them babies go." The two stand there for a couple of minutes and watch as their classmates nod, shake and kick their way around the hall and are starting to find this funny.

The rest of the class are looking back at them, wondering why they're not joining in.

"Well, well, well! I suppose you two are Misters O'Neill and Wolfe?" They turn their heads towards each other, then notice a man's head slightly behind them and Matt jumps. "Oh now, look who it is! Mister…?" Matt stands there silent with wide eyes.

"He's Wolfe and I'm O'Neill." Pauli says.

"Surely you are both in the wrong class? Architecture is on the third floor. And you, Mister O'Neill, would want to make haste for your test or," he looks at Matt, then back at Pauli. "Phttt! Out the door, no more college." Pauli looks at him with a confused face.

"What?!"

"You're both," he looks at Matt again. "Training. To be architects?"

"Nah, you've got us mixed up with someone else, pal."

"Oh, well, maybe I have. Good morning, Mister Wolfe and thank you for the bar, it was very nice. First time I had one. Personally, I don't go for that type of stuff, but I think you have converted me to the fruit bar, well done!" Matt continues to stand there in a state of shock, but Pauli twigs it now and remembers the train.

"Eh… and who are you supposed to be?" he asks, with annoyance in his voice.

"Oh, pardon my manners, Mister O'Neill. I'm your new P.A teacher, Mister Collon." he replies, with a smile.

"Where's McCa… Miss McCabe?" Matt asks, eventually defreezing enough to speak.

"Pregnant!" They look at each other, then back at Mister Collon. One of those tumbleweed moments pass before he speaks. "Okay boys, I think you both have had a nice long rest doing nothing, so go out there and join the rest of the class."

"And what are they supposed to be doing?"

"Warming up of course, Mister O'Neill." he replies, as he glances down at his clipboard for a moment before looking back up with that smile.

"For what?" Matt asks.

"Dance!" The two look at each other with dread.

"Well, it is performing arts," he says, while still smiling and walks around to face them. "Acting, singing, dancing and so forth. So today I want to try and fit in a bit of each. I just want to gauge where you kids are at so far."

"For fuck's sake." Pauli whispers, under his breath.

"For fuck's sake indeed. Okay boys, out you go and warm up, and don't worry about looking silly." The two stand there and watch him walk to a table with a portable sound system and a bag on it.

"You go first."

"Ah, fuck it! I'm gonna run behind Becka and check out her arse." Pauli says, and runs off.

"Ya dirty bastard! Why didn't I think of that?" Matt says, before running across the floor while waving his arms in the air.

CHAPTER THIRTEEN

A few minutes later, Mister Collon speaks through a microphone plugged into the sound system.

"One two, one two, testing," he holds it up and looks at it. "One two, one two three, testing."

"It's on!" a female voice shouts.

"Where did he pull that from?" Matt asks, bent over with his hands on his knees, trying to catch a breath.

"I've a better one. Why do people say that into a mike?"

"Alright class," he looks at the microphone again, then walks to the system and raises the volume. "One two… can you hear me?"

"I think the Isle of Man can hear you!" the same female voice shouts.

The class laugh and Pauli looks around to try and see who said it, as he doesn't recognise the voice. But with everyone laughing, not a chance.

"Alright class, I think you can all stop now," he says, only realising that they stopped seconds before. This is not lost on the class and they laugh again. "I'd say you are all hot enough now." Somebody wolf whistles and there is more laughter. "Okay okay, enough of that malarky!" Matt looks at Pauli.

"Mahwhat?!"

"Never heard that one before."

Mister Collon stares slowly around the room, making sure to make eye contact with each student. 'A little bit of the old 'show them who's the boss' look on them to make them feel uncomfortable. Then they will bend to my will,' he thought.

"Ha ha!" The last two words he said aloud, straight into the microphone. The class look back at him in silence, for seconds, before laughing again.

"What's he laughing at?" Matt asks, looking at Pauli.

"You call that a laugh?! I've heard more realistic laughs in comics." Whatever trick Mister Collon was near pulling off, was blown out of the water by those words. Note to self. Sell this mike at next Sunday's car boot sale. Start again.

"Hello, class. My name is Mister Collon, and that's with two L's: Collon."

"Yes, sir!" Pauli shouts. "Sorry, sir, wasn't supposed to be that loud. My eardrums are still getting used to your mike."

"Okay, let me clear the air first…" The students laugh and he closes his eyes and thinks, idiot, don't give them fuel.

"I like this class, it's a funny class!" Matt says, grinning as he looks around.

"Let me rephrase that. I've heard them all before. So no matter what you think you can come up with, I've heard it already, and my name is not pronounced like that. As I said, it's Collon," he looks around the class again. "Right then, I want to gauge you, so we are going to start off with some dance first." All of the girls give a cheer and they are also joined by the two gay lads. It begins with six five-minute sessions of dance. From classical to hip hop, salsa, disco, Bollywood and for the last, you just do your own thing. The two dance with each other to Pachelbel's "Canon" first. Matt rapidly bats his eyes at Pauli.

"What am I… the bird or the bloke?"

"Anyone ya want, just pretend I'm not here."

"It's just as well we watched them films that you're into, because I'd be just standing here like a knob." They dance around for a couple of minutes before Matt notices that everyone else has either stopped or are slowing down, but all are looking at them. "Hey P, everyone's looking at us. Does my bum look big in these jeans?" Pauli opens his eyes and takes a glance around.

"They're not looking at your rectum, ya ponce. They're trying to copy us." They dance for a few more seconds before Matt stumbles and gets freaked out by all the looks and starts freezing up.

"Can't feel it anymore, bro. Now we're like two plebs."

"Four plebs," Pauli corrects him. "Becka and Lucy are still going and they're a lot worse than us. They look like a three-legged cow dancing with a one legged cat." Matt laughs loudly and the music stops abruptly. They look towards the sound system to see a frowning Mister

Collon pulling the mike from his pocket and plugging it back in.

"Mister Wolfe, are you okay?"

"He just swallowed a bit too quickly," Pauli says.

Matt sees Becka and Lucy staring over while giggling and whispers to Pauli. He looks and sees Becka, then notices a smile under a mass of hair standing beside her. He shivers for some unknown reason and hopes that it wasn't too obvious. "Shit Matt, I feel nervous." he whispers, but before Matt can say anything, Mister Collon taps the top of his mike.

"Misters Wolfe and O'Neill. Are you two the class clowns?" The two look at each other. "Because if you think you can clown your way through this class on my first day, than maybe you should clown yourselves into a different class." They don't know how to respond to this so end up staring back at him, and the silence is long and uncomfortable.

"Mister Colon!" a female voice calls, pronouncing it as the rectum equivalent. He looks towards where the voice came from and so do the rest of the class. A petite girl walks a few steps forward, with most of her hair covering her face except from the end of her nose down to her chin, and stares at him. He looks puzzled as he stares back at her and wonders what she wants. "Mister Colon," she begins again. "As you said yourself just now, it's your first day. In other words, you're not here long enough for the time it would take me to fart and it to pass through my knickers." He slowly lowers his mike and wonders if he has just heard her right. As he is staring at her, she looks to her left at Pauli and grins. He stares back at the hair with the grin, and all this seems to be happening in slow motion. She looks back at Mister Collon. "So… if you want a class to teach, I suggest that you treat us as equals to yourself and as adults. Because as far as I know, everyone in this class is 18 or over. It is your first day, so build a bridge and get over it. You don't know us so don't even pretend to. And don't threaten any of us either, or you'll be teaching an empty class. How long do you think that would last, Mister Colon?"

This time the silence seems to last for much longer than it should, and the class have turned back to see if he has a response to the statement. As he is standing there holding his microphone and looking at this girl, he looks shell-shocked. He looks at the window for a moment before looking back at her.

"Excuse me?!"

"You're welcome!" Matt shouts, while thinking that there is nothing like kicking someone when they are down, especially when they deserve it. His conscience is clear concerning Karma as he thinks it will understand. Mister Collon, out of confusion and embarrassment, removes the mike from the system and presses play. Pachelbel's "Canon" begins again. "P, mate…" he exhales. "After that, I think we should begin."

"Yeah, me, too." he agrees, while looking over at Lucy.

"Are ya ok, P?" Pauli looks back at Matt.

"Eh… yeah. So what do we do?" Matt bends slightly with his arm outstretched.

"Would you do me the honour?"

"I accept." Pauli says, in a high-pitched upper-class English accent while taking the tips of Matt's fingers. "Oh, you Pimpernel, you."

"Hey, let's do pardon me but your teeth are in me neck." Matt says.

"It's MY neck." Pauli corrects.

"Okay, your neck then!" The class try to imitate them again when they start. Mister Collon seems to have forgotten about his incident with Lucy and intently watches the two. When the song is over, they go into hip hop. The last music to be played as the class is nearing break time is the Bollywood music. Some of the girls go into the change the light bulb and pat the dog routine, but the rest start moving and don't have a clue. They start to cop on and imitate the bulb and dog gang. Of course, the two gay lads know their business and when they start, they get everyone's attention.

"They must have watched the bleedin' Indian music channel as well. What are we gonna do, P?"

"Dance... and we're better than them."

"But if we do, we're never going to get any... ya know. All the birds might think we're a bit... well... gay as well."

"Matt, I don't know what planet you've been living on since we started this class, but we haven't got anything from ANY of these birds. Well, not me!"

"Okay then, here's what to do. Throw your balls in the air and hope that a steam roller doesn't do a job on them when they land."

Pauli winces and unknowingly presses his knees together and covers his crotch.

"What does that even mean?!"

"It means that we've nothin' to lose. What say we kick their arses, boyo?"

"I say, ya should've said that first," he takes a breath. "Okay, roger that! Let's go."

They break into dance. The two had indeed watched a lot of the Indian music channel, and still do on occasion. It all started when they were thirteen. Matt's house didn't have the satellite back then so they spent a lot of time at Pauli's. On one of these days they came across it by accident. Both were immediately attracted to a music and dance that they had never seen or heard before. Within weeks, they could dance along to any video that came on. Of course, all of this happened when everyone was out. MTV was another favourite, and Matt can do a mean Beyoncé to rival Pauli's Michael Jackson. They had also practiced some 'Classical dancing' as Pauli had called it. This all started after they had watched *Plunkett and MacLean*, *Dance of the Vampires*, and Pauli's favourite, *The Scarlet Pimpernel*. "Every little bit helps," he had said and Matt agreed. That was once the two had decided to do the performing arts, as they both wanted to be actors. Well, you never know, James Bond might have to dance his way out of a perilous situation sometime. They accidently came across *Fame* on a channel that showed old programmes, and it nearly turned them off the whole idea completely. But a few days later they recovered, and after promising to never speak of it again, decided to stick with the plan. As the song is finishing, they realise that they are the only ones still dancing. They look around the room and see that everyone is looking at them, again.

"My my, I am impressed, Sahibs Wolfe and O'Neill. That was very... energetic."

"Yeah well," Pauli coughs. "It's something we just sort of threw together."

"Last moment." Matt adds, as he takes deep breaths.

"Yes... right. If you say so," he says, turning and walking to the table. Minutes later and the class breaks for lunch. Pauli and Matt are about to leave when Mister Collon calls them. They walk over to the table just as he's placing a light blue see through plastic container on it. They can see sandwiches, an apple, a banana and something else, but they can't make out what it is. Next to come out of his bag is one of the biggest, oldest and ugliest flasks that they have ever seen, with a red tartan design. He then completely baffles them by pulling out an aircraft magazine and placing it on the table beside the lunchbox.

"Listen, lads, I know we got off to a bad start, but credit where it's due. I am really impressed by the overall dancing, but the classical and the Bollywood were excellent." They stand waiting on a punchline as they watch him remove the lid from the lunchbox and decide what to go for first. Seconds pass.

"You like planes?" Pauli asks.

"No, I love them! I'm actually going for my licence in five weeks and two days."

"No way! Then you'll be a pilot?" Matt asks.

"Well… yes. If I pass, which I should, then I'll be a qualified pilot. My aim is to become an instructor." Matt gets interested in the magazine and moves closer to get a better look.

"Does that mean that the teaching would go out the window?"

"Here, I'll show you what I fly." he says, not answering the question and picking it up. After flicking through some pages, he stops and hands it to Matt.

"Do ya own your own plane?"

"I'm paying a mortgage, so no. I go out every week and take lessons for an hour, sometimes two," he says, sitting down.

"Well, fair play to ya," Matt says, while browsing through the pages. Mister Collon is taken aback at this and now it is his turn to wait for a smart remark to be added, but it doesn't come.

"My sister is into planes as well, but the military type."

"No P, your sister is into ANYTHING military. No matter if it flies, drives, walks, floats, goes under the water, whatever!"

"Can't disagree with ya there, Matt. She is a bit obsessed with it."

"Tell him about the huge poster in her room." He looks down at Mister Collon.

"Yeah, she has this cool poster, even if I do say so myself."

"I say so as well. Every time I see it, I just stand there staring at it, and for some reason, it makes me feel happy, don't know why. Weird." Mister Collon is sitting there waiting to find out what is so cool about this amazing poster that makes people happy for no apparent reason.

"So… what's on the poster?"

"Oh yeah! It's an F-14 Tomcat flying through the sky, and the two guys in the cockpit are looking at the plane that's taking the picture, and both have their thumbs up. Maybe it doesn't sound that cool but it's one of them that you'd probably have to see for yourself."

"Actually, it sounds extremely cool! Where did she get it?"

"She sent away for it a few months before Christmas."

"Could you find out where?"

"I'll ask her tonight. But when I signed for it, I think USAF was on the tube." Mister Collon is nearly foaming at the mouth on hearing this.

"Really?! Will you find out how she ordered it and the postage for me tonight?"

"No sweat, I'll ask her the minute I get in. But it's a big poster," he looks at Matt. "What size would ya say it is, Matog?" he asks, while spreading his arms as wide as he can.

"About that, P mate. I think it's six foot by four. Or if not, close."

Mister Collon has now jumped up and his eyes are nearly on stalks.

"P, mate. I mean. Mister O'Neill, will you definitely find out for me, please?"

"No problem, consider it done." Matt's just found Collon's Achilles's heel and he's enjoying this.

"Tell him about her binoculars." he says, while he pretends to browse through the magazine.

"Yeah, she has these massive binoculars, and when she sees a fighter, or as she calls them, a fast jet, they're out to get a closer look."

"She must know what she's looking for. They fly so high that sometimes you can't even hear them. They're only noticeable by their vapour trails."

"That's what she's says. You and Em would get on really well." Matt slowly raises his head.

"Yeah, only problem is… Em's seventeen." he says, closing the magazine and handing it back to Mister Collon who, while taking it, smiles uncomfortably.

"Well, lads, it won't be as active after lunch. How is your singing?"

"Nuts!"

"I think there was a similar reaction to the dancing, Mister O'Neill. But you owned that floor when…"

"Eh… time is ticking down P, and I'm starvin'."

"Yeah, me, too," Pauli says, turning. "Later, Mister Col…"

"Charlie." he interrupts. The two look around. "Yeah… I'll tell the rest of the class after lunch. All this Mister and Missus stuff is a bit too formal. First names would be much more relaxed. Right so, off you go, the clock is ticking down."

He looks back at his lunchbox and takes out a quartered roast beef sandwich. He takes a bite and looks towards the window and shakes his head. "Oh yeah, you owned that floor. Note to self, don't go overboard on the compliments." He takes another bite as he puts his feet on the table.

CHAPTER FOURTEEN

"Well, I don't know about you, but I think we owned that floor." Matt says, and they giggle, but Pauli not as much as he would normally. He has seen a different side to Mister Collon, and maybe he's not that big of an arsehole after all. "Are ya really going to ask Em about her poster?"

"Of course I am. Did ya see the face on him? That guy likes planes, and all I'm doing is getting a web address." As they near the edge of the campus facing the garage, Matt's the first to notice.

"I think we've just been invaded."

Pauli turns to him. "What?"

"Our spot… look who's there."

Pauli looks over, but has to squint. He eventually recognises Becka and someone else. "Who's that there with Becka?"

"Ya mean the girl?"

"No, the fucking Elephant! Yeah, the girl!" Matt smiles and takes a quiet deep breath before answering, but it's that deep, that Pauli looks at him because he's taking that long. "So… who is it?!" he asks, with an impatient face and voice. Matt pretends to have another look and waits a few seconds before looking back at a confused Pauli, who is staring over at the girls.

"I think it's... Lucy."

Pauli looks at Matt, then back at the girls who start waving. Before he realises what he's doing, he's waving as well. Matt also waves.

"That's not Lucy."

"I think you're wrong, P mate... because it looks like her."

"So where's all her hair suddenly gone? Considering we've just come from class and she looked like a Kerry Blue."

"I don't know. Maybe she just pulled it back. Ya know the way it can get really warm when you've got a lot of hair, don't ya?"

"No... I don't actually!"

"Look, why don't we get our grub and sit down beside them and get a-chatting?"

"Matt, I'm really not that good, ya know?"

"Look pally waaly..."

"Pally waaly?!"

"Heat of the moment and all that shit. C'mon Pauli... please! Let's land them babes. I mean babe! Did ya see the look we got off Becka?"

At that moment, Pauli could have sworn that he heard a choir in the background and looks over both shoulders.

"Did ya here that?"

"What's wrong, man? Trying to get me back for yesterday?"

"You know what, Matt? You should go for Becka, just you on your own."

"Surely ya jest? Really, P? You're not interested anymore?"

"Yeah Matt, really. Go for it," he answers, as he looks towards the girls. "My fascination with Becka and her boobs is over!"

While waiting in line at the garage to get served, Matt is continuously in Pauli's ear, and persisting in trying to persuade him to join the girls at the spot with their lunch.

"After all, it is our spot, bro!" he keeps repeating. Eventually, Pauli folds and they do. To be perfectly honest, after he got there and found that it was Lucy, and seen her up close without any hair to conceal her face, he was delighted that Matt had worked the head on him to do it. Matt is being himself. Funny, vulgar and funny. Becka seems to enjoy his performance, for lack of a better word, and seems to be constantly laughing. Lucy on the other hand, is a different kettle of fish. She lets out the odd giggle, but other than that, sits there nibbling on her chicken baguette.

'Does everyone in college have chicken baguettes for lunch?' Pauli wondered. Matt is sitting to Becka's right, and as Pauli starts to sit down beside him, Matt gives him a nudge which makes him stumble slightly. At the end of that stumble, he is in between Becka and Lucy. So as the plan at the garage was for him to sit beside Lucy in the first place, and with Matt's subtle and barely noticeable reminder, that is where he ended up. For some unknown reason when he sits down next to her, he says sorry, and closes his eyes as he waits for the laughs to come, but they don't.

"Are you on the chicken today as well?" she asks.

"Every day. I'll turn into a chicken... or an egg." he replies, while looking at her. At this, she laughs loudly and it isn't a false one. After a few minutes, he starts to feel a bit more relaxed. But it is good that Matt is there, because his mouth is constantly going, so there are no awkward silences. Pauli actually admires him. Girls never make him nervous, he is just Matt. What you see is what you get, whether you like it or not. From the moment they got there, Pauli did try to take more than his fair share of sly glances at Lucy. From her ankles that showed between her socks and jeans, to the bit of her side between her T-shirt and jeans, that was visible when she would lean slightly when talking to Becka. But what it is that amazes him most is her face. All these months she had kept it hidden, or that hairstyle had. But now, with her hair tied back, he can see everything, even the tiny freckle on the side of her nose, and she is stunning. He tries not to over eye contact her, but most times when he tries to take a sly glance at her face, she is already looking at him. Either she has very fast reactions, or she is staring.

CHAPTER FIFTEEN

The next day as they are leaving college, Pauli needs to use the toilet. Matt waits outside and when Pauli comes out, there is no sign of him. He goes back to the class, thinking that Matt had probably forgotten something, but it is empty.

"'Where the hell is that ginger ponce?" he keeps whispering, as he retraces his steps back the way he had come, scanning as he went. He checks the toilets in case Matt had come back from wherever he went, and then gone in search of him, but they are empty. He decides to go out front and have a look see and wonders why he had not done this in the first place. When he gets there, still no sign of Matt. He decides to count to two minutes. After which, he starts to get pissed off and worried in case they miss the train. Because if they do, the wait for the next one will be a very boring hour and a half one. He takes out his phone and rings Matt's number. A car horn beeps a few times as he waits for him to answer.

"Answer, you bloody dope! Where are ya?" The car beeps again and he puts his finger in his ear.

"Hello, may I be of assistance?"

"Matt, ya bleedin' doorknob! We're gonna miss the train! Where are ya?!"

"Look slightly to your right, my dear chap." Pauli looks to his left and right.

"Look around for what?" The car horn beeps again and he looks at a red Opel Astra SXi.

"Hello again, handsome. Want a lift?" Lucy calls with a smile.

He stands there stunned as Matt reaches over the passenger seat and opens the door, "C'mon big fella!" Pauli has not even noticed Matt, never mind heard him. He can only see Lucy's face staring at him from the driver's seat with that lovely smile. He smiles back as he walks to the car, and is still holding his phone to his ear and his finger in the other one. She looks over the seat and says something. "P, ya can hang up and take your finger out of your ear now." He stops and looks at the phone, then stares at his recently removed ear finger before looking back at the car. He sees three giggling faces looking at him as he walks to it, gets in and buckles up.

"That damn finger has a mind of its own and... okay, I'm lost. What's going on?"

"Me and Becka are bringing you boys home."

"But we live in..."

"We know! Brains in the back told us." Lucy interrupts. While on the N1 heading south, Lucy has a question that she just has to ask. "So, lads... me and Becka have talked a bit and have decided that for blokes, you are really good dancers. How the hell did that happen?"

"Well it..." Matt begins.

"No, let Pauli tell us." Becka interrupts. "And you better have a good excuse... sorry, reason. Well. None of them sound good," she thinks for a moment. "How about explanation? How can two blokes dance like that who aren't gay, tell us that?" They came off the N1 at the Walshestown exit and took their time down the old road. Becka brought up food. She said that they would normally be at home by now and that she was starving and would love a burger and chips. This she said seconds before a garage came into view just before the turn for the boys' village. Pauli looked around at Matt and both thought that it was a bit coincidental. They know the garage well, as it is about two miles from their village, and it has a burger joint franchise inside.

The two never realised that the idea of getting food was already well planned. Before they even had time to protest, Lucy was pulling into a parking spot. They were asked what they fancied and both said that they were full, but the girls knew they were lying, especially after listening to the sound effects that Matt's stomach was continuously making, even over the music, on the drive down. So they said that they would be back in a few minutes and turned and entered the garage.

The truth is that the lads have nothing. Two euros something between them, and would that even be enough to get one portion of chips? They decide that this could never happen again and that they would always try to carry a bit of extra cash, just in case they were offered another lift home. Matt comes up with the idea of just sitting back and acting cool when the girls are eating, and reminds Pauli that they are studying to be actors, so it should be "easy peasy." It is about ten minutes later when the girls emerge, and what they are carrying seems like a lot of food for just two people. When they get in, a bag each is handed to Matt and Pauli. They look at each other and it is like their worst nightmare has come true. They know that the girls know that they have no money, and Pauli has never seen Matt look so uncomfortable. If his face is anything like Matt's, then they would never make it as actors.

"We would have felt really weird with just the two of us eating, so we thought that the four of us eating together would be more normal." Becka announces. Lucy nearly looks as worried as the lads, but when Matt opens his bag, followed by Pauli, she smiles with relief. The girls have played it safe and got double cheeseburgers, fries and strawberry milkshakes all round, and the lads make short work of it for being "full" a few minutes earlier.

The four spent close to three quarters of an hour in the car between eating and talking except for a little incident. Becka and Matt were just short of opening their mouths and emptying the contents of the bags into them. There were no niceties when it came to eating burgers this size, and they didn't seem to care what faces they were pulling while taking bites or trying to chew. Lucy and Pauli were going the opposite route. He was turning away from her every time he took a bite, and that was when she would take hers. Nice and sly. He glanced at her while he was chewing and she pointed out some mayonnaise on his chin, so he wiped it off and checked his face in the mirror. It was then that Becka said something, and when Lucy turned to answer her, he noticed a streak of ketchup running from her mouth to her ear. How she managed to do that, he did not know. When she turned back around, he pointed at her face and when she saw it in the mirror, she nearly choked with laughter and spat her food onto him. This time his tracksuit top got it as well as the jeans. She had to get out of the car and walk around while she was trying to get her breath back in between coughing. Becka had wanted to get out as well, but decided not to after Pauli jumped out and walked around with her. Matt also reminded her of the plan, so she stayed put.

Lucy sits on the small wall surrounding the garage and he sits beside her. He keeps watching her as she stares at the grass and eventually she looks at him.

"I'm really really sorry about that, Paul. Honestly I am."

"Don't worry about it. I'm sort of getting used to it." From the look on her face, he decides to explain what he means by telling her about what happened a few nights before, when Fran had been eating spaghetti.

"And the whole plate landed upside down?!"

"Yeah, it was like a sandcastle. When I lifted the plate up, the food was in the exact same shape as the plate." She laughs and he watches her until she starts coughing again, and then without thinking, he starts rubbing her back for a few seconds and stops suddenly. She looks up at him as his face changes colour. He forces a smile. "Now it's my turn… I'm sorry."

"Sorry for what?"

"Well… ya know the way when babies have wind or something, and ya rub their backs? I thought that it might help a little. Again… sorry."

"It did help… thanks."

"You're welcome." he says, and looks to his left quickly.

"Pauli?" He slowly looks back and now he is trying to get a breath. She is staring at him and he notices that she still has that streak of ketchup on her face but it has dried in. "Sorry for what?"

"Eh…" he swallows hard. "When I was rubbing your back… I sort of felt your bra. It was an accident. Really!"

"It's okay."

"No really, it was! A total accident."

"I said it's okay, Paul."

"There's still ketchup on your face." he blurts.

"Oh no! I forgot about that. Come on, big boy." she says, getting up and the two walk back to the car. After all was said and done, the lads still had a big problem with not donating towards the cost of the food. Pauli begins to say, "Next time…'"but he is cut off mid-sentence by Becka. She seems to be running the show now and says that it is their treat as they don't live here, which makes no sense to Pauli. But as Matt is thanking them for the food and the drive home, Pauli decides to just shut up and keep quiet. They are dropped at the entrance to their estate and both wave until the red Astra is out of sight. Pauli exhales and looks at Matt.

"So… what do ya make of that?"

"Actually, P, I think it was very nice of them to bring us home and buy us a bit of grub."

"A bit of grub?! Did ya see the size of them burgers?! Of course ya did… I mean, between them

117

being in our spot yesterday and then bringing us home today, and then the food? I'm not happy, Matt."

"Not happy? And why? Ya seemed pretty happy when ya were rubbing her bra! AND... the two of you seemed to be gettin' on well together."

"We were getting on well. I only rubbed her back because she started coughing again. The bra just happened to be there."

"What are the chances of that? Look, the main thing is that you got on well."

"I suppose. But do ya not think it's a bit weird... the way it happened?"

"Okay... it's a bit weird. But did ya never hear of *Wacky Wednesday* and *Freaky Friday*?"

"Okay. I'll put it down to a *Freaky Friday*. That was a mad film, wasn't it?"

"Freaky!"

CHAPTER SIXTEEN

"Cuckoo… cuckoo." Pauli pulls the quilt over his head and snuggles deeper into it. Seconds later, he exhales while smiling. "Cuckoo, cuckoo… cuckoo, cuckoo." He frowns and thinks, 'What the heck?' He listens, but after hearing nothing, he turns onto his belly and tries to get back into that dream about Lucy and he smiles again. "Cuckoo, cuckoo… pieces of eight!" His eyes blink open under the quilt. 'You've gotta be fecking kidding me.' He turns and slowly pulls the quilt down. Matt's face comes into view, with him doing a Stan Laurel grin. "Morning!" Pauli puts his left hand over his eyes and nods his head.

"How the fu… and I'm trying to give up cursing, but how the fuck did ya end up here?"

"Mammy!" he replies, in a high pitched voice.

"What time is it?"

"Twenty two minutes to noon, as in… ya know what!"

"Ah, nice one, Matt! I would've missed it."

"Really? Do ya think I'd let ya miss Soccer Saturday? No fracking way, pal! And when's the last time that I didn't watch it here, tell me that, bro?"

"Never?"

"Exactly! Plus, me thinks that our…" he puts his fist to his mouth and pretends to laugh. "Favourite manager… ahem!" he says loudly, pretending to clear his throat. "Is gonna get put to the sword, and a serious tongue lashing from the lads after Tuesday's exit from the Champions League. I can't wait! I'm dying to see that post-match again, homes."

"Shit, that's right! Is it that good?"

"That good?! Aw man, all he says is…" Matt changes to a Spanish accent. "'My shquad this and my shquad that,' and he keeps blaming the ref. It's ace, and he looks like he was just after a good long cry. Total and utter classic!"

"Good on ya for waking me up, Matt." he says, throwing back the quilt. Matt looks down at Pauli's boxers. Well, truth be told, it's not like he could miss them.

"Ooh, Matron!" he says, in quite a good Kenneth Williams, while pointing. Pauli looks down and starts to go red. "Who, and I mean who, have you being thinking about?!"

"Well… I was havin' a bit of a dream about Lucy," he covers himself quickly with the quilt. "And I was trying to get back into it until that bleeding cuckoo started, and then the parrot! Thanks, mate."

"Sorry, stud. If I'd known, I'd have kept shtum and ya could've saddled that filly."

"If you'd known?!"

"Yeah," he sniffs the air and inhales deeply. "Sausages! Breakfast is served."

"Let's keep that appointment," Pauli looks under the quilt. "Look, I'll follow ya down in a minute."

"That poor girl." Matt says, with a grin as he leaves the room. While having breakfast in the kitchen, he winks at Pauli who tilts his head inquisitively. It is then that Rita turns around with a cup of tea in her hand.

"Okay for ye boys?"

"Oh, em… magnifique!" Matt replies in a French accent and kisses the tips of each of his fingers. Rita gives the old slanty eye while thinking to herself, 'It's a bit of food and I nuked it. Ah well, a compliment is a compliment. I'll have to pass it on to the caff… or maybe not.' She grins.

"Dad, what's the story?! How long before it begins?!"

"Any minute now, son!" Rita walks towards the sitting room.

"This is massive, Rita. My compliments to the chefette."

"Yeah, right, Matt. It's a bleedin' fry, get over it."

When she is gone, Pauli looks at Matt.

"What was the wink in aid of?" Matt looks over at the door, then back at him.

"Ya know the way your da's gone all George Bush?"

"Huh?" Matt tries to chew quickly so he can explain before the show starts and he swallows, but it's a hard one. Pauli winces.

"I felt that."

"So did I," Matt says, rubbing his throat.

"Take your time, it's not started yet."

"Okay, as I was saying. We're American… look at us crooked and we'll kick your arse all over the planet." Pauli scratches his head. "Ya know," he whispers, "the prepping."

"Aw, right… George Bush." he laughs.

"Anyway, I know some dude that has a container and he's willing to take a few hundred for it."

"You're joking?!"

"Nah, truth."

"Lads, you are pushing it close!" Fran calls.

"Look, tell ya later, let's go."

"Right." Seconds later, just as they sit down, *Soccer Saturday*'s music starts. On the break, Matt points his thumb towards the door and pulls a face.

"Go for it." Pauli says. Matt gets up and jogs up the stairs and Pauli thinks about going after him. Was that a, can I use your jax? Or was it a, can I use your jax and follow me and I'll give you the lowdown on the container? He decides to play it safe and stay put. Jesus, how weird would that look? Seconds pass before he looks at Rita.

"Where's Em and Em?"

"Gone out early with Jade, Jessie and Michaela. Over to the park to do the farm animals, the playground routine and a picnic."

"I was wondering, because I didn't hear that brat this morning. A different brat woke me up for a change."

"Pauli," Fran sits forward in his seat. "He's not a brat... he's a blinkin' torment!"

"Bullseye!" Rita agrees.

"Okay, torment. But it was just like... peace. Normally I hear Em... ya bleedin' this and I'll feckin' that. Ya can't stay under there forever. Ma, bring up the brush!"

Rita and Fran start laughing, "He does have a thing for that bed... or underneath it," he says.

"Can ya imagine him when he gets older? His wife wakes up in the middle of the night only to find herself in the bed," he hightens his voice. "Emmet dear, where are you? And his head pops out. It's okay, love, I'm under the bed, see you in the morning." Rita and Fran start laughing again.

"Or under the bed," Fran starts. "Emmet, where are ya, love? And his head pops out while holding some ribs on a fork. Felt a bit peckish love, fancy one?" Pauli claps his hands and lets out a yelp type laugh. The other two start again. The bathroom door opens and Matt comes down and walks into the room smiling.

"What was that sound?" Fran points at Pauli while still laughing.

"Pauli just spoke dog." Rita says, giggling. Matt sits down and looks around at the three.

"I love this gaff!" *Soccer Saturday* restarts.

CHAPTER SEVENTEEN

Approximately two miles away, in the park at the same time…

"Johnjoe, mind yourself, do ya hear me?!" Emma, Jessie, Jade and Michaela look at the person who has just spoken those words, as she walks towards Johnjoe, then they look at each other.

"How and why is she here?" Jade asks.

"I was just wonderin' the same thing." Emma says, and the three look at Jessie.

"Look, it's not my fault. She started talking to me when we were in the queue in the P.O on Thursday, just before we went to Swords."

"That was Thursday, Jess. Today's Saturday. That's one hell of a chat." Michaela says, in a slightly deeper voice than would be expected to come from a girl with her pretty face and athletic frame, standing at five eleven, with shoulder length black curly hair and unusually dark blue eyes.

"Here, check this out. Oh Sharon?!" Emma calls. Sharon looks around at Emma, then follows her pointing finger, which brings her eyes to her five year old daughter.

"Azure, ya little tramp, ya! Pull your fuckin' skirt down and fix your knickers!"

"I wonder where she learned that?" Jade asks, and the four giggle. "Johnjoe and Azure? Who came up with them?" Emma, Jessie and Michaela look at her.

"Jade?!" they ask together.

"Ya would've fit in perfect there." Emma adds. Jade suddenly looks really freaked out.

"Stop it, that's not funny." Michaela puts her arm around Jade's shoulder.

"We're only joking, for God's sake. You couldn't be anything like her, even if you lived in a sewer."

"Thanks… I think." They giggle again and it's now that Jessie notices Sharon walking towards them.

"Em, if I knew all the stuff you know, I'd say something coming at such o'clock. But that thing is heading our way." They watch in silence as she nears them.

"That fuckin' little tramp! Her skirt up and her knickers."

"We don't want to know!" Michaela butts in, while staring at the oncoming face of Sharon. An uncomfortable moment is shared.

"Ok… what's with this picnic?" Jade asks.

"Oh, yeah," Jessie looks around. "What about over there?" she points to a patch of grass at the edge of a tree line, "Oh my God, that looks lovely!"

"Fair enough." She is going a bit overboard, but feels responsible for Sharon's presence and rightly so.

She knows the way Michaela is and she's not known for her diplomacy. She normally hits first and doesn't bother asking or answering any questions later.

"Perfect. If Johnjoe wants a shite, he can go into the trees and have one." Sharon says, then turns and walks back towards the playground.

"What's Johnjoe, a bear?" Michaela asks, in a whisper. The four laugh, but try to do it quietly until Sharon shouts for Johnjoe and Azure to

"Get your fuckin' arses over here now, cause yizzer gonna get fuckin' fed!" The other parents, up until now, were trying to avoid looking at Sharon. They do take the odd glimpse, but are still hoping that she will leave soon with her four mates, as they are an imposing bunch and nobody has the balls to say anything. Even the ranger in charge of the playground, after being notified by a woman who had the nerve to disturb him by continuously knocking on the door of his hut until he opened it while he was having his third coffee in a row and trying to do the crossword in the paper, is not happy. He comes out with a gnat in his ear and listens to her moan. But even he weighs up the odds. After checking out Michaela in more ways than one, he decided that it would be in his own self-interest not to get involved. He doesn't relish the idea of returning home, bloody and bruised, only to tell his wife that five girls were responsible for kicking the shit out of him in his own playground. He put it to this woman that, as she is so concerned about it, that maybe she should do something herself or ring the Garda. Then he could get involved, he lies. He asks if her children are upset, only to find out that she doesn't have any and came to the park to read a book. The park is about a mile from east to west and the

127

same from north to south, plus the surrounding areas. In other words, it is a really big park. Then this bitch decides to read a book in a playground full of screaming kids? On hearing this, he wants her away from his door as quick as possible, so he lies again and says that he will ring the Garda instantly. Once back inside his hut, he puts the kettle back on for a fresh cup and thinks to himself what a cheeky bastard she was for interrupting him at work for something that feeble. As he rinses his cup, he remembers that he has a chocolate bar and a packet of crisps in his bag and smiles. In a few hours he would be out of there and could go to his local and do some real work. Until then, he will stay in the hut and mind his own business. Plus, that crossword won't do itself. As the four push their buggies in the direction that Jessie has deemed perfect for the picnic, Jade looks at her.

"Don't ever do that again, Jess. I mean it."

"We second that." Emma and Michaela say together. In the background they hear Sharon shouting at her kids.

"Come fuckin' on! Hurry up Azure or there'll be no bleedin' food left for yiz!" On hearing this, the four look at each other as they are nearing the spot.

"Did THAT even bring any food?" Michaela asks. Emma and Jade stop and look back as the other two go on to park their buggies.

"I don't think so," Emma says, while scanning it. "Her buggy looks empty... ish."

"It's not emptyish because what you're looking at is rubbish. The thing even has a weird smell off it."

Sharon is heading towards them from the playground while trying to push her buggy across the grass with one hand, and it is going everywhere but straight. She is pushing Azure's head with the other and swinging wildly at Johnjoe with her right foot, but has missed him twice so far.

"Let's be ladies and break out the food." Jade says, as she removes a bag from the buggy tray.

"If we were half ladies," Michaela says, dryly, "We'd be out in a beer garden right now on this fine sunny day, with some blokes trying to chat us up. Not sitting here with a pack of prams around us. I feel like a fucking cowboy surrounded by these buggies."

CHAPTER EIGHTEEN

Meanwhile, back at the ranch…

"How are ye for a can, Fran?!" Rita calls from the kitchen.

"On me way out!" he says, getting up. "But I just have to hit the head first!" Seconds later, her face slowly peeks around the door and he gets a fright on seeing it. Even the lads jump.

"Jesus, your ma can be creepy when she wants." Matt whispers.

"Ssh, this'll be good." She stares at Fran, who has frozen mid-stride, feet from his chair.

"Say that again."

"Now Re, ya know… like the… well… if…"

"Forget it, Fran, you're grand." Matt and Pauli look at each other, then at Fran, who still has a slapped with a wet sock look on his face. "Ye heard me, Fran. And get that face off ye, it's creepy. We use it in the job as well. I came out with it one day by accident and ever since then, it stuck."

"But ya tell Em not…"

"I know, but that's only because it could be construed the wrong way. Jesus, sure ye were there when I explained it to her, remember?"

"I do, love."

"Well, Dad, you'd want to hurry up and go to the head because *Soccer Saturday* is back in a couple of minutes." Fran smiles at Rita and makes for the door. She looks at the boys.

"Don't tell Em."

"Are you mad?! I like living here."

"And I like getting fed here and hanging with you nuts." She smiles.

"Right, the story is this. I'm doin' a coddle for the dinner and before ye ask, it's a white one."

"YES!" they say together.

"So, I suppose by that yes, Matt... that you're staying for dinner?"

"Well," he swallows. "Missus O'Neill, I..."

"Don't Missus O'Neill me, Mattaus Wolfe! I knew ye were staying. That's why I'm gonna make two big pots, so there'll be loads." Matt looks at Pauli with a smile on his face, then back at Rita.

"Thanks, Rita, I love your coddle. My ma only makes the brown one, which as far as I'm concerned is a stew. She makes tripe for me da cause he loves it but I won't touch the stuff."

Rita is tempted to say, "I wouldn't blame ye." But if it got said back to Maria, now that wouldn't be good. So she smiles and says nothing.

"Right Mam, how many sausages are ya going to use for the two pots?"

"Thirty two."

"Now they're not the cooked ones from the cafe, are they?"

"Pauli, for fuck's sake! I take pride when I cook something. I'm hardly going to put deep fried sausages into a bleedin' soup," she shakes her head. "I mean a coddle."

"Just checking."

"Well, I can make an exception for your bowl, and nuke some at the end and put them in it for ye, if ye want?"

"No, Mam, really… honestly. I love your coddle, Mammy."

"Mammy!" she smirks, nods her head and leaves the room.

"The old mammy trick, it always works."

"I know, it's deadly. Here, did ya want to tell me about that yoke or were ya just going the jax?"

"Wouldn't have enough time now, bro. So it'll have to wait till later around at my gaff," he smiles.

"Thirty two sausages for fuck's sake. When my ma makes that poxy brown one, she puts about six in and halves them."

"Nah… no way, homes! I wouldn't be too gone on eating half a sausage. It would just look like someone had taken a bite out of it and thrown it back in." Matt pats his belly.

"Well fed and loads of bread… heaven."

"Jesus, Matt, if I was going to say heaven, I think I'd set me sights a little higher than some buttered bread and a bowl of soup!"

"It's not soup, it's a coddle! And I heard that mammy remark as well!" she shouts from the kitchen. Just then, Fran tiptoes into the room with his finger over his lips. After a few seconds, he takes it away and smiles while nodding his head towards the kitchen.

"So, Franner, you're back, are ye?!" The three look towards the door.

"Your ma has a set of ears like a dog." Matt whispers.

"I know." Pauli whispers back and Fran nods in agreement.

"I heard that! And it's not too late for me to put some fried sausages in your soups… I mean coddle! ARGH!"

The three snigger.

CHAPTER NINETEEN

Back at the park, the picnic is going along much better than anyone expected. The girls thought that they had brought too much food, but considering the unexpected guests, it is just as well they did. Jade was right about the contents of Sharon's buggy and she was also right about the weird smell coming from it. Sharon has no problem with helping herself to the spread and seems to be constantly picking up food for her and her kids. As Jessie's, Emma's, Jade's and Michaela's kids are all around the eight month mark, they seem to nibble on bits of food for ages and the girls are also nibbling. So they watch as the other three eat their food as if their lives depend on it. Everything is going swimmingly, but then Sharon stops chewing and decides to speak.

"So, Emma, what's the story with your brother Pauli, is he gay?" The four freeze mid-chew and look at each other. Emma wants to say something, but suddenly it's hard to chew, never mind swallow.

"Are you a fucking simpleton?!" Michaela gets out first.

"Wha' do ya mean?' she asks, still eating, no fuss.

"I mean... you think that Pauli's gay?!"

"Well…" she takes a bite from a chicken drumstick and a bit of skin falls onto the grass. She picks it up and throws it in her mouth. "Ya never see him with a bird or anything. He's always with your man with the red hair."

"I don't know whether you've noticed it, Sharon, but you and your kids have red hair. Not that there's anything wrong with that, but compared to Matty… your Johnjoe looks like a fucking carrot!" Jade says, while staring at her. Sharon stops eating and puts her drumstick on the grass.

"I don't like the way ya say me son looks like a fuckin' carrot. And another thing, as far…" It's just as Sharon is saying "thing", that Emma, who is sitting to the right of her, knuckles her just below the shoulder. It is so fast, that by the time she pulls her arm back, Johnjoe, who felt the breeze across the top of his head, looks up at Sharon before looking at Emma with a confused face. He finds Emma smiling at him and as he looks around anti-clockwise finds the rest of the girls smiling as well. He smiles and goes back to eating the crisps and sandwich together. Azure's attention had been taken long before that when she spotted a Robin on the grass not far away, picking at bits of food. She decided to throw whatever she could find at it, which were mostly chicken bones. She threw an unopened yogurt as well, before Jade moved the rest out of her reach, and then her shoe.

"Did ya just punch me, ya tramp, ya?" Sharon asks, after looking at Emma, who starts to get up. But in a flash, Michaela is already up and standing behind Emma with one hand on her shoulder.

"Relax Em."

"Yeah, I did poke ya! Don't speak about my brother like that or I'll boot ya up and down this field."

"Yeah, right! In your dreams!" she says, smirking.

"Do you want me to let her up?" Michaela asks, while dead staring Sharon, who breaks eye contact.

"Can't even come out for a barbecue and there's fuckin' trouble."

"Firstly, this is a picnic. And second, why did you ask about Pauli?" Jessie asks.

"Well, I was thinkin' that if he wasn't, ya know... gay an' all, that I was gonna ask him if he wanted to come around to me apartment for a few cans or somethin' one night. Does he smoke the hash?"

"You stay away from Paul!" Jade growls. Emma, Michaela and Jessie are taken aback by the ferocity of Jade's statement.

"Jasus, I didn't know he was such a stud. If I'da known earlier, I would've asked him out long ago... probably still will."

Emma makes a move but, Michaela continues to hold her down. She is pinned. Sharon looks around at the kids.

"Ohh... I get it now."

"Get what?" Jessie asks.

"Yiz want to keep him for yizzerselves... so he's not gay. What about the redser?"

"I'm gonna fuckin' KILL her!" Emma says, trying to get up again but Michaela keeps her on her bum.

"You're very defensive of your bro… any secrets?"

"Sharon." She looks up at Michaela and her face starts to drain. "If I let go of Em," she glances quickly around, then back at her. But in that glance, she catches Jade's and Jessie's eyes, "You're going to be in a world of serious hurt, believe me." Jade gets up, and with her hands outstretched to Azure and Johnjoe, grasps theirs gently.

"Let's go back to the playground," she says, sweetly. Azure points at the robin.

"I need to get me shoe from that fuckin' bird first." When they get the shoe and are about twenty feet away, heading towards the playground, Michaela releases her grip on Emma's shoulder and sits down next to her. Sharon is not looking at all comfortable.

"You're a real shithead, Sharon. Do you know that?" Jessie says.

"Takes one to know one."

"Keep goin', Sharon! Cause your kids aren't here anymore and I'll drag ya into them trees and kick the shit outta ya!" Emma says.

"Yeah… go on and try it! Me kids are witnesses. If I look any different when they come back, yiz'll be all fucked, bigtime! I'll have the Gards on yiz so fast that yiz won't know what's bleedin' goin' on. Can yiz imagine it? Me out with me kids in the park and the four of yiz try to rob me?! There's a few years locked up for starters," she looks at them one by one and lingers on Emma. "Ya think you're all that and a battered burger, don't ya? But you're shit! You're just like me."

"So, ya admit that there's a smell of shite of ya then?" Emma asks. Jessie and Michaela start giggling. Sharon stands up.

"Jade ya bastard! Bring me kids back here now, ya fuckin' tramp, ya!" The giggles stop and the three are speechless. They can only imagine how Jade feels. Jessie is looking at the grass and has her hand on her forehead, trying to hide her face. Emma wants to ring Sharon's neck off her shoulders but her chance is long gone, with parents and children looking in their direction. With that shout, she just got more witnesses than she would ever need if Emma was to make a move now. Considering everything, with the abuse exchanged and received, Michaela picks up a small triangular ham and cheese sandwich and starts on it.

"Come on! We're getting' away from these fuckin' scumbags right now!" Sharon says, then grabs Johnjoe, turns him in the direction that they are going to go, by twisting his head, and gives him a boot in the arse. "Walk, you!" The three walk a few feet before Azure turns around.

"Yiz are bastards, yiz!" The four watch them walk away, and Sharon is still trying to kick Johnjoe as she pushes Azure's head every few seconds.

"Them poor kids," Jessie says, still watching Johnjoe dodge Sharon's foot. A few seconds pass in silence.

"I think that went quite well," Michaela says, while giving her daughter on the grass beside her a crust of bread to chew on. The three look at each other, then at her.

"Mikey, were you at the same picnic… as in the one we're having now?" Jade asks.

"Do you's think that she'll ever want to come on another one with us?" she asks, looking around at the three. "Yeah, me neither. Oh yeah, Em… lovely deadner." The four laugh.

CHAPTER TWENTY

Sharon had done two sensible things. The first was to get out of there and the second was not to give Micheala any backchat. She always had an unnerving presence on people and a low tolerance rate for idiots, as some of the girls in the Loreto had found out. Maybe it was her height? But whatever it was, everyone who met her never really felt at ease except for the girls.

The four have been friends since kindergarten. They were in the same class from the beginning of primary school until they left the Loreto in Balbriggan. When they got their Junior results, and all had done very well, they went out that night to celebrate with the rest of their class. The celebrations never really stopped after that. They were no strangers to alcohol before that night, but their sessions would normally occur in someone else's house when their parents were out, or in the local park. The four had also lost their virginity in that park. Over the summer holidays, they were constantly out in pubs and clubs and had one hell of a time, even though the three months were a bit of a blur to remember. They never went back for fourth year.

On one of these nights out over the holidays, they decided to go to Humphreys, the local pub, for a few before they headed off for their hard night of clubbing. They were all wearing miniskirts, but Jade took it a little bit too far even for the other three. The bottom of her butt cheeks could be seen by anyone who was standing up, so needless to say, a lot of men had suddenly taken to sitting down in front and behind her.

It was the height of July, and with a few mobile home parks less than two miles from the village, there was always an influx of out of towners in the summer.

This day was no different, and five of them took over the only pool table in the pub. The regulars watched on as their table was commandeered and were not happy. Their answer to this was to do what they did best, which was nothing. When the girls walked into the pub hours later, Jade took their attention away from the pool table and gave them something else to whisper about.

With it being a Saturday night, the pub was packed and something happened that never normally happened, no matter if you were a visitor or a regular, you had to queue to be served. There were also a number of different nationalities, which gave it a cosmopolitan touch, so it did not feel like a little pub in North County Dublin that night. Whether it was the hours of drinking or the part of Jade's bum that was showing from beneath her skirt, one of the five got it into his head to have a gander at the full bum. So as he was second in line for the pool table, he told the lads what his plan was, gave them a wink and went and ordered another five pints of cider. As he walked past Jade, he gave her a wink and a "click click" on his way to the toilet. She didn't even notice him. The girls were getting the drink into them, as it was 3.50 a pint here, but in the club it was 9.50 a bottle. They had their vodka and energy drinks in their bags and they would get a death just before entering the club.

Anyway, Brains emerged from the toilet and passed Jade again while staring at her. He did try the wink and the clicks again, but again he wasn't noticed and he started to get a little peeved. He stopped at the bar to pick up the drinks and in two trips brought them to the lads. The game was nearly over, so within ten or fifteen minutes, he would be on the table. As he said that he was going to pull up Jade's skirt on the way back from the toilet and didn't, the four were giving him stick for being full of shit. Now this he was not going to have, so he took a nice long slug of his pint and began his walk over to her. He stopped behind her and looked back at the four, who had their phones out recording and waiting. He turned back, and with his right hand, gently took hold of the hem of her skirt and raised it above her waistline, to reveal a freshly sunbed tanned bum with the red lace of a thong going up the centre. She didn't even notice it being raised, so her bum was exposed for about eight seconds before she saw Micheala moving towards her quickly from the toilet. Brains was standing there with a big smile, as he held up her skirt with one hand, while pointing at her bum with the other.

He was thinking that YouTube were going to love this, when he got a tap on the shoulder. He looked around and Micheala headbutted him and broke his nose.

Only when the warm blood splattered onto Jade's bum, did she realise what was happening. He hit the floor like a sack of shit and the pub went quiet except for, ""You're the one that I want"" which was playing on the CD jukebox on the wall. The four blokes stood there in shock, still holding their phones. They had just recorded Micheala flooring their mate with her head. They only snapped out of it when Brains, who was still lying on the floor, started screaming.

'Me fuckin' nose! Help me for fuck sake!'

With two of them playing pool, they were already holding cues and turned them back to front. Another picked up a chair, and the fourth took a ball in each hand off the table. These boys were not happy.

'Don't even think about it!' The four looked at Aoife, the head bargirl, who was standing with two barmen. Two more came in from the bar on the far side. She pointed at the ceiling to one camera, then to another at the opposite end of the room which just happened to be pointing at them. 'I can have the Gard's here in five minutes, and I think that yous have posed nicely just there for the perfect picture.'

'That fucking slut just broke his nose!' yelled one of the blokes who was holding a cue, as he pointed it at Micheala.

She had just looked back up from the guy lying on the floor after telling him "If you look up my skirt, I'll stand on your throat."

She stood there wearing a waist length black biker jacket, a red and black tartan mini which was a lot longer than Jade's, four inch platformed black strapped leather boots that stopped just below her knees, and red and black Argyle socks peeping over the top of them about two inches. She looked an imposing sight, standing six foot three as she stared at the remaining four, after taking one of them out of the equation already. Brains scrambled along the floor to the safety of his mates without looking back. Once there, he asked Aoife for a towel.

'Fuck off!' she replied.

With the cue holder being down the girl's end of the room, Jessie, Emma and Jade took one each and also turned them back to front. People had come from the bar and were trying to squeeze into the lounge to get a better view of the action, but still all of the patrons kept quiet. This was a stand-off that you didn't see every night.

'Ok, we can do this one of two ways,' Micheala began matter-of-factly. 'First, yous arseholes drop what yous have and yous can leave and that'll be that.'

'Ohh, we can, can we? Well what's the other way, ya lanky fucking slut?!'

The same bloke that had called her a slut already, asked the question with a smirk on his face while tapping the cue menacingly into his hand.

'The other way is quite similar. We will let yous leave… but there'll be a few Ambulances outside and yous will be getting wheeled out while having a nice look at the ceiling.'

Him and the guy holding the chair started laughing, but the other three stayed mouse quiet, not even a smile between them. This was not a good situation to be in. Considering they had only arrived out the previous night, and had the mobile home for another twelve days before returning home to Tallaght. So either they start swinging and stop standing there like saps, and risk ending up in the cop shop for assault and god knows what else? Thanks to the cameras and a hell of a lot of witnesses. Or they put down their weapons, put their tails between their legs and leave quietly like the tall slut said. They would have to stay away from this village and count down the days until they got out of here. Whatever option they chose was not going to do their reputations any good, as there were now camera phones pointing at them from most of the people behind the lanky slut. This wasn't going to be an easy one to live down, and getting locked up for a look at a tonged arse and four slappers wouldn't be worth it. Especially as three of them were on probation already.

'Miss, will ya get me a towel for me nose please?'

'I said fuck off!' Aoife repeated.

Just then the song ended on the CD player and after a few seconds of silence another began. ""Thriller"."

'Ok, ya lanky tramp! We'll let it go for now. Lads!'

The chair was put back on the floor, a cue was put against the wall and the other guy put his balls on the table. Mouthpiece was still holding his cue and decided to play to the cameras, as he knew that this was going to find its way onto the internet. He pointed it at Micheala and slightly shook it as he kept that smirk on his face, then slowly placed it on the table.

'Right, let's get the fuck out of this dump! It's full of wankers!'

The crowd behind the girls moved back to make a space for the five to walk out, but Emma, Jade and Jessie held their positions and their cues. Brains was first to leave, then the chair holder, handy balls was next, followed by the first to put down his cue. Mouthpiece was last and stood looking around the room for a few seconds before picking up his pint and necking it. After putting the empty glass upside down on the pool table, he belched loudly and grinned as he held both hands in the air, each showing the middle finger. At least he would look good whenever it was seen.

'See ya around, lanky,' he said, walking towards her but she didn't budge, she just stared at him. When he passed her, she gave him an unmerciful boot in the arse which caught him on the tailbone. It lifted him inches off the floor and he howled while holding his arse with both hands.

'And that's for calling me a slut!' she said, as she watched him sort of hop walk out of the pub, while still holding his arse and screaming in pain.

There was an eerie silence for a few seconds after the door had shut, until Aoife broke it. 'Ok, who ordered the rum and cola?'

The room exploded into laughter, talking, and suddenly there was almost a party atmosphere. Micheala looked at Jade.

'Ring your mam and get her to bring up another skirt and baby wipes. Then go into the jax, get that blood off your arse and throw that rag in the bin. And never wear anything like that again, clear?'

'I won't Mikey.'

'Girls!' Aoife shouted, and beckoned them to her with her finger. 'Four vodkas on the house and there's another four after that.'

The three thanked her and were soon joined by Jade. 'Me Mam's on her way up and its knee length.'

'Good, because I don't want to be doing that all night.'

'Jesus Micheala, that was some loaf you gave him. Is your head ok?'

'Fuck me head, Aoife. How's me hair? It took me ages to get the fringe the way I wanted it.'

The five laughed.

'I thought you were going to take them on all by yourself.'

'I had these three, and four against four... they wouldn't have stood a chance.'

Again laughter.

'Excuse me Miss.'

They turned to find six teenagers, three guys and three girls. They introduced themselves and just happened to be Spanish students over for the summer from Valencia. Aoife pretended that she didn't hear the student part. They chatted for a few minutes, and after showing the four the standoff that they had recorded on their phones, and a bit more laughter, they asked for a photo with the girls, who agreed. Aoife came from behind the bar and took some of the ten hugging and smiling. Ramon, the person who had spoken first, asked if they could put some pictures up on their internet page and the girls agreed and exchanged info.

A few minutes later, the four were in the toilet and Jade's skirt was in the bin. She stood in her tong as Emma wiped the blood off her bum with baby wipes. Micheala, Jessie and the other eleven girls, three of which were the Spanish girls, were all chatting away as this was happening.

'Right, your bum is clean. Jesus Jade, you've a lovely colour.'

'Thanks Em. Give me that skirt, Jess.'

Seconds later and she was fully dressed. 'Right, Aoife said four more on the house, and our taxi should be here soon, so let's get outside.' Micheala said, opening the door and the fifteen left.

Twelve minutes later and the taxi arrived. As they were leaving, the six Spanish students stood up and started chanting. 'Chickas! Chickas! Chickas!'

The name stuck and that's what they were known as from then on in the village.

CHAPTER TWENTY-ONE

After Soccer Saturday and two bowls of coddle each, with plenty of buttered bread, the lads ended up around at Matt's house. In his bedroom, Pauli sits on a two-seater sofa watching a paused game on the TV screen. It is minutes before Matt reappears with four bottles of beer and gives Pauli two.

'Get them down ya, lad! But slowly, because that's all I could scab off me ma,' he sits on the bed, takes a sip and moves his head slowly from side to side. 'Mmm, that feels good,' he looks at Pauli. 'Are ya not playing?!'

'Container?'

'Oh yeah, here's the read,' he positions himself facing Pauli, with one leg on his bed. 'Your man had a van in some estate in Coolock. But accidently, as the story goes, even though it wasn't an accident,' he shrugs his shoulders. 'After only four days of the van being there, well... I mean ON the fourth day, he turned up to open it and there was a car burned out inches from it.'

Pauli is looking at him and wonders where this is going, but decides to try and listen to a bit more without going asleep.

'Anyway, he thinks nothing of it. The natives are restless so they burn cars, who knew? When he opens the van, most of the stock is burned or melted. He spends half the day clearing it out and cleaning it up a bit, then goes and gets a load of new stock. After putting it in and arranging it, locks up for the night and thinks, a fresh start the following morning.'

'Was this in the winter or summer?'

'Don't know P, can't be sure. Anyway, when he gets there the next morning, he finds another car burned out exactly where the first one had been. Oh yeah, I forgot to mention that the first one was took away a few hours after a phonecall to the Corpo.'

'Don't tell me… the stock he replaced was destroyed as well?' Pauli asks, trying not to yawn. But this story, or lack of one, and the minutes sitting in front of the TV are taking their toll on his brain.

'Ya catch on quick. So he thinks, what the fuck?! Two cars, two nights in the same spot, and goes and rings the Corpo again. They tell him that it'll take a few days to move it, so he opens the van and starts cleaning it out again.'

'Hold on… what are the Corpo?'

'We live in a Council estate, but Dublin Corporation own that one. So they're called the Corpo for short.'

'Why do people keep burning your man's van? And what's this got to do with a container?'

'Oh yeah, I should've explained that part earlier. From what your man told me da, back in the seventies and eighties, there were caravans all around that estate because there were no shops built at the time.'

'So a van is a caravan that's a shop?'

'Yeah.'

'But caravans can burn, especially when there's a burning car parked next to it. Or should I say... two burning cars at the same spot, two nights in a row. So how did it not burn down?'

'I'm getting to that part!' he takes another sip of beer. 'As ya said, caravans can burn because they're made out of plywood or something. But that also makes them very easy to break into. So, someone along the way thought... a caravan or a shipping container? And that was the new shop.'

'So now it's a container, which means van, which means shop?'

'Yeah.'

Pauli yawns.

'Am I putting ya asleep?'

'Nah... just had a bit of a restless night. Carry on.'

Matt looks at the TV screen. 'I bet ya did, and I don't think I'll bother.'

'Ah c'mon, Matty! Tell me the rest.'

He looks back at Pauli. 'Ok. But only cause ya called me Matty. I know you're sincere when ya call me that.'

'I'm sincere.'

'Right, now ya have to imagine this. The container is in an unused carpark with a row of houses about ten feet away from it. So far, two cars have been burned out next two it, within two nights, at the exact same part of the va... container.' Pauli can suddenly feel this going somewhere at last, if the sudden change in Matt's eyes and his slight change of sitting position have anything to do with it. He is intrigued and stares back at Matt, waiting.

'Right, shock of shocks. He arrives down the next day to open the van and make some money, and the burned out car is still there... joined by another two. One is behind the container, and the other is between the container and the houses.'

'You're fucking joking?!' Pauli asks, sitting forward with widened eyes.

'No I'm fuckin' not! The Fire Brigade evacuated the first three houses nearest it, just in case.'

'Holy shite!'

Matt takes another tiny sip of beer while looking at Pauli.

'I can't take anymore, tell me what happened.'

'What do ya think happened? He got the fuck outta Dodge!'

'Just packed up and left?'

'There was nothin' to pack! He opened it and everything was melted to bits.'

'Did he know why the cars kept getting burnt next to it?'

'He thinks that he was taking business from another van shop not too far away from his one.'

'Well, I suppose it wasn't the brightest of ideas just sticking a shop into some estate without doing a bit of recon beforehand.'

'Nah, he knew about the other three that the same person owned, and thought it would be grand. But obviously it wasn't.'

'He sounds like a dope to me. So, what did he do with the container?'

'He left it there.'

Pauli stares at Matt before taking a gulp of beer.

'Hey go easy, that's all we have!'

'So let me get this straight. This bloke you know has a container in Coolock or somewhere. As far as we know, three cars have been burnt out next to it in three days, on three different sides. And how long ago was that?'

'I think he said it was about fourteen or fifteen… years ago,' Matt is trying hard not to laugh. He keeps telling himself, imagine you're on camera, imagine you're on camera. 'Or maybe it was sixteen.'

'Years?! I thought you were going to say months!'

'No, he definitely said years.'

'So god knows how many other cars have been burnt next to it since then. That's if it's still there. For fuck's sake, we were only out of nappies back then.'

'Four cars.'

'What?'

'Four burnt out next to it. One, then the next night another one, and then the following night, two.'

'I apologise, pardon my maths. But this bloke told ya he'd take how much for it?'

'A few hundred.'

'What does that mean… a few?'

Matt thinks for a moment. 'Yeah… what does that mean?' he jumps up and as he is walking out the door, looks at Pauli. 'I'll be back in a minute.'

A few minutes pass before Pauli hears him coming up the stairs. He sits back on his bed and takes a good long breath.

'I rang me oufla and guess what? Your man's there with him. They're in a darts competition out in some boozer in Ashbourne, so I had to wait till he threw,' he looks at his half full bottle on the floor, then back at Pauli. 'He said he'll take six hundred cash for it.'

Pauli double takes. 'Sa… say that again, the last part.'

Matt starts laughing. 'He said,' he tries to speak while looking at Pauli's stunned face. 'He, he said,' he splutter giggles and is happy that he hasn't got a mouthful of beer. 'He'll take… six hundred fo… for…' he can't finish and falls back onto the bed laughing.

What he was trying to say has just sunk into Pauli's head and he bursts into laughter. The two are like this for nearly a minute before slowly recovering.

'Aw man… that was awesome!' Matt says, wiping his eyes before reaching for his bottle. 'But me chest is in bits.'

Pauli goes for his one as well. 'Don't say anything. I don't want to spit this all over the place.'

'Now that would be a waste.'

The two take minuscule sips, and just after Matt places his bottle beside the TV, his mother calls him from downstairs. He jumps up again and is out the door. Not long after, Pauli hears Maria laughing. He can only assume that Matt has relayed the story to her. Footsteps sound on the stairs and Matt enters the room carrying a box of beer with a big grin on his face, and puts it on the floor.

'Me ma gave us this.'

'What?!…Why?!'

'Ya know her mate, Joan, that works in the supermarket?'

'No!'

'The one with the limp and the spanner eye?'

'Ah her? Ya should've just said the one that always gives out the wrong change.'

'Well she was supposed to be coming over here to have a drink with me ma, but she's been stitched up by her daughter to do a bit of babysitting while she goes clubbing. So me ma said, fuck it! She's not going to drink on her own, so there ya have it. She gave it to us to drink for her.'

'Firstly, my mam wouldn't fall for that. Secondly, tell Maria thanks from me.'

Matt goes to the door. 'MA!'

'Yeah?'

'Pauli says thanks as well!'

'Don't mention it. Yous two chill out up there and do your thing. Oh yeah, I've decided to get a Chinese, so do ya's want anything? I'm buying.'

Matt looks at Pauli. 'Two three in ones and some chicken balls?'

Pauli puts his two thumbs up and grins. Matt shouts down the order.

'I'll be ordering about ten. Is that alright for yous?'

'Perfect!'

'You can go out and get it, Matt. I'll be in me pyjamas.'

'Not a bother, Mammy!' he grins while nodding his head downstairs, then sits back on the bed. 'That worked out nicely, me ould chum,' he says, rubbing his hands quickly together before picking up his bottle. The two get stuck into the beer and while playing the game, Pauli thinks, what a great way to spend a Saturday night.

CHAPTER TWENTY-TWO

Sunday morning finds Fran in the kitchen making scrambled eggs, toast and tea for Rita's breakfast. He even went to the shop and picked up some orange juice and a croissant, just in case she prefers it to the toast. He glances at the clock on the wall, knowing that she will soon be awake. She always seems to rise around the half ten mark on days when she has no work, and at the moment it is 10:22. He decides to "gear up" and "deploy" himself up to her. Just as he is putting the orange juice and tea on the plate with the croissant, he hears her heavy heeled barefoot walk, going from their bedroom to the toilet. He uses this chance as a covert infiltration opportunity and brings the plates upstairs, stealthily taking them two by two after his slippers are removed. When she walks out, she passes the bedroom on her way downstairs. Seconds later, she appears at the door after walking backwards and stares at him. He is standing at the top of the bed with a smile and a plate in each hand. She scratches her hair and looks confused.

'Good morning, honey! Breakfast in bed for ya.'

Her confused look changes to suspicion, but she decides to play along and gets back into bed. When she settles herself, he hands her the plate of eggs.

'Ooh lovely! I haven't had your turmeric eggs for ages,' she says, licking her lips. 'Special occasion that I don't know about yet, is it?'

'There's toast or a croissant, or even both if ya want them.'

'Oh the croissant, I don't want toast.'

'Right, I'll have the toast then,' he says, rounding the end of the bed and placing the plate with the tea and orange juice beside her feet.

'What are ye doing?! It's no fuckin' good to me down there,' she says, while she slices open the croissant. 'Give me the tea and juice up here!'

He picks it up and holds it out to her. She takes it, places it on her locker and looks at him while shaking her head as she hands him the toast.

'Oh my God, these eggs are massive!'

'Right so, I'll leave ya to brek in peace. Just give me a shout when you're nearly finished and I'll be back to get the plates and stuff.'

She doesn't answer, just nods as she eats. He leaves the room and starts down the stairs to scrub that bloody pot and tidy the kitchen. Halfway down the stairs he hears a bang, then Emma.

'Emmet, ya little boll... I'll fuckin'...wait till I get me hands on ya! No ya don't ya little baldy fu... come 'ere!'

'Fran, will ye bring it up?' Rita calls.

'I will love,' he smiles and thinks, another day in paradise.

Minutes later, while he's in his chair watching a Prepping for D-day episode that he has already watched, he hears the noise of plates in the kitchen. He gets up and goes in to find Rita on her knees with her head in the dishwasher.

'Are ya alright there, love?'

She looks up at him. 'Where's the egg pot?'

'The egg pot?'

'Yeah, the egg pot! The one ye done the eggs in, the egg pot.'

He points at the press. 'It's in there.'

She stands up and looks at him.

'It's clean.'

She glances at the press while biting her lip. Seconds pass before she can't resist any longer. 'I have to see this,' she walks to it and looks through them all, then starts smelling them. 'Which one did ye use?'

'That little one beside your knee,' he replies, folding his arms.

She picks it up again and checks it carefully.

'Don't forget to smell it again,' he says, smugly.

She looks at him, then back at the pot and smells it. 'This is definitely the pot?'

'Yep, dat's de pott!' he replies, in his best rapper accent.

'Like… ye made scrambled eggs in this pot that I have in me hand?'

'Yeah! And I cleaned it, so there!'

'How did ye clean it, Francis?'

'I used steel wool, then rinsed it in washing up liquid. I'm not that thick and don't call me Francis,' he says, all of this through clenched teeth.

She puts the pot back in the press, then walks slowly to him and wraps her arms around his waist. 'I'm sorry, Franner. I don't think you're thick. Fair play to ye, that's all I can say... because scrambled egg is a BASTARD to try and clean.'

'Will ya stop talking about the pot?'

She stands on her toes and kisses him. After a few seconds he pulls away.

'Egg breath,' he says, grinning.

'C'mer ye,' she kisses him again. 'Hmmm,' she says, glancing downwards.

'Get a room!'

Both flinch when they see Emma looking at them and pull away.

'Do ye want anything... like a can of tea?' Rita asks, flustered. Emma has just taken a yogurt from the fridge and looks around at Rita.

'A can of tea?! Jasus Ma... actually DA, take her upstairs and do the deed. I'll just pop this and a biscuit up to Emmet and come down and blast the radio while I'm havin' me breakfast.'

'I'm gonna...' he points towards the sitting room.

'Yeah yeah, go ahead. I'll bring it in.'

'Thanks love. Mornin', Em.'

'Mornin', Da.'

Rita gets two cups and watches Emma, but she is still standing with the yogurt. 'You're a bit light.'

She looks at Rita. 'Oh, ya mean torment? He's upstairs under the bleedin' bed.'

'And you're leaving him there?'

'Well... yeah. I'm gonna bring up some biscuits and this, and if he comes out, fine. If he doesn't, then... he can eat them under the bed. It's not like he'll stay there for the rest of his life.'

Rita looks at her without saying anything.

'What Ma?'

'Ye seem very... laid back. Ye got the brush, but obviously didn't use it.'

Emma is still standing with the yogurt but her eyes are staring past Rita.

'Em, what's wrong love?'

'There's nothing wrong. It's just...' she leans back against the worktop and folds her arms.

'Do ye want a cup of tea?'

'Yeah, Ma, go on. I just want to bring this up to Emmet.'

'Don't forget the biscuits.'

She takes two chocolate biscuits and goes upstairs. When she comes back, Rita has already been in and given Fran his tea with some biscuits. She is sitting at the table waiting. Emma sits and takes a sup from her cup, then a deep breath.

'Right. Remember me, Jade, Jess and Mikey brought the kids to Newbridge yesterday for the picnic?'

'I do.'

'Well… Jess accidently told this… THING, about the picnic while we were getting our money on Thursday, and your one ended up inviting herself along. Now she has two kids but… you'd want to see the way she treats them and the names she calls them. Like the girl is only five and the young fella is three, but not a bother to her. I mean, calling them heavy language and swinging boots at them, and this was at the playground.'

'Do I know this person?'

'Her name is Sharon.'

'From where?'

'The apartments on Chapel Avenue.'

Rita takes a sup of tea. 'Does she have red hair?'

'Yeah.'

'And manky teeth?'

'That's her!'

'Em, ye don't want to be seen with someone like that. She has a really bad rep.'

'How bad?' Emma picks up her cup but waits for Rita to tell her.

'When she was younger she had a nickname.'

'What was it?'

'It was always said in Irish, but ye know what, an rothar dearg means, don't ye?'

Emma is astonished. 'The red bike?! Really?! Ohh… I didn't know that. Actually, how do you know it?'

'I heard this years ago when she was just a kid, and I mean ten and eleven. She was supposed to be going off with sixteen and seventeen year olds and doing the business, and I mean, the works! Then me and your da was in Humphreys one night, on one of the rare occasions that I got him to go out for a drink, and she thought SHE was the business.'

'What happened, Ma? I know there's more.'

'Well, let's just put it this way. He was about fifty and she left with him. The girl shouldn't have even been out that late, never mind in a pub. Months later, she was pregnant. It's a wonder she only has the two kids.'

Emma is still holding her cup but slowly puts it back on the table. 'Oh God, wait till the girls hear this.'

'Yeah, and ye make sure that ye tell them. And the lot of ye stay away from that tramp, because if ye are seen with her, ye will be branded as well.'

Emma takes a sip of tea.

'So you're cutting torment some slack because of this?'

'Mam… I treat him like the way she does her kids,' she starts crying and Rita gets up and hugs her. 'And I call him horrible names.'

'Em, you're a young mother. But now, thanks to what happened yesterday, ye have learned something. And from where I'm standing, that's a good thing.'

'But, Ma, what about when he gets older? He'll have mad memories of crawlin' around underneath a bed and being chased with a bleedin' sweeping brush. If he says something when he's older, or asks me about brushes chasing him under the bed, what am I supposed to say? Ah you're grand, son, that was only me?! Things like that stay in kids' minds. I'm a horrible mother!'

'No you're not!' Rita says, still hugging her. 'And don't ye ever think that way. Plus... we'll go half on his therapy.'

The two laugh as they hug again.

'Get a room!' Fran says, gliding silently past them.

CHAPTER TWENTY-THREE

A while later, Fran is watching an episode of Magnum P.I. This is one of eleven that he has tracked down and recorded on the satellite box and he is chasing the rest. Magnum is looking for something and empties a press, taking out a number of random items. One happens to be a rubber chicken. Even though he has seen this numerous times, Fran laughs. Pauli is sitting on the sofa and starts giggling. Fran looks over at him. 'It's class that part, isn't it?'

He looks up, then at Fran. 'What?'

'The rubber chicken part.'

'Rubber chicken? Where?'

'So, what are ya laughing at?' he asks, pausing the programme.

Pauli has just woken up and is still a little drunk. He scratches his head. 'Eh… ya know the way me and Matt went around to his gaff last night?'

Fran nods.

'Well, he said something when he was here and when we got there, I quizzed him about it.'

'I'm with ya so far.'

'Well, he said that he knows a bloke with a container and he's willing to sell for a few hundred euro.'

'A container of what?'

'Nothing. Just a shipping container on its own.'

Fran sits forward on hearing this. 'I'm looking for something like that for me shelter,' he says, excitedly.

'That's why Matt said it to me, because he thought ya might be interested in it.'

'I do... I mean, I am! Ring him, ring him now!' he says, looking for his phone.

'Dad, relax. We checked it up and your man's a sap.'

Fran sits back in the chair, deflated.

'Let me explain.'

And explain, he does. At the end, the two are laughing their heads off. This story just gets funnier to Pauli. Rita walks down the stairs, enters the room and stands looking at them.

'What's so funny? Ye can hear the pair of yous upstairs.'

Pauli puts his hand up. 'I can't repeat that again. Me stomach's in bits from last night and now.'

'I'll tell ya love, but give me a few minutes cause me belly's a bit jumpy.'

'Ok. But don't forget, because I could do with a good laugh,' she turns around. 'Ahh, here's me big boy!' she walks to the bottom of the stairs. Emma comes down, hands Emmet to Rita and she kisses him. 'Ye little divil!' she says, and walks back into the sitting room. 'Emmet... here's the laughing boys! Your uncle is the one who has one and a half eyes open. Say hello.'

'Gnnng!' he says, glancing around the room.

'Why didn't we just call him Gnnng?!' Pauli asks, giggling.

Rita, hostile, stares him and he stops. Something is very wrong.

'And here's your grandad. Say good morning, Grandad.'

He looks at Fran momentarily, then at the window. 'Gnnng!'

On seeing this, Pauli lets out a little, 'Bpp!'

Fran looks towards the window, trying not to laugh. Pauli gets up, walks very quickly to the door, out through the kitchen and into the back garden. As he gets to the side gate, he bursts out laughing while hunkering down and leaning back against it. This laughing lark is not all it's cut out to be, and his stomach is really sore at this stage. When it is not that funny anymore and he is giggling on and off stupidly, he decides that he will stay there until Emma goes out. If he sees Emmet again, especially after the look he got from Rita, it will be all over.

'Gnnng!' he says, shaking his head.

'Gnnng!'

He looks upwards at the direction that the sound came from, only to see Emma sitting crosslegged on the wall with her arms folded, while smiling down at him. The shock of seeing her there renders him speechless and drains a certain amount of colour from his face. It is seconds before he regains the ability to speak again.

'I'm sorry, Em, but… he's a mad kid. He just made me laugh.'

'Don't worry about it. He has that effect on most people.'

'I think them programmes are rubbing off on ya. You should've been a SEAL,' he squints. 'How the fuck did ya get up there so quietly?'

'As ya said… they're rubbin' off on me.'

'Are ya there long?'

'When ya went out the back, I went out the front. Then when I heard ya laughing away, I jumped the wall.'

'So, I was my own downfall?'

'Yep! Ya gave me cover sound. Ok, turn your head.' When he looks away, she turns and lowers herself, then drops the few inches to the ground and fixes her skirt. 'Are ya gonna stay like that for long? You'll end up getting cramp.'

He looks back at her. 'Am I forgiven?'

'Nothing to forgive,' she replies, with an outstretched arm which he takes and she pulls him up. 'I know what he is. And as ya said, he's a mad kid. Let's go in.'

'Roger that!'

The two enter the house and Pauli gives Emmet a better goodbye this time with no laughing. Minutes later, and they are gone.

'Close call there, kiddo,' Fran says, as he raises a can to his mouth.

'I know! But she was alright about it, different than normal. Before, she'd tear your head off. But today, she was… I don't know. Mellow? Relaxed?'

Rita sits there listening and stays quiet.

167

'Oh shit! Dad, can I have the remote?'

Fran tosses it to him. He goes straight to planner, finds what he is looking for and deletes it. He scrolls through the stations until he gets to Military and finds a programme about snipers. He presses record, then exhales as he sits back.

Rita and Fran look at each other.

'So boy, do tell.' Fran says.

'I had to delete something to make room for a programme Em wants to record about snipers. Just made it too as it's starting in six minutes,' he gets up. 'Does anyone fancy tea?'

'I'll have one, son.'

'Right ya are, Mam,' he says, and leaves the room.

They look at each other again. Rita winks and Fran gives a nod.

CHAPTER TWENTY-FOUR

When they have the house to themselves, Rita brings up the breakfast in bed. 'Fran, that breakfast was beut, thanks.'

'Well thank you, love.'

The match will be starting soon so she has to be swift. She is going to get to the end of this breakfast in bed shenanigans if it's the last thing she does. Once it's before the match starts that is, so her window is short. She is looking at the TV, but out of her peripheral vision, she is watching Franny boy as well and he is playing it cool. A bit too cool for her liking, so she lets out a little cough.

He quickly glances at her, then looks back at the TV. Something is coming, he knows that for sure. And he knows her false coughs all too well.

'Fran,' she says, slightly melodic.

Damn it, he thinks, closing his eyes. 'Yes love?' he asks, looking at her.

'What's your plan?'

'My plan, love?'

'Your plan! Breakfast in bed… turmeric eggs?' she acts shocked. 'Washing… oh, I'm sorry. ACTUALLY cleaning a pot. Tell me and don't mess about.'

'Ok… I could try and lie, but you'd see through that.'

'Well thank ye, and yes I would. Carry on.'

'I didn't do the breakfast to sweeten ya up, Re.'

'Well obviously ye did, because ye just said it there. Right there!'

'Do ya want the truth, Re? I mean… can ya handle it?'

She lowers her head while putting her left hand to her forehead. 'Two of yous. Bleedin' two… three!' she looks at him. 'Three. I have to put up with ye, Pauli and Matty Mc Fly!'

On hearing those last three words, Fran's jaw slowly extends outwards and his eyes widen. He is not impressed. At the sight of those eyes and that extended jaw, she thinks, what did I say? Whoops! And whoops, bigtime! Those eyes and that lower jaw only come out on very select occasions, and never the good ones. He stares at her hard and raises his right hand and points his finger at her. 'Don't you EVER say that again! There's only one Marty Mc Fly in this house, and that's Pauli!'

'What?!' she asks, confused.

'Matty Mc Fly! Do ya think that's funny, do ya?!'

'Oh shite! I'm sorry, Franner, I didn't think. It just came out. The three of yous are always doing different voices and quotes from films and all.'

His face starts to mellow, but he keeps pointing his finger at her. 'YOU know that I love me films, especially them ones. They helped me through a horrible time,' his eyes start to moisten. 'And Pauli loves them as well. How else could he do such a great impression of Marty?'

'I know, Fran. I'm sorry.'

He exhales and seconds later, his face takes on that placid look that is Fran, all back to normal. His mouth turns up slightly as he tries an apologetic smile.

'Can?' she asks, getting up.

'Yes please, love,' he takes her hand as she walks by and looks up at her. 'I'm sorry, love.'

'I'm sorry too, Franner,' she bends and kisses him on the cheek before leaving the room. When she comes back and is sitting with her tea, after giving him a can, she goes back to her original question. 'So, Fran... what's with the breakfast in bed? Ye are up to something. What is it?'

He decides to come clean, but takes a good gulp before doing so.

'Me bunker.'

She fights the urge to close her eyes and scream. 'Tell me.'

'Well...' he struggles to continue and looks around the room with panic on his face. She knows this look and behaviour all too well and stays quiet. No smart remarks or anything else that may make him feel any more uncomfortable than he already is.

'In your own time, honey.'

He sits there looking from his pad, to the carpet and back. Eventually, he looks like he is about to speak, and weirdly enough, does not pick up his can beforehand. She takes a sup of her tea which doesn't taste that great and wonders if the teabags have gone off. Can that even happen? She also notices that the match is about to start and he has not made any moves to watch it, or reached the normal cut off point. This thing is really playing on his mind.

'Re, I need a bunker and… well, I don't know what to do. Pauli told me earlier about a container that was going for a few hundred quid but… well, that's the story I have to tell ya, the funny one.'

'It better be funny!'

'Well, maybe it's not that funny, but it's weird in a funny sort of way.'

'Fran, did what ye just say make any se… CONTAINER?!'

'Yeah, a shipping container. Ya know the ones that do be on the…'

'Yeah, I know. The forty-foot trucks. The huge things for fuck…,' she takes a deep breath. 'So what happened?'

'It's a no go… no show.'

'Stop doing that!'

'Doin' what?'

'Ye know. The three of them in Fluglemans at the beginning. Well… sort of.'

Fran is in shock and smiles. 'Re, that's brilliant! That's the exact part!'

She smiles and is happy with herself, but it is one of her favourites. So right back at ye, movie boy. 'Shit! Ye swine are rubbing off on me!'

'Welcome to the family.'

He starts to tell her the story about the container somewhere in Coolock, but is constantly laughing while trying to finish it. She sits there, straight faced with arms folded, looking at him and is gumming for a cigarette and a decent cup of tea. She wonders if he will ever get to the funny part, that's if there even is one.

'The match'll be starting any minute,' she says, looking at her bare wrist, only then remembering that she doesn't wear a watch anymore. Big mistake. He sees this and now she realises that whatever chance she had of hearing the punchline before it starts, is long gone. Fran is hanging over the arm of the chair in bits. 'I'm goin' out the back for a smoke!' she says, with a pissed off tone in her voice and leaves the room. In the kitchen, she rinses a cup while waiting for the kettle to boil and listening to Fran in the other room. She takes the teabags out and smells them, then checks the date. Everything smells and looks good. She holds her hand in front of her mouth and breathes out.

'Shit!' she licks her teeth and they need a good scrub. She will give them one after this cup. She goes out to the back garden and sits on a patio chair and looks at the tea, wondering if she should have a bottle of beer instead. She decides to have the tea and then go on the beer. She sits back in the chair and is enjoying the sun with her tea and smoke. Just as she is finishing her smoke, she hears footsteps in the kitchen.

'Not still laughing, are ye not?!' she asks, sarcastically.

Fran doesn't answer. He just walks out, places a folded page beside her cup and retreats back inside. She glances at it a few times, then looks around the garden at her plants. After a few seconds, she looks at the kitchen window and can't see any sign of him, so picks up the page and reads it. At the end, she crosses her legs as she starts laughing.

'Ye bastard! I'm going to wet meself!' she shouts, as she runs inside.

CHAPTER TWENTY-FIVE

Rita decided to stay out in the back garden and take in a little sun, and she went on the beer. Well, it was a day for it. Her belly is not feeling that great after that laugh and she knows that if she goes back into the sitting room and sees Fran's face, it will most likely set it off again. He did venture out to the kitchen a few times to get cans, but had gone straight back in to watch the match.

She did actually wee herself while running up the stairs, but only a dribble.

The knickers got a quicky in the sink, but both them and her pyjama bottoms are in the washing machine at this very minute getting a good going over. She also had a sink wash, but as she calls it, a wee whore's rinse.

She is sitting with her feet crossed on the table while admiring her garden, when she notices a broken branch on one of her bushes.

'Those poxy kids with their feckin' football,' she whispers.

"Those poxy kids" are next door's. She looks away, but within seconds looks back at it. She is no good for stuff like that, especially where her plants are concerned. They get watered every morning and evening except when it rains. Her eyes narrow behind her sunglasses as she stares at it.

That wasn't like that this morning when she watered it and there isn't a football in sight. The little bastards must have climbed over, got their ball and broke the branch while making their escape. The feckin' cheek. She takes a sup from her bottle, then places it on the table. She will break it off so that it looks neater or it will annoy her for the rest of the day. Because it is so hot, she is not wearing any socks and walks barefoot on the grass towards it. She stares at it before bending down and reaching for it, when a low growl comes from the bush. She tries to move her feet too fast to stand up, but her left foot slips and she ends up on her bum with her glasses flying onto the grass. She scrambles using her fingers for grip and gets up. 'Oh Mammy!' she shouts, as she runs for the backdoor. While she is running through the kitchen, she nearly slips again. Barely keeping her balance, she keeps going while shouting.

'Fran! Fran!' she runs into the sitting room and he slowly looks up at her.

'Hello love, you're getting a bit of a colour there.'

She stands staring at him with her eyes widened that much that he thinks she looks like a lunatic. She swallows a few times as she rubs her bum.

'There's something in me bush and it growled. It sounded really big... it could've took me hand clean off!' His eyes drop from hers to her pyjama bottoms and he leans forward slightly.

'Ye dirtbird! I mean me bush,' she points towards the front window. 'I mean the one in the back garden,' she starts crying. 'And it broke me branch.'

Seeing Rita cry, ever, melts his heart. She is really serious and she is on about the back garden. He gets up and hugs her. 'Relax love. Both of us will go and check out your... plant.'

175

As he is walking ahead of her through the kitchen, she grabs his arm. 'Wait,' she whispers and gets the sweeping brush. 'Just in case.'

'What end am I supposed to use?'

'Any… anything. Just like…' she doesn't finish but does a poking movement towards the back garden. 'Like that.'

He takes the brush and heads for the backdoor. Once he steps onto the patio, he sees four beer bottles on the table and looks back at her.

'For Jasus's sake, love, four bottles and you're gone?'

'One of them is half full. Ye walk down to that bush with the broken wing, I mean branch, and you'll know,' she whispers, while pointing at it.

'Fair enough,' he says, and spins the brush in his hand so that the sweeping part is behind him.

'Chuck chick!' he says, while sliding his left hand back along the pole, imitating a pump action shotgun. He walks over to the bush and looks back at her with a grin on his face, while nodding down at it. 'This one?'

'Yeah yeah,' she whispers, from the back door.

He looks down at it while pointing the brush at it.

'Hey ya'll in there! Git yer yella bellies outta ma town, it's past noon,' he says, in a cowboy accent. Rita puts her hand to her head. He tries again. 'Hey varmint! Git yer lily livered carcass across the county line!' he pushes the front of an invisible cowboy hat up and looks at her. 'Guess there's nobody home.'

'Oh oh, there's somebody home alright, ye just gotta knock,' she says, pulling slightly behind the door while closing it a bit.

Fran suddenly remembers the match and he forgot to pause it. He decides to get back in quick and watch it, so he raises the handle and starts to hit downwards.

'Not me bush!' she shouts.

Laughs come from a few gardens away, followed by a solitary, 'GAAAY!'

But he is already committed and the handle hits the top of the bush and a roar comes from it. He drops the brush and turns towards the door. 'Keep it open!' Once he is inside, she slams the door. They look out the window and see the brush been dragged into the bush and stare at each other.

'That's either a dog or a bloody big cat.'

'It's a cat ye moron, and it's a tom… I think. They only get that big, don't they?'

'We haven't seen it.'

'But the sound of it,' she nods. 'So… there goes me brush and me bush. Gone!'

'I bet ya never thought you'd say that.'

She starts giggling nervously, then suddenly raises her hands. 'Hold on!' she shouts, inches from his ear.

He jumps and looks at her while patting his ear quickly.

'Sorry, but I know what to do,' she turns and runs towards the sitting room and he checks out her bottoms. She walks back in with his phone at her ear and looks at him, then squints her eyes slightly. She knows that look. She tilts her head to the side as if to try and look around him, but he is facing the garden. She shakes her head in mock disgust while fumbling to get a cigarette out of the box with her free hand.

'Hello, Da.'

Rita is trying to light her smoke, so presses loudspeaker.

'Da?!'

She takes a long pull from it.

'Da, if ya don't answer me, I'm gonna hang up.'

'Sorry, Em,' she says, blowing smoke everywhere. 'Look, there's an emergency. I need ye to come back.'

'What's wrong?'

She takes another pull from her smoke, then exhales. 'Em, there's something in me bush and it's big. Your da went down with a brush handle, but a weird sound came from it and he ran off and left it there.'

There is the sound of laughter from the phone and she looks at Fran. 'Em... Em, can ye hear me, love?'

Seconds pass. 'Ma, that was sick! Ya just made a show of me. I'm in Mikey's, and her mam and dad are here, plus Jessie, Jade and the kids.'

'What are ye talkin' about?'

'There's a broom handle stuck in your... bush, and ya want my help?'

Suddenly it dawns on Rita. 'Em, do ye have me on loudspeaker?'

'Yeah... like you do.'

'How do ye know I have?'

'Cause I heard Da fart.'

Rita looks at him.

'It was only a smalley,' he whispers.

'Wasn't that small,' Emma says.

'Where are ye now?'

'Outside their house,' she replies, sounding like she's about to cry.

'Go back in and tell them to shut up.'

'What?!'

'Go back in and I'll explain.'

'Ma, I mean it. If ya—'

'I'll sort this out, just go back in,' Rita interrupts.

When Emma goes back in, there is still some giggling and someone mentions the Fire Brigade and more laughs are heard.

'Hello?' Rita waits but it's still the same. 'Shut up!' she shouts down the phone. Emma has one hand holding up the phone and the other covering her eyes. It gets quiet quickly.

'Your ma's mad,' someone whispers.

'Who said that, Em?!'

'Eh... someone walked by outside,' she lies.

'Yeah whatever! Ok, I know what I said may have sounded a bit weird. But, Em, ye know the bush I'm on about, because ye got it for me birthday a few years ago and it was bald on one side.'

Even Emma tries to stifle her laughter with the rest. Rita hears this and puts the phone on the worktop. She fills the kettle, then looks at Fran. 'A can?'

'I have a full one in the sitting room, I'm grand,' he says, staring out the window. She goes in and gets it for him. The kettle is nearly boiled when she picks up the phone. There is a bit of chat and the odd laugh but it is quieter than it was.

'Ma… Ma?'

Rita looks at the phone.

'Ma?!' Emma repeats.

'Yeah Em, can I help ye?'

'Tell me the rest.'

'Right. The story is, that the bush has a broken branch, so I went down to take it away and something in the bush growled,' on the other end there is total silence and she looks at Fran and grins. 'Have I got your attention now?'

'Go on Ma, keep talkin'.'

'Well, I ran in and told your da, and when he was on his way out, I gave him the sweeping brush. Long story short, he hit the bush with it and the thing growled again, but this time even louder. The brush slipped from his hand and it got dragged into the bush.'

'But what can I do?'

'Do ye remember that ye really wanted something for your birthday two years ago and I sent Pauli in to pick it up?'

'Give me ten minutes and I'll be there,' she hangs up.

'What was all that about, Re? Could ya have been anymore cryptic?'

'Don't worry, Fran. Sit down and enjoy your can.'

It is about six minutes later when there is a key in the front door. Emma, Jade, Micheala and Jessie pull into the kitchen with their buggies and Fran looks confused. There are "Hello, Rita" and "Hello Mister O'Neill" here and there.

Jade walks to Rita. 'I'm sorry, but it was me that said you were mad.'

'I suppose it did sound a bit mad so we'll call it even, ok?'

Jade nods with a smile and the rest of the girls seem to relax on hearing this.

'Right, I'll be back in a minute.' Emma says, walking out of the kitchen.

'Em,' Rita calls, catching her on the stairs. 'We don't know what that is. It might be a fox and I don't want ye going out in that skirt. So put on them bottoms ye have and tuck them into the boots. And cover your face. Do the works, ok?'

'Copy that, Mam,' she says, turning and trotting up the stairs.

Rita turns to find the girls looking at her. Then Fran's face comes into view.

'Excuse the oncoming French, girls and babies. But Rita... what the fuck is going on? What's all this? Two years ago birthday present, and tuck your bottoms into your boots and the works stuff?'

'Ye'll see,' she says, heading to the fridge. She takes out a six pack of baby yogurts and holds them up. 'Who wants?'

The kids go all grabby so she hands them to Jessie, who is the nearest.

'Spoons are... well ye know where the spoons are. Right, girls, who's for tea and coffee?'

Except for Rita, it is coffee all round. They help themselves as they all have their own way of doing it, so she feeds Emmet in his buggy. Minutes later, the sound of heavy footsteps are heard coming down the stairs and everyone looks towards the hall. Rita knows what to expect, as she bought the stuff for presents here and there through the years. But she is a bit worried about Fran's reaction, especially as it was done without him knowing.

Suddenly Emma, or who they assume to be Emma, comes into view wearing a blue camo jacket under a black tactical vest. Her blue camo bottoms, as mammy told her, are tucked into her black boots. She has a blue camo kevlar helmet on her head, goggles and a black and blue check scarf wrapped around her face, just below the goggles and tucked into her jacket, so that it is covering her neck.

The faces on the girls is a picture. Shite! And it would have made a good one.

It is now that Rita is worried about how Fran might react when he sees what she is carrying in her gloved hands. She moves a little so that she can see the two clearly and without thinking, crosses her fingers.

'What the fuck?!' he says, when he sees it. He stares as she walks to the kitchen door and stops. 'An M4?'

'Yes, Dad. Standard issue to the US military.'

He looks at Rita. If it is going to happen, it will be now. Then the girls will definitely think they are mad. He nods towards Emma. 'Re… she looks good, don't she?'

Rita can feel the relief at the same time the words, thanks be to god, goes through her mind and she smiles. 'Yeah Fran, she looks the part.'

'Em, I never thought I'd say this about anyone wearing camo gear… but you look really cool.'

'Is that the best ya can do, Jade? She looks awesome!' Jessie says.

'Right, well I didn't get dressed up like this for a fashion show. There's something living in me Ma's bush, so I gotta go see what it is,' she walks to the door. 'When I'm out, close it.'

'Yes, Ma'am!' Fran says, as he gives her a salute and she nods.

At this point, the kids have been left to feed themselves as everyone else is positioned between the window and the backdoor. They watch as she moves diagonally to the right, across the patio to the grass. She has her gun trained on the bush in question, which is on her left, while working her way up the garden. She passes it by a few metres, then slowly drops to a crouch, moving sideways to the right, until she comes to within about two metres of where the brush handle is sticking out, while facing it head on. As she looks down her sights, she moves slowly towards the bush a few feet before she stops suddenly.

'Easy does it, Em.' Fran says, quietly. Rita looks at him, then back at Emma, who works her way closer to the bush and stops when it moves.

'Oh shit!' Jade says.

Emma stands firm, M4 still aimed. After a few seconds, she starts moving back.

'It must be big, she's retreating.' Jessie says.

'She got what she wanted… to find out what it is.' Fran says, before taking a sup. As she is moving, she glances at the grass and picks Rita's glasses up. She falls back to the side of the garden she walked up and stands, while walking slowly backwards and lowers the rifle. When she gets to the patio, Fran opens the door and she turns and walks in. She hands him the gun, the glasses to Rita, pulls up her goggles and lowers the scarf. 'I am bleedin' sweating!'

'What is it, Em?' Rita asks, putting her glasses on her head.

'She's a bloody big cat, Mam, and she has kittens,' she releases her helmet lock. 'And they're tiny and SO cute!'

CHAPTER TWENTY-SIX

Whatever plans the girls had before Rita's phone call, were put on hold. But after Emma's performance, they were flung out the window until tommorrow. They stayed on for more coffee and Rita threw together some sandwiches. They left just over an hour and a half later and Emma decided to give Emmet a mashed banana. Rita enters the sitting room with a bottle of beer and sits on the couch. She looks at Fran for a few seconds and smiles. 'What's wrong, narky knickers?'

'Wrong? The bleedin' noise of yous. Bibibibibibibibi!' he says, quickly moving his thumb and index finger as a mouth.

'I don't think we sounded like that, Francis.'

He looks down at her feet and slowly looks up at her face.

'Don't start looking me up and down, Franny boy.'

'Stop callin' me them names.'

'Well, as Pauli, a.k.a. Marty, your son would say, stop going on like a dick, doc.' He looks back at the TV and she continues to watch him.

'Go on... ye know ye want to smile.'

A smirk appears, then broadens to a grin before he starts to chuckle.

A few seconds pass.

'So, who won?'

'City.'

'So that's good?'

'Bleedin' right! Another three points gained. If they can win there next match, they should be out of the relegation group.'

She looks confused. 'But Fran… ye don't even follow city.'

'I know that, but I don't want to see them go down.'

'Ok,' she takes a sip. 'So… what did ye think of Em, Sarge?'

His eyes widen as he looks at her. 'She was bloody brilliant! I thought I was seeing things when she came down the stairs all kitted out. And her positioning while moving towards the tango,' he shakes his head. 'I mean the target. I just couldn't fault it, not one bit. She did everything right. I wanted to tell her, but with all those girls there, it would've been a bit awkward. Whatever that stuff is she's watching, she's learnt a lot. She'd make one hell of a Soldier, tell ya that.'

Rita is just about to take another sup from her bottle, when she does a double take at the door. Emma is standing there holding Emmet, and Rita freezes.

'What's wrong, Re?'

Emma walks in. 'I just came in for the babybag cause I fed him a banana in one hole, and out the other it came as he was eating it. I'm gonna bring him upstairs and clean his bum up.'

On hearing this, Fran starts chuckling again.

'Fran, you're feeble. She's cleaning a baby's bum.'

'It's the way she said it.'

Rita looks at Emma, who has a silly grin on her face, and one of her eyebrows is unintentionally raised a bit.

'Ye look knackered, Em.'

'I feel a bit, but I'm not going for a while. I wanna watch Strictly later and have me dinner.'

'Ah feck! I knew there was something that I forgot in all this excitement,' she looks at Fran, then nods her head. 'Don't go... ah, go on then.'

'You.'

'Inspector Callaghan, happy?'

'Delighted,' he replies, picking up his can. 'Oh, and you'll be able to see your little boyfriend tonight, Re.'

'Don't start that crap again, Franner.'

Emma giggles.

'Or ye, missus,' she says, looking at the faint stain on the carpet where Pauli's dinner ended up. 'Anyway, it should be ready around the hour mark.'

Fran rubs his hands together quickly. 'Lovely. Did ya get the yorkie puds?'

'There's three bags of them in the freezer.'

He wrings his hands while looking back at the telly.

'I'll put the potatoes on for the mash, and the roasties are on already. So all I have to do is prep the croquettes. In other words, open the bag.'

Fran and Emma laugh.

She gets up and comes over to Emmet, while smiling. 'Are ye gonna have your Sunday dinner, me little man?'

He stares back at her with a grin. 'Gnnng!'

Fran starts laughing, but seconds later the aroma from the nappy reaches him. 'Holy jasus!' he says, pulling his jumper up over his mouth and nose.

'Right, mister, let's get your arse changed,' Emma says, but looks at Rita. 'Mam, will ya take him for a second?'

'Give me the menace.'

She hands him to Rita, then goes to Fran and gives him a hug. 'Thanks, Dad. I heard what ya said and it really means a lot coming from you.'

'Thanks for handing me your weapon when ya came back in.'

'I'd trust no one else with it.'

CHAPTER TWENTY-SEVEN

Pauli had gone back around to Matt's and stayed there all day. It is 23:41 and he has just walked in the door. He goes into the sitting room to find Rita lying on the couch asleep. He then sees Fran sitting in his chair with an assault rifle on his lap.

'Alright son? I would've told ya anyway, but your mother made me promise to tell ya that your dinner's in the plant,' he says, looking up with a big smile.

'What's with the…'

'It's an M4. But I think ya already know that, don't ya? The newer version of the M16. Ya know the one they used in…'

'Vietnam.' Pauli cuts in.

'Very good, son.'

'Hello, son.' Rita says, with her eyes still closed.

'Sorry for waking ya, Mam.'

'You're alright. I just dozed in and out,' she says, sitting up.

'So…, everyone knew except me, eh?'

Pauli looks at Fran in silence.

'Your mam told me all about Em's fifteenth birthday present. That YOU went in and picked it up for her.'

'They wouldn't have sold it to her, she was too young.'

'Fran, stop it! Pauli, don't mind him, we told him everything. He's only winding ye up.'

'Dad, ya swine ya! I didn't know if ya were gonna go ape or something.'

Fran has a good giggle. 'For a BB gun… it's like the real thing. She's some baby, isn't she?' he asks, while looking at it and gently rubbing it.

'Oh it's… lovely, Dad. But you've just reminded me of something and I'm glad ya did, because I would've forgotten. Speaking of some babies. Remember that container in Coolock that everyone and their pet burns cars beside?'

Rita and Fran look at each other. 'We do,' they say together.

'Well, your man who owns it rang Matt's da today to find out if we were going to buy it. Because amazingly enough, someone else is suddenly interested in it, and it seems like they really want it.'

Rita and Fran look back at each other.

'The cheeky wee bastard!' she says, scrunching her nose.

'You were right, son, he is a sap.'

'I know, and both of yous are right. But listen, he said he'd knock fifty euro off if we picked it up ourselves, but that's as low as he'll go… if it's a quick sale.'

'So what did Billy say to that?' Fran asks, raising a can to his mouth.

'Well, it seems that when Maria was making breakfast this morning before I got there, she told him about last night and he was speechless. He couldn't believe that he wanted that much from Matt and he wasn't happy. So when your man rang him today about it, Billy told him that he was a fat moron, and only for they're on the same darts team, he'd blank him for life. AND... to shove it up his arse because there's more than enough room.'

Fran claps his hands. 'Good on ya, Billy. He never minces his words.

'And what did your man say?' Rita asks.

'He never had a chance to say anything because Billy hung up after that.'

'Proper bleedin' order!' Fran says, taking another sup.

Pauli looks at the M4 as Fran removes its magazine. 'Hold on, Dad... how did ya find out about it?'

Rita stands up. 'Sit down, son. I'll nuke your dinner for ye and we'll tell ye about our day.'

CHAPTER TWENTY-EIGHT

The next morning on the train to college, Pauli fills Matt in on the previous day's excitement and Emma's bravery.

'But P, mate, that could've been anything! Like, well… a cat, which it was but, it could've been a mad cat, or even a,' he looks up as if in thought, then back at Pauli. 'What are those mad dogs called? Ya know the real ugly ones that have a lockjaw? The heads used to walk around with them thinkin' that they looked cool until they got banned?'

'Yeah, I know what you're on about. They're a real rancid looking yoke. It's like a mastiff… a pitbull!'

'That's it! It could've been one of them, and they don't have to be injured to be mad because they're savages anyway.'

'Who said anything about it being injured?'

'Well, I'm just saying, that's all. Ya know what they say about injured animals? That they're worse than ones that are not.'

'Well, I'd rather go up against a lion with three broken legs than a fully fit one.'

'That's a really good point. But suppose it fell out of a tree and landed on ya and the fall broke its legs? I don't think you'd have much of a chance then because you'd be stuck.'

'Matt... I think if a lion fell out of a tree and landed on ya, you'd be brown bread. They're huge! Remember the one we saw at the Zoo? It kept coughing and it sounded like it had a sore throat.'

'Shit! Now that frightened me,' he looks away and thinks again before looking back at Pauli. 'It could've been a fox.'

Pauli is wondering if Matt was on the drink this morning.

'Matt, a wolf and I'd say, fair enough, your fertiliser. But a fox? Just give that a boot in the jaw and that would be the end of that. They're tiny yokes. And yeah, I get it. She was brave to go out on her own knowing that there was an animal there, whether it be a mad cat, dog or fox. But she had her BB gun, and we both know what damage they can do to a beer can,' he folds his arms. 'She did take a chance alright. But imagine if it had've been a pitbull or something?'

'Jesus stop, P!' Matt says, wincing at the thought.

'Anyway, she kicked ass without firing a shot.'

'I'd say the mates think she's a fruitcake.'

'Las chickas?! I think they're all fruitcakes! Especially Micheala. But Em's a bit, well not mad, but... on a different wavelength. Sure look who Emmet's da is,' he snorts. 'Locked up for three bells, as they say.'

'It wasn't her fault, he's an idiot! I mean, who goes around setting fire to wheelie bins and telegraph poles? And then getting caught while trying to set fire to an all-weather pitch after days of rain?'

193

Pauli watches him for a few seconds. 'Ya still like her then?'

Matt just stares.

'To be honest, I would've liked the two of yous to get together.'

Matt looks in shock. 'Really?! Ya wouldn't have minded me going with Em?'

'Why would I?'

'Ya know in the films. It's always... don't go near my sister, even when they're best mates. And when it happens, it always ends up bad.'

'Phppppf! They're films, Matt. And it seems like it's always a similar story. Remember the one we watched and they were bank robbers? Now they were really close. But the mate went with the sister on the sly and the brother shot him. Then cries like a baby and says they would've been good for each other?'

'I forget what it was called.'

'Exactly! So do I. That was a chore to watch and it depressed the fuck outta me.'

Matt looks to his left at the passing countryside and smiles.

'What?' Pauli asks, taking out two strawberry bars that he stole from Emma and hands one to him. 'What Matt?'

'It means a lot to me that ya said that.'

'Don't, Matt, I didn't bring any hankies.'

The two snigger.

Matt shoves the whole bar into his mouth and when it's gone, he stretches.

'Do ya think Colon is on this train?'

'Oh yeah, he must live down our side. What would you do if he walked up now and said, hello boys, I have something for yous. Here's a fruit bar each?'

'I'd check the wrapper very carefully.'

They snigger again.

Matt clears his throat a few times and Pauli knows that something is coming.

'And now I'm going to embarrass ya, homes. But… what was with the boner on Saturday concerning Lucy?'

'Boner and Lucy? And you were going to join the Garda?! Why ask?'

'Because I'm scarred, man, scarred! That quilt shouldn't have been moved, at all.'

'Fair enough, I got up a bit too quickly. But it seemed like I was dreaming about her all night. She's lovely,' he looks out the window, then back at Matt. 'And ya know the weird thing?'

'No, no I don't.'

'Remember when she cut into Mister Collon?'

'Colon!'

'Ok, Mister Colon. Happy now?'

'Yeah thanks.'

'Anyway, the part when she said about him being there and the time it would…' Matt false laughs way too loudly and when he is finished, stares at Pauli.

'About the length of time it would take for a fart to go through her knickers?' he slaps his forehead lightly with his left hand, while over-exaggerating his sudden enlightenment to Pauli's preferences in what he looks for in a girl. 'Of course! You're into a girl that can tell ya how long it takes for a fart to leave her arse, break through her knickers and float to freedom,' he clicks his fingers. 'Sorry, I forgot her jeans.'

Pauli folds his arms and just sits back and smiles.

'Look, Matt, we all stood there like a pack of dicks! Maybe we were in shock because we only found out about McCabe being preggos and gone, then we had a different teacher? So us saps were running around like saps, waving our arms, shaking our legs and whatever else. And I bet old COLON, got the laugh of the day watching us. He probably couldn't eat his lunch thinking about it. He probably laughed like a simpleton all the way home on the train. Maybe he even woke up in the middle of the night, falling all around his bedroom thinking of us saps running around like… saps!'

'So… ya think he thought it was funny then?'

'Yeah, I do! And who was he giving stick to at the time?'

'Me and you.'

'Exactly! But one thing stands. She was the only one that grew a set and stood up for all of us in that room, who were acting like… plebs!'

'I'm glad ya said plebs, I thought ya were gonna say saps all day.'

Pauli sits forward slightly and looks at Matt with a little intensity. 'I was always blinded or… mesmerised with Becka and her boobs, both of us were.'

'Were?! AM, ya mean! I still am.'

'Ok, but I'm not, not anymore. Lucy was always in her shadow… their shadows! But when she said her stuff, she looked at me and gave me a tiny little grin, as if to say… I don't know. But when she looked at me, I thought… oh my God, the bottom of her face is beautiful. Well, I hope she was looking at me.'

Matt rubs his hands together in that really quick way that makes Pauli feel ill, and has a big grin. 'Oh… she was definitely looking at ya, pal!'

'How do you know?'

'Let me put it this way, chumster. It's just as well she didn't tell us all how she goes to the toilet, step by step, or you my boy would be planning your wedding right this minute.'

'Matt, tell me.'

'Remember the day after we kicked all their arses off that Bollywood floor?'

'Yeah.'

'Well, ya went to the jax and I sort of disappeared with them back to Lucy's car, and we sat there chatting for a few minutes.'

'Yeah, and we could've missed the bleeding Enterprise!'

'That was the whole idea. Becka was giving her guff in the car, telling her to just ask ya out, but she was afraid to. Especially after what she said about, ya know yourself. Isn't irony ironic? The thing that she was most worried about is what got ya to notice her. Then they just happened to be in our spot for lunch? No alarm bells go off that day, P, no?'

Pauli is looking at him but Matt can see his brain working behind his eyes.

'I'll make it easy for ya… she fancies the caks off ya, pal!'

'Matt, don't bullshit me!'

'Me? Never, buddy. Then there was the garage when ya felt her bra.'

'I was rubbing her back because she…'

They stare at each other.

'Exactly! When's the last time ya rubbed a girl's back and felt her bra?'

Pauli thinks for some seconds. 'It's sad to say… but never.'

Matt stretches again. 'Well, me little back rubbin' friend, you'll be doing a lot more of it in the very near future.'

'And how's that going to happen?'

'You just leave that to your uncle Matty,' he says, with a grin and a wink.

CHAPTER TWENTY-NINE

It's quiet in the cafe, and Rita and Sophie are standing behind the counter drinking tea and coffee while the system is playing a burned CD. There were a handful in for breakfasts, but since around eleven, there is only one person left since opening time at nine and it is the same person. She is an old girl about seventyish, who is a regular, and she is still reading the same metro magazine that she came in with.

Rita looks at her bare wrist, then at the clock and exhales with boredom.

'I'm getting sick of that bleedin' CD. Find a different one, will ye? I'll go see if Mary wants another top up. And don't put any dance music on, Soph.'

Mary is delighted. Rita gets fresh tea bags, fills the pot and brings it back to her with a newspaper that somebody left on a table. She tries to pay even though Rita said it was a top up, so she refuses any money and returns to the counter.

'You know he counts those tea bags?'

'Yeah, like he goes around his four shops counting the bleedin' tea bags? Well, the miserable bastard can recount them, give him a bit of exercise. Like he's going to miss a few bleedin' tea bags? What are we supposed to do, use the customers' old ones?'

Sophie starts laughing.

Rita thinks about all the stuff that they take from the shop. He obviously doesn't count them well enough, so she is wondering why Sophie said that.

'Are ye ok, Soph?'

'Ah, just have them… and they're really bad,' she puts her arm across her face and takes a few deep breaths. 'Ohh, I have to go the head, Re,' she says, jumping up and running to the toilet.

Rita is just about to say something but she is at the door and disappears inside.

Suddenly it gets dark and seconds later, hailstones pound onto the road and against the window. Rita's phone rings and she checks it before answering.

'Sophie, what's wrong?'

'Re, what the fuck is that noise?'

'Hailstones, and they're bating off the windows.'

'What's Mary like?'

'She's still sitting there reading the metro, not a bother to her. So much for the newspaper, that's on the floor. I'm going to bring her down a few biscuits. How are ye doing?'

'Mouldy! That noise just frightened me. I'll see you in a while.'

'Ok,' she places her phone on the counter and goes to Mary's table. 'Mary, do ye fancy a few biscuits with your tea? Now they're mine so they're free?'

'Well... if it wouldn't hurt anyone,' she replies, after looking up. Only then does Rita notice the sticky tape across one of the lenses.

'No no, I'll be back in a sec,' she says, turning and walks back to the counter. She decides that not mentioning the hail was a good move, as it obviously doesn't bother her or else she hasn't even noticed it.

A while later, Sophie emerges from the toilet and she is a sickly white.

'For fuck's sake, get around here and sit down.' Rita says, taking one of her arms and bringing her to a seat.

'Oh Re... I don't feel well.'

'Just sit there and relax. Do ye want something, water or...?'

'Yeah water. Do you have any painkillers or headache tabs?'

'I have them good painkillers, but they're not the dissolvable ones.'

'Anything, this is rotten.'

'Do ye want a nerve tablet as well, to chill ye out?'

'Oh yeah, the lot... anything at all. This is... awwgh,' she takes a few breaths. 'I can't go home, Re... I need the money. I've two weeks credit union and I'm not asking John again.'

Rita gives her the tablets. A few minutes later, she is a different girl and looking a lot better. The hail stops and within seconds, the sunlight is so strong coming through the windows, that the two are sitting there squinting at each other.

Mary gets up and comes to the counter and Rita takes the till.

'That will be four euro, Mary.'

She looks at her in shock. 'But I had a breakfast, four pots of tea… and your biscuits. By the way, they were lovely. Did you make them yourself?'

'Honestly… no, I didn't. I just opened the packet, but I have loads for me kids.'

Mary looks cross. 'Don't be giving me your kiddies' biscuits, Rita. Keep them for the little ones. Even though they were lovely,' she winks.

Rita smiles and winks back. 'They're far from little ones.'

'How many do you have?'

'Just the two, thank God.'

Sophie coughs and Rita glances over at her, then back at Mary.

'Well, sort of three. The young one has a baby.'

'What's their ages?'

'The boy is nineteen, Emma is seventeen and her wee lad is eight months.'

'You're a grandmother?! I'd never have guessed that you were that old… I mean, that you have kids that old. Sure you only look like one yourself.'

Rita smiles over at Sophie for a few seconds, before looking back at Mary. 'Ah, that's very nice, Mary. Isn't it, Sophie?'

'Oh definitely, Re.'

Mary looks up at the price board for a few seconds.

'No that's wrong, I had more than that. I had loads of stuff! It comes to more than that. I... I had four pots of tea...' she looks up at the price board again.

'Mary, they were only top ups, they're free. And the biscuits were mine.'

She thinks for a moment. 'Well, if you're sure. I don't want to get you into any trouble, you know the way jobs are these days.'

'No trouble at all, Mary. Was the breakfast nice?'

'It was lovely! Everything was, and the service. Yous two are great girls,' she says, looking at Sophie, then back at Rita as she opens her purse and hands her ten euros. She takes it and gives her back six.

'There ye go, Mary. Now it was raining... I mean hail, so be careful where you're walking, won't ye?'

'Oh I will, I will. And the noise of that hail, it was very loud for hail,' she puts a euro in the tip bowl, turns and goes back to her table and starts to get her things together. Just before she leaves, she comes over to the table where the two girls are sitting. 'Thanks girls, I'm going now so god bless,' she turns, puts her stuff in a battered old pram and Rita goes to the door and holds it open for her as she leaves the cafe. Then Rita returns to the table.

'Jesus, you look after her, Re. Fair play to you.'

'That could be our mother, or even us in a few years. Ye know what they say, what goes around, comes around.'

'Yeah, and Karma can be a real bitch!' she says, before finishing off her water.

'So, how are ye feeling?'

She looks at Rita with a big smile. 'Brilliant!'

'Do ye want a fresh cuppa?'

'Please.'

'Tea or coffee?'

'Tea, at least I know where I am with it. I'm off the coffee now for a while.'

Rita makes two teas and sits back at the table.

'Soph, my Fran, well... I think he's going through the change.'

'You mean the crisis?'

'Yeah, maybe that as well. Now he's fifty in July, and that's not to mention the rest. I was expecting this a few years ago, but nothing. Now, suddenly out of the blue... I think this is it,' she takes a sip from her cup. 'Ye know the way they start wanting motorbikes, sports cars, more hair, younger birds... ye know where I'm going, don't ye?'

'I do. So what does he want, which one?'

'None,' she takes another sip of tea. 'I'd love a smoke now.'

'Me, too.'

Rita plays with her cup for a few seconds. 'Ok... don't laugh.'

'I won't.'

'He wants a... eh, shipping container.'

Sophie stares at her.

'Well, ye weren't lying, ye didn't laugh.'

Sophie takes a sip of tea and looks back at Rita.

'Are ye ok, Soph?'

'What does he want it for?'

'Well… he's got mad into this progra…'

'Fuck, fucking off!'

This time, it is Rita's turn to stare.

'Are you for real?!'

Rita hesitates before answering. 'Yeah, I am. Why?'

'So does John. Something about the end of the world. It's called D-day.'

'Prepping for D-day.' Rita corrects.

'Yeah, that's it. I knew there was something else. I thought, here we go, John's losing it.'

'Sophie, your John is near Fran's age, so maybe it's a midlife crisis for the two of them.'

'Re, as you know, I'm twenty six and he's forty-eight. I don't think I could put up with that.'

'It could be worse.'

'How?'

'Actually, I suppose this is bad enough. At least he won't be looking for the younger woman because he has ye, and he has that big jeep thing.'

'Landcruiser.'

'Yeah. Well, maybe it's not the crisis, I don't know.'

The two sit there thinking for a few seconds before Rita breaks the silence. 'Well Soph, the reason that I brought it up is that Fran nearly had one but…'

Here is where Rita tells Sophie the story about the container that gets burned on a regular basis. Needless to say it has the same result. The two are nearly falling off the chairs laughing. Just as they are coming down to giggles, the door opens and two middle-aged couples walk in.

'Ah well, back to work.' Rita says, standing and going to the counter for her pad and pen. Sophie goes back out to the kitchen.

From then on, it got busy up until lunchtime, when it got chaotic with the regulars in, plus the school kids for their sandwiches and rolls. The place started to empty slowly after the lunch rush, and with three people scattered here and there on coffees and teas, they decided that they would have a cup of tea too. This time they stayed behind the counter, and keeping their voices low, took up where Rita had left off.

'Right, Soph, back to Franner's near container.'

She giggles. 'I have to tell John about this when I get home, but I'm going to try and time the end just as he has a mouthful of cider.'

'Ye evil bitch!'

'I know,' she says, with a giggle.

'Right, I was wondering... with John having his fingers in the building and the transport trades and all that, if ye would ask him about the price of one?'

'No problem. I'll ask him tonight and I'll ring you.'

'Now, ye know the size of my garden, so nothing like a forty foot or anything. Just the smallest to shut Fran up.'

'No probs, and I'll make sure you get it for a good price.'

'Ah thanks, Soph. It's just to keep him happy if it is a midlife.'

They take a sip of tea and Rita's eyes widen as she remembers something.

'What? What is it?'

'What I'm going to tell ye… I'm not buzzing off Fran or nothin' like that. But the other day, he wanted to go to,' she finger quotes. "That German shop" as he calls it, and buy loads of jars of gherkins and make Pauli eat them. Only to fill the empty jars with sausages. I didn't really listen to him after that.'

Sophie starts laughing. 'I'm sorry, Re.'

'Laugh away. I know, it's a bit mad, isn't it? Anyway, I explained to him that he didn't have to do that and turn Pauli off them for life, because he loves them.'

'So does John. He's like a vulture, looking at me sideways when I get a burger, just waiting for me to offer it to him. Sorry, carry on.'

'Well, I explained to him that they already do them in jars and that they're called hotdogs, and he was amazed. Like, he's months away from turning fifty and he's only finding this out. So I brought him to the shop and we got eight jars of hotdogs, ten of tomatoes, beans, peas, six or seven bags of pasta, the same of fish and four boxes of rice. It doesn't bother me because he went half and I'd probably get that anyway when I go for a shop. Except the hotdogs and that much rice, but I didn't tell him that. All of that will be gone within a few weeks, the hotdogs and rice may take a wee bit longer.'

Sophie is trying not to laugh, but Rita is going to let her have one anyway. But she will omit the part where he lost two years along the way.

'And guess where he keeps the food? Under the bed.'

Sophie laughs that loud that the three heads turn to look. When she is finished, she wipes her eyes before looking at Rita.

'Re, there's these meals that the military use and they last for ages. John's thinking of getting some off the net.'

'Do ye think he'd mind getting me some for…, I don't feckin' believe this!'

'What?'

'Now I'm trying to get Fran some meals in case the world does end. He's worked the bleedin' head on me.'

'You were saying.' Sophie says, biting her lip.

'Will ye see if John will get me some for… Fran, as a surprise?'

'I don't see why not if he's getting them anyway. I can't remember what they're called though.'

'Fran would know, but I can't ask him.'

'Think younger.'

'Younger?'

'Ask Em.'

CHAPTER THIRTY

Fran waited about an hour after Rita left for work before going to the bus stop. His timing was perfect and minutes later, he was trundling his way down the road from the village to the old N1, or what is now called the R132, on his way into Swords. As the bus was nearly empty, he sat at the front, up top, just as he did as a kid. He felt a bit stupid for an adult but it was a good sensation. He also noticed the TV screen on the way up the stairs and it totally confused him. Only after looking at it and its changing views, did he realise that there were cameras on the bus. Where he was sitting had a blind spot, so he decided that he would try and sit there on the way home while he was having a can. Today's trip is going to end at the library, but before that, it is an outdoor sports shop that he has in mind for the first stop.

He had passed it many times when he, Rita and the kids used to go for lunch to an Indian restaurant years before, and hopes that it still exists. He can smell the food long before reaching it and stops outside the restaurant and reads the lunch menu. After a quick check of the prices, he nods and thinks about bringing Rita back for one soon. She would really like that.

He walks the few metres to the corner with fingers crossed, and takes it while purposely looking to the far side of the street so as not to make it obvious. Obvious to who?

he wonders, just as he sees the reflection of the shop in a hairdresser's window and smiles. He crosses the narrow road and stands staring between the two windows, either side of the door, at their contents for minutes. In one of the windows, they not only have one of what he is looking for, but two. He enters and meanders to the boot section. After giving it the trice over, he decides that a few are not bad and that he might invest in a pair someday. But today's objective is prime, and one thing at a time. Turning to the counter, he notices a number of BB guns hanging on the wall. But one in particular stands out and it is a Sa80, one of the weapons he used when he was in the Army. But again, first things first.

'Ow do?' he asks, in a Somerset accent for some unknown reason.

'Sound, and yourself?'

Grand… grand,' he looks at the window that has what he wants. 'That black bow, the small one. How much is it?'

'The price that it has taped to it…99 euro.'

'Can I have a feel of it?'

'Of course, sir,' the guy says, rounding the counter and walking to the window.

He removes it and hands it to Fran. 'Powerful thing that!'

Fran takes hold and draws it a few times but releases it slowly.

'Not your first time?'

'More of a crossbow man, meself,' he says, in his normal accent. 'My dad used to bring me hunting when I was a kid.'

'You know they're illegal now?'

'Why do ya think I'm lookin' at this yoke?'

The assistant smiles and looks at the bow. 'So… what did ya hunt with your dad?'

'You name it. Rabbits, pheasants, wood pidgeons. He caught a fish twice.'

'With a crossbow?!'

'Yeah. The second time it was to prove that the first time wasn't a fluke… and it wasn't the same fish.'

The assistant false laughs. 'Must've been one hell of a shot?'

'He was. He was a Soldier.'

The guy smiles again and looks back at his phone on the counter.

'Ok, I'll take it.'

His head snaps back to Fran, 'Good! Do ye want arrows as well?'

Fran looks over at a range of different types hanging on a wall.

'One pack of them… and the flight kit.'

After he pays for the stuff, he walks back and faces the wall with the BB guns. 'So… the P-90, how much?'

'230.'

'What about the MP-5?'

'225.'

'Ok…, the AR-15?'

'220.'

'The AK?'

'215.'

'The Sa80?'

'210.'

'So... everything goes down by a fiver?' he exhales, while glancing around the shop, then looks back at the assistant. 'My daughter has an M4 and she got it for 165,' he lies. He looks back at the rack of guns for a few seconds before quickly turning and staring the guy in the eye. 'How about doin' a deal on the AR?'

The assistant looks at the gun wall for a few seconds before looking back at him. 'Make me an offer?'

Fran makes him an offer and gets it for 180 after saying that his daughter is a BB gun collector. With this much potential business, he falls into Fran's trap.

Fran wasn't entirely bullshitting and he knows what Emma likes. As he had nothing to do with her fifteenth birthday present, a.k.a., the M4, he's buying her its predecessor, the AR-15. With the choices that they have, she'll have a nice little collection of at least three at Christmas. That should ruffle Rita's feathers and make her think twice before she goes Black Ops behind his back again.

Next stop is the library. He gets help from an assistant who finds a website that has what he is looking for. He tries to order the items but it is not as easy as it is made out to be. After some websites appear on his screen all by themselves that he didn't want, never mind even heard of before, he realises that computers are too difficult for him and not his style. Plus, they are a dangerous little bunch.

He accidently finds the original website again and decides that further help from the assistant is unnecessary. He takes down the catalogue numbers for the items that he wants and a contact number. In the back of his mind, while repeatedly looking over his shoulder, he doesn't want anyone else knowing what he is up to. Just in case they get the same idea. He will ring England using the good old phone and speak to someone, man to man. Avril is very helpful, and under two minutes later, she tells him that his order is being prepared and that he should have it within five to seven days. He bids her farewell and checks his phone credit immediately. The call cost him just over two euros and he is well chuffed with himself. With a smile on his face and a swagger that hasn't been seen in a long time, he walks the ten or so feet to the door of the supermarket. A tub of potato salad, a packet of sliced corned beef and two cans of beer are picked up for the journey home. On the bus, he gets his front upper seat again, out of the cameras view and demolishes the meat after taking two sups from his first can.

The potato salad will have to do for a snack later, as he forgot to pick up a plastic fork to eat it with. He is excited thinking about his expected delivery next week and about how Em will react to the AR. He decides to wait until the soaps are over before presenting it to her. For Christmas, he'll get her the Sa80 and she will like it, he is sure of that.

CHAPTER THIRTY-ONE

Rita gets home just after twenty past four and walks from the front door to the kitchen without stopping.

'Heya love! Got rashers, sausages, pudding and goujons if ye want some.'

Fran enters the kitchen to find the food wrapped in tinfoil on the worktop. She fills the kettle and once her cup is teabagged, sits down at the table.

He stares at the food. 'How are ya, darlin'?'

'Don't how are ye darlin' me, just go for it,' she opens the backdoor and just as she reaches for her cigarettes, she stops. 'Ah feck it! I'll hold on until me tea's done,' she looks out the door at the sun filled garden.

Fran roots through the package and takes a sausage and two pieces of pudding and stands looking at her while eating them.

'Nice?'

He nods his head. 'I love your robbed food.'

'Who's in?'

'All, and upstairs.'

'Anything new with that cat?'

He nods again, 'Ya know that moggie that lives here?'

She stares at him before starting to get up. 'Ye mean OUR cat?!'

'I'll get it, love,' he makes the tea and brings it over to her. 'Here ya go.'

'Thanks. Grab your can and we'll go outside and ye can tell me.'

After going to the sitting room and getting it, he arrives at the backdoor. 'Nothing to tell now.'

She smiles at him. 'Our one's the da. Oh God, no wonder she gave birth in the garden. And look at him lying beside the bush.'

'Yeah… it would almost bring a tear to your whisker.'

'Hardy har har! Jesus, Dad, you're almost as funny as Eamon Dunphy.' Pauli says, from behind.

'I'll take that as a compliment.'

'How are ye, love? How was your day?'

'Nothing to complain about, Mam, all's well. Oh yeah, Matt'll be around shortly.'

'Well, there's a rake of food there.'

He rubs his hands together. 'Grand cake, Nora!'

The two look at him.

'What?' he asks.

They look at each other, then back at the bush.

'Pauli, will ye get a rasher and sausage and throw it onto the grass?'

He turns without answering, gets the food and comes back to the door. 'Alright, where do I throw them?'

'Between two slices of bread with some brown sauce!' Fran answers.

Now Rita and Pauli look at each other.

'Da, you're downgraded to Liam Brady.'

'What about Johnny Giles?'

'What about him? Ya don't mess with the Johnny!'

'Son, will ye get me a beer from the fridge? I need something stronger than this with…' she trails off while glancing at Fran and nodding her head.

'I will, but where will I throw this food? Me hands are getting all greasy. Do ya know that there's some amount of fat on these rashers?'

'Be thankful ye have food!'

'Yeah, I know. There's loads of people out there…' he starts snoring.

'Pauli!'

'Sorry, Ma. Where…,' he doesn't finish. He just tosses the food to the edge of the patio. 'Come on Zeus… fetch!'

Zeus gets up and moves lazily towards the food. He picks up the sausage and walks back to the hedge and enters slowly. Then comes back for the rasher.

'Dad, no one liners about him giving her the sausage.'

Rita looks around. 'Pauli, ye dirtbird!'

'I left that one for you, son… sucker!' Fran says, chuckling.

Zeus helps himself to some of the rasher before bringing the remains to the hedge and leaving it just inside again.

'Ahh, he's providing for his children.' Rita says, smiling.

'Pauli lad, I'm runnin' low. Would ya do the honours?'

'Yawohl!' he replies, before turning on his heel and going to the fridge. He gets a can and another bottle for Rita, just in case, and brings them out to the table. She picks up the ashtray which is full of butts and holds it out to him. 'Would ye empty that as well, garçon?'

'Ya know what? I'm going up to me…'

'Gnnng!'

They look up to find Em and Em looking out their window. 'Gnnng!' they say.

Emma giggles.

'How's me little man?' Rita asks. Emmet looks up at the sky, then left, right, behind into the room, back out, down, then left and so on. 'Em, are ye staying in for the night?'

'Yeah Ma, me going nowhere; bed, food, telly…, but not in that order.'

'Good, because I want a word in your ear later.'

She looks puzzled. 'Gossip?'

'Affirmative!'

'Em, can I have another go of one of your…'

'Sssh! No, Da, not out here. When you're back inside I'll bring one down for ya. The AR? And thanks Daddy, or the M4? And thanks, Mammy.'

'The AR, and that's what I meant love, good girl.'

'Oh, I thought ya meant like now, out here?'

'Jesus, I'm not that thick, and have the fuzz at the door?'

The five end up looking in different directions before Emma breaks the silence. 'Ma, could I have one of your beers?'

'Of course!' she replies, getting up.

'It's cool, Ma, I'll bring it up to her. When Matt gets here, just send him up.'

'Sure will. And Paul, bring her up two.'

'Will do,' he says, turning and starts to hum.

She thinks, what better time than now? 'Paul, son?'

He turns around. 'Yes, Mother?'

'I need to have a chat with her so I'll bring them up. I'll do chips with that food when ye want it, so shout me.'

'Will do… later!' he turns and starts humming again.

'Re, before ya go, what are we gonna call that new moggie?'

'Well, Franner, with all the crap that's happening, I didn't even think of that cat, never mind naming the bleeding thing. Anyway, it's too big. It'll be off in a few weeks, never to be seen or heard from again.'

'What crap?'

'Ah, it's… crap in work. All new prices,' she lies.

'Ma, I'm still here with mutton head and I heard that I'm getting two bottles.'

'Sorry Em, me neck was starting to ache from looking up,' she looks at the dribble in her bottle. 'And I forgot ye were there.'

'So we won't bother callin' it anything then?'

'Fran… ye don't even like cats. Why do ye want to name it?'

'How about Daisy?'

Rita looks up. 'I don't think it's a Daisy, Em. Have ye seen her?'

She thinks for a moment. 'Actually… yeah, Ma, I did! Yesterday with her babies.'

'I'm sorry, Em. I'm still winding down from work. I told Sophie and she said that I should've taken a picture of ye. She told me to tell ye, fair play.'

'Ma, you're gonna make me cry,' she says, grinning.

'Honey, I'm on me way up now with your bottles, ok?'

'Beer, yehaa!' she shouts.

'Ok, Hammer, I need to talk to Em and spend a little time with her and mutton, so ye know the crack? If we're not down when the soaps start, shout us, ok?'

'Ok, my lovely. Go on up. She seems a bit…' he waves his hand.

'Finally ye can tell the signs. It's not rocket science, is it?' She kisses him and he pats her bum as she walks away. She knows that he is watching so she wiggles.

He wolf whistles.

CHAPTER THIRTY-TWO

Rita enters the room with four bottles of beer and Emma and Emmet are still looking out the window, so she sits on the bed.

'I'll be with ya now, Ma. We're just watching a jet and there's a liner coming any second as well. Sweet!'

She walks to the window. 'Where's the jet?'

'See those white trails way up there? That's it.'

Seconds later, Rita hears the sound of a plane.

'And that's the liner.'

'Where is it?'

'Look up at the gutter.'

She does, and a plane appears almost instantly, heading westwards away from the house and lower than she expected. Planes are planes, and other than the two jets, days before when she was in the garden with Fran, she never took an interest in them or even noticed them flying almost directly above the house. Now that she thinks of it, she has been in the garden on numerous occasions and the sounds of planes would be heard every now and then. But to bother looking up to see where it was coming from, never came into her head. She just put it down to background noise that was annoying when trying to talk to somebody. 'What's a liner?'

'Jet liner... passenger plane. See,' she points at it. 'Ya can see how many engines it has. But the fighters are up so high that the white vapour trails are all ya can see unless it's a really clear day, and ya might make out a tiny bit of the plane.' She looks from the white trails high up, heading east, to the fastly disappearing passenger jet heading west, then at Emma, who is already looking at her.

'Ok, let's have some beer.'

'Copy that!' Emma says, putting Emmet in his playpen.

The two sit on the bed and Emma speaks first. 'Ma... is this about that slut?'

'No, nothing like that,' she opens the bottles and hands her one. 'Chin chin.'

They clink bottles. After a sup, Rita is just about to speak, but puts her finger across her lips. She goes to the window, looks down at Fran and quietly shuts it, then goes back and sits on the bed. She takes another sup.

'Your da can hear a fly blink.'

Emma takes one as well and waits.

'Right, Em, here's the story. I'm thinking of getting your da a shipping container, but a small one, because I think he's going through the change.'

'Why do ya think that?'

'Because he's gone on a mad survival buzz since watching some shows on telly.'

'And?'

Rita is taken by surprise. 'Ye think that's normal?'

221

'I recorded those shows. Da was probably going through the telly and found them by accident.'

'Ye recorded them?!'

'Yeah. I wanted to see what their plans were if it was to happen. It shows foraging, hunting and there's weapons involved. But after watching a few of them, I wasn't impressed and lost interest. I just forgot to delete them.'

Rita looks towards the window and smiles. 'It all makes sense now.'

'What does?'

She stares into Emma's eyes. 'Em... what I'm going to say now is meant in the best possible way, but... ye are one of a kind.'

'Ah thanks, Ma.'

'Here, do ye remember when ye would be out pubbing and clubbing, and then ye would come back at mad times? Sometimes dawn even, and would get on the settee? One thing I'll say for ye... ye always knew where your home was.'

'Ma,' she nods at Emmet.

'Ok, well most of the time ye did. Then you'd get comfy, but wouldn't come up and get a quilt or anything, ye would just cover yourself with cushions and wait for your shows to start and watch them... or try.'

Emma looks puzzled, 'Try?'

The two take another sip.

'Em... did ye never wonder how ye were always covered with a quilt when ye woke up? Or find a bottle of cola and some crisps beside the couch?'

222

'To be honest, Ma, most of the times I don't even remember gettin' home.'

'Well, a lot of the times I'd be waiting for ye to come home and then I'd, or we would, if your da was still awake, listen for ye to come in and go to bed.'

'But?'

'Ye would get in eventually. I'd let ye use your key, but the minute ye were inside, the door would close over and I'd wait a minute, then go down and you'd be either asleep on the floor or on the stairs, key in hand.'

'So I never locked the door?!'

'Most times ye did. But there were the nights when ye were that gone that once ye were inside, that was enough.'

'Oh, Ma, I'm sick! I'm disgusted with meself.'

'Em, ye were young. Puberty and all that crap!'

At this moment, Emmet looks around and smiles.

'Will I get him a slice of cheese?'

'Yeah Ma, thanks.'

She is back in under a minute with a slice of cheese, a slice of pork, onion and tomato and two more bottles, and Emma does not look at all happy. After she gives the meat and cheese to Emmet, she decides to change the subject a little. She begins by talking about the first of the shows that Emma used to watch and about the good looks of the lead character. Emma agrees with her and recounts some of the episodes which Rita adds to. Her subtle change of tact has worked and Emma is back to normal and enjoying this. Then they move on to the show that followed it. Again some characters are mentioned and some plot lines.

She looks at the ceiling for a moment before looking back at Rita.

'Ma, how do ya know the names and the stories?'

'Because when ye were asleep, I'd be down the end of the couch and then they would come on reminder and I'd end up watching them.'

'Hold on for a second. The first one ya mentioned was Zeke.'

Rita blushes a bit. 'He was a Sergeant… and reminded me of your dad.'

Emma smiles. 'A likely story. But I found him more of an uncle figure.'

'T-minus five!' Fran shouts up.

'Copy!' Rita shouts back.

Emmet looks around with a confused face, then goes back to rubbing the cheese into the netting of his playpen.

'Right Em, to the point. Ye know the food that Soldiers get and it lasts for ages, what's it called?'

'M.R.E's.'

'How do ye say that?'

'M.R.E's.'

'What does that mean?'

'Meals ready to eat.'

Rita looks confused.

'Just think, Meals, Ready, Eat. Forget the, to, part.'

'Good,' she smiles. 'Meals ready eat, meals ready eat,' she repeats a few times, looking and sounding drunk in Emma's opinion.

'Yeah, Ma… why?'

'Because it seems that Sophie's fella, John, is a bit ma… getting a container as well, because he watches the same shows. But he's going one step further. I told her about the sausages in the jar episode, and she said that he's gonna try and get some of them… M.R.E's.'

Emma looks in shock. 'You're jokin', Ma!'

'No, I'm not. He watches them as well and is getting a few containers. At least now it doesn't feel as weird with someone else in the same boat.'

'Ma… I mean the M.R.E's! He's getting some?!'

'Yeah, so I was thinking of getting some for your dad as a surprise. Depending on the price, of course. Do ye think they'd be dear?'

'I don't know, but I want some as well!' she looks at the giant poster of the F-14 Tomcat on the opposite wall. 'Why didn't I ever think of doin' that?'

'Well, Sophie said that she'd ask him about the smallest container and the M.R.E's. She's going to ring me tonight, and Sophie's no bullshitter.'

'Ma, don't forget me now.'

'Don't worry. If they can be got, they'll be got,' she takes a sup from her bottle. 'What type of food are they?'

'From what I've seen on telly or read, they come in a pouch. Some ya put into water and heat up, others ya put something in and they heat up. And others, ya can just eat from the pouch. I read this book about this tank squadron, and for some reason the logistics got mixed up,' she sees Rita just about to ask. 'The supplies got mixed up or something, and the only food they got were boxes and boxes of bacon and beans M.R.E's. And because they were

225

on a mission, they had to stay in the tank for nearly a full day… no getting out for fresh air.'

Rita makes a face. 'How many are ye talking about in the tank?'

'Four! For a full day on coffee, smokes and bacon and beans. Yum!'

'Jasus… that doesn't bear thinking about. What do ye think the other flavours would be?'

'It could be spagbol, chicken curry, shepherds, lanky hotpot, stuff like that. They come in desserts as well. I know,' she closes her eyes for some seconds and Rita watches her. 'Sticky toffee pudding is one of them. Ma, I never tasted that, but it sounds lovely. Will ya see if he can get that one as well?'

'I'll ask when she rings, and that does sound lovely,' both finish their bottles and Rita opens another two. 'All of what ye said there sounds nice, Em.'

'Look Ma, they wouldn't give them to the troops if they were rubbish.'

'These tank fellas, were they Americans?'

'No, Brits.'

'It's about to start!' Fran shouts up and then they hear the music.

'Right, we better make shapes. Ye get the bottles and I'll get fathead and we'll talk after she rings.'

'Roger that, Mam!'

CHAPTER THIRTY-THREE

True to her word, Sophie rang after the soaps. Emma was upstairs trying to get Emmet asleep and Rita went out to the kitchen to take the call.

'Right Re, here's the story. I said it to him and he said that he knows of a few that are lying on sites and are no longer being used, as the building has been completed. Sometimes they can be left there for months afterwards before getting picked up, so leave it with him and he'll find one that's suitable.'

'Did ye find out the size of the smallest?'

'He said the smallest they use is twelve foot, but that would be too small and a waste of time. It would have to be at least a twenty foot. I told him the story of the burnt one and I timed it to perfection. He spat cider all over the kitchen floor and nearly choked in the process.'

On hearing this, Rita holds the phone away from her and looks at it for a moment before putting it back to her ear. 'Ye bitch!'

'I know! Anyway, he said it wouldn't be mad money, and I told him it better not be or I'll be going on strike.'

'Jasus Sophie, don't do that! I don't want to be responsible if anything happens between ye two.'

'Re, I'm just buzzing with him… kinda. If he can get one, he will. And it will be reasonable. They're used for storage and offices so it will be in good nick and not a burnt out shell, let's put it that way.'

'Ah Sophie, you're so good and so is he. I feel a bit weird now because I'm asking again.'

'You mean the M.R.E's? Did Em know?'

'She told me. She knew exactly what they were.'

'Well, he still has to check them on the net.'

'Well, when I said it to Em, she said that she wants some, too.'

Sophie starts laughing. 'That's your girl! But he will check them out and he's dying to try them. He just has to find out if they can be gotten by civilians, and he wants to check between the US and the UK. He's even thinking about Germany as well. I'll say one thing for him, he's thorough. He says he wants to check the different meals, prices and the shipping and stuff like that. He's on top of a job at the moment and it's a bit behind, so he doesn't have as much free time on the laptop as normal. Then when he comes in from work, it's the drink. I'd try but I wouldn't know what to look for.'

'Me, too! I'm useless at technology. Jasus, I can just about use the till and that debit card yoke,' she takes a quick sip from her bottle. 'So, what are ye up to?'

'I'm having a few bottles and making some cocktails. He keeps eyeing up the Chinese menu so I think that's on the cards for later. I have those aroma candles burning in the bathroom, so I'm gonna make a pitcher and bring it up while I have a bath. I can constantly smell chips and I know it's off me.'

'Ye lead a great life! Candles and cocktails while you're taking a bath?'

'I know. I must think I'm some sort of royalty but… hold on, Re. John, don't dare go near that bathroom. I'm going up now for a bath! I don't care!…Use the one under the stairs!…Re, sorry about that. He's a fuckin' weirdo!'

'What's wrong?'

'He wanted to have a piss, so I told him to use the downstairs jax. Now he's in the garden waving at me while he's pissing on the flowers.'

Rita laughs.

'Oh, I'll drink some drink tonight and I need it. Thanks be to God you're in the kitchen tomorrow.'

'Oh shite, I forgot! I've to open up.'

'Yeah, and I'll be cruising in at nine. So have a cup of tea and a toasted cheese and ham ready for me, won't you?'

'Of course I will. And ye enjoy your extra few hours in bed.'

'He's on the drink, then there's gonna be a Chinese involved. I'll end up on the sofa because if I sleep in that bed with him, I'll need two baths in the morning.' Rita laughs again. 'Too much info. I've heard enough about blokes farting.'

'Tell me!'

'I'll tell ye in the morning, I need to go the head.'

'Right so, and don't forget me toastie.'

'I won't, missus. See ye in the morning.'

CHAPTER THIRTY-FOUR

It is Wednesday, and Matt and Pauli's class started at ten and has just finished now at twelve exactly. This means that they can have a nice leisurely walk to the train station and make the twenty to one, be back in their village just after half one, and pick up some chips for the walk around to their estate.

They leave the old class of Miss McCabe, which is now the new class of Mister Collon, and are metres from the front door and the beginning of their walk.

'You boys fancy some lunch?' a female voice asks.

Both recognise it as Becka's and are already smiling as they turn. Matt is facing her and Pauli faces Lucy. There are grins all around from the four and Pauli finds himself unable to stop staring into Lucy's green eyes.

'Does a fart smell?!' Matt asks, breaking the moment. 'Sorry, Lucy.'

The four laugh.

'I'm starving and could do serious damage to a piece of food!' Matt adds.

Becka laughs again but Lucy raises an eyebrow and glances at Matt, then back at Pauli, who shrugs his shoulders.

'This… is what they give me to work with,' he says, arms outstretched at Matt. The girls giggle.

Minutes later, the four are in Lucy's car and curiosity rears its tiny head.

'So… where are we going for lunch?' Pauli asks, again in the passenger seat.

'A little place we know,' Becka replies, from behind him. Seconds later, a song ends on the radio and leads into the beginning of another one. 'There's a good omen, Lu, they're playing one of your songs.'

She raises the volume and the music flows through the speakers.

Pauli looks behind at Matt, then at Lucy. 'Ya like the old stuff then?'

'I love all the sixties and seventies stuff, O'Neill. Sorry, Pauli.'

He keeps looking at her. 'Sorry for what?'

'Calling you by your last name.'

'Well from now on ya can call me by it, I insist. And I'm not being corny, but ya said it… natural like, so I'm cool with it,' he instantly looks out his window and grimaces. Why did he even think he had to talk that much? And to make it even worse, about a name? He wants to shake his head in disgust but he imagines that the three are watching him and maybe even laughing very, very quietly.

But in the back, Matt and Becka give each other a thumbs up and a grin.

'Eh yeah, and old misery arse COLON doesn't have a problem calling people by their last names, so I think he's used to it, isn't that right, P?'

Pauli nods but keeps looking out the window. When the song finishes, Lucy lowers the volume and for some reason, he thinks he needs to say something. 'Ok,' he turns and looks at her. 'My turn, Lucy 000.2 thousandth of a second for a fart through your knickers record holder, Weaver. What would you prefer?'

Matt and Becka laugh and Lucy goes beetroot.

'I'm sorry to do that to ya, it was uncalled for.'

'Well, I did open the door to it when I said it,' she says, grinning. 'And I didn't know what else to say. He really annoyed me that day.'

'Well, Lucy,' Matt begins. 'Other than knowing how fast your farts travel, ya were the only one that spoke up for the whole class, so fair play to ya!'

Pauli looks behind at Matt and thinks... thanks for stealing me line, ya red louse!

'She also said about his mike being on and the Isle of Man thing.' Becka slips in.

'No way! I looked around to see who said it but nobody stood out.'

'When we saw you looking around, Lucy hid behind me.'

'I was peeking over her shoulder with some of her hair covering my hair.'

Pauli, Matt and Becka laugh but Lucy just grins and he stares at her again.

Jesus, she has a beautiful profile and her teeth are immaculate.

'What's wrong, O'Neill?' she asks, without taking her eyes off the road.

'Eh… nothing. I was just looking at… the sea!'

Not long after, they see a sign. Welcome to Carlingford.

'Are we across the border?!' Matt asks, excitedly.

Nobody answers, so he and Pauli just take in the view. Looking from the sea on the right, to the fields and hills to the left. Matt takes off his seatbelt and moves between the two front seats with a hand on both, for a better look.

'Woah… this is really nice. Check out them cliff mountain things there, P.'

Pauli looks out his window. 'Hey Matty, there's your bird!'

Matt moves back and bends across Becka to get a better look. 'Where?'

'That good looking sheep, second from the left.'

The girls laugh.

'Hardy bleedin' har har!'

'Only kiddin' with ya.'

It just happens to be the perfect day for someone's first visit to Carlingford. The sun is beaming, the sky is blue and almost cloudless and the sea is perfect. The girls picked the right day, and the weather forecast that they had watched before leaving for college was spot on. So it had to be today with the boys. The last thing they wanted was a rainy day, which would have left them sitting in a restaurant until they got the hint that it was closing after lunch. Then back to the car which would have ended up as boredom central after a while. They pull into a carpark facing the beach and spot some water lovers in the sea. Some are on surfboards and some are on surfboards with sails attached to them. Pauli knows the name of the second version from watching a

233

Hawaiian based Police series. But as usual when under pressure, his brain lets him down, again. He doesn't want to come across as a dope by asking Matt in front of the girls.

'This is beautiful,' he says, playing it safe.

'But are we over the border?!' Matt asks, again.

'No, Professor. The border's a few miles up. See those mountains there? Well that's the Mourne, that's Ulster.' Becka says, releasing her seatbelt.

Matt stares at the mountains for seconds, then looks back at Becka. 'But we're not far from it?'

'What Lu… about eight miles?'

'Near enough, sweetie, give or take a few feet.'

The four get out of the car but Matt and Pauli walk to the front of it and continue to take in the scenery. The girls stand watching them.

'I'd love to live here.'

'Me, too.' Matt agrees.

'Don't worry, boys, it won't go away. So lunch, what do yous fancy?' Becka asks. Truth be told, when the girls asked them to lunch, both were caught off guard. Pauli was thinking, maybe the old chicken baguette and a drink from the garage across from the college. Get the food and drive to the station, eat in the carpark, then a goodbye and a good luck and get the train home. Nice and simple.

In his pocket he has just over sixteen euros.

Matt was thinking something similar. The garage does a chicken baguette for two euro, so three fifty and you're sorted with a drink as well. The train ticket is prepaid so there is no problem. Except now there is. He knows this because he counted his money last night on his bed before going to sleep, and carries it in a see through money bag, the sort banks give out. The only saving grace is that it is tucked safely out of sight from all eyes, in his jeans pocket. They stand there looking around, catching each other's eyes momentarily every now and then.

Matt is thinking about his stomach right now as he can smell the food in the air.
But Pauli is thinking about something altogether different. Is this some sort of a date? Well, the girls did invite them after all. No they didn't. They asked if they fancied lunch, that's innocent. Maybe there's no food involved and they just wanted to talk. But about what? This is a hell of a long way just to come and say a few words. Lucy drove a good few miles to get here near the border. You can almost touch the Mourne mountains and they're in Ulster, for fuck's sake!

'So… what's it to be boys?' Becka asks, again.

Matt looks around frantically. 'There,' he points. 'That's a shop! I fancy a chic.'

'Me, too!' Pauli cuts it.

They look at each other and nod in agreement.

'How about an Indian?' Lucy asks.

Pauli's head turns slowly to face her and he is thinking of the takeaway in Laytown. Oooh, a mixed grill, mmm. 'There's a takeaway here?'

'Yes there is…, but that part doesn't open until five thirty. So for now, it will have to be the restaurant, and they do a lovely set lunch.' Becka replies.

Pauli suddenly feels uncomfortable. We've been set up, and big time!

These bitches are taking turns asking and answering questions. Well-rehearsed. A bit too well rehearsed, in fact. For fuck's sake, we do acting classes together.

'I can't eat spicy food.' Matt says, rubbing his stomach.

Pauli smiles. Good lad, Matty, we'll get the fuck outta here.

Becka is staring at him with a bemused look.

'Why have you got that ridiculous pained face on for? And why are you rubbing your belly? You weren't rubbing it when you were going to get your spicy chicken roll a few seconds ago.'

Pauli is looking at Matt and agrees with Becka. Over acting to the extreme.

'Lads, I got some vouchers for this restaurant at Christmas, and me and Becka were coming here for lunch today anyway. You get loads for nine ninety nine, so the four of us eat for free.' Lucy says, with a smile while holding the voucher. Becka walks closer and puts her arm around Lucy's shoulder and tilts her head so that both are touching and she smiles, too.

The boys are thinking… what a pretty picture. Plus, they know their maths. With their money combined, they can pay for their part of the meal, just in case. It won't be the most pleasant sight in the world, but it can be done.

Phew! Relief. Almost telepathically, they smile. 'Sounds good,' both say, and look at each other.

'Ok, well let's go in then.' Lucy says, turning and the two link arms as they walk across the sand covered carpark.

'Are ya checkin' out Lucy's arse?' Matt asks, in a whisper.

Pauli looks at him before pulling away with longer strides after the girls.

'Only asking,' he says, taking longer steps to catch up.

CHAPTER THIRTY-FIVE

The starter and the main course come and go. On the drinks front, they all went for diet cola's which were two fifty each, so her fifty euro voucher did cover everything. When leaving, she leaves a two euro tip and so does Becka. Pauli leaves one euro and Matt leaves nothing. As he brings up the rear, the other three don't know. When they get outside, they stand there looking around.

Becka breaks the silence and the awkwardness. 'Fancy an ice pop, Matt?'

But before he can answer her, Pauli calls him over and he looks a bit confused.

'Don't forget, thing wants us to suss out that yoke when we get back, ok?' he says, slipping a five note into Matt's pocket on the blind side of the girls.

Matt twigs. 'Oh yeah, I didn't forget. That yoke gives thing nothing but trouble,' he says, with a grin followed by a wink.

'Now go and get your ice pop, and make sure there's no vegetable oil in it, ok sonny Jim?'

'Yes, Daddy!' he replies.

He watches them walk off towards the shops for a few seconds before looking at Lucy, who is already looking at him.

'Thing and yoke?! That is the weirdest... what was that?'

'Ah, just reminding him about something.'

'Ok. So, do you want to go to the beach, or do you want an ice pop as well?'

'By the way Becka said it, it sounded like a two person deal so I don't want to interfere. Plus, I don't eat that sh... stuff.'

She giggles, turns and walks slowly towards the beach.

'What's so funny?' he asks, following.

'You are! You're a funny guy.'

'Don't have me go all Joe Pesci on ya. And... I'm actually not that funny.'

'Oh... you are, believe me.'

When they reach the sand, she sits and takes her runners off. He stares down at them and then at her toes, thinking that she has beautiful feet.

Why haven't I ever... how could I have seen her feet?

She looks up at him. 'What's wrong?'

His stomach goes jumpy and he starts to boil up. 'I gotta sit down, I feel a bit weird,' he replies, plonking himself on the sand and stares out at the water.

He hopes that it's not food poisoning because it will be embarrassing.

She moves a little nearer to him and pushes her feet into the soft sand. 'I don't want you to smell my feet,' she says, with a smile.

He smiles back and they sit there for about a minute in silence.

'Are you feeling any better, O'Neill?'

He takes a deep breath with his eyes closed. Whatever that was, it wasn't the food. 'Ya know what? I am, I mean I do.'

Suddenly he gets a smell which he knows is from her. That lovely smell that girls have. What is it? Shampoo? Deodorant? Shower gel? He looks at her to find her looking at him. Then the corners of her mouth rise into a tiny smile, only enhancing her lips and making her even more beautiful this close.

His stomach goes weird again and he looks back at the sea.

'O'Neill?'

He faces her. 'Yes, Weaver?'

'Are you ok?'

'Eh… I don't know, Lucy.'

His stomach is bombing it again and then it happens. She moves towards him and he freezes, but she slowly keeps coming. He can't believe this is happening. Maybe she is just going to whisper something. But her eyes start to close, then his do and their lips meet. The kiss is just a slight touch. When he opens them to find this girl inches from his face, he moves forward and kisses her again. This one lasts longer and life has suddenly got good, and about time. When they do part, she grins at him.

'I've wanted to do that for so long… but I know that you and Matt had Becka's boobs on your minds.'

He starts to get embarrassed. 'It was more Matt,' he lies, but stops. 'You're right. It was the two of us. But that's in the past, for me anyway.'

'It better be, young man!' she says, with mock sternness.

'Ok, my turn. What's with you and aromas?'

'Aromas?!'

'Yeah. Between what ya said in school about the length of time…'

She looks amused. 'Oh, that will haunt me forever. Go on.'

'And burying your feet in the sand.'

'With me not wearing socks with runners, the feet sweat and… well, smell a bit.'

'I don't believe it!' he says, loudly.

This starts her off laughing. 'They do… honestly!'

'Let me test them then.'

'What?'

'Your feet. Take them out of the safety of the sand and let me test them.'

'Test them? How?'

'By giving them the once over with this beak.'

'You will not!'

'Oh, but yes I will.'

She thinks for a moment. 'Ok then, but on your life be it,' she slowly takes her right foot out of the sand and he reaches for it. 'Hold on, not yet,' she puts her hand in her jeans pocket and takes out her phone and pretends to dial.

'What are ya doing?'

She takes a deep breath. 'Ok… you can go now, 999's on standby.'

CHAPTER THIRTY-SIX

Seconds before, a few hundred feet behind Lucy and Pauli. Matt and Becka are sitting on a low wall with a half-eaten choc-ice in his hand, and a brunch that has been nibbled around the edges in hers.

'Well, I think that's what ya can call... it worked. And about bleeding time! The persuading that I had to do the day both of yous were in our spot wasn't funny. I thought he rumbled me, but only that it happened so quick and that he was nervous, well... he probably would've rumbled me. It was touch and go.'

'Was he really that nervous?'

'Nervous?! When he realised that it was Lucy, he sort of went into a trance, and then started to shake. Even his teeth chattered, and he said he could hear music.'

Becka thinks while she continues to look at them. 'I thought you were making it up about him being so shy.'

'No way! If he was any shyer, he'd be wearing a balaclava.'

'And he really said that he didn't like her?'

'No Becka. I didn't say that HE said that he didn't like her, I said that HE said that he didn't think much of her.'

She looks at him. 'Is that not the same thing?'

Matt looks at the ice cream dripping onto his hand before looking at her.

'Ya know as well as I do that it was her hair. All he could see, in fact, all anyone could see was the tip of a nose, mouth and a chin. He couldn't see her face because if he had of, they would've been going out months ago. Only for ya told her to put it up that day at the spot, well, ya know the rest. It's amazing what pigtails can do, isn't it?'

'It was a ponytail, and yes it is. She was always wondering why he wouldn't even look at her and I kept telling her, wear your hair up, back or sideways, but let your face be seen, then he'll notice you.'

'So what took so long?'

'She's actually very shy, too, and she was afraid in case he saw her and still didn't notice her, or find her pretty.'

'Well, he's definitely noticed the girl now.'

Becka smiles. 'At least there's no more sneaking around to us because even I thought it was getting a bit risky. Are you ever going to tell him?'

'What? That the three of us were in cahoots trying to get him going with Lucy? Of course I will... when they have their second baby.' She laughs.

'Did you see that kiss, or kisses? He gave her a good one the second time,' she picks up her phone and puts it on screen. 'Look at that.'

'Jesus! That phone has some zoom on it. Now that looks like something out of a holiday brochure.'

'Oh, I can't wait until she sees these, she'll love them. I know I've said it loads of times, but she's totally mad about him and constantly talks about him. And if I know my

Lucy, she'll print these out on A4 and use a magnifying glass to look over them.'

'What the hell?!'

She looks at Matt, then follows the direction he's staring.

'Is he licking her foot?!' he asks, as ice cream now covers most of his hand.

Becka switches to camera, points, zooms in and gets it. Then checks it.

'Oh that's class!' she looks at Matt who seems in shock. 'Want to see?'

'Did he lick it?'

She shows it to him and he's left staring at the image for seconds. 'Now I've seen it all. That boy of mine is a fast worker.'

'There's nothing more for us to do after seeing that,' she puts her phone in her pocket. 'When you finish your ice pop,' she stares at his hand. 'Or when it's completely melted, we can go sit in the car if you want?'

'What about the keys? It's locked.'

'Lucy left it open. Just in case we want to sit in, know what I mean?'

'Aw, that know what I mean?!' he gets up. 'Well, this bad boy is gone right now,' he throws it on the ground. 'And when we get to the car, another bad boy will make an appearance, do ya know what I mean?'

She drops hers on the grass and winks. 'I'll have to save my energy then.'

'Ooh, ya filthy girl, ya!'

The two laugh as they walk towards the car.

CHAPTER THIRTY-SEVEN

Lucy is enjoying this even though she was a little worried at the start because her runners really do make her feet smell. But when he start rubbing the sand off her foot, and then blowing it from between her toes, it felt like heaven and she tried hard not to wriggle too much. Her feelings are confirmed, but she knew that anyway as she had fallen for him a long time ago. She just finds it hard to believe that her foot is in his hands. Then while she wriggled, her foot jerked and touched his lips. He smiled and continued to blow the sand from it. She moves it back and gets into position for another kiss. They lie on the sand, with him underneath her, and kiss for a while before she sits up on him and starts fixing her pony tail.

'People might get the wrong idea with ya like that.'

'Oh shit!' she says, lying back down on him while peeping around with a worried look on her face. 'I live here.'

'What?!' he asks, quickly sitting up. In doing this, she rolls off him backwards onto the sand.

'Nice move, O'Neill. Now there's sand in my hair,' she says, lying on her back looking at him. She gets up slowly, removes the bobbin and starts rubbing and shaking her hair in an attempt to get the sand out.

'Ya live here?'

'Yeah. We both do, why?'

'Of course! The coupons for the Indian. I didn't cop that part.'

'My mam says that I'll turn into an Indian because I eat that much of it.'

He smiles and she smiles back. 'What?'

'You're lucky. I mean, growing up here.'

'Been here just over ten years and I've loved every minute.'

'Where did ya live before here?'

'England,' she replies, bending her head again to try and get the sand out.

'What were ya doing there?'

'I was born there.'

'Really?!' he asks, staring at her as she shakes her head from side to side.

'I'll just have to give it a good wash in the shower before bed and probably again in the morning,' her full attention returns to him. 'Sorry, just thinking out loud... and yes, I'm a Brit. Well, I was, but now I'm an Irish citizen. But I have a British passport as well.'

'Snap! So do I.'

She freezes and looks through her draped over hair at him, then smiles. Lucy says 'Ha ha, very funny.'

'Ok, don't believe me then,' he purposely over smiles back at her. 'And ya don't sound English.'

'You don't sound Irish!'

'Do I not?'

She thinks for a moment as she moves her hair so that he can see her face.

'Top o' the mornin' to yee!' she says, in an accent which would be more at home coming from a Leprechaun. 'Sure t'isn't it a grand day, bejasus!' she adds.

He laughs.

'I'm glad I could see your face when ya said that, and the voice was classic.'

'Thank you,' she fixes her hair back into the bobbin. 'But see, you don't speak like that. Or let me put it another way. Do you ever watch those talent shows?'

'I do, but only because of the talentless attempts that are way too funny to miss.'

'Me and Becka watch them for the same reason. But do you remember one of the judges asked two Irish lads why they were speaking American?'

'Yeah. They said everybody in Ireland speaks American.'

'Exactly! Even up here, especially the girls,' she changes her voice. 'Oh my god! Hi! French fries! Shut up! You look SO awesome!' she grins. 'And these girls have been born here. Sorry about the accent, I know it wasn't that great. That needs a little more work. Anyway, I rest my case.'

'Good case! And concerning your accent that time, if I had my eyes closed, I would've imagined myself sitting on a beach in Beverly Hills.'

'Yeah, billies!'

He smiles but he can see that she is not finished yet.

'Here's a better one. Becka... what do you think of her accent?'

He looks at the sky and thinks for a few seconds before looking back at her.

'She does have a slightly peculiar way of saying some words. Is she Welsh?'

Lucy bursts into laughter with her head in her hands. He watches and laughs a bit because she is laughing. She eventually brings it down to a stutter and looks at him with wet eyes. 'You think... Becka sounzzz...' and she's off again.

'Welsh!' he finishes.

This just makes her worse than before and she ends up falling backwards onto the sand, regardless of her hair. While she's like that, he takes this opportunity to check out the curvature of her bottom and he really likes what he sees. Well, he did already, but not from this angle. Then his belly goes weird again, but it's a good weird. Will I get to... touch? See? Then he remembers them kissing.

Oh shit! Are we boyfriend and girlfriend? He looks back at the laughing beauty and her bum, which is moving from side to side as she turns. Oh I hope so, he thinks, as he licks his lips. Not long after, she sits up and removes the bobbin from her hair and it falls with sand, again.

'I said you were funny,' she starts shaking her hair from side to side again. He doesn't say anything, he just watches her. He thought she looked good with her hair up? She continues again to try and remove as much sand as she can and while doing so, catches him staring at her and she stops and parts her hair again so that she can look at him clearly. Her face has changed from joy to worry.

'What's wrong?'

'Nothing.'

He stares at her and from nowhere, hears a faint voice.

Tell her, yee sap. Look at her. A few seconds ago she was laughing her head off and yee made that happen. Now look at the pretty wee face. Tell her how yee feel or yee'll regret it, I mean it lad, yee will because…

'Ok!'

She looks even more worried now. 'Ok?!'

'Lucy… you are lovely…'

If he thought she looked worried before saying anything, it has trebled now.

'But?'

'But… when ya took your hair down. Well, it probably sounds corny but… you're beautiful. When ya can see your face, that is.'

The worry drains from her face on hearing this. She stands and walks the few paces to him and sits down on him with a leg either side. His belly goes weird again but he likes this feeling now and he knows it is all her. They stare at each other for seconds before they begin to move closer and closer, then they kiss.

He is enjoying her sitting on him and the kissing, but then the voice starts again. Feel the bum lad and feel it now… because if yee don't, well…

He stops mid-kiss. 'Ok then!'

She pulls back slightly and looks at him confused. 'Ok then?!'

He puts his hand on her bum and she nods her head to the side. 'Ohh… ok then.' They start kissing again.

'BANG! And that's the money shot!' Matt says, looking at Becka's phone. The image is of Lucy and Pauli kissing with his hand on her ass.

'Bang indeed!' Becka says, smiling at Matt.

CHAPTER THIRTY-EIGHT

The four joined up again after Lucy and Pauli had stopped kissing while he felt her bum. He noticed what looked to be Matt and Becka over beside the water. Lucy looked around to see what he was looking at and saw that it was them and waved. She reached for her phone because shouting was out of the question as they were way out of earshot, and had not made a move to come any closer, so she rang her. She told them to come over and then put her phone away.

'I wasn't sure if it was them.' Pauli says, still squinting in their direction.

Nearly two minutes later, they pull up and sit down.

'Are you nice and comfy, Lu?'

Lucy wiggles her bum while still sitting on Pauli, then starts to get up.

'Don't get up,' he whispers, while gripping her hips.

She looks at him, moves a bit and grins.

'Ooohh,' she whispers back.

'So we went to the car but it was all locked up.'

'Oh, Beck, I'm sorry. I don't remember locking it.'

'Went to the car for what?' Pauli asks.

'I found the sun a bit too hot,' Matt lies. 'A bit of shade and all that.'

'Beck, you should've come over and got the key.'

'It's alright, Lu.'

Lucy looks back at Pauli. 'How you doing?' she whispers.

'A bit better.'

She gets off him, turns and sits down on the sand between his legs, facing out, and takes his hands and holds them around her belly.

'Are ya ok, P?'

'Yeah yeah, grand. Thanks for asking, Matty.'

'I bet you are!' Becka says, nudging Matt gently.

The four are sitting there for a while before the sea air kicks in and they start to feel peckish. After a food conference that lasts all of four seconds, it is decided unanimously that they will have chips and chips. The lads start walking the few hundred feet to the chip shop. When they get there, for a lovely sunny day in a beautiful little village by the sea, the place is empty and has the same ambience as a funeral parlour.

'Now this… I'm not sure about.' Pauli says, quietly.

'The chips smell nice though. Well, at least from the outside, and we don't have to queue.'

'Ah, it's after lunch, that's why it's empty.'

'Right. Oh yeah, and thanks for the fiver, P. Now that would've been the total of embarrassing moments never caught on camera, if I'd resorted to me pouch.'

'You don't still carry… it better not be the same bag!'

Matt smiles. 'I've grown attached to the old bag.'

'I'm gonna buy you a wallet.'

'No you're not,' he says, looking up at the list of food. 'Me bag's grand.'

Pauli looks up as well. While looking at it, the two would love to have more money because the choice of food displayed is making chips on their own look and sound quite scabby.

'Ah no, these do curry rolls!'

Pauli looks at him. 'What's a curry roll?'

'It's like a...,' he thinks for a moment, then starts scratching his head. 'It's like...'

'Did ya ever even have one or does it just sound good?'

'No, I really had one. A few actually, but it was in town.'

Pauli thinks he is bullshitting so persists in the questioning. 'Keep talking.'

'Remember Lar who lives on the North Strand?'

'Ya mean that nut?! Your man that gets locked up all the time but keeps escaping from everywhere he's been?'

'Yeah, that Lar.'

'His parents should've called him Papillon. How is he anyway, keeping out of trouble?'

'He's on the run again. Got locked up and.'

'Escaped again?!'

'Yeah. Anyway, when I was in with him a few times, we went to the chipper down the road and they do these lovely,' he closes his eyes. 'Curry rolls.'

'Curry rolls, two?' asks a bloke that must have crawled in on his knees, as the two didn't see him until he spoke. But as he stands facing them, his head is inches from the ceiling and he is built like a door.

'Four and four chips, please.' Matt says.

Between what Pauli has and Matt's few cents change from the fiver, plus his pouch, they don't have enough for the full order. So Matt changes it to four curry rolls and two chips, but asks that they be wrapped together. They are left looking at each other when the curry rolls are put on newspaper. The door of a chipman goes to get the chips.

'Now that can't be hygienic.' Matt whispers, watching the fella at the fryer.

Pauli looks at him in disbelief. 'Matt, a few weeks ago when ya were in me gaff having spaghetti, a…'

'That had to be a Tuesday, am I right?'

'Well, yeah! But remember a meatball fell off your plate and ya chased Zeus out of the sitting room, through the kitchen and caught him in the back garden?'

'I do, and he's not that fast for a cat.'

'My point is ya walked back in eating it, and this is not hygienic?'

'That was different, we don't know these people.'

Before he wraps the food, the door of a bloke puts two extra scoops of chips on top of their food and grins. 'Can't have your ladies thinking yous are tight, boys.'

The food is wrapped and the lads thank the chap and try to give him what little change they have left, but he refuses.

After they walk across the road to the beach, Matt looks at Pauli. 'He was a nice bloke doin' that, wasn't he?'

'He was too!'

As they are approaching the girls, Matt looks at Pauli again and sniggers.

'What's so funny?'

'You felt her ass!' he says, in a perfect Butthead voice and sniggers again.

Pauli thinks about that part for a moment. 'Matt, I think I'm going weird.'

'In what way, brah?'

He has second thoughts about answering that question but if he can't confide in Matt, then he can't confide in anyone. 'I heard a voice tellin' me to do it.'

Matt laughs. 'Don't worry, mac chum, it's only your horny voice helpin' ya out.'

'Me horny voice?!'

Matt stops and so does Pauli. 'Is this the first time ya've heard it?'

Pauli thinks for a moment. 'Yeah, but I heard it twice today.'

'Tell me what it said.'

So he tells Matt about the first time when it told him to tell Lucy that she was lovely, and then the second time when it told him to feel her arse.

'The first time was the pre-emptive strike, the soften up approach. But the second time... now that was the real deal. See? Your horny voice! What did it sound like?'

'Really really Irish. Like a Leprechaun in me ear.'

257

'It's in your mind, P. You're the only one that can hear it.'

'So… you have one as well?'

Matt starts walking again. 'Everyone has one, but mine sounds Jamaican.'

'Jamaican?!'

'Ya; think that's cool? Lar's one sounds Native American.'

CHAPTER THIRTY-NINE

While they were gone, Becka showed the photos to Lucy.

'Oh Beck, that's a lovely one,' she says, about the second kiss.

'I know. Matt said it looked like something from a travel brochure.'

'Matt's seen this?'

'He's seen them all.'

Lucy looks at her. 'All?!'

'Scroll to the right. I couldn't get the first kiss good but... well, see for yourself.' She pulls the phone closer when she sees the next one and stares.

'Was that a kiss, Lu?'

'I... I sort of barely brushed my lips against his,' she keeps staring at her and Pauli just before they close their eyes and she knows that this is her favourite.

'Becka... I need this one.'

'Don't worry, you'll have them all. Now keep going.'

After some seconds, she changes the picture and laughs. She stares at what looks like Pauli licking her foot. Then she moves to the one where she is sitting on him and his hand is on her bum. 'I didn't know he had such a good hold of it.'

'Did you like that?'

She looks back at Becka. 'Hmm-mm!'

'I think he enjoyed it more.'

'Do you think I'm coming on a bit strong? I mean… am I being… Becka help!'

'Relax! From what I've been told, when you were sitting on him when we came over, it's not the first time that his little friend has come into the equation.'

Becka relays the wake up for *Soccer Saturday* story that Matt has told her and Lucy is beaming. 'So he dreamt about me and I gave him one?'

'Well, you definitely gave him something considering you weren't there. Yeah, I suppose you did give him one in a way.'

'Oh Becka, that's… well, it hasn't made my day, but it's made it much better.'

'So… how was it meeting the little fella?' she asks, with a wink and they laugh. Lucy remembers something and her eyes widen.

'What?' Becka asks, with a serious face.

'It came up earlier about here and I told him that we lived here, and he said that he would have loved to have grown up here.'

'That's nothing, Matt said the same.'

'I might have mentioned that I moved here from England when I was eight.'

'Might have. Or DID?'

'I did.'

'Lucy, why?! We've been told enough times never to mention that stuff.'

'It's innocent. I told him I was born in England and moved here, nothing more.'

'That's all?'

'Yeah, but it gets better. We got talking about accents and I brought you into it.'

'Oh no.'

'Do you know where he...,' she giggles. 'Where he thinks you're from?'

'Go on, tell me.'

'Wales!' she starts again and Becka laughs, too.

When they regain their composure, Becka is the first to speak. 'Do you think we should say anything or not? Now you know the way my dad is, and yours isn't much better.'

'Or my mam,' she thinks for a moment. 'You're getting on well with Matt, right?'

'Well, we would have got on a whole lot better if you hadn't locked your car up.'

'Don't want to hear it! That's my car, Beck.'

'I know, heat of the moment and all that.'

'Both of yous had your heat of the moment the day we brought them home. What if Pauli had looked around to find your hand down.'

'Stop, Lucy, please! I know... that was stupid.'

Lucy looks at Becka's face as it turns red. 'Yes, my girl, I've not forgotten.'

'So… what will we do, or not say?'

'Nicely put. How about nothing? This is parents' stuff and nothing to do with us and the boys, so we'll keep mum.'

'Mum it is then, and here come our chips.'

Lucy smiles.

'What are you thinking about? Your kiss to lover boy when he's leaving?'

The smile instantly disappears.

'I'm sorry, Lu. I feel the same about Matt.'

'Beck, I know I have a free house four days a week, but it would be weird to ask them to stay tonight, wouldn't it? Well not you, your ice is broken. But with Pauli… asking him out to lunch, then me kissing him and…'

'You're right, Lu. It would be a bad start and way too fast.'

'Maybe next week?'

'That's a good idea. But say something like… your parents have gone away for a week. And if they want to,' she raises quote fingers. 'BUZZ UP…for a barbecue? That's always a good one. Then well…' she grins.

'So we're sorted?'

'Yeah, guv, we're sorted!' she replies, in a gruff cockney accent.

As the boys approach, the girls are laughing at Becka's impression.

'Yes yous are, and that was really good, Becka.' Pauli says.

'And here's your bleedin' chips! Me hand is scolding!' Matt says, kneeling down and dropping them a few inches to the sand. He lifts his hand and blows it as he waves it past his face. 'Have they never heard of bags up here? And why do they put chips in newspaper? Ink will be all over them. I think even those famine countries give ya a bag, even if there's nothing in it. For fuck's sake! Me bleedin' hand! I'm gonna have to run over and stick it in the sea.'

'Matt, shut up, you're moaning.'

'Of course I'm moaning, me bleedin' hand's killing me!'

They watch him get up and run away towards the sea. When he gets there, he puts it straight into the water. After a few seconds, he waves back at them with his other hand.

'That must have been really sore if he did that.' Becka says, staring over at him.

They watch him walk back and as he gets closer to them, he smiles.

'That feels better, but it's still a little warm and numb.'

When he sits down, the food is placed between them and Pauli feels Lucy nestle into his side. Before they start, Matt makes them hold up their curry rolls and do a toast. They touch the rolls together. 'To Lar!'

'Who is Lar?' Lucy asks.

He tells the story of the escape artist while they eat, leaving out the part about his Native American adviser. When they are finished, they all give the rolls the thumbs up and Matt is delighted with himself. It comes time for the lads to head home and Lucy offers to drive them, but they instantly refuse. Carlingford to their place and back? They are having none of it. Becka checks the train times on her phone and they decide to jump the 17:22 Enterprise to

Drogheda, then swap to the Commuter, which should have them back in their village for about six thirty. Now this they are happy with.

The time comes for them to make for Dundalk station. Once there, the girls explain to the ticket guy that they just want to stand on the platform with the lads until the train comes, and he lets them through. It is a seventeen-minute wait and they go their separate ways to say their goodbyes. The boys will never look at this station again without thinking of this day and this moment. When the Enterprise pulls in, they know they have a minute or two before it leaves. They cut it to the last few seconds before an Irish Rail guy asks them to get on, as he has to give the wave to the driver. Becka and Matt say goodbye as if they'll never see each other again, forgetting that they are in college the next day. Lucy and Pauli's goodbye is low profile in comparison.

'So tomorrow then?'

'Yeah,' he replies, with his hands around her waist.

Then she does something that he finds a little weird. She kisses his throat, each side of his neck and then his lips, while feeling his butt. 'Time to go, O'Neill.'

'Come on, lads, for Jasus's sake! It's got to go!' the Irish Rail guy says, pointing towards the front of the train.

One last peck on the lips and they are on the train in different carriages. Matt comes into the carriage where Pauli is sitting and eyes up the food and drinks trolley as he squeezes by it. He sits next to Pauli who is staring out the window. 'It's not a good feeling, is it, P?'

'No, it's not,' he replies, as he stares at the quickly disappearing station. He's not being blunt with Matt, it is just that today has been his first real experience of being with a girl. Matt has had a few girlfriends and isn't backward in going forth, but Pauli is in a boat in which he has always been alone. Until today, that is. What happened was amazing and unbelievable, and all in a matter of hours. And with it being spur of the moment from college. He can't believe that they were leaving today to go home when Becka asked them to lunch. That part feels like days ago. A word comes to his mind which he never had much time for or even thought he would ever use in this lifetime. But if it means anything, even though he still hasn't grasped it fully, he would take the chance and use it for what happened from lunchtime until now. Today was surreal.

He only starts getting back to normal when they are on the Commuter.

'Now if that was my groundhog day, I'd be happy with it.'

On hearing this, Matt perks up. As the time on the Enterprise had been mostly spent in silence and looking out at the fast passing countryside and houses.

'It was one hell of a day P, that's for sure! And we get to see our girlfriends, tomorrow. How good is that?'

Pauli looks at Matt's smiling face. 'Pretty damn good, Matty. Pretty damn good.' When they get back to their estate and are at the splitting point, Pauli asks if Matt wants to come around for food and he might try and scab some drink.

'I think the ink on that paper the chips were in is after wreckin' me belly. Ya didn't happen to notice the date on it, did ya?'

'No Matt… that was the last thing on my mind.'

'Well to be honest, I have to go home and have a good crap.'

'Ya know where I am if ya feel any better.'

Matt nods.

'If I don't see ya tonight, tomorrow at the station, ok?'

Matt nods again.

'Well… enjoy your dump.'

'Oh, I will, big time! Night man,' he says, and walks away holding his stomach. Pauli watches him for a few seconds before turning towards his house and walking away, humming.

CHAPTER FORTY

Rita had been in work three days in a row, but on the third day, Sophie was off. She was on with the boss's sister and that meant that there would be no dossing, and she wouldn't be able to take home anything for the dinner. She would have to stop off in the supermarket on the way home and spend her own money on the evening meal. Then she remembered the catering size lasagne in the freezer that she took from the cafe months before, and grinned.

She found it very hard to be around the sister for that long and that made the day seem to drag. What made it worse was the hour and a quarter they spent in the empty cafe before closing up, and the boring conversation which took up most of that time. Rita never liked her and found it hard even to pretend to, so she let her do most of the talking as just looking at her drained Rita of energy. She had first experienced it a few months before and this time was no different. Bragging about this and that, of holidays that were coming and of ones that had long past. Having to upgrade the car because it is weeks away from turning two years old. Then her children got mentioned, and Rita is pretty sure that the story she told was the exact same one that she heard months before. She fake called herself twice and stood outside the kitchen door and had a pretend conversation, making things up on the fly while having a smoke. The second time she did it, she wondered why she didn't just text Fran or Sophie and get them to ring her.

The cafe is a peculiar place and is positioned poorly for passersby. Every day at a certain time, it would just die and nobody ever came in. They would walk by and maybe even glance at it, but then just keep on walking. On those occasions, Rita and Sophie would shut up shop early and go home. Why sit around like idiots if they can get home earlier and go on the beer? But today, she had to wait there until five o'clock exactly. Only then did they take in the tables and chairs, the hanging menu boards and wind back the overhanging cover outside. Then the chairs inside were placed upside down on the tables and the mop was brought out. Rita volunteered to do the floor while the sister done the till. Then she made sure everything was switched off and waited at the back door. Sixteen minutes past five and the place was locked up. After a false smile and a quick goodbye, Rita turned her back and tried her best not to storm over to her car. Once in, a cigarette was lit and then the journey home began.

When she gets home, she walks straight from the front door to the fridge and after taking two bottles and grabbing the radio remote on her way by, goes out to the back garden and sits in the sun. Her favourite radio station is now on in the background at a nice volume. It is her favourite because she pities them, as she believes that they only have between ten and fifteen CDs. Every time she listens to it, the Djs play either the same songs or different songs from the same albums. She thought it was on a loop at the beginning, but after some careful listening when the news came on, or when there was a competition to give away a T-shirt or a ten-euro gift voucher for the local Chinese or chip shop, she realised that it wasn't. They would always mention the names of the lucky winners who were never the same people. After the first few days of listening to it, she got a pen and paper and took down every song that was played for nearly two hours. The next day, she did the same and compared the list. Then she realised how sad she was to be doing it, and how sad her life must be that she had even came up with the idea in the first place, so she stopped. Now she just listens without thinking about the songs or CDs.

She is just putting her second bottle down on the table after taking a sup when her phone rings. As always, she checks the ID before answering.

'Hello, Missus, what's the story with ye?'

She chats to Sophie and fills her in on her day, and of the verbal diarrhoea spewing forth from the hole beneath the boss's sister's nose. After a while, Sophie brings up the results from her mission brief.

'Are you ready, Re?'

'Go on, tell me.'

'Firstly, the M.R.E's can be got, but the US. military don't sell them to civilians. There are places that do something similar, and John says that there wouldn't be much of a difference, if any.'

'Cool.' Rita takes a sip from her bottle.

'Now pricewise, they're weird. I think John said you get either six or twelve meals for thirty five dollars, that's about twenty euros.'

'Jesus!'

'I know! Then they have to be shipped from the US, and so…'

'I get ye,' she says, trying to light a smoke.

'He hasn't checked the British or German ones yet, but if they're the same price, maybe Fran has the right idea. Ok, the container. Are you sitting down?'

'I am, and I'm dreading this part. Go on.'

'Well they're peanuts.'

'What?!'

'He looked them up and there's two that he checked out. One is the twelve foot one which as I told you before, he said would be a waste because it would be way too small. Then there's a twenty foot.'

'What's he getting?'

'He's getting a forty foot to start with.'

Rita has just inhaled and nearly chokes on her smoke and coughs for a bit.

'To start with?!'

'Re, you seen the amount of land at the back of our house. There's seven acres of it just doing nothing. So he said he'll get another forty later.'

'What would he do with them?'

'Re, did Fran record any of them shows?'

'Well, to be honest, it was Em who recorded them and he just came across them by accident. Probably after waking up half asleep and half drunk.'

'Now that makes more sense.'

'That's what I thought.'

'Well, John showed me an episode and this bloke has loads. He welded them together and cut doors in them and basically made a giant house from them.'

'No way!'

'Yeah. See if Fran has… Em has the episode and you'll see what I mean.'

'Ok. So the twelve is definitely too small?'

'I know twelve foot sounds big, but he said that it would be the size of two graves long.'

'Shite!'

'I know. Not the best way of describing something but… it's to the point.'

'So how much is the twenty foot?' Rita asks, getting up to get another bottle.

'Twenty-five euro.'

She stops suddenly. 'What?!'

'You heard me right, twenty-five euro. And your man in Coolock wanting six hundred for a burnt one?'

'Are ye joking?'

'Re, I swear. I seen it myself.'

Rita takes a bottle from the fridge, holds it between her knees and opens it with her free hand. 'Shite!'

'What's wrong?'

'Just spilt half a bottle on the floor,' she puts the bottle on the worktop and starts mopping. While this is happening, Sophie asks where the container is going to go in the back garden and it suddenly dawns on her. She abandons the rest of the floor and leans the mop against the sink. Then with a fresh bottle and her half on the worktop, goes back out to the garden.

'Shite, Soph, I never thought about it. I just wanted to get it for Fran,' she looks around the garden and tries to

271

imagine a twenty-foot shipping container just sitting there.
'Oh no!'

A hard day at work, just want to get home, grab a beer and go out back and sit in the sun and wind down. But instead, there's a dirty big container sitting on the grass? She explains this to Sophie.

'I know where you're coming from, Re. But John said he would put it a good bit away from the house until it gets buried.'

'Buried?!' Rita asks, nearly choking for the second time in minutes, but this time on beer.

'Well, you wouldn't just leave it sitting in your garden. The neighbours would think you're mad and report you to the council. This is John's land so it doesn't matter to him.'

'Oh God, maybe I'll just forget it. I mean... what was I thinking?'

'Did you tell Fran?'

'No, not a word.'

'Ah, well then you're alright. I'm just going along with John. Yes love, I knew there was something missing. A nice container will brighten up the garden, and it'll look lovely out beside the washing line and so on. But I'm thinking in a few weeks, it'll all be forgotten. Maybe he'll want to be an Astronaut or something.'

The two laugh.

'Men they're mad, aren't they?'

'Yeah, Soph, they're just bigger boys.'

The two talk for a bit longer before saying goodbye. Rita goes in and takes a huge lasagne from the freezer and flings it in the oven. Then she gets a can for Fran and another bottle for herself and heads into the sitting room.

'Heya love, here's a can for ye. Sorry I didn't come in sooner, but that prick's sister was on with me and I needed a bottle to unwind with out the back.'

'You're grand, love. I saw the way ya drove into the garden, and then the state of your face getting out of the car. So I held me breath as ya walked by the room.'

She laughs. 'Well, I'm ok now. I know ye don't like me been freaked out.'

'I don't like it one bit, love! So… was that poxbottle wreckin' your head all day?'

She laughs again.

'Thanks, love,' she hugs him. 'Ye just christened someone a new name.'

'Well, it's my pleasure. Now all I have to do is swim up Mount Everest, then pitch a tent on the Moon and my wish list is complete.'

She takes a step back and looks at him. 'Are ye trying to be funny? Or trying to be smart?'

'Funny, my lovely,' he says, walking to her and kissing her.

She has had a few shocks today but this is the biggest.

'Fran… what's going on with ye?'

'I'm just happy that you're happy, baby.'

She suspects something. 'How long have ye been in this room?'

'All day, bar when I went to get a can or to the head.'

'I mean, since I got home?'

'Since just before ya got home.'

'And ye didn't leave it?'

His face changes as does his attitude and he moves back a few steps. 'Am I under room arrest or somethin'?'

She knows him long enough to know that he is telling the truth, and that he is getting annoyed because he has to try and prove that he is telling the truth. She goes to him and gives him another hug and a kiss on the cheek. 'Sorry, Hammer, I'm just a narky bastard!'

'Don't say things like that, love!' he says, sincerely.

This is what she loves about him... what she sees, is what she gets.

She salutes. 'Sar'nt O'Neill, of the Royal Regiment of Fusiliers. How does chips, lasagne and potato salad sound for your scoff at chow time, SIR?'

'Well, ma dear,' he twirls the end of an invisible moustache on one side of his face, then the other. 'It doesn't sound too jolly bad! And if ya don't mind me saying... the next time ya address a Sergeant in the Royal Regiment of Fusiliers, you'll do it in the proper fashion. By asking the same question while being bent over with your buttocks facing me! Is that clear, ma dear girl?!'

She covers her face with her hands while laughing.

'And don't call me sir... I work for a living!'

She salutes again. 'Yes Sar'nt!' Fran goes to the toilet. When he comes back, she is still standing in the same spot but has changed the station and is watching a cookery show.

'Is Pauli in?'

'No, just Em and the nutter.'

She watches him put the A4 pad on his lap after sitting back in his chair. 'Still makin' plans for your bomb shelter?'

He looks up at her. 'Sit down, Re, you're makin' me nervous just standing there. And it's not a bomb shelter... it's a bunker!'

She stays standing. 'A bunker for what?'

'You've interrogated me enough times, and have asked the same questions over and over. Nothing... ok? I'm having a massive hit, and it was all just an illusion.' He looks at the TV and the narrator says something funny and he laughs.

She watches him for nearly a minute and he is showing no sign of noticing her, considering she is less than a foot away from him. Now this is really starting to annoy her. He seems to have switched off completely as if she's not even in the room. This is not normal for him.

'Fran.'

Nothing.

'Fran, I know ye can hear me because we're in the same room.'

He stares at the television.

'Fran!' she yells.

Nothing again, not even a blink. He continues to watch the show and while picking up his can, the narrator makes him laugh again. This is not good and it's been a while since he has been like this. She should have recognised this from before, and now she has got to get him back quickly. She sits on the arm of his chair and puts her hand on his shoulder.

'Fran?'

'Yes, love?' he asks, still watching the programme.

'Are ye ok, love? Do ye want a can?'

'Grand cake, Nora! No honey, I have one… thanks.'

She looks around the room, then back at him for a few seconds. 'Tell me about your bunker, will ye?'

'Rita… you never know what is around the corner.'

Shite! He has gone back to speaking the way he did when they first met, again.

'Like what, Fran? What's around the corner?'

'RPGs, IEDs. And the worst… Snipers! And they are the worst. You never know they are there until it is too late… and some of your mates are lying dead or wounded on the street. Then most of the time, they just disappear. They're like the fucking wind, they are,' he raises his left hand and closes it. She watches it until he opens it slowly. 'Poof! They were there… now they are long gone.'

'Francis?'

He looks at her. 'Don't call me that, Re, ya know I don't like it.'

'Right. After this, I won't ask any more questions about your bunker, ok?'

'What do you want to know… again?'

'What's the bunker for?'

'You never know what's going to happen. The world is going fucking mad. It's better to have some sort of plan in place, or else we are gonna be like everyone else who does nothing. We'll be standing around, holding our dicks, and not knowing what to do when it starts.'

That dick word is being bandied about a little too much lately for her liking.

'And your bunker's goin' to save us from all that stuff... if it happens?'

'Well, it'll give us more protection than this house will.'

She takes a sup from her bottle and proceeds with her subtle third degree.

'It would need to be pretty strong.'

'I've drawn up a scaled plan of the back garden.'

'And?'

'Well, on those shows, the most popular thing used for a shelter is...'

'A shipping container,' she finishes.

'Yeah... well, it would have to be something like that.'

'I suppose then ye could put the food under the bed in it?'

'Exactly!' he perks up. 'That's exactly where I'd put it.'

She feels sorry for him at this moment but she needs to go a little more.

'Fran, do ye not think that a container sitting in the back garden would look..., well... a little odd?'

He moves forward while still looking at her and winks. 'But that's the beauty of my plan. It would only be there for a day.'

She looks at her bottle and mentally counts how many she has had, and it comes to nearly four so far.

'Are ya ok, love?'

'Fran… a container in the back for a day?'

'Sorry Re, I meant it would only be seen for a day. Not even a day, a few hours.'

She thinks back to her phonecall with Sophie. 'Before it's buried… you're going to bury it, aren't ye?'

He smiles broadly and taps the A4 on his lap.

'So what are ye going to do? Get your shovel and start digging?' she asks, as she looks at her wrist and still no watch. 'Shite! Why do I keep doing that? Anyway, Fran, it's a major operation for ye to get a bucket of coal from the shed, and you're thinking of digging a hole… a pit, for a shipping container? Well, ye would want to start now, because from my calculations, you'll be about eighty by the time it's finished.'

He keeps quiet and after some seconds, his eyes glance at the A4, then at her.

'Ye have that covered… in your little book, don't ye?'

He nods and she drains her bottle and gets up. 'I need another one of these. Yourself?'

'I'm grand, love.'

While in the kitchen, she checks the lasagne. 'ARRRGH!'

'What's wrong, Re?'

'The fuckin' thing's not even on! Damn that whore!'

Seconds later, she wiggles past him and sits on the couch.

'Damn that whore?'

'Ye know, your one today? Poxbottle! Anyway, tell me.'

'Well… ya know the way we have a corner house and a bigger garden?'

'Yeah, Fran, I live here!'

'Well, ya know the fences beside the gate?'

'I do. The wooden ones that were here when we moved in, and that I have to woodstain because…' she remembers a few minutes ago. 'Go ahead, love.'

'They are wooden… and ya can slide them up and take them away.'

She takes a good gulp from her bottle, 'Keep goin'.'

'If one of the concrete pole things that they slide into was removed… let's say for a day or two, then put back with the fences…'

'Spill it, Fran!'

'Well… a digger could fit through and dig a hole for the container,' he lifts his can and takes two long gulps while looking at her nervously.

Without moving her head, she looks at the TV for a few seconds, then her eyes move slowly back to stare at him. Seconds pass. 'Ok… ye win.' His eyes narrow.

'Ye get your container.'

'Really?' he asks, disbelievingly.

'Yeah, but on one condition.'

'Name it.'

'Me garden… ye better not wreck it,' she thinks for a moment before she pulls a face and looks at the window. Am I stupid? Me fence is coming down and a digger thing

279

is going to dig a twenty foot hole, and the rest! And I'm saying he better not wreck me garden? 'Let me rephrase that. I'm going to take a picture of the garden and the fence before anything happens, and if it doesn't match up afterwards... well,' she smirks and points at his crotch. 'See him... he'll never get anything from me EVER again! Do we understand each other?'

'We understand each other, Re. So, I'm really getting it?'

'Lord give me strength! Yes, you're really getting it!'

He stands up and starts doing a jig around the room. Pauli has just got home and walks into the sitting room and stares at Fran twirling around with his arms in the air. He looks at Rita sitting on the couch, then back at Fran who spots him.

'Marty, Pauli, you're back!' he says, continuing to dance.

Pauli puts his right hand to his ear. 'Eh... yeah, doc, I'm back.'

On hearing this, Fran claps his hands while still jigging. Pauli watches a little more before going into the kitchen and Rita follows him.

He opens the oven. 'Aw cool, lasagne.'

'And chips, coleslaw and potato salad.'

He shuts the door and faces Rita. 'So, what has dad so happy?'

Minutes later, she finishes telling him and awaits his verdict.

'Fair play to ya, Mam.'

'Ye agree?!'

'Bigtime! A hobby or interest is what dad needs, we've been told that for years. This is good. Mental health and all that. At least he won't be stuck in that room all the time for days on end.'

'Ye know… I never thought of it like that. Thanks, son. Oh, speaking of mental health, he had another episode today, only a while ago.'

'How bad?'

'Not as bad as they used to be, but I didn't see it coming. It only lasted a minute or two but it was about the same stuff: RPGs and the IEDs and snipers. But as ye can see for yourself, he's back to himself now.'

He stands looking at her. 'Mam, ya done good. Especially after telling me that.'

'Thanks, son.'

'Ok… now down to business. Can ya spare a bottle?'

She goes to the fridge and gets two, then grabs the opener. 'Let's have them in the sun before it goes, and after this, help yourself. And speaking of people helping themselves, where's Matt?'

'Right now, I'd say he's on the khasi.'

The two are sitting at the table taking in the sun, when she looks at him from behind her glasses. 'So tell me, why home so late?'

'We went for lunch with two mates.'

'It must've been some lunch!'

He begins by telling her that they went to an Indian. As this is her favourite food, he has got her full attention. The starter gets mentioned, then the main course. By the time he is finished, her mouth is watering at the thought. She looks into the kitchen at the cooker.

'Thinking of getting an Indian, Mother?'

'As Em would say, roger that.'

'And Em is saying it!'

'Hello Em.' Pauli says, without looking up.

'Brother. Anyway, Ma, if you're…'

'I am getting one. What do ye want?'

'Yahoo! Will ya get me a mixed grill?'

Pauli looks up. 'Copycat!'

'Well, ya shouldn't have let me taste your one then, shouldn't ya… brother?'

'Is that it, Em?'

'Well if ya want to get me a few chips, ya can.'

'I'll do oven chips with the lasagne. The bleedin' lasagne! I forgot about that.'

'Mam, don't worry about it. I'll have a fair chunk of that because I'm starving. And I think dad will demolish his fair share of it after the booze.'

'Right Em, just ye and me for Indian. Are ye sure that's all ye want?'

'Ok Ma, I'll have a portion of pakoras as well, if ya insist, and don't forget to get poppadoms as well.'

'Now… are ye finally finished?'

'Yeah, but, Ma, will ya lace me chips with pepper as weOWW!' The two look up.

'What happened?' Rita asks.

'The little fu… art, scrawbed me leg. Ouch! Stop doin' that! Ma, I gotta go and stick a DVD on for this fella. So ya know what to get me?'

'Yeah, love, what time?'

'Whenever you're getting yours!' Em shouts from the room.

Rita goes inside and comes out with another two bottles and gives Pauli one.

'Ye can get the next ones.'

'I will, Mam. Is he still dancing?'

'I don't know. So, where's this Indian?'

'Eh, Carlingford.'

'Ye nearly crossed the border for an Indian?!'

'Matt thought it was across the border. So much for a C in geography in the Leaving. But it's only about five or ten miles from it on our side.'

'Oh, I know where it is, son. I'm from just down the road. So was it dear?'

'Nine ninety-nine a head, but we had Cola's, so it was four cent shy of fifty euro.'

She thinks for a moment. 'Twelve fifty each? Do ye and Matt always take that much with ye?'

'No, we just about had enough. But we didn't pay for it… Lucy had a voucher.'

Rita raises her sunglasses and looks at him while smiling, 'Who's Lucy?'

CHAPTER FORTY-ONE

Fran got up extra early this morning because he couldn't sleep, which is nothing new, but today he is expecting his delivery from England. He knows that this will have to remain a sealed lip situation concerning Rita, as her sneering smile is really starting to get on his wick. He checks the clock on the telly every few seconds and wonders if she is even in work today. He is tempted to bring her up a cup of tea as an excuse to wake her, but she is not that thick, she would know that he is up to something. So he picks up his can and takes a sup. Just as he is putting it on the table, he hears her phone alarm go off.

'Yes!' he shouts, throwing his arms into the air. Then he slowly looks around the room with a frozen look of horror on his face. He hears her get out of bed and her heavy heeled walk cross the bedroom floor to the landing.

'Fran?!'

'Yes love?'

'It's half seven in the morning, why are ye shouting?'

'That wasn't me, love.'

'Fran, I'm not going to argue with ye from the landing, but it was ye!'

He plays it safe and says no more. Seconds later, she enters the bathroom.

'Thud!'

'Emmet!' Emma yells, as the sound of something rustles across the floor.

He brings the brush up to her, then goes and makes Rita a cup of tea. It is cold by the time she comes down as she had a shower, applied her makeup and done her hair. She makes a fresh one and enters the room and sits on the couch.

'Well, it looks like I don't need to alarm me phone anymore.'

'Ok love, it was me. I'm sorry.'

'Why would ye do that?'

He cannot tell her the truth. That he cheered because she eventually got up for work, and when she is gone, he can wait for his delivery in peace. So he looks at the telly.

'Fran, why the scream?'

He looks back at her. 'I…I think I'm gettin' tourettes, love.'

She looks at him for a moment before getting up and going out to the kitchen. After he hears the radio come on, he sits back and smiles as he picks up his can and whispers to himself. 'Won't be long now, lad.'

Emma came down minutes later with Emmet and gave him his breakfast in the kitchen. Rita asked Fran if he wanted something before she left and he went for a cheese and sausage toastie. When he came into the kitchen to get it, Emma put her hands over Emmet's ears and as he passed her, screamed. 'Mornin', Da!'

After the initial shock, he joined in on the laughter as he thought it was funny. When Rita was leaving, she came into the sitting room and asked if he fancied anything in particular for the dinner, and he picked pork chops. After she gave him a peck on the cheek, she was inches from his ear when she screamed.

'See ye later, Franner!'

When she left, he was thinking that if things were to continue like this, that he'd have to take more nerve tablets just to get around the house. So he decided that when she came home, he would tell her that he had dreamt that he had tourettes and that should be the end of it. If not, he will just have to play them at their own game and scream into their ears when they are not expecting it.

Pauli came down not long after and asked why everyone was screaming. When Emma told him, he just said "Ok" and made his breakfast. Matt knocked soon after and the two left for college.

A few hours later, Fran needed to go to the toilet, but did not want to miss the postman, so he asked Emma to keep an ear out for the door. As luck would have it, he was only sitting down a few seconds when the doorbell rang. 'Shite!'

Emma signs for the delivery and Fran comes down about twenty minutes later. He walks in and counts the small boxes that she neatly arranged on the sofa. 1 of 5, 2 of 5, until he gets to 5 of 5.

She sits watching this with Emmet on her lap. 'So, Da, what's the story?'

He doesn't reply. He places a box on the floor and tries to rip it open, but it is taped up too good. After going out to the kitchen, he returns with a scissors and takes his time cutting the tape, then opens the box and removes a gasmask. Emma stares at it with an open mouth, but no sound.

'And this is for you, Em,' he says, holding it out to her.

She runs to the kitchen and comes back with the buggy, puts Emmet into it and then takes it from him. 'Really, Da... this is mine?!'

'Yeah, and I have one for everyone in the audience,' he says, looking around the room. Emma starts laughing and so he does. He opens the rest of the boxes and takes the masks out. Emma is wearing hers so Fran tries his one on as well. She mumbles something and he mumbles something back. They repeat it and then take the masks off.

'Da, I said you're a mad bastard!'

'Oh, I couldn't make it out. And less of the cursing there, young lady.'

'Sorry, Da, but this... these are the real thing, aren't they?'

'I paid good money for them so they fuckin' better be!'

The two start laughing.

After putting the smallest one on Emmet, who seemed quite happy sitting in the buggy with it on, he filled Emma in. He got them just in case of a pandemic or a chemical attack. Now that they have arrived safely, he is planning on getting the suits as well. He told her of his visit into Swords last week and that he'd have to go back in to make another order. Emma went upstairs and came down with her laptop and got onto the website and he was delighted. There would be no more trekking over to the library, but he would miss the corned beef and the can on the bus home. While he sat with a can, she sat with a cup of coffee and the two scanned through the items. Emma was nearly drooling as this was happening. They picked out five suits and Fran rang. Avril answered again and was glad to hear that everything had arrived safe and sound. She took the order and gave Thursday or Friday as possible dates of delivery. She also gave him a discount for this and the previous order for being ex-service after he gave her his details. When he put down the house phone, he sat back in his chair and smiled over at Emma. She heard everything as it had been on loudspeaker.

'Da, I have to say, when I saw them programmes, I thought that the people were a bit weird. But now, we're them people and I feel normal.'

'Because we are normal, love.'

'Da, this has made my day, thanks.'

'Don't mention it love… and don't mention it to your mother or she'll think I'm a bit mad.'

'Da… that ship has long left port!'

CHAPTER FORTY-TWO

Rita tells Sophie that she is going ahead with the container, and about Fran's plan to bring a digger through the side of the garden to dig a hole to bury it in. According to him, she won't notice a thing after about a week or two, when the grass grows back.

Sophie laughs.

There are only two men in the cafe and they are at different tables. Both look towards them and for some reason, one of them starts laughing as well, as if he's in on what has just been said. After some seconds, he goes back to eating his super extra-large breakfast.

Rita smirks. 'Get him,' she whispers.

'Idiot,' Sophie says, also in a whisper. 'So, what changed your mind?'

'I said to meself... self, if Fran asked for a sports car or whatever, how much would that cost? And against a container, well, the container wins hands down. He isn't going to be doing too much posing in one of them now, is he?'

'Aha! So it's to keep an eye on him?'

'Of course it is! He's my man and that's the way it's going to stay. Plus, ye know the way he doesn't leave the house much, not even to the back garden unless it's a special occasion like getting a bit of coal?'

'I do.' Sophie replies, trying not to laugh.

'Well, Pauli said it would be good for him, and Em agreed. They said it would get him outdoors a bit more and give him something other to think about. As I've told ye before, if we still lived in England, there are loads of charities and things that support veterans.'

Rita goes on to tell her about a programme that she watched with Fran a couple of months ago. There were different ones on each week about veterans who found it hard to reintegrate back into society, or as it was phrased in the programme "Civvy Street" after leaving the Armed Forces. Whether it be by choice, end of service or through injury. Some had turned to crime and were incarcerated, as they could not cope, especially after returning from tours of Afghanistan or Iraq. Others carried much longer memories as they had served in Northern Ireland, Bosnia and even the Falklands. They still found it hard to adapt and felt alone after being with a unit of men for so long that they new had their back wherever they would be. Then there were those who had either physical disabilities or the harder to spot ones, the mental ones, such as PTSD. She goes on to tell her of one place in Scotland where "the vets" spend a week, basically being cowboys after been given a horse to look after.

Then another in London where there is an enclosed garden that they tend to. Looking after and growing flowers and plants. Fran pitied "the lads", but said that even if they still lived in England, he wouldn't join up with something like that as there are more deserving than him that would benefit from it. And as they live in Ireland, the chances of finding something like that for ex-British service personnel would be non-existent. So that is where the container for his doomsday bunker comes in.

Rita notices Sophie's eyes welling up. 'Soph, I shouldn't have said anything. I should have just left it at getting the container and said nothing more.'

'No, you're ok, Re. I just never knew it... well, we're Irish. That's the last thing we would think of, British soldiers with difficulties. But Fran brings this much closer to home in a weird way. Did what I say just make any sense?'

Rita reaches for a napkin and hands it to her. 'It made perfect sense. At the end of the day, we're all human and can relate to others who are not so fortunate.'

Sophie covertly tries to wipe her eyes. 'It will do him the world of good, Re. Out in the fresh air, pottering around the garden and not stuck in that room thinking about the past that much, please God.'

'That's what Pauli said. Well not exactly, he said mental health.'

'That's what I was trying to think of, but he's dead right. You never know, this could be the making of Fran.'

'Touch wood.'

She sniffles and then smiles. 'Ok, well I bet you're glad that you know me.'

'Well, yes, Sophie. I'm actually honoured to know ye.'

'Well then, missus, as Fran would say, make me a brew and we'll have a chat.'

Rita goes with the flow and makes two teas. 'Ok, bitch, what's this about?'

Sophie blows the tea a few times before taking a sip. 'Mmm, nice tea, Re.'

'Sophie?'

'Ok, it's funny what you said. Not the part about… I mean at the beginning.'

'Is it?' Rita asks, trying to remember what she said at the beginning.

'Yeah. Because behind our house in that field where Johnboy's container is going to go is… a dumper and two JCB's just sitting there.'

'You're joking?!'

'Would I?'

'You'd be dead if ye did!'

'That's why I wouldn't, biatch!' she says, with a grin.

'Will ye ask?'

'I will,' she takes another sip from her cup. 'I love this tea.'

The two are chatting away for a few minutes before the idiot that laughed out of turn, looks over and points at his plate.

Rita starts to get up. 'I bet ye this is trouble.'

'No Re, I served him so I'll see what's up.'

Rita takes a sup of her tea and watches. Within seconds of Sophie getting there, she looks around at Rita, who gets the hint and follows her over.

'Good morning, sir, and what seems to be the problem?'

Sophie moves back a step and keeps quiet.

'Well love… the problem is… that I found this on that sausage there,' he says, holding up a hair.

Rita looks at the plate, then at the hair he is holding up, then at him.

'Right. So, what do ye expect me to do?'

'I want a refund.'

She looks at Sophie, who is nibbling on her nail while trying not to laugh. Rita is also trying hard to keep a straight face. 'A refund? Sophie… this is a super extra-large breakfast, right?'

She nods.

'So that's fourteen fifty.'

'Re, extra toast by two.'

'Right, so now it's seventeen fifty. Is that right, sir?'

'Yeah. That's about it,' he replies, still holding the hair up.

Sophie lets out a sound and when he looks at her, she rubs her chin.

'Ok. Well there's just three problems that I have, and here is the first one. This is the largest breakfast we do, and from what I can see, there's only a segment of tomato and one sausage left on your plate. And that hair just happened to be on that last sausage, after everything else is gone?'

'That's not my fault, love. It must've been underneath.'

'Fair enough. Now here's two, look at her,' he looks up at Sophie and smiles, showing a set of teeth and gums that she would rather never have seen. 'What colour hair has she got?'

'Blond of course!' he replies, with a snigger.

'Now me, what colour is my hair?'

'Black, love. You've got black hair.'

'Good, so you're not colour blind. That thing you're holding up is grey, and it looks like the rest of the stuff that's hanging out of your shirt.'

He looks down at his protruding chest hair, then back at the one he is holding.

'No… no, it's not the same.'

'Well is it blond or black?'

He stares at it, then looks from Sophie to Rita. 'No… it's grey.'

'Good. Well at least we got that sorted. It's not from us two, so ye can keep it for yourself. Now, there's one more thing, and this is number three.'

'And what's that?' he asks, starting to sweat and looking like he cannot wait to leave quick enough.

'Ye haven't paid for the food yet, so how can ye have a refund?'

'Well, I'm not happy with it. That ruined me breakfast.'

'There's nothing to ruin, it's all gone! So… whenever you're ready, that will be seventeen fifty, please.'

He looks from Rita to Sophie, who is staring at him with a weird grin.

'Eh… I'll have to go out to the van and get me wallet,' he says, standing up and reaching for his phone, but Sophie snatches it from the table and folds her arms.

'You can have this back when you've paid the bill,' she says, then notices the other man looking across and smiling, while holding a book with one hand and giving her a thumbs up with the other.

The idiot stands looking between the two of them, then turns for the door. He goes outside and gets into his van.

'He had no intention of paying if his wallet is in the van.'

'I know, but I have a plan,' Rita whispers, as she watches him. 'Are ye alright for about thirty seconds?'

'Of course!' she holds up the phone. 'That fat fool is a broken man at this stage.'

Rita runs behind the counter and grabs some plastic forks, then runs through the kitchen and out the backdoor. The bookreader who gave Sophie the thumbs up is intrigued, so he puts his book on the table and folds his arms. He looks at the guy getting out of the van and coming back towards the cafe. Once he is inside, bookreader notices Rita running over to his van and kneeling at the front wheel. He looks at the counter and Sophie is adding up the bill again, but throwing a sly eye out at the van. He looks back out the window and sees Rita sneaking around the other side and dropping out of sight. The fat guy is getting impatient now and just wants to get out of there. The bookreader spots Rita's head pop up, have a quick look around, then disappear again and tries not to laugh.

'This bloody machine! Always acting up,' she lies.

'Look, I need to go to the toilet.'

Sophie points at the door while thinking that this is just getting better. 'Straight through there on your right.'

Once he is inside, she runs to the door and whistles. Rita's head pops up.

'Your man's in the jax, how you doing?'

'This one's nearly flat. Is the fork still in the other one?'

She looks at the wheel, then back at Rita. 'Yeah, and that's nearly flat, too.'

'Right, I'll be in in a minute.'

Sophie runs back to the counter and waits. She is listening for the flush but nothing is happening and she is dreading the worst. If he comes out and says that he got food poisoning, the smiles will be wiped off their faces good and proper. She is just about to run back to see how Rita is doing when the toilet door opens and he walks out.

'Is it working yet?'

She shivers, knowing that if he did not bother to flush the toilet, the chances of him washing his hands are minimal. 'Yeah... you just have to enter your pin.'

As interesting as this may be, the bookreader keeps his attention on Rita.

This time he sees her look out from the back of the van, then vanish. Almost instantly, she appears at the front and makes her way around it. As she is passing the first wheel that got the plastic fork treatment, she grabs it from the valve and continues past the window, out of sight. Seconds later, she walks through the kitchen and stops beside Sophie at the till.

'Ok, Soph, that bin is full now.'

'Good,' she looks at the idiot. 'Ok, you can take your card now and here's your receipt,' she puts it on the counter, not taking any chances of handing it to him. He takes them and turns to go. 'Don't forget your phone,' she says, picking it up with a napkin and putting it on the counter as well.

He picks it up and as he walks by his table, takes the sausage and sticks it in his mouth. Once he is gone out the door, Sophie turns to Rita.

'You done the two of them?'

'That was the plan, but I ended up doing the back one as well.'

Sophie laughs. 'He won't be able to move that thing with three flats.'

'Well that's his problem. It had to be done, Soph. The bleedin' cheek of him.'

The two laugh and spot the bookreader looking at them.

'Do ye want a cup of tea or coffee? It's on the house.'

'Yes please, and I won't say a word,' he turns and watches as the van moves a bit before the revs get louder and louder. It eventually manages to drive out of the carpark and he wonders how far it will get before the bloke realises that there is something wrong and pulls over. Then he looks at his car.

'Don't worry. That Avensis hasn't got a fork anywhere near it. Tea, Soph?'

'I'd love a cup. I just want to wash my hands.'

'I'd hold that thought. Ye have to get your man's plate first.'

'Biatch!'

CHAPTER FORTY-THREE

Not long after, some miles up north, and it is minutes away from the end of first class. Matt and Pauli have just finished their, as Mister Collon put it, "unusual version of Macbeth." Considering that they had not been told to rehearse it, and the last time they did give it a read over was a few months before, at the request of Miss McCabe, the two are quite happy with it. And it seems that the girls are too. With their rapturous applause and very loud whistles, much to the dismay of Mister Collon. The two gay lads are now starting their version coming up to the break, but even Mister Collon cannot take anymore.

'Ok, lads, leave it there till later.'

An audible sound of relief goes around the room. Pauli looks across the class where the girls are, and Lucy smiles at him and nods to her right at Becka. He is confused and she nods again. He looks and notices Becka's fingers moving ever so slightly. He looks to his left at Matt, who is also working his fingers.

Damn it!

In the midst of this, Mister Collon is yattering on about what he expects from the rest of the class after lunch. Pauli looks back at Lucy. When he saw Becka and Matt communicating by using sign language, he felt jealous for a moment, quickly turning to self-disgust. He knows how

Matt came to learn it because of Lothar. Matt had always wanted Pauli to learn it as well, and he said he would, but he put it on the long finger. But Becka? Now that's a question that will need to be asked sometime soon. Eventually the class is dismissed and the lads walk over to the girls, who have not budged an inch.

'Hey!' Pauli says, smiling.

'While the sun shines.'

Matt shows less restraint than Pauli and grabs Becka's hand and they make for the door. Seconds later, the only two remaining in the class are Lucy and Pauli. He looks uneasy. 'Are we ok?'

'Why do you ask?'

'I don't know. I just…'

'I was being innovative. We're in PA, remember? And before you ask, I do know that there's a, make, in there.'

'In where?'

She grins while looking at him, then kisses him quickly on the lips and he smiles back with obvious relief. 'You didn't think I had second thoughts, did you?'

He doesn't know what to say, so as Fran always told him "say nothing."

She takes his hand. 'It was me who chased after you, remember? Let's go get some lunch.'

They catch up with the other two who are waiting outside for them.

'Come on, man, me starving!' Matt says.

Becka gets Matt's hand and puts it on her head. 'Me hungry… get food!' she says, in a deep voice and the two walk away like that in the direction of the garage.

Pauli and Lucy laugh.

'That would have been a good Macbeth.' Lucy says.

'Damn it! Yeah, cave Macbeth meets cave Witch.'

'What do you think Mister Collon would have thought of that?'

'Mister Collon would have thought... very inventive. Oh yes, thanks O'Neill. Fifty seven minutes,' he says, passing them. 'And no, I'm not,' he calls back, walking towards the carpark.

Lucy stares after him, then looks at Pauli. 'What did that mean?'

'I got him a web address for a poster.'

'And the last bit?'

'I was gonna ask... do ya think he's gay?'

The four make their way to the spot. Pauli volunteered to stand in the queue to get the food but Matt and Becka overruled him. So he and Lucy sat on the grass in the campus across the road. Becka turned and waved over and Lucy waved back with a big smile.

'Yous two are really close.'

She looks at him. 'As close as you and Matt.'

'Really, that close?!'

'Do I really want to know?' she asks, giggling. 'Yeah, we're close. My mam used to call us the shadows. I like them as well. Not big on words but... that guitar!'

'Ya know your music for been...'

'For being... so young?' she finishes. 'I grew up on all that type of stuff. My mam and dad were always playing music, and still do when they're home.'

He stares at her, and those eyes are either getting greener or she wears contacts. She smiles. 'What is it?'

'Eh, did ya get your wig chopped or something?'

'You mean, did I get my hair cut?!'

'Yeah. It looks like… well, not as much as before,' he looks at the grass and mentally curses himself. Pauli, could ya be any more awkward?

'Well, yes I did actually,' she says, reaching behind and tightening her ponytail. 'I realised that I had a little too much hair for my liking. In fact, and you will probably think that this is funny, but I felt like a Kerry Blue Terrier. Do you think that's weird?'

At the mention of, Kerry Blue, he swallows hard.

'O'Neill,' she grins. 'Are you alright? You look a bit… pasty.'

She knows! And the only other person that knew… he looks at the garage but cannot see Matt. The louse must be inside. He slowly looks back at her and forces a smile.

'Ya see,' he swallows. 'The thing is, was.'

'You're ok. I'm just having a bit of fun with you, and you were right. Becka was always telling me that my hair was a bit extreme.'

'So everything's alright between us?'

'Well, I got my hair cut specially for you. So what do you think?'

The relief on his face is immediate and she is glad. He places his hand on hers.

'Did that hurt, O'Neill?'

'Not as much as something else would've, and I've been building up to that since last night.'

'Good, and don't take as long in future,' she takes off a flip flop and purple sock with her other hand. 'I've got a real itch!'

'I thought ya don't wear socks?'

'I know. Socks with flip flops or sandles is a no no.'

'Is it?' he looks at her foot and realises that he knows it. 'We've met before.'

She looks at him while scratching her toe. 'Huh?'

'Yeah, and we have the proof. Licking her foot in the light of day on a public beach? Shame!' Matt says, then hands him a baguette and drink.

He and Becka sit down and get stuck into their rolls. Pauli looks at Lucy who is still scratching that toe of hers. She brings the top of the baguette to her mouth, bites the paper and peels it down until it tears away and spits it onto the grass, then takes a bite from it. She must be hungry to have done that. As she is chewing, a tiny crumb clings to her upper lip. Just as he is about to tell her, she glances at him and her tongue comes out, gives it a lick and it is gone. For some reason he cannot take his eyes off her. Even when she is biting through paper to get at her food, she is stop-a-breath beautiful. He watches her while still holding up his unopened roll.

'Are you going to eat that or just sit there holding it in the air?' she asks, before taking another bite and winking at him.

He lowers it, and as he is gracefully unwrapping it as opposed to what Lucy just did, he notices that Matt and Becka are looking at him, so he takes a huge bite.

'Me and Becka were wondering if yous,' Lucy looks at her, then back at Pauli, who has a mouthful of food. 'Would be into… buzzing up, to mine after college on Monday for a barbecue?'

'Sounds good! What do ya think, P?' Matt asks.

Pauli can barely move the food around his mouth to chew, never mind answer a question in understandable English, so he shrugs his shoulders and nods.

'Good. But there's one condition.'

'What's that?' Matt asks, looking at Lucy.

'Yous have to bring a toothbrush,' she replies, looking up at a now able to chew Pauli with her grin, then takes a smaller bite of her roll.

Matt waits until Pauli has swallowed his food, then makes it obvious to all that he is thinking of something before looking back at him. 'P, mate?'

'Yeah Matt?'

'I still have that thong that ya left in me gaff. Ya know the gold one? So I'll bring that for ya so that ya won't have to bring a change of undies.'

Pauli's face is a picture and the four laugh their heads off.

CHAPTER FORTY-FOUR

The following day, Rita and Sophie are on again. Sophie opened up so Rita arrives in just before nine thirty.

'Morning.'

'And a good morning to you, too. I have a brew ready for you.'

'Ah thanks, Soph. Where's your car?'

'I didn't bring it, John dropped me down.'

'At half seven?!' she asks, putting her jacket in her locker.

'The reason is, he got the wheels turning about the JCB and the other stuff.'

This is probably too early to remind Rita about all that. She walks out and stands looking at her and her face seems whiter than normal.

'Are you alright, Re?'

'Let me have the tea first and then tell me.'

A few sups into her tea, and her brain has adjusted to what it has just heard. It is now prepared for what Sophie has to tell it. 'Ok, tell me.'

'Right. I'm only the messenger. He said that if he told me what to tell you, that most of it would go on the missing list. Or I'd probably tell you something completely different.'

Rita takes another sup of tea. 'And ye would.'

'I know. I'm useless at relaying messages if it's anything longer than such and such rang, or your dinner isn't ready yet.'

'Sure I'm your sister! I would've forgotten the part after such AND…'

'So, he's dropping in after work to tell you himself, and I'll be holding on as well to keep you company.'

'And for your lift home.'

'That, too.'

'So what time will he get here?'

'He said about half four.'

'Ah grand, we'll be empty by then.'

'Like we are now,' Sophie picks up her cup but stops before putting it to her lips. 'Did you see the van down the road?'

'I did! Up on the path and the tyres are wrote off.'

Sophie giggles before taking that sip of tea. 'Re… that was a bit of a mad thing to do. Do you think he'll ever come back?'

'Soph, he was chancing his arm, and he knew he was caught and couldn't wait to get out of here. Imagine how often he pulls that stunt and doesn't pay?'

'I suppose.'

'Look, if we were to let everyone off who held up a hair after eating most of a fry or a dinner, me and ye would be out of a job, and standing outside shops tryin' to sell the big issue.'

Sophie giggles. 'You're right. Oh, and I told John about it.'

'Ye didn't?'

'I did, and he said your man deserved it. Although he never heard of anyone doing that before. So, I said I'd ask you today. Where did you learn the thing with the forks?'

'Ohh, that was all Em.'

'Em?! How did she learn it?'

She gets up. 'Ah, it was years ago, when we rented a farmhouse up in Donegal.'

'Where are you going?'

'I just got a mad craving for chocolate so I'm getting a bar. Want something?'

'Yeah, I'll have one of the yellow ones.'

She takes a quick trip into the kitchen and sees that the bread and scones are made, then returns with the bars and starts on the first finger.

'So?' Sophie asks, after taking a bite.

'So?'

'So the rest of the story?'

Rita shakes her head. 'It's nothin' special, Soph.'

Sophie needs to find out how all this started. Firstly for herself, and secondly, because John was in bits laughing when she told him last night. He ended up putting down his laptop for the night, and they continued to have a chat and a laugh while drinking, and it went on for a while. Then one thing led to another, and that wouldn't have happened if the story had not been told. As he is under a bit of pressure with some jobs that are behind in work, she is not going to let it take over his life, or theirs. He let off some steam last night and seemed the better for it this morning. Tonight, her plan is to make him some chunky chips with a couple of T-bone steaks, which are his favourite. A bottle or two of wine to go with some beers and then dessert. And another bit of "humah humah" just before bedtime. That is her plan, so she needs to hear this story. Another thing, she is wondering what the connection is between plastic forks sticking out of car tyres, a farmhouse in Donegal and Em is?

'I want to hear it, Re.'

'Look, I'll tell ye the short version.'

'You started this yesterday, so I want the director's cut version.'

'Sophie, this isn't one of those mad funny things, it's just.'

'Re, tell me!'

She finishes off her first finger, takes a sup of tea and begins.

'Right. Years ago,' she looks up for a moment. 'I think Pauli was about eleven, so Em would've been nine. Everyone in the estate seemed to be going abroad for their summer holidays. So Fran got a bit uppity and suggested that we bring the kids away as well, instead of probably been the only family left in the estate. Only problem was, we couldn't afford to bring them foreign. We even priced bringing them to a theme park in England for a week, but that was too dear. Fran was losing patience at this stage so he suggested somewhere in Ireland. We looked through the papers and there were loads of caravans and houses, but we picked this one in Donegal because of it having been a farm at one stage. We were thinking... let the two of them run wild around the fucking place and give us some peace.'

Sophie finishes her bar and nods her head for Rita to continue.

'Well, from the moment we arrived there, it was a disaster. There was no water the first night, and after that, it came on when it felt like it, but it was never hot. If we wanted to have a cup of tea or a wash, it was back to the eighteenth century and boil up pots of water on the cooker. And as for the shops, they were fuckin' miles away. Six miles in fact, back in Donegal Town. Now that's a pain in the arse if ye just got back and realised that ye forgot to pick up butter to go with your toast, or milk to go with tea or cereal. So we rang the slut who we'd dealt with when we rented it, and told her that we wanted our money back as it wasn't as advertised. But she said, no way!'

'So, what did you do?'

Rita looks towards the door, then slowly back at Sophie. 'Well, Fran wanted to burn it,' she narrows her eyes and moves her head slightly from side to side a few times. 'Well..., not actually burn it. More blow it up.'

Sophie's eyes widen. 'You're joking, right?'

She shakes her head. 'No I'm not. And I have to say, he had a good plan.'

'I'm almost afraid to hear it. Tell me.'

'As I said, if we wanted a wash or a cup of tea, we had to boil pots of water on the cooker. But the cooker was gas. Fran wanted to put all the rings on and leave a burning candle upstairs in one of the bedrooms. "That should do it," he said, "Boom!"'

'And where would yous have stayed?'

'Ah, we only lasted four days before we admitted defeat and decided to go back home. He wanted to do it the day we were leaving.'

Sophie is engrossed. 'Well?!'

'Even I thought that was a bit much. I just wanted to break all the windows and leave the taps running for when the water came back on. But just before we left, I bottled out and eventually persuaded Fran to just leave it and go home.'

'Jesus! Remind me never to get on Fran's bad side.'

'I will.'

'The forks?'

'Oh yeah. Well we took the old N4 home, as he doesn't like dual carriageways. After a while, Em started saying she was hungry, then Pauli and Fran joined in. So we pulled into a roadside restaurant outside Kinnegad. Anyway, Em ate her food like a savage and was the first to finish. Then she went to the toilet. After about maybe ten minutes later, she still hadn't returned, so I got worried and went looking for her. I checked the toilets, womens and mens, but nothing. So I went outside to see if she was at the car. I'd only walked out the door when I heard this hissing sound. I thought it was insects or something. I looked around and spotted a white fork sticking out of a tyre valve, then another one. Then I spotted Em walking through the carpark and bending down and I followed her.

As I was walking through the carpark, all I heard was hissing and it was getting louder. Every car I passed had forks sticking out of their tyres. When I got to her, she was on her knees trying to stick a fork into another one.'

Sophie starts laughing. 'So what did you do?'

'I told her to drop the remaining forks, which was about ten or fifteen, grabbed her by her hair and marched her back to the car. I went in and whispered to Fran to get outside quick and took Pauli and went to the car. Fran walked out minutes later after going back and filling his plate with food again, and cruised over to the car as if nothing was wrong.'

'You mean he...' she starts giggling.

'Yeah... walked across the carpark eating it. We still have that plate. Oh, and he forgot to pay for the food. Then on the news that night "Fork menace in Meath."' Sophie goes into hysterics. Her head is on the table so Rita moves her cup in case she knocks it over. It is minutes before she can breathe normally again, even though she does fall back into the odd giggle. John is going to love this story, if she can ever get around to finishing it. She looks at Rita while wiping her eyes.

'Re, you've the weirdest family I know.'

'Tell me about it,' she takes a sup of her tea and makes a face.

'Freezin'. Do ye want another?'

Just then, the door opens and six Japanese tourists walk in with about fifteen cameras between them.

'Heads or tails?'

Sophie gets up and goes to the counter, gets the pad and pen, and comes back to the table and places it in front of Rita.

'Can't blame me for trying,' she says, standing up.

CHAPTER FORTY-FIVE

Fran didn't feel like sitting in front of the telly again and drinking himself into a familiar state of drunkenness. Instead, he decided to venture back into Swords and take another look around that camping shop. Surprisingly, he wanted to get out of the house. The thoughts of standing at the backdoor with a brew, looking around the garden, just wasn't cutting it today. He also had an urge to hold the Sa80, and wondered why he hadn't the last time he was there. Just to look down the sights and release and insert the magazine gave him shivers. This would be so close to holding the real thing that it felt almost creepy. Thinking about it now, he should have bought that instead and got the AR-15 for Em's Christmas present. He left the house and caught the 11:15 bus and at 11:21, he got off it. He had gone with Rita on many occasions to Swords but never had she done it in a little over six minutes. This driver was either in a serious hurry to have his lunch or had played a racing car video game the night before. While taking two different bends, Fran had felt the bus sway to the side as if it was just about to topple over, but it came out of the bends upright and seemed to fly up the road. After the second bend, it even overtook two cars, and that was a first for Fran. He was sitting in the front seat that didn't have the camera blind spot, and could imagine his face if they were handing out pictures when he was getting off.

He would need to pick up another two cans for the return journey, just in case it was the same driver, but picking up the beer was going to happen anyway.

As he was getting off, he told the driver that he should enter for Le Mans and he laughed. Fran watched it slowly crawl away up the main street and wondered had he imagined it all. Everyone else on the bus either had earphones in their ears or were talking. None of them seemed bothered at the excessive speed with which the driver had used to get them to Swords, in what must be a record time for a double decker bus. He only start forgetting the journey the nearer he got to the camping shop. He could see the corner where he would take a left, go under an arch and the shop would be on his right. He kept his eyes on the corner that much, that he walked into a sign on the pavement outside a shop. He looked down and read the chalk writing and smiled. A breakfast roll for two euro.

He went in and picked only two items for his roll even though the girl told him he could have four. But he stuck with his choice, just the two. He took this as a sign that maybe he did just need to get out a bit more. He would have the roll on the bus with a can of beer on the way home. Fuck them and their camera. He walked in and greeted a different sales assistant from before. He worked his way around stacked boxes and looked at the boots again. Then he had a look at their rain gear. He didn't last long there as everything was overly priced and it was a bit too designer for his taste. As he was walking to the rack with the BB guns, something caught his eye and he stopped. He picked it up and played around with it for a few seconds before deciding to buy one, but not this display model, he wanted one in an unopened box. He went to the gun rack and stood looking at the Heckler and Koch Sa80. He took it down and gave it a good going over, releasing and inserting the magazine a few times. The sales assistant took this opportunity to bring his smiling face over to him.

'A fine weapon, just not a big seller. Most of the people that come in here look for the AK-47 or handguns.'

'Really? I bought an AR-15 here a few days ago.'

The assistant goes on to tell him that the AR is the second best seller of the assault rifles, but that the handguns are the favourites with the youngsters.

Only a handful of adults are interested in the rifles for airsoft purposes. As he's talking, Fran notices more boxes getting brought into the room, but not through the front door, but from the back. The assistant from the other day is one of two people carrying them. This does not add up and Fran looks at the new assistant.

'What's with all the boxes?'

'We're closing down. What we're selling lately isn't even covering the rent.'

'Is that so? When are ya's shutting up?'

'Today at five.'

'So… would any of this stuff be on sale prices?'

'Whatever we don't sell today is going back to the suppliers,' he looks at what Fran is holding. 'I can do you a deal on that if you're interested?'

Fran played the game well and quoted the assistant about it not being a big seller. After some cat and mouse between the two, he parted with some money. When he left, he had the Sa80 which he got for 60 euro instead of the 210 price tag from a few days ago. An MP-5, which would be put up for Em's Christmas present, for 70 instead of 225. Ten packs of arrows for 20 euro. And not one, but two Black Widows in their boxes, both for 10 euro. He had to haggle hard for a pair of boots but eventually got them for 55 euro, which was miles away from the 225 price tag that was on them. They even threw in some Polish camo combat trousers and jackets for free. When he left, he was 215 euros lighter, but a very happy man with a smile to match. He struggled from the shop to the main street which was only about twenty yards, and decided to go back into the shop where he bought his roll and picked up a six-pack there, instead of traipsing up to the supermarket beside the library. He had a can on the bus home but didn't get off at his stop in the village. Instead, he stayed on and went the two or so miles to the beach and got off across from the terminus. He had about a forty metre walk across grass until he got to the edge, when it became sand. Where he sat looking out at the sea, was metres away from a chip shop almost directly behind him. The chips he would leave for another day, when he would come up with Rita. He started on his sausage and bacon roll while drinking a freshly opened can, and looked around at the nearly deserted beach, except for two people in the distance with dogs running freely. Some seconds were spent looking to his left, at the coastline of Rush in the distance. Then his attention was drawn to the small island probably a mile or so across the sea in front of him. What had Rita said it was called? Ireland's eye or something? He stares at it and can make out houses or maybe one very large house at the bottom of it. He finishes the roll and it feels like the old days with a Sa80 beside him, even if it is in a box and wrapped in two black bin liners. He has another can before catching the bus as it passes the front of the chip shop. Once home, he tries on the combat bottoms and boots and stares at himself in Rita's full-length mirror. When he hears the front door open, he gets a start and wonders how long he was standing there admiring himself. He recognises the two by two footsteps coming up the stairs, and goes to the door just as Pauli reaches the landing.

'Son… I have a mission for ya.'

Other than Pauli's head moving back a few inches with widened eyes, his hand stops inches from his door handle and he freezes. 'Dad… are ya ok?'

Fran looks down at his camo bottoms and black boots, then back at Pauli. 'This? Don't mind these, I got them for free. Well, not the boots… but they might as well 'ave been,' he shows him the two rifles, gats, the arrows and the other sets of clothing. Pauli puts Em's present, the arrows and the gats in the attic beside the bow and the other arrows. Once back down, he stands facing Fran. 'Who do ya tell and what do ya say?'

'Nobody and nothing.'

'Good lad. Another thing, when you're down in the village, will ya pick me up a few bags of marbles in that euro shop?'

Pauli doesn't even want to ask why. 'Of course I will.'

'Grand. Now help me find that T-shirt I won a few months ago, will ya?'

Within minutes, Pauli finds it and hands it over. Fran looks at it through the see through unopened plastic. Pauli waits, then decides that he needs a bit of a push.

'Dad… you don't even know what it looks like. Open it and try it on.'

Fran's hands start shaking and he looks at Pauli. 'You do it, will ya?'

'No! You spent weeks texting that radio station trying to win that so… go on.'

Fran opens the taped edge and takes it out and holds it up. He stays like that for seconds without moving. Pauli wants to see the front of it and what all the fuss was about, but he decides to stand and wait like a good little Soldier.

Seven seconds later, he coughs. 'Dad… show me, will ya?'

'Wait till I put it on,' Fran turns and goes into the bathroom. 'Won't be long.'

Pauli is sitting on his bed when the bathroom door opens. He bends forward and Fran walks towards him with a walk he has never seen before. He stops on the landing and Pauli goes to his door and looks over the T-shirt, then at Fran.

'So, Sergea… sorry. Sar'nt O'Neill. You look good, dad.'

'Thanks, son. I feel it too,' he walks down the stairs and into the sitting room.

As he sits in his chair, he keeps glancing down at a blue silhouette of a Soldier, with a partial sun behind him on his T-shirt. He switches TV channels to his radio station. Pauli hears it from his room and walks onto the landing and looks down the stairs.

'Waiting for another competition, Dad?'

'I am, son. It's not too loud, is it?'

'Not a bother. Ya never know, you might win another goody bag while listening to the reports as well as the music.'

'That's the plan, Pauli.'

'Roger that, Dad!'

CHAPTER FORTY-SIX

Sophie and Rita are standing behind the counter having a chinwag when John pulls up outside. Both of them look at the clock, then back at him as he gets out.

'There's my fella and he's thirteen minutes early.'

He walks in and looks around. 'How long will I have to wait for a seat?'

The two laugh.

'It's been like this for nearly an hour, not a sinner. Are you hungry, babe?'

'A few chips will do me with a mug o' tae.'

'How about chicken kiev, chips and the mixed salad?'

'What's the mixed salad?'

'A normal salad with coleslaw.'

'Do yous work for coleslaw?! Everything at home is... do you want coleslaw with that? Are ya sure, there's loads of it?'

'It's the same in my house. Fran thinks we make it,' she looks at Sophie. 'Even though we do. But he's testing me now by asking for potato salad.'

'Have yous got potato salad?'

The two look at each other before Rita goes into the kitchen.

'Sit down there, Johnboy, and I'll get that cup of char for you.'

'Don't mind if I do, Sweetocks.'

Sophie brings down his tea and a paper. 'There you go, big fella,' minutes later, she arrives down with his food. 'Here you are, service with a smile,' she turns and he pats her bum as she walks away.

'Hey, I saw that!' Rita says, pointing.

He grins and starts devouring the food. The two cash up while he's eating. When he is finished, they go to the table with a tea each and Sophie gives him a can of orange.

He rubs his hands together. 'Now that was lovely!'

'The potato salad and coleslaw, I made fresh this morning.' Sophie says.

'You make some potato salad and coleslaw, Sweetocks!'

Rita puts her hand over her eyes. 'Oh god,' then looks at them. 'Sweetocks?'

'It's short for sweet buttocks.' Sophie explains.

'That's… new.'

John reaches into a satchel on the chair beside him and takes out an A4 pad. 'Ok, down to business.'

'Ah no! Not ye as well?' He looks from one to the other while placing it on the table.

'What?'

'Fran never goes anywhere without his one, it's always in his hand.'

John and Sophie laugh.

'Ah, ye dirty bastards! I didn't mean...' she laughs as well.

When they finish, John points at the pad.

'This has the prices, times and days of delivery and so on in it. Because Rita, if I told you what I'm going to tell you without it being on paper to take home with you, would you remember any of it by the time you got to your car?'

'Eh... no. It would be gone in one ear and long gone out the other.'

'Exactly! This will only take a couple of minutes to tell you, and if you're happy, then it can go ahead.'

'Fair enough.'

'Right. First, the container. There's a few twenties lying around the yard for a while doing nothing other than taking up space. So there's your container for free.'

She is shocked. 'No way?!'

'Yeah, and they're wired with lights and sockets.'

Now she is stunned.

He then goes on to explain that to send the container down will cost fifty euros. The crane to move it from the truck to the garden is a hundred. Diesel for the JCB, with it having to run all the time, will work out about another fifty euros, but the machine is free. Then there is the two lads doing the work.

'Hopefully they can have a hole done in two days, big enough for it to fit into, but it will cost a hundred each per day.'

She doesn't even think about it. 'Yeah... ok, I'm happy with that.'

'Do you want to talk it over with Fran?'

'No, I don't have to. As I said, I'm happy with that.'

'Ok. Now I'm sending down my two best lads, and they'll do their best to get it done in two days. But if they can't… you'll have a piece of container sticking out of your garden and will probably have to cover it up as is. Or… have a big hole in your garden until the following Saturday, but it'll cost you another two hundred for them to come back and finish it.'

'I'll take the chance.'

'Well, it's six hundred all in for the works. Beats paying six for a burnt one.'

The three have a giggle about that again.'Oh yeah, sorry Rita. Three more things.'

'Go on.'

'Once the hole is dug to the depth, then my lads are gone.'

'Ok, that's fair.'

He looks at Sophie, then the two look at Rita.

'What?'

'Ok… one of the lads is a devout Muslim.'

Rita's eyes widen.

'I know what you're thinking,' he puts his hands up. 'But this lad is sound!'

'Re, I met him and he's a really nice fella. He looks like,' she looks at John. 'That fella out of that mummy film. And a bit like that other fella who does be on that yoke that you watch when I'm asleep. That… apollo thing?'

'He looks like both of them, because that fella out of that mummy film and that apollo thing, is the same bloke!'

'Yeah,' she looks at Rita. 'He looks like him,' then looks back at John. 'That's the same fella?'

'Yeah, that's him! Do you want me to tell Rita the rest?'

She squeezes his leg. 'Go on, Johnboy.'

He looks back at Rita. 'Right, he prays five times a day. So when he's there, he could just stop out of the blue and disappear for about twenty minutes to go pray. The reason I'm telling you this, is that you might think he's dossing and say something to him.'

'That's if you're not working that day.'

'I'm glad you brought that up, Soph. As Fran will need to know as well so he.'

'I get ye,' Rita interrupts. 'That's no problem. I'll let him know.'

'Right then. The last thing I need is your address. I know me and Soph have been down a few times, but I don't know what the estate is called.'

She smiles. 'It would be handy for the container, I suppose.'

'That as well. But I need to give it to one of me lads who works in the Council.'

Her smile vanishes and she turns white. 'The Council can't know anything about this or they'll evict us as insane!'

'We need to make sure that there are no underground pipes or cables where the boys are going to dig, and my lad is bang on. Luckily he has a bit of clout there now, so he can get me a copy of the plans. If it's all clear, grand. But if there's anything under the ground, then the container idea is out the window. Well, at least burying it is.'

'Shite!'

'Look, I get your address, ring him, and in the morning he'll have a gander and tell me by lunchtime. And don't worry, he won't say a word. Actually, he's going to give me a hand when I'm doing mine.'

'Ye really trust him?'

'Yeah, I do. And he owes me one bigtime, but I won't go into that.'

'Ah go on! Tell her so as she knows what you did for him.'

He looks at Sophie, then back at Rita.

'Ok. He was working away, not a bother, and bought a house. A few years later and he got laid off and couldn't pay the mortgage. I heard this through one of me lads who happens to be his mate.'

'You forgot about Megan.'

'Ok. Megan is his daughter, but she was only a few months old when this happened. So him, his wife and kid are under the cloud of losing their home.'

Sophie looks at Rita. 'He never likes saying this part as he gets embarrassed.'

He turns to her. 'Thanks for that, Sophie.'

'You're welcome. Now tell the rest.'

'I told the mate to send him down to me and we had a chat. He told me that he had a feeling he was going to be laid off, but not as quickly, and had applied for a job with the Council. So I gave him a job until or if he got it, which he did, five months later. So he took it.'

'Ah John, that was very good of ye. Ye saved his home.'

'I wouldn't put it quite like that.'

'Well I would!' Sophie says.

'How old is the wee one now?'

'She's five,' Sophie looks at John. 'She's six next month. Just as well we brought this up or I would've forgot.'

'Yeah, just as well,' he looks at Rita. 'So will I go ahead?'

'Well, after telling me that story, I suppose ye know him really well, so... yeah.'

'Ok. Everything is written down here,' he takes two pages from the pad and hands them to her. 'Well, that's it! You decide what weekend you want it done.

I've told the lads, so they're ready whether it be next weekend or next month sometime. And lastly, the container will be down the Monday morning. So if they get it done on Saturday, which is doubtful, but if they do, it means that there'll be a massive big hole in your garden all of Sunday. So let's hope it doesn't rain, and tell everyone in the house to watch where they're going if they go out back.'

'Will do! Right so, when do I pay ye?'

'I'll ring Soph tomorrow and she'll let you know about the plans and if it's a go. Then we'll get the hole dug, drop the container, and any time after that. A bit one week, a bit the other. You don't have to pay it all in one go. I'll sort the lads out with their money.'

'Ah yous are very good!'

He looks at his watch. 'Right so, we make a move?'

Sophie looks at Rita. 'Your address, Re.'

She gets up, goes to the counter, writes her address on a page and comes back and gives it to Sophie, who gives it to John. 'Go! Ye should've been gone ages ago. Shoo!'

They say their goodbyes and she watches them drive away and starts to grin.

'Fran… ye got it, ye bollox!'

CHAPTER FORTY-SEVEN

When she gets home, she goes straight into the kitchen and puts the foil-wrapped booty and her handbag on the worktop counter.

'Are ye alright for a can, Sarge?!'

'Just got one, love, thanks!'

She takes her jacket off and flings it towards the counter and it lands on the food. Fuck it, she thinks. It's not like she doesn't smell like food already, and she is determined to have a nice long bath tonight. She takes a bottle from the fridge, opens it and grabs her handbag as she goes into the sitting room.

Fran glances up as she cuts across the room and she seems to be moving quicker than normal. Her wiggle has also taken on a form of its own. Curious.

After sitting down, and a few swigs from her bottle, she looks over at him.

'Ok, ya either had a shit day or someone was driving really slow in front of ya?' She reaches into her bag, takes out the pages and hands them to him.

He starts to read them with a bored expression. Any second now and Bamm! A mega face change. He reads the

325

second page, then the first again, then glances back at the second before looking at her. 'Is this a joke?'

'No, no joke. But we won't know for sure till tomorrow, when Sophie's John finds out if there are any pipes or stuff under the grass. If there is, then it can't be done. But if there isn't ye pick when ye want it done,' she takes two swigs from her bottle. 'But it has to be a weekend, so ye pick which one.'

His hands drop to his lap and the pages fall to the floor as he leans back into the chair. She waits while staring at him, but nothing. He is looking towards the TV, but not at it. She sits forward slightly while continuing to stare at him, but still nothing, not even a blink.

'Fran!' she yells, starting to get up.

He jumps and looks at her. 'What?'

She sits back down. 'Jesus, Fran… I thought…'

'Thought what?'

She takes a few deep breaths. 'Nothing! I need a smoke after that.'

She goes out to the back garden after picking up another bottle on the way. After a few minutes, he comes out with his can and the pages and sits beside her.

'I thought ye would be happy.'

'I am happy… but I think I'm in shock.'

She looks at him through her sunglasses. 'So you're really happy?'

'Re… I think I'm gonna break into another dance.'

'Ah… so that's what ye call it?'

He chuckles. 'You and your one liners,' he looks around the garden for a few seconds, then back at her. 'Thanks, Re. I know that ya must think I'm a weirdo.'

'Think?! I know you're a weirdo… but ye are my weirdo.'

The two laugh. They sit there for a few minutes drinking and for some reason, both looking around the garden. Fran wants to see a big rectangular pit now. But Rita is thinking about her poor garden and how long it took her to get it like this. When Fran does decide, the feckin' thing might look like no man's land.

'Jasus, what's goin' on?! Dad, you'll melt. Quick, get in outta the sun.'

'Pauli, you're back.' Rita says, stating the obvious.

'What's wrong with it?'

'Badumchish!' Fran adds, playing invisible drums.

'Thank you, folks, I'm here all day,' he says, bowing a few times.

'So, did ye go for lunch again?'

'We had lunch, but it was a low key affair with the ever favourite chicken baguette!' he does jazz hands. 'Mister Colon kept reminding us of the time.'

'Colon?!' asks a voice from above.

He looks up. 'Em, ya flower pot!'

'Brother, and I can hang out me window and earwig if I want.'

Rita squints upwards. 'So, that's what ye do be up to?'

'That and takin' in the view. I have to keep an eye out for the odd fast jet going past, ya know yourself,' she holds up a set of binoculars and checks the sky.

'Well, Em, your view is going to be seriously messed up in a few weeks, because your Da,' she whispers the next part for fear of the neighbours hearing. 'Might be gettin' his container.'

The binoculars get lowered and Em looks down. 'No?' she whispers back.

Rita goes back to talking normally. 'Yeah. We'll know for sure tomorrow and if it's good...,' she thinks and shakes her head. 'Ok... good news, then he just has to decide the weekend.'

Fran gives Pauli the pages and he reads both of them. 'Sweet!' he looks up at the sky and spreads his arms. 'Roll on Super Volcano, Solar Flare and... whatever else Matt said because I forget. We laugh in your faces. Ha! Ha! Ha! And as for you Aliens... yous can go and kiss my.'

'Pauli!' Rita shouts. He looks at her, drops his arms and hands the pages back to Fran.

'Are ye ok, son?'

'Can I have one of them, Mam?'

She points at the kitchen. 'I think ye feckin' need one, and quick!'

He turns to find Emma standing beside him with Emmet and jumps. He looks up at her window, then back at her. 'How did ya do that?'

'I was in a hurry, now outta me way. Da, let's see.'

A few hours later and everyone is fed. Tonight's dinner was just a quick slap together job which resulted in chilli, pasta and breadsticks. The last of which Rita had liberated

328

from the cafe and it went down a treat. Em disappeared after the soaps with the menace to try get him asleep. While eating her dinner, Rita was watching Emmet and thought that he was going on weird. Then corrected herself and changed weird to weirder. Maybe another tooth is on its way?

Anyway, she asked Fran about the container and it was decided that it would be the following weekend if all went well tomorrow. If it was a go, he was worried that it didn't give much notice to the lads doing the work. But she explained, for the fourth time, that they were sort of on standby, so didn't mind. She also asked him for a look at his pad and he willingly handed it over. She went through it, reading what he had written and checking his diagrams. He really had drawn a scaled model of the garden, with centimetres representing metres, and what she saw didn't half look that bad. If all went to plan, nobody would even notice that it was there, eventually. Once the grass had regrown and blended back into the rest of the garden, it would look normal again.

She gives it back to him.

'Franner, ye missed your callin'. Well, I mean if ye hadn't been a soldier. Ye could've been one of those... ye know, the gardener fellas, that design stuff and turn wrecks of gardens into something nice?'

'Landscape artist?'

'That's it! Ye could've been one of them.'

'Thanks, love,' he says, looking at her with a smile while thinking of doing some landscaping of his own with her in bed in the morning.

CHAPTER FORTY-EIGHT

It is Monday afternoon and there are minutes left before second class finishes. That is the part Matt and Pauli are looking forward to and whatever happens after that. It's not long before they are heading to Carlingford and Pauli is riding shotgun once again. When they get there, they drive down the road with the sea on the right and the Indian and chip shop on the left and continue into the town.

It is a lovely sunny day again and second time in, the place has not lost any of its appeal on the boys. They go through the town and leave on a road heading north. After a little over two miles, Lucy turns left and about twenty feet from the turn, they pass a sign which reads, Private Road. A little further up, the road bends to the right and something a couple of hundred metres ahead has grabbed the boys' attention. Pauli looks behind to find Matt staring with his mouth open, then turns back around. 'Are they gates?' he asks, instantly chastising himself mentally for asking the obvious.

'A gate.' Lucy replies.

Seconds later, they come to a stop and she presses one of two buttons on a thin grey box clipped to her visor, which up until now hadn't been noticed. The gate starts sliding to the left. When there is enough room, the car takes off through it and stops outside the third house on the left.

'Holy shit!' Matt says.

'O'Neill, will you let Becka out your side?'

'Yeah… yeah, of course,' he says, fumbling at his seatbelt release before getting out. Becka hops out, walks to the gate and presses an intercom. Seconds pass before the gates start to open and she waves at the pillar opposite her.

'What's she doin'?' Matt asks.

'Saying hello.' Lucy replies.

She slips through the gap while the gates are opening, so she has a head start on them. By the time Lucy drives in, Becka has already gone in the front door.

'Ok, chaps,' Lucy releases her seatbelt. 'We'll be back in a minute,' she gets out and seconds later, disappears through the front door as well.

'Oh yeah, I agree.'

'Agree with what, P?'

'Holy shit!'

It is minutes before the girls emerge from the front door with an older woman, who is built like an East German athlete. Her hair colour is a mixture of brown and grey and it is in a bun. She is wearing a khaki shirt with the sleeves rolled up above her elbows, and a white apron over it. A brown skirt is just visible at the bottom, and on her feet are what look like black army boots.

The three walk towards the car and Becka is carrying a shopping bag. Pauli is watching as they get nearer and only the girls are smiling. Matt tries to hide behind one of the headrests. Before they get to the car, Pauli notices Lucy move her head slightly, then she does it again. He takes this to mean get out of the car, so he does. Matt stays put behind the headrest. The two girls stop each side of the woman about four feet from the car.

'O'Neill?' she asks, looking down at him with her right eyebrow slightly arched.

'Yes, Ma'am,' he replies, shocked at the sound of his voice. He expected it to come out all crackily, but instead it had a strength to it and he is pleased.

She nods her head and he nods back. Then she looks at the car and her head moves from one side to the other, trying to find the person she knows is inside.

'Volfe!' she barks.

Matt's head slowly appears from behind Lucy's headrest and he gets out smiling. Pauli looks at Lucy and she is standing there as cheeky as you like. Hip to one side, arms folded, biting her lip and nodding her head slowly while looking up at the sky. He looks at Becka and she is looking behind her at the house, but her shoulders are shaking up and down and he twigs it. He has got to do something fast or Matt is not going to come out of this looking good in any shape or form.

He who dares wins… and so on.

'That accent'

The woman looks at him and Becka and Lucy look at each other.

'South African?' he finishes.

She smiles broadly. 'Ya! You know Afrikaans?'

'No, but Volfe… Wolfe knew. He said it to me many a time, that Becka has a beautiful South African type lilt to her voice.'

She is beaming now and puts an arm around each of the girls' shoulders and squeezes them tightly. 'Yous did good. I like these boys.'

Becka starts coughing. 'Mam, you're hurting my neck!'

She releases her grip on the two. 'I am sorry, precious,' she looks to her left. 'Are you ok, Lucy?'

She tweaks her neck. 'Oh... I'm fine' she replies, rubbing the side of it.

'I almost forgot the salad!' she turns and jogs into the house.

'P... thanks man. Here, what the hell's a lilt?'

'I think it's a musical thing, and thank me when I stop shaking.'

Almost immediately, the woman runs back out the door with a plastic bag. 'Becka, you take this as well. Lucy is driving.'

'Well, it's been a pleasure meeting you, Mrs MacDonald.' Matt says, with new found confidence.

She looks from him to Pauli with a smile.

'Greta.'

Lucy says something to Greta, in what the boys assume to be Afrikaans, and she replies in the same tongue. She hugs her and Becka and both go to the car. Matt waves and gets in, but Pauli nods and grins slightly which she returns. He gets in the back with Matt and when the girls are in, they wave and leave the garden, turning left. Seconds later, the car stops at another gate and it starts to open after Lucy touches her visor device again. She pulls in and parks.

'Ok, we're here!'

The four get out and Matt and Pauli look at what may as well be the same house they left seconds before. Even the plants in the garden look identical.

'Ok, so… yous live what… ten seconds from each other?' Pauli asks.

'Me, neighbour, Becka's,' Lucy answers, as she takes a bag from her. 'Mama done good,' she says, and the two walk to the front door.

'You know my mama, Lu? Food for a dozen when two will do.'

The boys look at each other.

'I think we're on a different planet.' Matt says, and looks around the garden.

Pauli looks at the house. 'I couldn't have said it better myself.'

They stay there for almost a minute before Lucy appears at the opened door.

'Yous know that yous are supposed to follow us in?'

Pauli walks towards the house. 'Yeah… just acclimatising.'

'With ya there, bro.' Matt whispers.

This is not what the two had expected. And try as they might, they could not hide it from the girls. They had been meaning to stop along the way and pick up some drink and munchies, considering the girls were doing the food. But they had forgot in all the excitement. They were brought out to the back garden, and after being asked what their preference in alcohol was, were handed a six pack each, just like that. But whatever the garden was supposed to do to make them feel more at ease, it didn't. It just seemed to make them worse. Both looked like they had been plucked from the earth and placed in the middle of Afghanistan. They just didn't want to be there.

'What the hell is going on?'

'I don't know.' Becka replies, in a worried voice. Something rare for her.

There is about twenty feet between the couples.

'P… I've seen football pitches that are smaller than this garden.'

Pauli is looking around trying to think of a different comparison to make. Matt's is good, but as he is thinking, he feels a pain in the back of his neck.

'Oow!' he yells, looking around quickly, thinking it's a bee or a wasp sting.

Matt jumps and looks at him, then finds Lucy standing there.

'What the hell is going on with yous two?!' she asks, with a side plate of venom in her voice while fixing her stare on Pauli, who is rubbing his neck.

For some reason, although he doesn't know why, Matt finds this funny and is trying not to laugh.

'What was that?!' Pauli asks, looking around for some sort of flying insect.

She stares up at him. Again, that cheeky stance. Hip to the side, hands on hips, but now her bottom lip is in on the act as well. He has seen Em do that plenty of times and every time she has done it, she was really annoyed. He puts it down to one of those girl-freaked-out things.

She slowly raises her hand and extends her index finger towards him. 'That was my finger!'

On hearing this, Matt sniggers and Becka looks at him. One down, she thinks, and starts signing with her left hand which is out of Pauli's view thanks to Lucy. He slowly moves sidewards away from Pauli, who is still looking at Lucy and her finger. Pauli saw Becka look at Matt after his snigger and he nearly did the same himself, but he kept his stare on Lucy, right into those eyes. While doing this, his peripheral vision noticed Matt seeming to slide away from him, but he kept staring at her. He has just realised that they haven't blinked yet.

Oh no! I hate having sore eyes.

Her finger is still pointing at him and he wonders how long she can hold it there before her arm starts to shake, and then it's… goodbye finger, nice knowing you, but you lost, adios! But suddenly he sees things differently. Especially the part when Matt was beside him one minute, and now he is over at the barbecue with Becka and they are taking food out of bags.

Nice one for having me back, Matt, he thinks as he looks at Lucy and her finger. This is one stubborn girl.

He puts his hands up. 'Are ya gonna put that away before it goes off?'

She holds it for a few more seconds before lowering her arm. He knows what is coming next. That cheeky little grin any second now. But it doesn't. Instead, her bottom lip starts to shake and then turns downwards. He looks back at her eyes, and already a tear is halfway down her cheek and moving fast. Then one drops from her other eye. He reaches out with his palm facing upwards and she places her hand down on it and grasps it. He slowly pulls her to him and gives her the best hug he has ever given anybody. Hopefully, the best hug of her life. Damn it! I made her cry. Hey! She poked me in the neck first and from behind. Ok,

I'm never going to annoy her again… but if I do, I won't turn my back on her.

She moves back and looks up at him, her eyes and cheeks still wet.

'I'm sorry, Lucy.'

'Kiss me you fool,' she whispers.

They kiss.

'You haven't got a clue! You can't cook!'

'I never said I could, I just said I would.'

Pauli and Lucy look at them. 'What's wrong?' she asks.

'Heston here, said he'd cook the sausages first. So he puts them on the rack and starts turning them every few seconds. Only problem is the thing's not even lit!'

Lucy looks at Pauli. 'Are we ok?'

'More ok than you'd ever believe.'

She kisses him. 'What say we put some life into this wake?'

'Fucking A, Ma'am!'

'I'll see you later about that language, Soldier,' she salutes, about turns and zeros in on the barbecue. 'Becka… DJ or cook?'

'I'll do fifteen on the grill, then be MC.'

'10-4!' Lucy says, walking inside.

Matt comes over to Pauli. 'Sorry, dude, had to skedaddle. Got the evil eye and all that from the missus,' he takes a swig from his bottle.

'The only evil eye you got is in your jocks, pal!'

Dance music breaks the silence just before Lucy walks back out.

Ha! I knew there was a grin around here somewhere, Pauli thinks, as he watches her saunter over to Becka after giving him a wink.

The girls know their stuff. They switched from cook to "MC" as Becka had put it, about every fifteen minutes. How had they worked that out? Pauli wondered. They also banned Matt from the Barbecue and Pauli was very happy about that. Food poisoning from Matt's hands again? No thank you! It had taken three days for him to recover, plus the two days before he could walk normal again.

When the food was done, it was put in a drawer under the grill to keep it insect free. This was all new to the boys as was this barbecue. The thing was about the same size as their single beds. Their version of having a barbecue, was to go to the supermarket and buy two small rectangular foil containers with charcoal in them. They would light one and put the food on it and about ten minutes later, it would die. They would light the second one and try and finish the food before that died as well. But it would always end up going into the oven or under the grill, so barbecues were a load of bollox. At least they were until today.

The lads were matching each other, five for five. Just one bottle left each, but Matt was carrying his around in a lopsided six-pack container. Pauli was tempted to say something just in case it fell out. But Matt start yawning and said that he needed to get out of the sun for a while and maybe have a cup of tea. This was good. He normally knew his limit and if he got drunk too fast, would then try and sober up a bit. With him being pale skinned and ginger, getting too much sun was another thing he had to watch out for. Between the almost instant sunburn and then his skin peeling like a snakes.

When Becka and him go inside, Lucy asks Pauli if he fancies a walk.

He exhales. 'I don't know. I didn't bring my hiking boots or a compass.'

'Ha ha! You're real funny!' she gets him another six pack and a four pack for her, and they walk down the garden and stop near enough midway. 'Sit your ass on the grass, O'Neill.'

They sit crosslegged for about half a minute.'You charmer.'

He looks at her. 'Me? I couldn't charm if I was charmed into it.'

She smiles. 'You've got a way with words, I'll give you that,' she sips from her bottle. 'But the way you won over Becka's mam today, and believe me, what I saw is a first. She never melts like that.'

'Ppphhfft! That was a set up!'

'No it was not!' she lies, unconvincingly.

'Look in the mirror, that face ain't working. I saw the two of yous when she was giving it all the Gestapo.'

She laughs.

'And I was just waiting for her to take out a monocle, stick it in her eye, then a Luger and put a bullet between mine!'

She lies back on the grass and is still laughing. He laughs as well but takes this opportunity to check out her bum again. Then that voice starts.

Oh baby… now that's a sight there for yee, lad. Yee will get your hands on…

Shut up and mind your own business! he says, mentally.

When she laughs herself down to a giggle, she sits back up, takes a few breaths and smiles. 'I told you, you are a funny guy.'

They sit there and he looks around again. He is starting to really like it here.

'So, what's with everyone speaking Afrikaans?'

She finishes off her bottle and opens another. 'Ok. Me and Becka moved here within months of each other. Our birthdays are seventeen days apart, different months though, and we live three houses from each other.'

'With ya so far.'

'She was born in South Africa. Then one day her dad decided that it was too weird and that it was time to live somewhere else.'

'So where does the MacDonald come into it?'

'Her dad's a Scot.'

'Oh right,' he takes a sip from his bottle. 'Her mam is a big woman.'

'Six foot three and a half. Her dad's about your height.'

He begins to laugh but stops.

'What?' she asks, turning her head slightly to the side. 'I'm just thinking… I'd say they look noticeable when they go out somewhere.'

She giggles. 'Oh, they do! They stand out like two peas on a plate of mash.'

Both giggle.

'Well, that's it! Be back in a minute,' she gets up and runs away in the direction of a hedge surrounding the garden.

'Oh no, we should've stayed at the house. Please don't go in a field.'

At the hedge, she bends down and struggles to pick up what looks like... he thinks he's seeing things, but then realises that he's not. She is walking back towards him with a very large umbrella and she is stumbling from side to side. But fair play to her, she hasn't fell over yet. He jumps up and jogs over to her.

'Ya never know what you'll find in a hedge these days.'

She drops it with another of her giggles and she is out of breath.

'What's this for?' he asks, checking the sky for clouds after picking it up.

'Shade. It gets very hot. Where we're sitting is where me and Becka sunbathe.'

He looks at her. 'Ya mean... knickers and bras?'

'No. The full length version from the beginning of the last century, and mine are black and white. Yeah! Knickers and bras!' she starts walking and he follows. Then she decides to have a bit of fun. 'We use some amount of sun cream between us. I have to rub it on her back and she does mine, every twenty minutes or so.'

He slows to a stop and stares at her.

'We just lie there, straps open, bare backed. You know yourself, tan lines and all that,' she starts walking. 'Ok, let's go,' he checks her ass out and she looks over her

341

shoulder and winks. 'Come on, big boy… and don't forget your pole.'

They get back to the spot and he opens the umbrella. 'Ok, where do ya want it?'

'Put it between us and the sun so as we don't get cooked.'

When it's up, they sit under it and she moves closer to him and takes a sip from her bottle. Minutes pass in silence. She turns to face him and he looks at her.

'You haven't asked.'

'I don't want to know. It's none of my business.'

She looks at him sharply.

'That came out wrong. I mean… it's none of my business.'

She kicks off her flip flops and it is another of those quiet, but this time, not awkward moments. He takes in the scenery and wonders what all the fuss was about at the beginning. The bottles of beer have probably helped accelerate the acclimatising part. He looks at her but she is already looking at him.

'Sorry for poking you in the neck.'

'Ah, you're grand. It doesn't hurt anymore… not that much anyway.'

She gets up on her knees. 'Let me have a look.'

'I'm joking.'

'Turn and let me see. Now please.'

He turns and she moves closer. 'Oh!'

'Oh what?'

Her head comes into view. 'I marked you. I'm really sorry.'

Oh oh! Her eyes look like they are about to start again.

'You're ok, really! I deserved it, and I haven't had a poke in the neck in a while.'

Her face disappears and seconds later he feels her lips on the back of his neck. After a few kisses, her face comes back into view again. She looks at him for a moment before kissing him. When she moves away, he smiles.

'That was well worth a poke in the neck.'

She smiles. 'Can we go and get some food? I feel a bit weak.'

He gets up and holds out his hand. She takes it and they continue holding hands until they get back to the house. On the patio, she realises that they left the drink back at the tanning spot. 'What are you having?'

He looks at the end of his bottle. 'Same.'

'Ok, back in a mo,' she walks inside and comes back with another six-pack.

'Where's yours?'

'I'm done! A few bottles and I'm talking double Dutch,' she goes to the barbecue. 'I need ribs. Becka's mam… Greta, had these marinating for two days, Afrikaans style, so this is authentic fare. Oh doodlecracker! I forgot the salad,' she turns to go but stops. 'Would you mind coming inside while I have my food? It's too hot out here.'

'No problem! You tell me what ya want and I'll bring it in.'

'Thanks. Eh… ribs, chicken and a sausage,' she says, before walking inside.

'And a sausage,' he repeats, quietly.

When he walks inside, the room is in darkness, thanks to the drawn curtains.

It takes seconds for his eyes to become accustomed. He sees Matt and Becka on a huge L shaped sofa to his right. A coffee table separates it from an identical one on his left, and Lucy is lying at the far end of it. As he goes between the sofa and the table, he notices that Laurel and Hardy are on a massive flat screen TV on a brick base. He doesn't remember seeing the TV when they were led through the room to the back garden. Probably still in shock. He looks at Matt.

'Thanks for telling me, pal.'

'Ya went that far away that I couldn't get a signal.'

Pauli grins.

'They've got everyone that was ever made in a box set, and Becka said that we can watch them anytime we want.'

'Sweet!' he turns to Lucy and stares at her for a few seconds before realising that she is asleep. He looks around at them. 'She was only awake a second ago.'

'Pauli... O'Neill,' Becka corrects herself. 'She is knackered. Now, I'm going to tell you something and you can't tell her, I mean it.'

He stands there with two bottles in one hand and a plate of food in the other. 'Ok, I won't. But please help this not to be bad.'

'It's not.' Matt says.

He feels nervous and confused. He puts the bottles and the plate on the table and sits on the same sofa as Lucy but at the far end.

'Ok. Remember the day we came up here and ya licked her foot?'

'I didn't lick it, I just blew th…'

'I know,' Becka cuts in. 'She told me. You blew the sand from between her toes.'

Matt starts laughing and they look at him. 'Ok, I'll stay quiet.'

'Long story short. For some reason since we started term, yous two have been watching my two and so on,' she looks from him to Matt and back. 'Well?!' she says, with a tone in her voice that makes him feel uncomfortable. 'You didn't even notice her from day thirty, never mind day one!' she looks at Matt. 'This guy only saw my boobs and I know it.'

'Guilty! But I told ya that already.'

She looks at Pauli and he nods his head. 'It's true.'

'So… what changed?'

He shakes his head. 'I don't know.'

'Yous checking me out and now you're with Lucy… what's changed?' she asks again, with a menacing tone in her voice.

He tries to think, but between Becka and her mam in the same day, maybe he's not that strong. He can't find anything to say.

'I'll tell you what changed. SHE went after you! You done nothing, not a thing. You never even gave her a glance,' she says something in what he thinks is Afrikaans and it doesn't sound that complimentary. 'She couldn't sleep properly for weeks before we asked yous to lunch, and all she does is talk about you, and I mean all of the time,' she looks at Matt, who looks at Pauli.

345

'That girl is in love, P.'

Pauli looks to his left at Lucy lying there asleep, and at that hair that kept him from noticing her for so long. It is partly covering her face again, but now he knows what it's hiding and he has an irresistible urge to touch her.

'This is weeks and weeks of thinking about asking you to have lunch, and then worrying in case you said no. Then to get you up here today? Ok, a few bottles down her throat and she's gone. But you're here, and that's the only reason she's asleep right now, which sounds weird. Because if you weren't, she'd be in a bad state, believe me,' she looks across at her, then back at him. 'Lucy is no drinker. She's a real… curl up on the sofa with a quilt, bickies, crisps and pop while watching the telly.'

'Pop?'

She looks at Matt. 'The border's up the road and that's where we shop. Pop or soda is minerals.'

'What's her favourite?' Pauli asks.

'Orange,' she replies, and smiles at Lucy's requirements for a good night in.

She groans and Becka gets up. As she is walking to her, Lucy bends her leg up. Pauli looks at Matt but he is already looking at him.

'I didn't look, P, I looked away. You'd do the same.'

'Becka's not in my eye view anymore, are we clear, Matt?'

'We're clear. Thou shalt not covet.'

All of this is said in whispers.

'Lu… Lu, can you hear me?'

'Mmm.'

'Lu, are you alright?'

'I–I'm a bit cold.'

Becka takes a throw that is draped over the back of the sofa, covers her with it and tucks it under her. 'Ok, honey, you're covered.'

'Is Pauli still here?' she asks, yawning, with eyes still closed.

'Yeah, he's here.'

'Is he staying?'

Becka looks at him and he nods, 'Yes, hun, he's staying.'

'You're staying as well…,' she yawns. 'With Matt?'

'Yeah, babe, we're all staying.'

'Good! I'm knackered, Beck. I'll see you…,' she yawns. 'Again… awhile.'

Becka waits a few seconds, turns and walks to the sofa and sits. 'She's bushed,' she looks at Pauli. 'See what I mean? She is mad about you.'

'Yeah man… the caks off ya!'

Becka looks at Matt. 'Don't talk like that. It's muck!'

'Ok, sorry. Never again.'

'Pauli, don't mess her up.'

'I won't,' he looks at her hair sticking out of the cover and smiles. 'I love her.'

Becka and Matt look at each other in shock.

CHAPTER FORTY-NINE

Lucy wakes up the next morning confused. It takes a few seconds before she recognises her surroundings, her room. 'How did I get here from that field?'

She gets up and goes into Becka's room to find her asleep in bed with Matt. Suddenly, she remembers that she was in the field with Pauli.

Oh no, what happened?

As she tiptoes over to the bed, she notices that she has a different sock on each foot. The least of her worries right now. 'Beck... Becka,' she whispers.

Becka opens one eye. 'Lucy–is that you?'

'Ssh! I'm down here,' she says, kneeling on the floor.

Becka looks down and finds her. After a lot of blinking and shaking her head, Lucy starts to come into focus. The second eye is staying open now as well.

'Lu, are you ok?'

'Yeah, I'm fine. Where's Pauli?'

'When we came up he was asleep on the sofa.'

'Who put me to bed?'

'I did. Who else?'

'Nothing,' she is happy. 'So he's downstairs?'

'As far as I know he is,' she replies, blinking.

'Hold on! I said I wanted strawberry, not vanilla, Pal!' Matt says, in his sleep.

The two try to laugh quietly and Lucy kisses Becka on the cheek. 'Later, honey,' she whispers, and tiptoes back to the door. She goes downstairs and checks both sofas but only finds a throw and a quilt on one. She tries, but still can't remember anything since the field. Suddenly, a face looks in the window, smiles and holds up a chicken drumstick. Lucy's frown has turned upside down.

She slides open the door. 'Good morning, handsome!' she says, sitting down, leaving a seat between them.

'Good morning, beautiful!'

She is reaching for a drumstick but on hearing this, her hand stops midflight and she looks at him. She continues and picks one, holds it up and he tips his half-eaten one against it.

'Skol!'

She grins. 'Ok then – skol!'

He watches her take a bite. 'Nice socks.'

She looks down at her feet on the seat. 'Yeah, it must be some new fashion that Becka invented,' she looks at him. 'She did put them on me?'

'She done everything, don't worry. She picked ya up off the settee and carried ya upstairs as if she was carrying a few towels. Either you're really light, or she's quite strong.'

'A bit of both – but more she is quite strong,' she takes another bite. 'So, how was your sleep in a strange house?'

'Pretty good. Yeah, no complaints.'

'Do you want a yogurt drink or something?'

'A yogurt drink, miss random?'

She giggles. 'Ok, it was a bit. But do you? I'm having one and I don't want to be a meanie and come out with just mine. So, do you want one?'

'Now I know you're not a meanie. What flavours have ya got?'

'What's your favourite?'

'Oh I see, it's like that. Ya have them all?'

'Every single one, even peach,' she says, as she stands.

'A peach yogurt drink?!'

'They're some anniversary special edition or something, they're actually lovely.'

'I'll take your word for it, but I'll go for a raspberry one, please.'

'No way! That's my favourite, really! Ask Becka if you don't believe me.'

At that little plead to be believed, that her favourite was the same as what he picked, he stares at her. Looking first at her odd socks, then pyjama bottoms, flowers of course, what else? Then up to her T-shirt, pausing ever so slightly at a certain part before looking at her face. Her hair looks like it just came out of a tumble dryer. If she looks like this every morning after just getting out of bed, he would so like to be there to see it on a regular basis.

'What are you thinking about?'

'Eh... the raspberry drink.'

She smirks. 'Yeah, I bet!' she turns and enters the house. When she comes back, she gives him one and sits and starts shaking hers and he watches her. 'Are you not going to give yours a good shake?'

Halfway through that sentence she tried to abandon it, but her mouth overruled her brain and just kept talking. She assumes that her face has changed a reddish colour but is determined to keep eye contact with him. He starts to shake his very gently while looking at her, but as this isn't like yesterday's stand-off, he blinks a few times with relief. She breaks the seal, flips off the lid and takes a sup. When she lowers her bottle, he taps his chin twice with his index finger.

'What's wrong?'

'You've got something…'

She sticks her tongue over her bottom lip and searches for the drip and gets it.

'Gone?'

'No, a little more,' he lies, and watches her tongue move around in search of the nonexistent drip of yogurt drink.

'Did I get it?'

'Oh yeah… it's gone.'

He knows it was a cheap shot but he could not resist, and it was so worth it.

'So, do you fancy a shower?'

He tilts his head while looking at her.

'I… I mean, I'm having a shower. After me you can have one… if you want to, that is. I'm not saying that you smell or anything!' she grimaces while covering one eye with her hand and looking at him with the other.

'Well, seein' as though ya put it like that, I have to say that's mighty white of ya,' he looks at the sky, then back at her. 'Yeah, a shower sounds good.'

'Settled then!' she rests her chin in her right hand and looks at the sky as well. 'You know what? I'm glad we're not in today.'

'Me, too.'

'Do you want to come up and you can watch telly while I have mine?'

'Do ya have the sports news?' he asks, hopefully.

'I have the sports channels!' she says, standing up and holds out her hand. 'Come on, sailor.'

He takes it and stands. 'Aye, aye!'

CHAPTER FIFTY

Her room looks like it was taken straight from a film. Her bed is a huge wooden four-poster with purple curtains tied back at each post. He is pretty sure that he saw this in a vampire film somewhere, and it is bigger than his room, of that he is certain. Contrary to what he was expecting, there is not a bit of pink in sight.

'Ok, I'm going in to scrub the grime off me so... see you in a while,' she walks towards the en-suite.

'Lucy, where's the telly?'

'Oh, I'm simple!' she turns and walks to a locker at the top of the bed and picks up a remote control. After pressing a button, she hands it to him and walks back towards the en-suite again. It is then that he notices something rising from the end of the bed.

'Holy shit!'

'If you take your runners off, you can lie on the bed. Enjoy!' she smiles, turns and closes the door.

He takes his runners off and does just that, then closes his eyes as he exhales. His bed compared to this? Is a complete joke and a total embarrassment. He sits up and checks for the sports channels and finds them. Then the movie channels and she has them, too. He switches back to the sports channels and goes through each one again. After all that, he puts the sports news back on and leaves it. It is then that he hears her singing. Would you like to swing on a star? Carry moonbeams home in a jar? And be better off than you are? Or would you rather be a fish? He smiles and leaves the telly muted as he lies back onto the pillows and listens to her. His eyes close and he thinks that it doesn't get much better than this. When that song is over, Bluemoon, comes from the bathroom and he grins.

He actually lied to her about how he had slept. When he saw Becka carry her to bed, he so wanted to be the one to do it. But as he has not been in her life a wet day, Becka is her number one, and boy is she a number one. After the lecture she had given him, and looking after Lucy from the sofa to bed, he realised how close they are and how strong their friendship is.

He said he loved her. Was that only because of what Becka told him? Or is it how he really feels? I do love her, he thought, as he lay on the sofa, smiling. That is the reason why he did not sleep, or could not. She was on his mind. He did doze a few times, but nothing that could be described as a sleep.

Fruit? What kind? Let me think. Ok…, I can smell lemon, and that is definitely strawberry. Hmm… mango or melon? What's the difference? I'm no fruit expert. Ok, I'll say both, just to be on the safe side. Is that a banana?

'Pomegranate,' she whispers.

He quickly sits up and looks around the room, eyes wide and looking scared.

'Pauli… Pauli?' she puts her hand on his cheek and feels him shaking. 'Pauli, look at me. You're in my room, remember? The barbecue?'

He continues to shake but it eases off after nearly half a minute. 'Lucy?'

She smiles. 'Hello... and welcome back.'

Without thinking, he hugs her. 'I didn't know where I was.'

'You were talking in your sleep.'

He lets go and moves back, so she holds his hand without him noticing.

'I smelt fruit.'

'That's my bodywash, and you nailed it except for the pomegranate. That's when you woke up like you were in a warzone.'

'I've done that ever since I was a kid and it always freaked my dad out.'

She squeezes his hand. 'One question.'

'Go for it.'

'Where did you get banana from?'

He is in the shower minutes later and is wide awake now. He checks the shower gels, or rather, bodywashes. After all, he is in a girl's bathroom. But after going through them, he cannot find the one she used. Cool! He does not want the two of them smelling like fruit baskets. So he decides on, Outer Mongolian Fusion. Whatever that is?

While going through the motions, he stops and cocks his ear slightly and smiles. She has put the Indian music channel on and raised the volume.

Ah well, grab your balls and throw them in the air! He thinks for a moment. Did Matt actually say that?

He does a little twisting of the bulb while patting the dog as he listens to the music, and emerges from the bathroom minutes later.

'Did you like that?' she asks, lying on her belly with a big grin.

'I did! It got me moving.'

'I've seen your moves, boy! And me and Becka want yous to teach us some.' He stops at the end of the bed and forces a smile.

Ah, here we go! That uncomfortable look again. She pats the bed. 'You can sit down, you know.'

He keeps smiling but doesn't move, so she pats it again. 'Come on… I won't bite,' he sits on the edge of the bed. 'You don't look relaxed, O'Neill.'

'Oh, I am!' he says, while nodding.

Ok Ok. Change of subject, she thinks, as this is not working. 'What do you think about another barbecue? And this time I'll stay awake!' she says, with her right hand out of sight but her fingers crossed.

'I'd like that.'

'So will you stay over again? Or if you want, I can drop yous.'

'Stay… if you don't mind.'

She sits up and kneels facing him while smiling. 'You have just made my day.' Seconds pass as they look at each other and she is getting frustrated. What the hell do I have to do, write it down for him?

He moves closer and they kiss.

CHAPTER FIFTY-ONE

Becka and Matt wake up starving and then they remember the food. She is looking forward to some of her mam's two day marinaded Afrikaans style ribs.

When they get downstairs, there is nobody to be seen. Matt follows her out to the patio. Other than two yogurt drinks, one of which is open, and some eaten drumsticks, nothing again. The trail is cold. She looks down the garden but even the umbrella is not there. She knows this is stupid but she just wants to see Lucy face to face. She barely remembers talking to her earlier.

'Food!' Matt says, after opening a drawer on the barbecue. He grabs drumsticks, sausages and a rack of ribs and stands facing her with them in his hands.

She stares at him. 'And how are you going to eat them?'

He starts to put them back.

'Stop! I'll get you a plate,' she slides open a door on the barbecue, takes one out and holds it under his hands. He pours the food onto it and she hands it to him. 'Do you eat like this in your home?'

'Eat like what?'

'Grab as much food as you can when you see it?'

'No, that was just a once off. I'm really hungry.'

'There's beer in the fridge,' she says, and walks back inside.

She goes up to Lucy's room and stops outside her door. If she is asleep, she does not want to wake her up so she decides not to knock. 'Lucy?' she whispers. Nothing.

'Lucy?' she repeats, a bit louder but still no response. She gently opens the door, only to see Lucy, naked as the day she was born, in midgallop astride a naked Pauli. She closes it and as she stands there, a smile slowly starts to appear.

'Go my pretty… go!' she whispers, and walks away.

She grabs a beer on her way through the kitchen and joins Matt on the patio. His face is destroyed with the marinade and his cheeks are huge while he is trying to chew. A sound comes from his mouth. She stares at him, then takes a good gulp.

'I hope I wasn't supposed to understand that.'

He keeps chewing and tries again. 'I said,' he swallows. 'Did ya find them?'

'Yes, I did.'

He looks at the open patio door. 'Where are they then?'

'They're… talking. Getting to know each other a little better.'

'Cool,' he takes a bite from a drumstick. 'I'm sure it won't be long now before they progress a bit further, know what I mean?'

'Oh, I know what you mean. Sex?'

He looks at the remains of the food on his plate and stands up. 'Yeah, let's go.'

She laughs.

'I meant the next step for them is sex. That's what you meant, wasn't it?'

'Oh… yeah! That's exactly what I meant,' he sits back down, picks up a sausage and takes a bite.

'I'd say they are much closer than we think.'

'Ya reckon?'

'Oh, I reckon good,' she takes a gulp after watching him throw the other half of the sausage into his mouth.

'Well, I think I'll leave it there for now. Ya didn't have your rib.'

'I think you ate enough for the two of us.'

He belches loudly. 'Sorry.'

'Them… I don't mind. It's the other ones I have a problem with.'

'Yeah. I have a problem with them, too.'

'I noticed. Ok… get cleaned up, as in your face and whatever, and I'll be in the bedroom waiting. And I mean everything, ok?!'

He grins. 'I'll be that clean, I'll even smell clean.'

She raises an eyebrow before getting up and entering the house. He picks up another sausage and sticks it in his mouth. After it's gone, he finishes his bottle, then hers and belches again. He wonders if Pauli will get his leg over before they go home.

He stands up and claps his hands. 'Right. A few farts, a good fuckin' wash and then I'll go to town on that girl,' he whispers, as he walks in.

CHAPTER FIFTY-TWO

A few hours later, Lucy and Pauli walk out onto the patio to find Becka and Matt having a few beers. The table is covered with empty bottles.

He looks at Pauli. 'I know what you're gonna gonna…'

Pauli helps him up. 'You're going inside, Pal! This sun will mess you up. No no ya don't!' he takes the bottle from Matt and hands it to Lucy, then brings him inside and sits him on the same couch from the previous day.

'P… I'm boholocked!' his eyes are half open and his head is rolling from side to side. 'Bolloxshed! How do ya say that again, P? Bolloilxed? Boxleckt?!'

'Keep your eyes open, Matt.'

His head is still moving and his eyes look as if they are going to close for good, so Pauli hits him a clatter. There is a sound from behind and he looks around to see Becka and Lucy, with hands covering their mouths and shock on their faces.

He says nothing and looks back at Matt, who is staring up at him.

'Matty, how much did ya drink?'

'Eh... well, I had some ribs... the... did I?... I,' his eyes start to close so Pauli hits him another clatter and Matt jerks his head back. 'Pauli... I need some tea.'

The same sound came from the girls at the second smack.

'Right, stay awake, you're good at this. Three cups of tea and you'll be back in the room, ok?'

'I'll stay awake. Hey man... that hurt!'

'I gave ya two,' he looks around at Lucy. 'Where are your tea bags?'

She swallows. 'In the kitchen in a jar... with tea wrote on it!'

He leaves the room.

'It's a white jar!' she calls after him.

Minutes later, Matt is halfway through his second tea. 'Thanks, P, I needed that.'

'You're welcome.'

The girls look at each other, then back at the lads.

'He hits you twice and you thank him for it?!' Becka asks.

Matt looks at her. 'I'm thanking him for the tea,' he takes a sup. 'Oh that's lovely, twice?'

'Yeah, Matt, sorry.'

'I'm happy with that,' he drinks more tea while rubbing his cheek.

'No no, this is a joke of some kind!' Becka says.

Pauli looks at her. 'You've got your way of looking after Lucy, and I assume she has hers for you. Our way... is slightly different.'

'You'd want to put a few exclamation marks behind that sentence.' Lucy says.

'I know it looked harsh but,' he looks at Matt. 'Another tea, old pal?'

'Yes thanks,' he replies, changed from the sloppy sleepy wreck he was on the patio minutes before, to a weirdly sober and normal Matt. 'One more and I'm there. Back in the room, as ya say.'

The girls look at each other again and are in disbelief at Matt's almost sudden transformation. Pauli goes to make more tea and Matt smiles at them.

'Sit down. It looks weird with ya's standing over there.'

'But it's easier to run away.' Lucy says, not moving.

'Honestly, the drama's over. Now comes the explanation.'

They hold hands and round the sofa and sit facing him.

'Ok, me and Pauli have this thing. We're not big drinkers but ya know yourself. Sometimes you can get a bit carried away and forget to stop.'

'So yous ARE big drinkers?' Lucy asks.

'No! But the odd time, it happens and...'

'My turn,' Becka says, interrupting him. 'So you do know that word exists?'

'What word?'

'The word YOU! All you ever say is, Ya! It sounds like you're saying yes every few seconds.'

Lucy giggles.

'Do I say ya?'

'Yes!' they say, in unison.

'All the bleedin' time!' Pauli yells, from the kitchen.

'Continue with your explanation!' Becka commands.

'Right. So we made a pact... no, that sounds a bit weird. A deal! We made a deal that if one of us gets into a state where it's not good or too sloppy, as we say, the other person tries to get that person sober.'

'By hitting him?'

'It's worked so far, and if it's not broke and all that.'

'So one of yous drink less?'

'Well... yeah. If the other drinks more.'

'And how do yous decide who does what?'

'We don't. It just seems to happen.'

They look at each other, then back at him.'So if Pauli got really drunk... you would hit him?' Lucy asks.

Pauli has been listening in the kitchen and hasn't got a clue what Matt's talking about. He's even wondering why he hit him in the first place, never mind twice. He won't mention the amount of times that the two have drank until they fell asleep, and woke up on Matt's floor on numerous occasions. Or the time when Matt staggered around the tree on campus while pissing and shouting. He must be getting mixed up with when they have the odd fight. Pauli has to go along with this now or the girls will not only think they are nuts, but dopes as well.

He enters the room. 'Answer the girl, Matt.'

'Well, he has got his fair share of clatters.'

He sits down beside him and gives him the tea. 'Number three, pal, you're nearly there.'

'Thanks, P.'

Pauli looks across at the girls. 'And Matt hits harder than I do.'

They are feeling more relaxed now that they have been given an explanation, if that is what it could be called. Lucy turns to Becka and gives her a weird look.

'What, Lu?'

'You started drinking the same time as Matt?'

She thinks for a moment. 'Yeah. We came out to look for yous, but yous were nowhere to be seen. So we had a beer.'

Lucy moves her head back slightly while looking at her. 'I'm not sure I like your pronunciation, Becka. I think you need a slap or two.'

Becka bursts into laughter, followed by Lucy.

'Converted?' Matt asks, before taking a sup.

'Affirmative.'

CHAPTER FIFTY-THREE

The girls bring up the idea of doing kebabs instead of another barbecue and the boys are on board. There is still loads of chicken, ribs and sausages, but decide to use only the ribs and chicken. The sausages are left for the boys to pick at. They realise that they will need tortillas or pittas, so Becka rings her mam and she tells them to drop down with the chicken and ribs, and she will "de-meat" it for them. After the food is bagged, the boys get some kisses and the girls leave them to watch Laurel and Hardy. The car is left there and they walk the few hundred metres to Becka's house. Matt runs back from the window he was watching them from and sits down on the sofa facing Pauli and looks at him. 'So... what do ya make of this little situation?'

'What little situation?'

'Lucy and this house! Firstly, her parents are supposed to be away for a week on holiday. But then Becka lets slip that she stays here four nights a week, every week. Just the two of them.'

'Matt, I don't like where this is going.'

'No, ya got it wrong. I'm not saying that they're lesbians or anything, but why does she stay here? It's a big bleedin' house! Like... does she have parents? I asked Becka, but she said... well, told me to mind me own business.'

Pauli laughs.

Typical Becka, straight to the point. But now he is thinking that it is a bit weird as well. Of course yesterday, he had the perfect chance to find out, but he didn't take it, even after Lucy brought it up. Mister Bigman. "I don't want to know. It's none of my business." But he does want to know and he knows that he jumped the gun yesterday. He wants to know as much as Matt does, but now it will be him who has to bring it up, as Matt has been put firmly in his place. The only problem is, he is happy just to be here with the three of them and doesn't want to mess up. But if Lucy was going to tell him yesterday, it can't be all that bad.

'Ok. I think it's a bit odd as well,' he concedes.

Matt exhales. 'Good. I thought I was the only one.'

'You were the only one! Until what ya just told me. I'll ask her about it, but not the minute she gets back.'

'When?'

'I don't know... the right time. What's wrong for fuck's sake? You look weird.'

'I just keep thinkin' about a certain motel.' The girls arrive back within the hour and they are in great form.

'Honey's, we're home!' Lucy calls.

'We're here, ladies!' Matt calls back.

They walk into the sitting room to find them sitting on separate sofas.

'Nicked a can of cola.' Matt says, holding it up.

'I stole my one wearing a mask.' Pauli says, holding his one up as well.

The girls laugh.

'Yous can nick and steal anytime yous like.' Lucy says, heading into the kitchen with a bag. Becka also has one and follows her. When they come back, they too have soft drinks and each sits beside their man.

'When we were down in mine, my mam was de-meating the food. So me and Lu were talking amongst ourselves about the unusual way that yous have for..., looking after each other,' Becka is straight-faced but Lucy giggles. 'Anyway, she overheard us.'

'She has ears like a bat.'

Becka looks at Lucy. 'She has hearing like a bat, her ears are normal.'

The four laugh. When they are finished, Becka continues.

'When she heard what we said, she roared and said that her brothers used to do the same. She has five brothers, my uncles of course, and going out for a drink in South Africa... well, you don't get into a state where you can't string a sentence together. But Uncle Pieter liked his drink and would always drink quicker than the others, so obviously he would get drunk faster. Then my uncles would slap his face, one by one, and he would understand and slow down. If he didn't, they would just keep slapping him until he did.'

The boys start laughing and Lucy is giggling while looking at Becka, but she is trying not to laugh as well.

'Ok ok, let me get this straight,' Matt says, with his hands raised. 'So if ya go out for a good night with the brothers and drink a bit too much, ya get a good hidin' and maybe a kebab before an Ambulance drops ya home?' he starts laughing while banging the cushion a few times with his hand.

The three stare at him.

'Yes, Matt, just like you and Pauli!' Becka says, with a stern face.

It is as if someone flicks a switch because he stops instantly. 'Aw yeah... I get it now,' he says, feeling like an idiot.

'But there's four of them and that's a lot of clatters.' Pauli says.

Matt nods. 'True.'

'Anyway, it must be a fella thing. So, at least we know now.'

'Indeed we do, Beck.' Lucy agrees.

Here is the chance for Pauli to ask the question and he clears his throat.

'Lucy... remember yesterday, down at the tanning spot in your field?'

'Not very much, and it's a garden.'

'Garden then. You said something like... I suppose you want to know, and I said not interested or something.'

'Yeah, I remember that part. That was before the umbrella, I think.'

'Right then. If the question is still open, I would like to know, both of us would.' Becka looks uneasy.

'What do you want to know?'

'The house... and the four night a week thing with Becka?'

'How...?' she looks at Becka, who drops her head for a moment before looking at her again, then looks back at

Pauli. 'So..., you want to know how I have here to myself, four nights a week?'

'That's the one.'

'Ok. Do you remember when I told you that I was born in England and moved here when I was eight?'

'I do.'

She looks over at Becka, who opens her hands as if to say… it's your call. Lucy stares at the window as if she is thinking, and she is. The thought that is going through her mind is honesty and not lying to Pauli. A relationship based on lies is not a relationship and is doomed from the beginning. She turns and faces him. 'Ok. When we moved, my parents continued to work in England and still do.'

'So when ya were eight, your parents would leave ya here for four days while they were in England?' Matt asks, in shock.

'They took six months off for us to settle in here.'

'And with me and Lu being friends and going to the same school, she stayed in my house for the four days.' Becka says, getting in on the action.

'Until what age?' Matt asks.

The two look at each other. 'Fourteen?' Becka says.

'Yep! And Greta was always in and out, making sure that we were ok.'

'Fair enough, that makes sense,' Pauli says, happy with their story. 'They must have some jobs for a house like this and to still be working over there.' Here is the moment and Lucy can feel Becka's stare.

'They do,' she swallows. 'My mam works for the CPS and my dad's a Judge.'

'What's the CPS?' Matt asks.

'Crown Prosecution Service.' Pauli says, before Lucy can answer.

She is impressed. But then she glances at Becka, and she has worry written all over her face and Lucy starts to feel nervous. She remembers all the years that her parents told her never to reveal anything to anybody, about coming from England or what they worked at. Maybe this wasn't the best idea in the world to come clean on, especially so soon. Only now are the two wondering how Pauli would know what the three letters stand for, and Lucy needs to find out quickly.

'How do you know that?'

'I've watched the Bill a few times.'

The girls exhale together and Pauli and Matt stare at them.

'What's wrong?'

'Nothing, O'Neill… everything is perfect.' Lucy replies, with a big smile.

Becka even manages a grin which is soon to be wiped from her face.

'Ok Becka,' Matt begins. 'Your mam is in the house so your dad must have a good job as well.'

She says something to Lucy in Afrikaans and she says something back.

'Ok, yes. He has a good job.'

Matt looks at Pauli, then back at her. 'That's it?!'

'His job is in security.'

To say that this is an anti-climax for the boys is an understatement, and their faces show it. They actually look really disappointed.

'Security?' Matt asks, half-heartedly.

Becka has not done her dad's occupation any justice by trying to be cagey, and she knows it by their almost sleepy reaction. But seeing as though Lucy took the chance and spilt her beans, she decides to go for the shock treatment and spill some beans of her own. 'Yes. He owns a security firm in South Africa.'

'And that's where he is now.' Lucy adds.

The lads look at each other and shrug with a, not bad, look on their faces. Lucy sees this and starts speaking Afrikaans to Becka, who at the end, nods.

'Becka, what type of security does your dad specialise in?'

Matt and Pauli look at each other again and both admire Lucy for trying.

'Personal Security.' Their heads turn to face Becka.

'How personal? I mean how would you describe the people who work for him?'

'They are ex-military.'

'And in layman's terms... what would they be better known as?'

'Bodyguards!'

Lucy does not say another word and rests her case. She smiles at Becka, who smiles back. Oh yeah, and the boys are stunned. The last two words impressed them. Between Lucy's parents' jobs and now this revelation about Becka's dad, they are feeling a little inferior, but Matt has a different idea.

If this was a game of poker, he would have folded long ago because he has nothing to add to the pot of the last three jobs mentioned. But as it seems to be playing out like a poker game, he has just found an ace up his sleeve. Well, not his sleeve, but Pauli's. And like any good cowboy, he's got a partner and he's about to show his hand, whether he knows it or not.

'Pauli, old buddy, old pal!'

The three look at Matt.

'Yes, Matty, old chum?'

'What are ya waiting for?… Tell them!'

He looks confused. 'Tell them what?!'

'About a certain soldier that me and you know... or I will!'

He looks at Matt for some seconds before looking at Lucy, then Becka and stares at the telly where Laurel and Hardy are paused. It's not that he doesn't want to bring Fran up, very much the opposite. He is proud of his dad. He just thinks that no one will want to hear or be interested. He looks back at Matt, who is nearly pleading with his face, and he WILL talk if Pauli doesn't. He looks at the girls who are also waiting, so he begins.

'My dad was in the Army for thirteen years.'

'What rank was he?' Becka asks.

'Sergeant.'

'My dad was a Lance Corporal. You must be very proud.'

'Yes, Becka, I am.'

372

This is where Matt decides to play the same game Lucy did.

'Pauli, old bean… what army was your dad in for thirteen years?'

'The British Army.'

The girls' faces cannot hide their shock. 'The Royal Regiment of Fusiliers,' he adds, then looks at Matt, who gives him a smile and a nod.

'Your dad must have seen a little action in those thirteen years?'

'Yes Matt, he did… and then some.'

'Can you tell us?'

He looks towards the window and realises what he is about to say. He heard it so many times, but had never really thought about it. This time is different.

'Yeah. He did three tours in Ulster… and while he was there… he was shot twice,' he looks at Matt again, but he's not smiling anymore. He gets up and comes over and sits on the floor beside him. Becka gets up as well and sits beside Lucy. 'Then there was Desert Storm. His Battalion was deployed from Germany to the Persian Gulf… so my dad was there at the beginning of it.'

Becka and Lucy seem entranced after hearing this.

'Tell the rest, P.'

He takes a deep breath. 'After that, came Bosnia. Three weeks before he was due to finish his tour, he was on patrol as part of a United Nations Peacekeeping Force, when two of his section were shot by a Sniper. One died straight away, and my dad dragged the other, who was shot in the back, to a building. Then a car bomb went off next to it. It was a set up. Me and my mam were living in Coventry at the time. I was two or something like that... so, I don't remember much. But he was in hospital for four months before they released him. Then a while later... we moved over here,' he looks at the girls and there are tears streaming down their cheeks. Then he looks at Matt and he is the same. 'Ok... well that's it,' he says, trying to put a brave face on it.

'No it's not!' Matt says, sniffling.

Lucy gets up and runs out of the room and comes back with a box of tissues. She goes to Becka, who takes some, then to Matt who does the same. She sits back down, takes some herself and starts wiping her eyes.

'Pauli, I'm sorry. But what does your dad do now?' Matt asks, wiping an eye.

He stares at the TV for some seconds before answering.

'He drinks a lot, and hardly ever leaves the house. He used to shout stuff when he was asleep... that hasn't happened in a while. Then there was the nightmares, but he doesn't get them as much anymore. Or if he does, he doesn't tell us,' he looks back at the two laughing faces, paused on the TV screen, then at the three sitting around him. 'He has PTSD... and suffers from depression. My mam said that before Bosnia, there was nothing wrong with him at all. He would've been promoted within the year, and they had a great life. But one night, not long after they met, she asked him if he was ever afraid that he would get killed? He just stared into her eyes and said, I'm a Soldier. If I die, it's my job. When the bomb went off in Bosnia, he was hit by shrapnel from it and parts of the car. Some of it couldn't be removed so he's still carrying it with him. He never recovered from that. And then having to leave the army. Having to leave was the hardest part for him, he loved it... and still does.'

Becka and Lucy are sobbing now, and Matt is lying on the floor with his arm covering his face.

'Can I get a bottle, Lucy?'

She nods and waves her arm towards the kitchen. He goes out and takes two. After opening one, he swallows half before taking a few breaths, then swallows the rest.

'Pauli, will you bring in a few please?' Lucy croaks.

He comes back with what the girls drink and some beer and lager. He finds the two sitting on the floor as well. Becka is beside Matt and Lucy's back is against the sofa. He puts the drink on the floor and sits next to her. She takes his hand. 'You weren't buzzing off me. You do have a British passport.'

'Well, I was born there.'

'So… I'm the only one that was born in this feckin' country?!'

'But, Matty,' he puts his hand on his back. 'Your origins are from Germany. The Black Forest, of all places! And that has one hell of a history.'

'Thanks, P, you're a real gent!'

'He sounds like a Brit to me.' Becka says, looking at him sideways.

The four laugh.

'Cool! We're all happy now.' Lucy says, just about to take a sip from her bottle.

'P… there's one more thing.'

'There's more?!' Becka asks.

Pauli takes another good sup from his bottle. 'A little. My dad gets the Army pension. And because of his injuries, he can't lift or carry anything in case he does irreparable damage. So he's on disability here as well.'

Lucy's eyes start to fill up again. 'That's so sad.'

'He is a hero!' Becka says, no nonsense.

'It's funny ya should say that.' Matt says, and looks at Pauli.

'He has a few medals.'

'P… define a few, please.'

He thinks while he looks at the ceiling. 'Seven… maybe eight.'

'It's eight, P,' he looks at the girls. 'And I saw and held them!'

'Eight?!' Becka barely gets out. 'My dad hasn't got one.'

'Aww! We're really sorry about that,' Matt says, trying to keep a straight face. 'And my favourite one is the cross, that's… woh!'

'The cross?' Becka asks.

'The Military Cross. He got that one for Bosnia. And Matt is right, it's my favourite as well.'

'Eight?' Lucy asks, still trying to get her head around the number.

'Yeah… eight!' Matt looks from her to Pauli. 'P… your dad's the man! How many times have I said it? Tell them, how many?'

'A lot, Matt. Really a lot.'

He puts his hands behind his head and smiles. 'Well, at least we won the pot!' The three look at him.

'What pot?!' Pauli asks.

'Ah... don't mind me. I was just thinkin' of... the bags of scraps in the kitchen,' he lies, and knows that it was a poor one.

Lucy folds her arms. 'What bags of scraps?!'

'That stuff ya's brought back from Becka's.'

Both girls look at each other and they don't look happy.

'Scraps?! That's the food you have been eating since you got here. My mam just took it off the bones for kebabs.'

'I think he's still a bit drunk,' Pauli says, looking from Becka to Lucy, before settling his annoyed stare on Matt. 'Isn't that right... pal?!'

He swallows hard. 'Yeah, that's it. But it smells really nice!'

Matt has barely got away with his Mister Collon. Speaking instead of thinking first. He will explain it to Pauli when they have some time to themselves. But he is very happy that they have just, thanks to Fran, kicked some ex-military and Judicial arses around this sitting room.

'Well, that's the end. No more secrets.' Lucy says.

'Damn right.' Pauli agrees.

It stays quiet for close on half a minute before Becka springs off the floor, goes to the TV and switches the channel to Indian Music. Suddenly, the mood has changed and the girls demand some dance lessons. It is six songs later before they take a rest, and then food gets mentioned. They go to the kitchen and the girls take the makings for the kebabs, the boys get the booze, and they head out onto the sun drenched patio. On the way out, Lucy put the dance channel on, so their background music was sorted. They spend hours outside before kebabs get mentioned again, so a second batch gets done. But Matt being Matt, has four and eats the remaining sausages. Just before nine, they decide to go their separate ways. So it is hugs and kisses for the girls, and the boys pat each other on the shoulder a few times.

When they get to Lucy's room, she goes for a shower. Then Pauli does the same. When he comes out, he is wearing Dennis the Menace pyjama bottoms that she gave him. The only problem is that the ends of them stop between his ankles and knees. She laughs wildly while pointing at him.

'Honestly, these are the biggest ya have?'

'I'm only a little thing! I can get you a pair of my dad's, if you want?'

He imagines her coming back with a long white sleeping gown, maybe even the hat as well. He definitely watched too much Laurel and Hardy today.

'No, these are fine.'

She pats the bed a few times. 'Come on over, O'Neill... I won't bite.'

CHAPTER FIFTY-FOUR

The next morning, Pauli and Lucy are back on the patio and he is on his second peach yogurt drink, just minutes after finishing his first. She brought two out, placed one in front of him and sat down. She did not shake hers as vigorously as yesterday, and once she started drinking it, he decided to give his one a go.

She is also eating bacon flavoured corn snacks.

'Are you sure you don't want a packet? We've tons of other stuff in there.'

'Nah. I usually have a fruit bar in the morning.'

'What type?'

'I can never remember the name, but they come in strawberry and blueberry.'

'I know the ones,' she puts her packet on the table and goes inside. She comes back and places a box of each in front of him, sits, and picks up her packet.

'I'll say this, yous don't do things by halves.'

'That's my mum. Over to Newry every Saturday for the weekly shop.'

'Newry?!'

'Yep! It's only up the road and she won't shop down here as it's too dear. I'm the only one who uses euros in this house. Well... Becka as well.'

He thinks about what she just said.

'Yeah, that makes sense. In England four days of the week, then drive across the border for the shopping, they wouldn't need euros. And she's right, it is too dear down here. My mam is always moaning.'

She munches away on her snacks while nodding her head. 'And if she saw me eating these for my breakfast, I'd get a right earfull.'

He is staring at her as she looks into the packet, picks one out and pops it in her mouth. She catches him looking and stops mid chew. 'What?'

'How is it that everything you do, you look lovely doin' it?'

She laughs. 'Why thank you, kind sir. But I don't think I would look lovely doing everything!'

'Eh... I don't know about that.'

'Go on, keep talking.'

He remains silent but a grin appears while he looks at her.

She leans forward. 'Are you talking about a number two?' she whispers.

'Are you not?' he whispers, back.

'Oooh! Yack!' she says, and makes a face.

'See? Even that.'

'Get that thought out of your mind, boy!' she says, with a giggle. She takes a sip from her yogurt drink as Becka walks out. 'Good morning, Becks!'

'Morning, Lu,' the two kiss each other's cheeks. 'Morning O'Neill.'

'Becka.'

'What's wrong, Becka? You've got a really weird face on.'

'I'll tell you in a minute. I'm just going to get one of them,' she goes inside.

'Arguement?' Lucy whispers.

He shruggs his shoulders and says nothing. When she comes back, she sits on the vacant chair between them and takes a sup.

'Spill it, Becks!' Lucy says, holding a snack inches from her lips.

'He smells!'

The two laugh.

'No really, he does! Farts all night and… ugggh! The smell from them. I can still smell them, here… smell,' she holds her arm out to Lucy, who quickly pulls away.

'Becka, I'm eating!'

She looks at Pauli. 'Here... you smell.'

He points at the drink on the table. 'Drinking.'

She brings her arm close to her nose, then pulls it away while closing her eyes.

'Becka… I don't think smells like that linger for that long.'

'They do! O'Neill, go up and smell the room.'

He looks at Lucy before getting up and going inside. When he returns, he has his T-shirt covering his nose and mouth. He walks past them to the edge of the patio facing the field, and only then does he take it down. After a few breaths, he turns around and there is panic on Lucy's face.

'Am I right?!' Becka asks.

'Yeah! I don't know what that is but it's not good. Can ya not smell it, Lucy?'

'It better be gone before my mum and dad get home!'

Minutes later, Lucy comes to the end of her snacks and rips the bag open and starts licking the inside.

'Won't let a crumb go to waste.' Becka says, watching her.

'Waste not, want not!' she crumbles the bag in her hand and sits back while looking down at the tanning spot. 'What say… we bunk for the day?'

Those words have changed Becka's face completely. She sits up with a smile while looking at Lucy. 'What are you thinking, Lu?'

'We could go to Belfast. Do a bit of shopping, get a bit of lunch?'

They look at Pauli.

'I'm game!'

'Settled then! So, I'm going for a shower. Would you like one, O'Neill? she asks, while winking at Becka, who sniggers.

'I would like one very much indeed.'

She stands, holds out her hand and he takes it. 'Right so, let's go.'

When he walks past Becka, she raises her hand to her mouth and turns her head slightly. 'Enjoy your... shower!'

They go inside and seconds later, Lucy's head peeps back out the door.

'Oh... we will!' she says, with a grin.

After their showers, they went for some light exercise in her bed. Afterwards, Lucy went back into the en-suite and minutes later, came out with a different hairstyle. He asked her what it was and she told him that it was a French pleat. She is wearing purple and green Bermudas with black palm trees on them, lilac flip flops, no socks this time, and coincidentally, a peach T-shirt. As they walk through the house with her leading the way, his eyes are glued to the back of her Bermudas. When they get outside, Becka is sitting at the table with Matt, and he looks like he just fell off a roof.

'Are ya ok, Matt?' he asks, with a worried voice.

'Eh... yeah, P.' he replies, moving his head as if to say, can we talk in private?

It would not be considered the most subtle hint in the world. Becka gets up and her and Lucy go inside. A few seconds pass before Pauli sits next to him.

'What's going on, Matt?'

'I think I just fucked up, bigtime!'

'How?'

'Becka said that I smell and it's like something that's dead.'

'You do smell! I went into your room and nearly puked. I had to cover me nose and mouth, and didn't breathe until I got back out here. But I think she's going a little overboard on the dead thing. Did ya crap your jocks and hide them in the room or something?'

'P, man, what do ya think I am?'

'Matt!'

'Ok! But I don't do that anymore. Plus I'm wearing them, look!' he pulls the band over his jeans. 'See?'

'Did ya check them?'

'Of course! That's the first thing I did after Becka said it to me.'

Pauli's eyes widen.

'Not in front of her! I ran back up to that toilet wardrobe thing.'

Pauli decides not to even bother correcting him. 'Matt, now listen to me. You eat a hell of a lot of food, but yesterday… that was pure greediness.'

He nods. 'I think it was all those sausages.'

'Well, maybe you should try and go to the toilet a bit more and… I don't believe I'm gonna say this, but… maybe fart a bit more as well. But at a good distance.'

'Pauli… ya know me, man. The best thing I can do after a false heart attack, is fart! Actually, maybe farting is the best.'

'So we're clear?'

'We are, pal. I just hope Becka doesn't blank me now.'

'Did she tell ya?'

'I just told ya she did!'

'No, I mean about today. We're bunking college and going to Belfast.'

'No fecking way?!'

'Yeah, and we're leavin' soon. So if ya don't get your shit... sorry Matt. Your act together, you'll be here for the day.'

'I will on me bollox! I'm goin'! I've never been over the border or to Belfast.'

The two hear laughing and look around, but see nobody.

'Matt, whatever's in there, get it all out and have a good long shower, ok?'

'I will, buddy! I'm goin' up and I'm gonna have a good hard crap! Thanks for the heads up, P. TTFN.'

Pauli watches him go inside and winces at the "good hard crap" part. He really hopes that Becka doesn't blank him. But if she keeps going on about it, he will play the – Hey... we're all human – card. Suddenly, he thinks back to Lucy up in her bed and their workout. He smiles, seconds before the two walk out and they smile back at him.

'You look happy with yourself. Care to share?' Lucy asks.

'Oh, I am... but later about that last part.'

'The two of yous are experts in tact,' Becka says, sarcastically. 'So, what was it?' It takes him a moment to realise that she is not asking him why he is smiling, but what Matt's problem is.

'Oh yeah, that. He thinks it was the chicken bague—'

'We heard!' they say together, as they cross their arms and stare at him.

'Heard what?' Pauli asks.

'Everything!' Lucy answers.

'How?'

Becka's head slowly looks up at the balcony above them.

'Damn it!'

'Ten out of ten for loyalty, O'Neill. Now we have two questions.' Lucy says.

'Shoot!'

Becka nods at Lucy to ask the first one.

'Firstly, what did he mean about a false heart attack?'

'And what did you mean about him crapping his jocks and hiding them?'

CHAPTER FIFTY-FIVE

Lucy reverses into a spot. 'Ok, chaps, we be here!'

'Nice parking, Lu.'

'Thanks, Beck!'

'Do yous do this often, I mean come up here?' Pauli asks.

'Every second week or so.' Becka replies.

'I don't believe it, I'm in the North! I'm in... we're in the fracking North, man!'

'Yeah, Matt, we got here eventually.'

'Come on, let's check out the shops.' Lucy says, getting out.

'So, what are ya getting?' Pauli asks, looking over the roof of the car at her.

'88s!'

He looks at Matt, then at Lucy as she rounds the car towards him. 'What's 88s?'

'Runners, or as they call them, sneakers! Did you ever hear of Happy Days?'

Pauli and Matt spread their arms with their thumbs up. 'Haaay!' both say. The girls are highly impressed and laugh.

'Well, they're the runners that they wore back then and I'm getting a white pair.'

'And with me being awkward, I'm getting black.' Becka adds.

'Are they the ankle jobs?'

'That's them, O'Neill!' Lucy says, with a little jump of excitement.

'Yous will have to get the jackets as well to look the part.'

'What are they like?' Becka asks.

'The sleeves always seem to be a different colour to the body part.'

'Have two, so does Becks.'

'You're joking?'

'No!' they answer.

'Right so, lead the way.'

They begin in Castlecourt and find the runners almost immediately. Then Lucy asks if they fancy lunch. The choices range from burgers to pizza and even a place that sells baked potatoes. They all rule the last one out as it sounds a bit too adventurous for the boys first time here. After looking at Matt's face, Pauli suggests that maybe the others should be given a miss as well. Maybe next time. They walk out onto Royal Avenue, then onto Donegall Place. Just before the end, the lads recognise the City Hall.

'No way! We're in the centre! I know this building from the telly.' Matt says. They walk over to it and after the lads touch it, the girls decide to do the same. They have been up here many times before and even had lunch sitting on the grass beside it, but touching it had never occurred to them.

They walk back down Royal Avenue and cut through Castlecourt. The girls have their footwear and they are happy. Nothing else catches their eyes.

They come out at the Smithfield Market side and the girls walk over to have a browse around. That is when the boys spot the military surplus shop.

'Shit! Em would love this. Is this gear legit?' Pauli asks.

'All ex-military.' Becka says.

'Aw, P, Em would move in if she saw this place.'

'Let's go in.' Lucy says, leading the way.

The lads have a good few quid on them between euros and their cards. Considering they haven't had to spend a penny since they came with the girls on Monday, and this is Wednesday. Pauli has just spotted something that he has to get for Emma and as far as he knows, she hasn't got one. He picks it up and goes to the counter. 'Do you have one of these in blue camo?'

A woman walks the length of the counter, rounds a corner, then reappears almost instantly with a water bottle in a blue camo cover wrapped in plastic.

'There ye go, son.'

He pays for it and puts the desert camo one back. 'That's Em sorted!'

'She's gonna love that, P.'

'I hope so.'

Becka looks at Lucy. 'Let's get some lunch.'

They go back to the City Hall and walk up a street on the right side of it. Becka and Lucy seem to know their way around quite well. They continue straight and after a few crossings, take a right. They enter an Indian restaurant a few yards up on the right side of the street.

When the orders have been taken, Pauli looks into the bag at the bottle.

'Ya done well, P. She'll be happy as Larry... whoever he is?'

The girls are listening to this, then look at each other and both look pissed off.

Becka gestures with her head but Lucy nods no. Becka goes ahead anyway.

'Nice water bottle.'

Pauli looks at her. 'It is, isn't it?'

'Who is this... M person?!'

Pauli looks at Matt and they realise. 'You or me, old bean?'

'I think me, old sport!' Matt replies, in a faultless upperclass English accent. Lucy looks like she is going to melt, and Becka looks like she is going to pick up the table and play tennis with the two. Matt clears his throat before starting. 'This... EM... person that you are referring to, or to use her full name... Emma, is a very attractive seventeen year old girl. She also just happens to have a little boy called... Emmet. A charming little rascal who looks the picture of his father. Would not you agree, my learned friend?' he looks at Pauli.

'It is as if he were cloned, my dear chap.'

On hearing that, Lucy is finding it difficult to breathe. Becka sees this and has had enough of Pauli and Matt's Barrister impressions and stands up.

'Hey, MacDonald, sit down and listen!'

Becka is taken by surprise. She does as Matt says and sits back down.

He looks back at him. 'Pauli... may I proceed?'

He waves his napkin. 'Be my guest as always, tiddley plonk!'

Matt double takes him before carrying on. 'Ok... this Emmet child is a lovely eight month old..,' he looks at Pauli. 'Did I just say lovely?'

'Loosely, Matt... loosely.'

'Ok,' he looks back across the table at the girls. 'He is my... godchild!'

The girls look from him to Pauli.

'And...,' he waits for them to look back at him. 'He is Pauli's blood relative... by way of being his... Nephew! Case closed!'

They look back at Pauli. 'Em's your sister?' Becka asks, as Lucy can't speak.

'Well, only since she was born.'

Becka looks at her and she has tears in her eyes, but then she starts laughing and hugs Becka for some reason. She gets up, rounds the table and stares at Pauli. 'Em is really your sister?'

'Yeah.'

She hugs, then kisses him. Matt looks at Becka and she points her finger at him, but eventually smiles. Lucy sits back down and all that is missing is a rainbow above her smiling face. She and Becka hold hands and they rest on the table.

Matt actually feels a bit guilty for dragging it out and Looks at Pauli.

'P… ya gotta explain.'

'Ok,' he looks across the table at the two. 'Here's the read.'

He begins by telling about Emma's ambitions from a young age concerning the US Navy, and the starters arrive in between. He continues to tell the rest about her fascination with all things military and Matt joins in on the way. By the time they are finished with their de-brief, the girls have the full run down on the up until a few minutes before, mysterious Em.

They look at each other and smile and wink at the same time. These girls are not called the shadows for nothing. After the main, all four go for dessert. When the bill comes, Lucy starts to raise her hand to take it but Pauli snatches it from the waiter's fingers. And by his face, that is the first time that has ever happened. As he walks away, he glances back more than once. The boys bring up the fact that they have been guests for three days and so far, as Matt put it, "haven't spent a Phennig." Pauli thinks that he must like that word. Then brings up the burgers, chips and milkshakes in the garage on the way home. Lucy goes red and mimes, "Sorry" then gives him a smile that makes it all worth while. He pays by card and leaves a ten euro note as a tip. Of course, Matt says that he will fix him up later. But the main thing is, they have took their girls for lunch and, eventually, paid their way. The two are now happy.

CHAPTER FIFTY-SIX

On the way back, they pulled into a retail park just before the junction for Dublin and stopped outside a supermarket. When they entered, the girls went straight to the clothes section. After a bit of browsing, Lucy pushed the trolley around to the snack aisle and picked up popcorn and potato hoops. Becka got peanuts, nachos and dips. They asked the boys to watch the trolley as they had forgotten something and vanished.

'Probably gone to get some girls stuff.'

'Deodorant?' Matt asks, looking at the contents of the trolley.

'No! You know... the gear! Tampons and... whatever else they use.'

'Aw right, with ya man.'

'And it's called antiperspirant for birds. I know that from Em's hoard.'

'Jasus, P, speaking of which. Lucy didn't look at all well before we told her about Em. I thought she was gonna barf all over the table.'

'Ya don't get out much, I thought Becka was gonna hit us with the fuckin' thing!' Matt titters.

'P, speaking of deodorant, do I still smell?'

He starts sniffing as he walks around Matt. 'You're cool, Matty. There's no smell of fart off you,' he thinks for a moment. 'I didn't think birds were that paranoid. I always thought that they only cared about tans, make up, nails and clothes. And Matt, those two could do a lot better than us two plebs.'

'Well, you're right about them doin' better than us plebs. But I went out with this bird once and she was a paranoid fuck! Where were ya today? What time did ya leave your house? Was there any girls on the bus?'

'Was there any girls on the bus?!' Pauli asks, in disbelief.

'Yeah. When I used to go in to see Lar. Remember I pointed her out that day when she came out to see where I lived?'

'The day you hid behind the wheelie bin?'

'Yeah! That nut job.'

'She looked a bit mad alright, with her eyes going from side to side all the time.'

'That's what I said P, she was a nut job. But one thing I'll say for the girl... once it was dark and ya couldn't see her eyes, she was a rapid r...'

'Right, I get ya!'

'Hold on, ya just said YA!'

'Did I? Oh shit!'

'Ah... now I get it. You're tryin' to speak normal in front of Lucy?'

'Matt, I do speak normal, and so do you. But that ya business... it sounds chavy.'

'Is it really that bad?'

'It's crap, man! And I'm not going to mess anything up with Lucy, even if it means speaking like them. Yeah, exactly! Do you notice how they speak? Their pronunciation and their diction?'

Matt grins and slowly shakes his head. 'I could see old Rochester coming from a mile away, pal.'

'That obvious?'

'Let's put it this way… here's Becka.'

'That's not a great comparison, Matt.'

'No really, here she is!'

Pauli looks around to find her walking towards them on her own.

'Where's Lu? I mean, Lucy?'

'The toilet.'

Becka slowly takes them on a tour of the same aisle for nearly ten minutes before heading to the checkout. Matt insists on paying for the few items in the trolley. When the three get back to Lucy's car, they find her sitting in it.

'Bogey belly?' Pauli whispers.

'No, just a number one, and get that number two out of your head.'

Then for some reason, he kisses her. Just a quick kiss on the lips. But when he moves back and looks at her, she is smiling. She didn't see that one coming. Neither did he for that matter.

Just before Newry, Becka gets a call and starts speaking Afrikaans. She laughs a bit and "mama" gets mentioned, so the lads assume that she is talking to Greta. When it ends, she tells Lucy to go to hers first. When they pull up outside, the gates are already opening, and Greta is standing at the door with her hands on her hips. They go inside and it resembles Lucy's except for different furniture.

Becka speaks Afrikaans again and Greta looks from her to Lucy and seems to ask a question. Lucy answers and her and Becka face the boys.

'Ok, we go outside now.' Becka says, and walks off. Lucy looks at them and nods towards Becka and follows her. The lads do the same to each other and feel like idiots, especially when Greta laughs.

They follow them through the kitchen and out the backdoor. There is a giant green shed a few hundred feet from the house. As they get closer, they see that it is one of the good metal ones and not a wooden barn, as Matt thought it was. It has two large doors in the centre which are closed. Becka goes to a smaller door to the left of them and presses some buttons on a keypad. There is a beep and she pushes open the door. The fluorescent lights take a few seconds to kick in, but when they do, the lads stand there in shock. In front of them are two vehicles. To their left is a tan coloured Humvee. On the right, next to it is a grey Armoured Personnel Carrier. Matt is the first to notice that it is on tracks.

'My dad is a bit of a military nut as well.' Becka says.

They hear her and want to say something, but seem mesmerised as they look from one to the other of the two vehicles facing them.

'Can we touch them?' Matt asks.

'Of course!'

Both go to the APC first and separate either side of it. Pauli has taken the blind side so Becka and Lucy watch as Matt checks it over. He gets down and rubs his hands along the tracks. They can only assume that Pauli is doing something similar on the other side. Matt continues slowly and goes out of sight when he gets to the rear of it. The girls hear talking so know that the two have met up. They walk to the Hummer next. This time both of them stay together while they give it a good going over. The girls were expecting this, so decide to sit on a sofa against a wall and wait for them to become bored. It takes a little longer than they thought it would. Nearly twelve minutes later, by Becka's watch, they come over to them.

'They're awesome!' Matt says.

Lucy holds out her hand to Becka. 'Five euros, if you please.'

She takes the money from her jeans and hands it to Lucy. The boys look at them and seem confused.

'We had a bet to see who would say awesome first,' she holds the note up to the light and seems to be checking it. 'This better not be another of those fake ones.'

'It's not. We got rid of the last of them today, remember?'

'Ya mean… yous paid for your 88's with false money?' Pauli asks, mouth agape.

'Of course! We always pay for stuff that way. Remember the garage and the burgers that day? It was all free food!'

'Don't forget you filled your car with petrol that morning as well, Lu.'

'Oh yeah! A handy sixty euros of petrol for nothing.'

Greta walks in laughing while carrying a tray of sandwiches. Pauli and Matt look at her and their faces have gone from shock to horror. Lucy and Becka start laughing and the boys are getting nervous now. Becka struggles to get up and walks to the back of the APC. They hear what sounds like a door opening and when she reappears, she's holding an AK-47, and still laughing. This only starts Greta and Lucy off again. Matt is eyeing up the door while Pauli is staring at what he thought was his normal girlfriend. At least her eyes don't keep going from side to side. Soon the laughter dwindles to giggles, and Lucy is now lying on the sofa holding her belly.

Greta holds up the tray. 'Here are sandwiches.'

The boys don't budge. So Becka walks to Matt and gives him the rifle, then continues over to the sofa, sits and takes a sandwich from the tray.

Lucy sits up and takes one as well. 'Oh... that was so funny. My belly is in bits!'

Matt is looking at the rifle when Pauli takes it from him and checks it.

'It's a fucking BB gun!'

The three females laugh again.'Sorry O'Neill, but we couldn't resist it.' Becka says.

'So, all that fake money stuff?'

'Joking.'

He looks at Lucy. 'You little...'

Suddenly, Matt starts laughing and they all look at him.

'Only gettin' it now, Matt?' Pauli asks.

'No... I was just about to run out the door and hopefully not get shot. I would've looked like a dope running across the field.'

After some giggles, Becka begins by telling them that the two vehicles are real. The Hummer is ex-US Marine

Corp and ex-Afghanistan. Her dad bought it on their online auction site and had it shipped from America two years ago.

The APC is ex-Russian Army. That was bought in the Czech Republic and shipped over only eight months ago. She points out the triangular Czech flag on a wire at the back, that they had missed while inspecting it. The AK-47 is, as Pauli said, a BB gun. One of five that are in the APC. Both vehicles are used at military meetings and exhibitions around Ireland and the UK. The most recent of which was two months before in Scotland, when Greta drove the Hummer, accompanied by Becka and Lucy. Her dad took the APC on the back of a flatbed truck.

'So... yous dress up in all the gear?' Pauli asks, now excited.

'Yeah. All kitted out in our choc chip combats and our boots.' Lucy answers.

Matt wants to say it sounds great, but is afraid in case it comes across as a hint.

Becka turns to Greta. 'Mam, when is the next one?'

'I think it's August in Dublin.'

'So, we all go,' she says, looking back at the two.

'And we get dressed up as well?' Matt asks.

'You have to!' Greta says, and takes a chunk from her sandwich.

The boys are relieved that their girlfriends are not villains, forgers, psychopaths or in any other way, mentally unstable. Now they are suddenly hungry and make their way to the food. Pauli takes a sandwich and looks around at the vehicles. Matt takes two and stares at the rest. When the tray is nothing but crumbs and the odd crust, Greta goes back to the house and Becka and Lucy give them the hands on tour. The Hummer is the first that they get into, and after both lads sit in every seat there is, the four move onto the APC. This is a game changer. The smell inside, the torn and worn seating, the front seats that go up and down so that it can be driven with hatches closed while under fire. Or with hatches open and seats up, when just out for a run of the mill cruise on a nice sunny day with a cool breeze in your helmet. The five AK-47's that are strapped inside and positioned in different areas of the vehicle just add to the effect. The boys don't want to get out if they don't have to... but they do. The girls are craving some alcohol liquid refreshment, and that means it can only happen if Lucy's car is back in her garden. But one more thing has to be done before they leave, and it was the main reason that they came to Becka's in the first place. After a quick phone call, Greta comes back and stands beside them.

'Ok, the real reason why we're here.' Becka says, hands on hips.

Pauli and Matt face the three and wait for the revelation.

'What size is Emma?' she asks.

Pauli puts his hand level with his eyes. 'About there.'

'Not what height she is, what size? Ten, twelve, fourteen?'

'Oh...' he looks at Matt. 'Becka?'

'Yeah Becka, she has your build. Well, not your...'

The three females laugh.

'Ok, she's about a twelve. So a fourteen because they are worn loose,' she says, looking at Greta and Lucy, then the three separate. Lucy and Becka go to the right of the APC and start going through different boxes that run along the wall. Greta goes to more boxes stacked along the opposite wall, on the left side of the Hummer. She is still laughing at Matt's aborted description of Becka's build, and she is the first to find what she is looking for.

'Dutch!' she shouts, holding up a pair of combat trousers and throwing them towards the front of the Humvee, where they land on the ground.

'Afrikaans!' Lucy shouts, holding up another pair of combats but with a different design. She throws hers towards the front of the APC and they also land on the ground.

'Russian!' Becka shouts, coming in last and holding up a pair with a different design and colour, and throwing hers in the direction of Lucy's.

Pauli and Matt look at each other and they have a confused look on their faces. They look back at the three, who have now moved to different boxes and are rummaging through them.

'It must be an Afrikaans game, but it's not that great, is it?' Matt whispers.

Pauli doesn't even look at him, never mind answer him. His eyes are on only one thing and that is Lucy, squatting down while searching through a box.

Now, those Bermudas fit.

'Done!' she says, standing and turning while holding a shirt above her head with one hand, as she pulls the back of her Bermudas with the other. She sees Pauli looking and gives him a wink, while grinning.

'This is a weird game.' Matt whispers.

'Ssshh!'

'Me, too!' Becka says, turning and holding a shirt above her head as well.

Greta says something in Afrikaans and the girls laugh. The boys assume it's a curse and smile. Seconds later, she stands up with a shirt above her head and turns around. 'Ok... me, too, eventually!'

The three pick up the bottoms and walk over to the boys.

'Right. Here's Russian shirt and combats, Lu has the Afrikaans and big mama has the Dutch.'

Greta says something and the girls laugh. Matt and Pauli just stare at them.

'I said, not as big as I want to be.' Greta translates.

The two smile and stand there silently until Becka saves the moment.

'Ok, they'll need a wash as they are surplus,' she thinks. 'Actually, two washes, just to be on the safe side. Plus, they have been in those boxes for God knows how long and before that, God knows on who,' she thinks again. 'Three washes.'

Matt and Pauli stand looking at her with identical blank faces.

'Lu, you explain.'

'These are for Emma.'

They look at each other, then back at her. 'Really?!' Pauli asks.

'It's nothing to do with me. It's all Becka and Greta.'

He looks at them. 'Really?!'

'Yes!' they answer.

'So,' Matt looks from one wall of boxes to the other. 'All of these boxes are full of combat gear?'

'No, just combat clothes. My dad gets this stuff all the time and for nothing. So if they are the wrong size for Emma, we have the right size here, believe me.'

'And he is a bleeding hoarder!' Greta adds.

The four laugh at her pronunciation of "bleeding."

'But he is a bleeding hoarder!' she repeats.

The clothes are put into two bin bags and into Lucy's boot. Then she drives the few hundred metres back to her house.

CHAPTER FIFTY-SEVEN

Lucy decides to wash the clothes and put them in the dryer, so that when Emma gets them the next day, they will be clean and ready to wear immediately. After putting on the first of three short washes, she comes into the sitting room.

'Ok, these are quick so we won't be here too long. So, what do yous fancy?' she asks, looking at her watch. 'Alcohol, juice or a nice cup of tea?'

The three laugh.

Pauli raises his hand. 'Beer please!'

'And I'm the lager man!' Matt announces, as if nobody already knows that.

'I'm going to do red today, Lu.'

'And I'll go blue,' she says, and her and Becka head to where the drink is kept. They are back seconds later and hand the boys their six-packs. 'The next wash goes on in seven minutes. So once it's on, what say you all to the tanning spot?'

'Yay, to the tanning spot!' Matt shouts.

'Yay to the tanning spot!' the three repeat.

They make a move once the second wash is on. Lucy decides to do the third when they come back later. When they get there, they sit facing each other.

'Pace yourself, Matt.'

'Oh I will, P.'

'Yes. We don't want any slaps today.' Becka says.

'Hear hear!' Lucy adds, raising her bottle and they all clink.

She carried, or rather struggled down the garden with, a large portable ghetto blaster and stubbornly refused to let any of them carry it. When they got there, she put BBC Radio 2 on.

'Even English stations?' Pauli asks.

'Not that there's anything wrong with the Irish ones, we play them in the car. But when we're here, we always seem to listen to this one, I don't know why.'

'My dad listens to one as well, but it's a forces one. They play good music too.'

Talk goes back to Becka's shed and the vehicles. The two ask what it's like to be in both. The girls explain between them that the Hummer is the smoother of the two and that it has a great sound. It also has removable doors, so they can cruise around on the sunny days at the exhibitions and not get baked. The APC is a whole different animal. As they already know, it is smelly. But it is also very noisy and Becka's dad drives it as if he is demented. He speeds across fields and they do be bouncing all over the place inside, even while wearing the newly fitted seatbelts. Then he does the spins and that is when it gets really exciting. The boys are nearly drooling while listening to them and cannot wait to go to the meeting in Dublin. The girls tell them about sitting on the roof of it, holding the

AK-47's, when they are in slow convoy with the other military vehicles, so that the spectators can get a good look. Then when they park up, the spectators take pictures of the vehicles and even of themselves inside and on top.

'Do you charge them much?' Matt asks.

'To take pictures with their own cameras and camcorders? Of course not! It is free!' Becka answers, as she looks across at a giggling Lucy.

Pauli is glad that Matt asked that question because he was just about to ask it.

'What are you thinking, Matty? Charging people for taking photos?!'

He looks at Lucy and grins while thinking that it was a close one, too close.

When they were in the Hummer, there were also BB guns strapped inside it. Pauli recognised them. Two M-4's, an AR-15 and the classic M-16.

He is wondering how he won't tell Em about this when Becka nudges him.

'Emma can come, too, if she wants.'

'But we'll have to give her choc chips and deserts for the Hummer.' Lucy says.

Becka nods. 'Get her foot size for next time.'

He looks at Matt, who is grinning back at him, and feels like screaming and running around the field. He wants to ring her this minute but decides to try and go on like a normal person. 'No mess, she can go?'

'Yeah. Normally it's just the four of us. But this way it will be much livelier,' she turns to Matt. 'How is your belly?'

'Not a bother! That won't happen again, don't worry!'

'I'm not! And I know it won't because if it does, I'll grab your ankles and drag you outside and that's where you will stay until the morning.'

He grins, but then realises that she is dead serious. 'It won't, cub's honour.'

Pauli watches as she gives him the old, Greta Gestapo eye treatment. Then he looks at Lucy, who is biting her lip and trying not to laugh. While looking at her, he makes out part of the umbrella over at the hedge.

'Hey Weaver, fancy a walk over and we'll get that big brolly just in case?'

'I do, Mister O'Neill. But first,' she points at her feet, then to his runners. 'They have to come off… and socks as well. Let your feet breathe.'

The two are barefoot as they walk away carrying a bottle each.

'Is everything ok with Becka and Matt?'

'She's only playing the tyrant to make sure that it doesn't happen again. When we get back they'll be all laughy.'

They look around to see them kissing.

'Ok… maybe not laughy.'

Pauli stops and after a few steps, she stops as well. She turns and squints as she looks at him with one eye closed. 'What's wrong?'

'I'm not letting them get away with that. Walk your little bum over here.'

She walks to him and they get even. When they resume their walk, after a few steps she takes his hand, looks up at

407

him and winks just before something catches his eye. He stops abruptly while pulling her hand.'Ouch! O'Nei..'

'Ssh! Don't move a muscle,' he whispers, while staring towards where the umbrella is. She looks around, shakes loose his hand and gives him her bottle, then walks away. 'Lucy... stop!'

'I've known him since he was a baby,' she continues walking before eventually kneeling on the grass. 'Caesar... come to mammy, come on.'

Pauli doesn't know what to do and just stares. Then he hears footsteps running up behind him. They slow to a walk and Becka and Matt appear beside him.

'So, your baby came back, Lu?'

'He sure did, and I think he's frightened.'

'P, ya know what that is, don't ya? Why don't ya go over and give it a boot in the jaw?' Matt whispers.

'Shut up, Matt,' he whispers back.

'Don't worry, O'Neill... he's part of the family.' Becka says, reassuringly.

He doesn't say anything as he is too busy watching his girlfriend kneeling on the grass, metres away from a fox. Her arms are open and it keeps looking for some seconds before slowly walking towards her. She puts her arms around its neck and the thing starts licking her face.

'See? Part of the family.' Becka says.

After a bit of catching up, she stands and turns while rubbing its head and walks towards them. It lies on the grass and watches her.

'Your fella was worried about you, Lu.'

'Did you tell him?'

'No. I thought I'd leave that to you.'

'Tell him what? What about tellin' me?!' Matt asks.

'I'll tell you. Now come back over to the radio.'

When Lucy gets near Pauli, she stops a few feet away from him. She tilts her head in a cheeky way and blows hair off her face while looking at him. 'Well?!'

'Well what?'

'You're going to say something, aren't you?'

'Actually yeah, I am. I've never seen anything like that before. How?!'

She looks relieved and takes the bottle from him. 'Come on, I'll tell you on the way to the house. We have to go get some food for him,' she takes a sup. 'Ok…, last year around May, Becka had to get her tonsils out so she was in hospital for a few days. I stayed with Greta at night, and in the day, I was in school and then would come back here and sunbathe while studying.'

'How long was this for?'

'Four days.'

'That must have been hard for you?'

'It was! We visited her every night, but I was lonely and really missed her. Anyway, one day I was lying back there and the radio station went dead, not a sound. So I sat up to see what was wrong with it and I heard a... squeaky noise. I looked up at the sky because I thought it was a bird or something, but nothing. They must have gone to the beach that day.'

He laughs.

'So I stood up and looked around, but nothing... not a sausage! I listened for the squeak and followed it. It led me to where the umbrella is and then I found this tiny little pup, as I thought it was. It could barely stand so I picked it up and brought it to the house and fed it.'

'Where did it come from?'

'That's the thing! I didn't know why a pup so small would be out in the middle of nowhere on its own, so I put it under my bed and went to see if there were any others. I searched for hours until we had to leave to visit Becka, but didn't find anymore.'

'The mother probably got hit by a car or something.'

'That, or either someone shot her. You can hear gunshots most mornings and evenings around here.'

'The set or lair, must've been close if it crawled out and could barely stand.'

'I know. I really did look hard for the rest, but I didn't know it was a fox at the time. You hear about bags of pups and kittens getting thrown into rivers, so I thought it was something like that. Except they just left them to die instead.'

He stops. 'Can you imagine if you had found the rest? There would probably be five or six of them lying over…,' he looks back at the umbrella. 'Where's it gone?'

She looks over at the hedge, but in line with where they are standing.

'Oh, he's a sly little thing. He mouches up the garden as I walk, so when we get to the house, he'll be over there,' she points at a corner. 'Watch how he moves.' They begin walking and when he looks over at the fox, it is shuffling sideways up the garden, so it is matching their walking pace.

'I've never even heard of that, and only for I'm seeing it... I wouldn't believe it.' Sure enough, when they reach the house, it is where she said it would be. Lying in the corner looking over at them.

'He just needs to get used to you. You could even be rubbing his head in a few weeks,' she looks at Pauli. He was never good at lying or hiding what he really thought, and this is written all over his face. 'Don't tell me that a big strapping lad like yourself is afraid of a little fox?'

He looks over at Ceaser, then back at her and forces a smile.

'Ok ok, I understand. If I hadn't have found him and a fox just walked into the garden, I'd be gone up this grass like Zola Budd!'

'Who's Zola Budd?'

'Come on, I'll tell you later.' When they go into the house, she gives her face a rinse, then goes to the fridge and searches it. 'Where the hell are those sausages?'

'Eh... in Matt's stomach.'

She looks around. 'The lot of them?!'

'He's a food merchant.'

She turns back to the fridge. 'Ok then... it will just have to be some rashers, this cheese... mm, ha ha! You think you can hide in there, do you? Well, I'm sorry, but you're somebody's dinner today,' she takes out black pudding.

Pauli is standing behind her and just taking in the view. She stands on her toes while searching the top of the fridge and he has to admit, although in his mind, that those Bermudas look real fine. Yes sir... real fine! He is enjoying the view that much that when she turns around quickly, she

411

catches him and he freezes. 'Hmm... I wonder what's going on in your mind, fella?' she asks, while pointing a chorizo at him.

'Am I allowed?'

'Well, let me put it this way. Only for we have a hungry fox out there waiting for his dinner, you would be more than allowed,' she glances up at the ceiling. 'Know what I mean?'

He swallows. 'Now that's something you don't hear every day.'

She giggles. 'Don't worry; you'll get some sugar later, Sugar. But in the meantime, will you take this stuff while I get a pot and a bottle of water?'

'Of course,' he walks to her. 'A pot and a bottle of water?'

'He'll be thirsty after all this, especially with the chorizo.'

'Lucy, I'm no fox expert, but is that not too spicy for... dog-type animals?'

'Spicy?! Ha! That bloody savage eats Chinese, Indian, pizza, chile, you name it! We even get extra when we order. But give it a wide berth when it farts.'

'So... you've smelt a fox's fart?' he asks, not believing what he has just asked, and almost afraid to find out the answer.

'Of course!' she replies, matter of factly while taking a pot from the press. 'And more times than I care to remember,' she starts rinsing the pot, then stops and looks at him. 'Rinsing a pot for a fox?! Now I'm going overboard. Ok... let's go feed that savage,' she takes a two litre bottle of water from the fridge and turns, raises her face with her lips pouted and they kiss. 'Good boy,' she leads the way out. When they are on the grass, she stops and puts the water and pot down. She looks down the garden and spots Becka waving and she waves back.

'Ok, from here on, I go alone,' she takes the food from him and puts it in the pot, then places it on her head. 'Don't laugh, I'd never be able to carry everything the normal way. See you in a min,' she winks, turns and walks away.

He goes to take a drink but remembers that they are in the kitchen. So he just stands and watches her walk across the grass towards her pet fox, with a bottle of water in one hand while trying to balance a pot on her head with the other.

When she comes back, she has her hands clasped together. 'I need to rinse these again and then we'll get some more booze and head back to the gang.'

'Sounds good, Lu.'

'That's the first time you've called me that.'

'Sorry. Didn't mean to rob it on Becka; it just slipped out.'

'I mean… I like it. It's more... well, less formal. More intimate.'

'Well in that case, I will rob it! But not right away, she might hit me a slap.'

After washing her hands and face, she puts a six-pack of beer and lager in a backpack which he wears. She puts two six-packs for her and Becka in another and she wears that. They begin their walk back to the spot with a bottle each.

'Ok, the rest of the story. One Saturday, me and Becka went to Belfast to do a bit of shopping and have some lunch. My mam was changing my bedding, and guess who walked out from under the bed? Now you have to keep in mind that he was only a few weeks old, so he was a little cutie. When we got back, she was sitting watching the telly with him asleep on her lap and Becka nearly had a stroke, but it was cool. She asked me where I got him and I told her the truth, in the garden. I told her the whole story and she tried not to, but she cried. And us being girls, we cried as well. So there was the three of us on the couch crying when my dad came back from golf. He thought that someone had died. But as my mam told him the story, he kept looking at Ceaser... but he didn't cry. He took a good long look and knew exactly what he was, but he said nothing until a few months after the Leaving Cert. Anyway, we struck a deal. When spring came, he had to move out. My dad was alright about it, he even bought him a kennel.

'You're joking?! Actually, you're not, are you?'

'Nope! It's at the side of the house, but... he never uses it, and that's the end.'

She takes a sup from her bottle and he takes one from his.

'Now that is one... remarkable is not a word I would use often, if at all, but it's the only one I can think of... story!'

'Thanks! And it is, isn't it?' she asks, walking along with a smile.

'Definitely!'

When they reach the spot, Matt looks up at Pauli. 'So, what do ya think of that?'

'Remarkable!'

'Damn! I should've went for a long word. I just said mad.'

As they take the backpacks off, the bottles clink.

'What have you got there, Lu?'

She sits, crosses her legs and stares at Becka for seconds. 'Your favourites!'

'Oh yes! Yummy, yummy, yummy!'

She hands over the bag. 'I knew you'd like that.'

'Lucy… we forgot the brolley.' She looks back at the house, then up at the sky. 'That bloody little fox!'

The four agreed that it was not needed and carried on chatting and listening to music. There was also many more questions about the day in Dublin and Ceaser again, plus laughs in between.

The boys felt like they were on holiday and did not want to go home. But they knew that things had to go back to normal, especially with college the next day. Even though they would not be saying goodbye until nearly one the following day, they knew it was creeping towards them. The girls felt the same, but with Lucy's parents coming back on Friday evening, they knew as well that normality had to be restored. Make the most of the remaining time and then next Monday, it would start all over again. There was no sloppiness in the alcohol department, and some was even brought back to the house when they returned around seven. Lucy checked the corner but Ceaser was nowhere to be seen.

After a vote, two pizzas went into the oven for the supper. Spicey chicken and a Hawaiian. They ate on the patio, and Pauli and Lucy had sided with orange to wash them down, while Becka and Matt went for Colas. If questions were asked about their absence, Lucy's car wouldn't start and the boys had suffered bogey bellies from some food, which was not really a lie. It was just after nine thirty when they said goodnight and went their separate ways. When she went in for a shower, Pauli knew what was coming and done the same. They said goodnight to each other in their own way, and under an hour later, her head was on his chest and the two were asleep.

CHAPTER FIFTY-EIGHT

The four are in from ten until twelve, and the plan is to get the usual for lunch. Then off to the station and wait for the twenty to one, which will have the boys home for just after half. The three days have taken its toll on them, especially the boys. So much seemed to happen in so little time. With no Enterprise today and no changing at Drogheda, this will be a nice mellow one train journey back to their village on the Commuter. The ticket guy lets the girls through and the four sit on the train, a few seats apart. It is empty except for them.

Lucy takes off her backpack. 'I have this for you.'

'Ah, thanks! I need something to carry me gear around in.'

She laughs. 'No, it's inside. Now it's only small, and Becka got Matt the same.'

'When was this?'

'Remember yesterday when we left yous with the trolley?'

'I do,' he replies, with a raised eyebrow.

'Well, we walked through the clothes section seconds before.'

417

'Yeah, I remember that too. I thought yous looked suspicious as we got nearer.'

'And I thought we had good poker faces. Anyway, we spotted something so we double backed for them. I went and paid and Becka went back to yous.'

'So you didn't go for a wee?'

'Oh, I did! But that was after paying for these,' she takes out a small bag.

'You little slya!'

'I know, I know. Little ole' sly me,' she hands it to him. 'Don't open it until yous can't see us, promise?'

'Promise.'

'Now as I said, it's only something small.'

'Lucy, I don't care if it's just this bag.'

'One more thing… I sort of tried it on for a while, so you might get a little smell of me from it.'

He smiles. 'Thanks, Lu.'

Some more people get on the train but only a handful. Before long, the driver announces that it will be leaving in two minutes, and anybody not travelling should disembark. The four go to the doors and after hugs, kisses and goodbyes, they look at the girls on the platform, inches away, and that horrible feeling is back. The two are not known for being impulsive types, and up until now, have never been. But they are thinking the same thing at this moment. Both are torn between staying on the train or jumping off there and then. But where would that get them? As hard as it is, they know that they have to go home.

'Don't forget the bag with Emma's clothes, and don't leave it on the train.'

'I won't.' Pauli says, and knows that he barely got that out.

The doors beep and then close. They stare at the waving girls through the glass and wave back as it starts to pull away. They walk to the end of the carriage while still waving. When they can no longer see them, they go back to where Pauli and Lucy were sitting. He takes the bag of clothes from the facing seats and puts it between his feet.

'If I forget them… I'll fall over them!'

'Good thinkin', bro! Ok… we can't see them anymore, on three?'

'Yeah.'

Matt actually counts down from three, but they take out their gifts at the same time when he gets to one, to reveal two identical grey T-shirts with Laurel and Hardy on the front.

'P…, I think I'm gonna cry.'

'Please don't, Matt… you'll start me off.'

They do.

CHAPTER FIFTY-NINE

They get back to the village and go to Pauli's house. When they go out to the back garden, Rita, Em and Fran are sitting on the patio chairs and all are wearing sunglasses. There are bottles in the girls' hands and a can in Fran's. They look at the playpen, which has a quilt cover over it, and cannot see Emmet, but can hear movement inside it.

'Pinch me! I must be seeing things! Is... is that my long lost son, Pauli, and my long lost adopted son, Matt?!' Rita exclaims, with a look of astonishment on her face while pointing at them.

'What, Ma?! Ya mean that I have a brother... and another... brother?!' Em asks.

Matt and Pauli look at Fran, who is shaking his head. 'No, Rita... no. I definitely remember that we only have one child... but,' he stands and walks to within a few inches of them and stares at Matt, then Pauli while moving his head from side to side. 'They do look a bit familiar alright.'

Pauli glances at Matt, but could hear him laughing before that, then back at Fran.

'Re, I think ya may be right. I think this is our son... hello, son, hello Matt.'

'Is that it, Fran?! Jasus, I thought we were going to drag this out for a while and have a big ending.'

'Hello, all.' Pauli says.

'From me too! Remember, the adopted son, brother and godfather?'

Em takes a sup from her bottle. 'Hello... all of the above.'

'Now ye two look like ye could do with a drink.'

They look at each other and smile lazily.

'Go on! Ye know where they are.'

'Matt, will you? I just want to see if I can spot me nephew in there.'

'Roger Wilco!' he says, turning.

Pauli goes to the pen, hunkers down and lifts the cover a bit. 'Hiya Popeye?'

'Gnnng!'

He smiles as Matt appears with the bottles.

'So, how did it go?' Rita asks.

They recount the events of the last three days in Lucy's house, only leaving out personal details and Matt's weird smelly event. For some reason, they forget to mention the contents of the shed in Becka's garden, and the upcoming meeting in Dublin which Em is invited to. More bottles are opened and they sit on the grass, both wearing a pair of Pauli's Bermudas after a quick change. Only now are they starting to recover from leaving the girls and beginning to chill. But the grass reminds the two of that huge field, minutes from the border, that a couple of girls call a garden. Pauli starts humming the song that was playing in Lucy's car that Becka said was a good omen. But Matt hears it and stands up with his arms in the air while looking at the sky. 'So good to me!' he shouts.

They laugh.

Some minutes pass before he hits Pauli on the arm.

'Ouch!' he looks at him. 'What the hell was that for, Matt?!'

His face is weird, as is his smile. 'The bag!' he says, without moving his mouth.

'Oh krud! I forgot,' Pauli says.

Rita, Fran and Em look at each other, then at Matt as Pauli goes inside.

'That was really good, Matt. Do ya practice that a lot?' Fran asks.

'All the time,' he replies, with the same face and without moving his mouth.

Em bursts into laughter, followed by Rita and Fran.

'Here he comes.'

'Matt, stop doin' that, it's creepy!' Rita says, giggling.

Pauli walks out with a large plastic shopping bag. Lucy did not want him carrying a black bin bag around so put it in this one.

'There's one thing we sort of forgot about,' he hands the bag to Em. 'These are from Becka.'

'Excuse me! But I think there may be more than one thing that we forgot about, and I think that Lucy was as much involved in this as well! Oh yeah, Greta, too!'

'Ok,' he looks back at Em. 'These are from Becka, Greta and Lucy.'

'That's Becka's mam, by the way.' Matt adds, looking at her.

'I remember, the meetin' the first time.'

'Well, open it then!'

'I'm afraid to. I don't even know these people,' she says, looking around.

'Em, don't be such a wuss! Open the bleedin' thing, I wanna see what's in it.'

'Right, Ma!' she says, emptying the binbag onto the patio. She takes a sup from her bottle and looks at Pauli, then at Matt. 'If this is a bag of rubbish, yous are gettin' the slaps!'

'Keep going.' Pauli says.

She takes another sup, puts her bottle on the table and starts ripping the tightly packed taped bag. After looking through a finger ripped hole, she freezes and looks at them. 'Oh my god!'

Fran stands up. 'What is it?'

The lads look at each other and Pauli nods for Matt to explain. He gets up, rests his thumbs through the arm parts of an imaginary waistcoat and walks to her.

'There are three pairs of bottoms and shirts. Dutch, Afrikaans and…,' he looks around at Pauli, who mimes, Moscow, and looks back at her. 'Russian!'

She is holding up a pair of bottoms, then searches for the matching shirt and plucks it from the bag and runs into the kitchen. Seconds later, she runs back out and tries to pick the bag up. Matt helps her bundle it into her arms, then she runs back in again. They begin the story at the military surplus shop in Belfast and Pauli remembers the water bottle which is in the sitting room, in a bag on the couch. He goes in and gets it just before Em comes downstairs and walks out wearing the Dutch combats and she is smiling

423

from ear to ear. He gives it to her, saying it is from him and Matt and she is now in heaven. They begin again and tell the whole story and she is entranced, as are Rita and Fran.

'Ya mean that I can go to this show and be in a Humvee and an Armoured Personnel Carrier?'

They nod.

'And this Hummer was actually in Afghan, and not a made up yoke with plastic panels that was bought in a garage somewhere?'

They nod again.

'And Becka and Lucy are goin' to give me choc chip camos and desert boots to wear at it?'

They nod again.

Fran asks them to tell him about the APC again, and they go over everything from the seating, the smell and the AK-47's strapped to the inside. Then about being bounced all over the place when it goes across grass at speed, and when her dad does the spinning. Em asks them about the Hummer again and about the weapons inside it. Rita is listening to this carefully and stealthily watches Fran from behind her sunglasses. He is as excited as Em is, and she knows that she will have to have a word in both Pauli's and Matt's ears, concerning trying to get him a seat in at least one of those vehicles, if not the two.

The boys decide to walk to the supermarket and pick up two boxes of beer. One for themselves and one to reimburse Rita. When they get back, the questions start all over again. Rita has tuned out at this stage as the same things are being repeated over and over again. Her main objective for tonight is to get an Indian for the supper, after being reminded of the one in the story.

Matt starts to look very tired and very drunk. He invites Pauli around for some game console therapy just after seven. But he looks in even worse shape than Matt and is continuously yawning. Matt starts yawning too and decides that he needs his bed and goes home. Within minutes, Pauli announces that he is going to the toilet but doesn't come back out. When they are just about to order the food, Fran goes up to see what he wants and finds him asleep in his bed, with a T-shirt in his hands on his pillow. He turns to leave but then looks back at him and double checks. He saw it right the first time, Pauli is smiling.

CHAPTER SIXTY

It is Friday evening, and Fran is in his chair going through the A4 pad while listening to the forces radio station in the background. He browses through the pages, looking over the plan of the garden and where the container will go, and has been doing this for the past two hours, over and over again. There is not really much to check and recheck. A hand drawn outline of the back garden and a hand drawn outline of a rectangle in the same garden. It's not rocket science and that page will never make the Louvre.

He is nervous and thinks that he will have to go to the toilet again. Rita should be home shortly and he might have to get a nerve tablet or two from her. After a quick think, he decides to get three. They should calm him right down.

He glances at the clock on the TV screen. She should be back soon, he thinks as he looks down at the pad. Some minutes later, he hears one of those extra slow road sweepers. Poxy Council! Them poxy things don't even clean anything. They only throw up dust everywhere and leave a useless wet streak on the road. What a complete waste of money. He sits back and ponders for a moment.

How long would he last if he had that job? Crawling around, looking down at paths and trying to get as close as possible without mounting the fucking thing, and hitting a lamp post or a tree or something. He could well see himself falling asleep behind the wheel from the boredom of it. Then holding up the traffic, and purposely not looking as drivers eventually go by and give dirty looks and honk their horns. He shakes his head. No… too strenuous a job. He'll just sit back and let that lad out there do it. He looks back at the pad as it gets closer and louder and then the sound changes. He lifts his head and leans it a few inches towards the window. That fucking thing needs a new exhaust or a service, he's thinking. Just as he is about to look back at the pad, the sound lowers and he gets up to have a look out, but jumps when he sees that there is a yellow JCB turning into the garden. He stares as it manoeuvres in and passes the window out of sight. Seconds later, Rita's car pulls into the garden. He walks to the front door, but she opens it before he gets there.

'Heya love!' she says, and gives him a peck on the cheek and walks on into the kitchen. He looks back at the open door to see Sophie enter and he jumps again.

'Hello Fran,' she says, with a smile, as she walks past him. 'John will be in now.'

He looks back at the open door again. 'John?'

'So, what do ye want, Soph, tea or coffee?'

'Tea please, and John will have a coffee, thanks.'

Fran walks to the door and looks out to see the back end of a JCB, then John appears. 'She's a beauty, isn't she?' he asks, looking at it.

Fran walks to the side of the house and takes in the full view of the machine.

'Yeah… yeah. She's a fine specimen.'

'Well, tomorrow it starts and Sunday it's over. I'll be starting me own in a few weeks. I haven't got time to scratch me arse at the moment, but I suppose that's a good thing, as washing it is out of the question.'

Fran looks up at John, who is about half a foot taller.

'Only jokin' with ya, lad!' he says, with an enormous grin. 'Right,' he claps his hands. 'They said that there'd be a coffee for me, so I'll leave yous two to get aquainted and I'll go and get me caffeine,' he slaps Fran's shoulders and walks towards the door.

Fran stumbles at the slap and when he turns, John is gone. He looks back at the digger and walks slowly around it while wondering whether or not to get in it. 'Fuck this!' he says, and starts climbing.

He is sitting in it a few minutes when three local lads, around eleven or twelve, walk by bouncing a football.

'Nice JCB, Franmeister! Give us a wheelspin!'

'Or a handbraker!' says another.

The third puts his hands up as if on a motorbike and twists one while making a revving sound. Fran smiles at them and thinks that the lad doing the motorbike is a bloody idiot. He watches as they walk away laughing.

'When the end comes, who'll be laughing then, yiz little fucks?' he says quietly, and laughs while going back to looking around the inside of the cab.

'Fran?!' Rita calls, then she walks into sight and comes closer while looking up at him. 'I should've known! So… what do ye think of it?'

'She's a lovely bit of kit!'

'She… IT… had to be brought down tonight because those two lads will be driving here to get started early.'

He keeps checking the inside and doesn't bother saying anything.

'Fran?'

He looks down at her. 'Yes, love?'

'Are ye gonna come in before they go? They're going to a fiftieth tonight.'

'Sorry, sorry,' he says, getting up.

'Don't fall off that! Ye be careful.'

He gets down and they go into the house. When they enter the kitchen, John is at the sink rinsing his cup.

'Jasus, I needed that!' he says, placing it on the side. 'Right, me flower. Let's get moving and get cleaned up and off to this do.'

Sophie takes a sup from hers and stands up. 'Right, Re, see you Sunday.'

'Oh shite! I'm on with that poxbottle tomorrow, I forgot.'

'Well, when you're slaving away, I'll be sleeping off a hangover.'

'That's what you think!' John says, with an exaggerated wink.

'Come on before you make a show of me.'

Rita and Fran follow them out. They say their goodbyes and watch as Sophie's car drives up the road and out of sight.

She looks at him. 'Did ye have any food?'

'Honestly love, I couldn't eat, I'm that nervous.'

'Do ye want one of your tabs to calm ye?'

'Two.'

'Well, ye know them lads will be here early?'

'I'll be up, love, I will!'

'And look after them with tea, coffee and food. Even though Sophie said that Fariq, now he's the Muslim fella, well he brings his own food. But she says that he really likes his tea, so make him plenty, won't ye?'

'It'll be like he's back in Iraq!' he says, smiling.

Rita's face goes white.

'What's wrong, love?'

Seconds pass before she regains enough composure to speak.

'Fran... he's not from Iraq! He's from England, but of Iranian descent. Whatever ye do, don't mention Iraq, ok?!'

'Ok, not mention Iraq.'

'In fact, don't mention anything outside of Ireland!'

'Got ya, love.'

She puts her hand over her eyes, and is thinking strongly about making up an excuse to tell the boss why she can't make it in, then she spots Pauli and Matt. She looks up at the sky with her hands clasped. 'Thank ye, lord!'

While Fran is looking at her confused, Pauli and Matt stop and stare.

'Pauli, come here!' she shouts.

They look at each other.

'O'Neill... I am glad that we didn't take that lift from the girls. Because you my friend, would be given an arctic cold shoulder.'

O'Neill has become Pauli's new name, thanks to Lucy's frequent use of it. But at this moment, his a.k.a is the last thing he is thinking of.

'Fran... he doesn't look well,' she walks a few steps. 'Pauli, come here, son!'

Eventually, with a nudge from Matt, he starts walking towards the house again, but both of their eyes are fixed on the JCB. They enter the garden and stop. Pauli looks in their direction but not at a particular face. He clears his throat.

'Matt's here for...' he trails off while pointing at Matt and looks back at it.

'What O'Neill means... what Pauli means is that..., I don't know.'

'Get in and I'll make yous something to eat,' Rita says, moving to let them pass. Once they are in, she stands back beside Fran. 'I think it's made an impression. Shite! I hope them workers don't start too early, ye know the way workers are. I don't want the Garda at the door, Fran.'

He looks back at her. 'Don't worry... I won't mention Iraq.'

CHAPTER SIXTY-ONE

Fran is sitting in his chair at 05:56, watching the sports news. He has been up since 04:38, which is about the norm for him. He thought that he would not have been able to sleep at all. Between the lads coming, the JCB, the container, and everything else running through his mind the previous day, but he did. It is business as usual, except he has a cup of tea in his hand instead of a can of beer. It is actually his second, as he had his first one standing in the garden admiring the black and yellow beauty.

He hears Rita's alarm go off at seven, and goes out to the kitchen and preps a cup for her and puts the kettle on. He thought that she would have taken longer, but seconds after the toilet flushed, he could hear her socked feet padding down the stairs. Her sleepy head enters the kitchen and she smiles at him as she walks to the table and sits down. 'I'm knackered!'

He puts a cup in front of her. 'There's a brew for ya, love.'

'Thanks,' she takes a sup. 'You're up, fair play.'

'Do ya want toast or biscuits?'

'Shite!' she runs to the fridge, takes out a leg of lamb and puts it on a large tray, then into the oven. She sets the timer and turns to face him. 'Fran, now I want ye to listen really carefully. That's on for two hours and when ye hear a BING! Do ye see this knob? Turn it all the way to the right, and two hours later ye will hear another BING! Don't touch the other knobs and don't open the door, ok?'

'Lamb?'

'Fran, listen to me. When ye hear the BING!' she repeats the instructions to him two more times. 'Matt will be here around nine so let him in. Our boys can feed themselves, but look after the workers with biscuits, crisps, bars, ye know the story. Then just go back into the room, and sit and watch telly or listen to your station. Matt will wake Pauli, but ye don't touch anything, and DON'T..'

'Mention Iraq… I know, I'm not thick!'

She goes back upstairs, showers and reappears just before eight. She crept down the stairs, just to see if she could beat his hearing and she did. Only as she was filling the kettle, did she hear "Love?!" She smirked and whispered, "Got ye!"

'Do ye want a can?!'

'No love. I'm gonna give a hand so no drinkin' till later!'

Her shocked face looks at the kitchen door. She does her tea and goes into the room and stops in front of him. 'Did I hear that right, you're not drinking?!'

'Yes love. I'm gonna help out so I'm on the tea.'

'No YE are not! Have ye forgotten the months ye spent in hospital and the way ye were when ye got out?! And what they said about lifting anything heavy and what could happen?! Them fellas know their stuff, they'll be grand! Now, do ye want a can while I'm standing?'

'I'll have one in a bit.'

She walks the few feet to the couch, then backtracks and stares out the window. After a bit of squinting and moving her head around a bit, she looks at him. 'Fran, there's a car parked outside our garden and there's a fella sitting in it.'

'Could be a taxi?'

'No sign.'

'Hackney?'

'Fran, he's staring at the feckin' tractor!'

He gets up and looks out. 'I think that's the Muslim lad.'

She looks at Fran. 'And how do ye know that?'

'Well... he does have that look to him,' he faces her. 'And he doesn't look Irish.' She sits down and starts nibbling on a fingernail. A nervous tell-tale sign which he has seen many times and knows all too well.

'Will I go out and ask if he's...?'

'If he's what?! Are ye that Muslim bloke that's here to dig up our garden?'

He pulls back his shoulders, sticks his chest out and turns his neck to the right, which gives a little click, while looking at her. 'No! Ask is he Fariq... and if he is, bring him in and offer him some tea!'

Her face drops and she puts her hand over her mouth and nods. He turns and leaves the room. She hears the locks coming off the front door and watches through the window as he approaches the car. The fella looks at him and lowers the window. They talk and then Fran turns as the window rises and comes back towards the house. He comes into the sitting room and looks at her. 'It's him!'

'So why…?' she sees movement out of the corner of her eye and looks out the window. Fariq shuts his door and walks towards the house carrying a bag.

Fran turns and faces the door as Fariq stops. 'Come in.'

'Thank you.'

'So, do ya want some tea?'

'Yes please, that would be nice,' he replies, in a Dublin accent.

Rita appears at the doorway beside Fran. 'This is my wife, Rita.'

'Good morning, Mrs O'Neill,' he looks back at Fran.

'Ok, let's do that tea. After you, straight ahead.'

When Fariq passes him, Fran looks at Rita and mimes, Dublin?

'Wife?' she whispers.

He pulls a face and walks into the kitchen. She hears the kettle and decides to have a cup of tea, forgetting about the one she just walked in with. When she enters the kitchen, Fran looks at her and does his double wink.

Oh no! He's up to something. Fran, please don't mention Iraq.

'Fariq,' he looks at Fran. 'As salaam alaikum.'

She looks from Fran to Fariq, who seems a little surprised.

'Wa alaikum salaam.' Fariq says, with a smile.

'Our teabags are in that middle one.' Fran points at three jars on the worktop.

'I brought my own, thanks.'

'Right well... help yourself.'

'Thank you,' he sniffs and looks at the oven. 'Lamb?'

'Yes,' Rita says, before Fran can say anything. 'For your lunch. It's halal!'

He arches an eyebrow. 'Really?'

She nods and then leaves the kitchen and goes upstairs. After something hits the floor and a curse, she comes back down, enters the kitchen and with a shaking hand, holds out a receipt to him.

He looks at it for a moment, then back at her. 'Mrs O'Neill, thank you for the proof, but there was really no need. And there is no need for your hand to shake. I am a Muslim, nothing else.'

She feels like crap and her face shows it.

'Thank you both, it's very thoughtful,' he says, looking from one to the other. He goes to the table and places his bag on it and removes a smaller bag and a cloth wrapped glass.

'Fariq, we're next door so if ya want to come in, you're welcome,' Fran says, and turns, but Rita turns quicker and walks out in front of him. He stops and looks back. 'Treat this as your own,' he continues into the room.

Fariq looks at the lamb for seconds before he begins making his tea.

To say things are awkward next door would be an apt description. Rita stuck her chin in and muddied the waters and she knows it.

'I'm sorry,' she whispers.

He winks. 'Not a bother, love.' Fariq stays in the kitchen with his tea. Minutes later, they hear a ringtone that they don't know, and both squint while trying to listen to what is being said.

'Right!'

They look at each other.

'Yeah, I'm in the kitchen. They brought me in and I made some tea… I was waiting in the car… you're outside? Hold on.'

Fran goes to the front door and opens it, to see a bloke locking up his car across the road. 'You're Fariq's mate?'

'I am!' he says, entering the garden.

'He's in the kitchen. Go in and help yourself to tea, coffee, toast... and there's biscuits in the press above the microwave.'

He stops and holds out his hand and they shake. 'Good morning, Mister O'Neill. I'm Jack, and thanks for the hospitality. We'll get it done, don't worry.'

CHAPTER SIXTY-TWO

When he comes back into the sitting room, Rita sits forward on the couch.

'What was that ye said to him?' she whispers.

'As salaam alaikum. It means…,' he puts his hand to his chin. 'Eh…?'

'Ye mean ye said something to him and ye don't even know what it means?'

'Look, when Em found out that one of the lads doin' the back was a Muslim, she said that I should greet him in Arabic.'

'So… what does it mean then?' she asks, still whispering.

'I think she said it means… peace be with you, or… Allah be with you, somethin' like that. But it's alright, love. I said it the proper way because she told me that he would say it the other way round, and he did.'

A bang comes from upstairs.

'Well, there's one we don't have to worry about being woke up.'

'Ya little shit!'

'Two.' Fran corrects.

'Oh shite! The bleedin' cat's in the bush!' she says, getting up.

'Hold your horses there, love. They're gone.'

She sits back down. 'Gone? Gone where?'

'The ma cat, and Em was right, she is a biggy. She took them one by one and put them in the shed.'

'What? She just walked up to the shed with a kitten in her mouth, opened the lock, then the door, and walked in?! Oh, and I suppose then she walked into the kitchen, on her back legs, and threw a pizza in the oven, and sat there with one of me bottles waiting for it to cook? She should've threw on a wash for me.'

'Re, ya know the way the glass is broke in the window?'

'Ye mean she jumped through that window with a baby kitten in her mouth?!'

'That she did... a baby kitten.'

'The tramp! She could've hurt them.'

'Well, she didn't. I checked a while later.'

She breathes a sigh of relief. 'Well, at least that's one less thing to worry about.' A few minutes pass before they hear the backdoor open and close.

'They must be gettin' started.'

She points her thumb towards the window. 'Fran, the tractor's out the front.'

They hear Pauli's phone ring and him talking.

Fran winks. 'Must be his moth.'

'It's great, isn't it? He has a girlfriend and he said that she's gorgeous! Oh, I'm delighted for him.'

439

'What about Matt?'

'I'm delighted for him, too, but he's had a few. This is Pauli's first real girlfriend. I can't wait to see her.'

Pauli comes down the stairs a few minutes later and stumbles through the door. 'Morning, folks!'

'Ye seem very happy.' Rita says, smiling.

'I am.'

'Did your moth wake ya?' Fran asks.

'Nah, she'll be out cold. That was Matt. He'll be around in about an hour.'

'He rings ya and wakes ya up to tell ya that he'll be around in an hour?'

He yawns. 'I text him first to see if he was awake.'

'Yous pair are mad!'

'Excuse me!' Rita says, and Fran looks at her. 'There's a big tractor in our front garden, and it's goin' to dig a feckin' big hole in our back one. To put a shipping container in it, and then cover it up as if there's nothing there. And ye say that they're mad?!'

He concedes defeat. 'Point made, and very well made, if I do say so meself.'

'Thank ye!'

'You're welcome,' he counts to three. 'Re… are ya in work today?'

'Aggh!' she screams, and looks at her wrist. 'What time is it?!'

'Ten to nine.'

She runs out the door and up the stairs, says something to the Ems, then runs down the stairs, back into the room, grabs her bag, phone and keys and gives Fran a peck while passing him. 'Don't go near the lamb!' she turns. 'Bye, love, don't let him near it,' and runs to the front door. 'Bye!' she yells and slams it.

The two are looking out at her when the JCB starts and she jumps and drops her bag. She sees them laughing and points her finger and shakes it, then gets into the car, reverses out and wheelspins away. Fran gets up and goes out front but the JCB's in the back garden now, and he knows that he is going to get it in the neck when she gets home. The wheels have destroyed the front garden and are quickly doing the same to the back. He watches as it reverses to about ten feet from the shed, then notices white spray paint on the grass. They marked it out and removed the pillar before they even started it up, and they were only out here a few minutes. These boys know their stuff.

'Eh... Dad?' Pauli says, from behind.

'Yes lad?' he looks around to see people standing at their doors and looking out their windows, staring over at them from the houses across the road. 'Mornin'!' he calls, then takes a deep breath and enters the house.

Em and Emmet are in the kitchen now and he is mesmerised by the big yellow noisy thing. Em is holding a spoon to his open mouth but nothing is happening. 'Come on, menace! If ya eat up, we'll get ready and go to the zoo.'

'Zoo? Nice one. Haven't been there for a while.' Pauli says, with his back to her, waiting for the toast to pop up.

'Why don't you and Lucy go?'

'We probably will,' he says, without turning.

'Ma told me that ya said that she's a nice lookin' bird.'

441

He turns. 'I never said that. I said that she's beautiful!'

Em smiles. 'I know, but I didn't hear ya say it, thanks brother,' she looks back at Emmet. 'Did ya hear that, Popeye? She's beautiful. Now come on and eat.'

Pauli goes to say something but wonders what, so turns back and looks at the toaster as Fran walks in.

'The natives didn't look too happy, did they?'

'Da, Saturday morning, ya know? A lie in like what normal people do.'

He looks at her. 'A lie in for what?! No one works in this estate. Well, at least they're not supposed to work.'

The toast pops up. 'And about flippin' time! That toast was really annoying me.'

Fran walks to the backdoor. 'Ah no, I can't have this!' he opens it and goes out. As he is walking up the garden, Fariq is pushing an empty wheelbarrow to the mound of earth already excavated. 'Ya can't do all that yourself, lad. I'll help ya.'

'We only brought one wheelbarrow in the bucket.'

'Have one in the shed,' he winks, and walks towards it.

Pauli meanders over to the window for a nosey while chewing on some toast.

'What's he up to now?' Em asks, while still holding the same spoon of food at Emmet's mouth.

'He just took that old wheelbarrow out of the shed.'

He watches as Fariq passes Fran on his way to the end of the garden with a full load. Fran stops at the mound and starts filling his one. Once it is full, he pushes it over to the corner where the fence was removed. Pauli stuffs the remaining toast in his mouth and runs to the worktop. He gives the other slices the once over with some butter, takes two slices of cheese out and slaps them down on a slice, then plants the other slice on top. He looks around and picks up the kettle, throws the remaining water in it towards the sink, then starts banging it down on the toast while splashes are going all over the place. Emma looks around at him and just then, Emmet leans forward and puts his mouth around the spoon. 'What the fuck are ya doin'?!'

He doesn't answer. When he stops, he checks how flat the sandwich is and starts eating like a savage while slurping tea.

'Did your Lucy see this side of ya?'

He tries to say that he doesn't have time to explain, but with a good bite of a cheese toasty and some tea in his mouth, English it doesn't resemble. Nor does it look too good, as tea dribbles from his mouth when he tries to speak.

Em continues to watch in disbelief, this contorted mess called her brother, as he tries to talk, drink, eat, chew and swallow at the same time. When he finishes, he looks like he just sprinted a few hundred metres, as he stands there breathing heavily with a worryingly red face.

'What the fuck was that all about?! Are ya tryin' to choke yourself to death?!'

'Da's out there working! Too much weight on the back and it's gone, remember?'

'Oh shit! Why didn't ya just say that?'

'I did! Tell Matt to follow me out when he gets here,' he says, closing the door.

She turns back to Emmet, who is sitting there with the spoon still in his mouth.

'Emmet, let go!'

'Hmmmm,' he says, as his gums stay locked around it.

CHAPTER SIXTY-THREE

'Dad! What are ya doing?!'

'Well, I'm not just gonna sit on me arse and let Fariq move all that on his own. Ten men can move a mountain… or somethin' like that.'

'Let me have a go, Dad.'

'Ya can have a go in a while, son. Go have your breakfast.'

Pauli grabs his arm. 'Remember what those docs said about your back? Too much weight, and it could be a wheelchair for life.'

'They were a pack of quacks! I'm rearin' to go.'

Pauli thinks quickly. 'How many is this one?'

Fran picks up the shovel and looks at him. 'Three.'

'Ok. Five each, then swap?'

Fran thinks it over. 'Ok,' he turns and starts filling the barrow. 'Five then.'

Matt comes out a while later and Pauli pushes the barrow past him.

'Roped in, were ya?'

Pauli empties it and on the return journey, fills Matt in while Fran is in going to the toilet.

'With ya, pal,' he says, taking off his jacket. He drapes it over a patio chair. 'Ok, I'll have a go after this one.'

'Wait till he comes back out and then you take it. Phase him out and all that.'

'Rogeroo.'

Pauli gets back to the mound and Fariq hands him the shovel, then turns and wheels his barrow away. When Fran returned, he was impressed when he saw how well Matt and Pauli worked together. With the wheeling from one while the other filled, then they would swap after the fifth load. He had gone in to use the toilet, and with what Pauli had said in the garden and then Em starting in the kitchen, he knew that they were right and it would not be worth the risk. Plus, if Rita found out, she would swing for him. He decided that the best place for him to be was out of the way. So he grabbed a can, went to the sitting room and sat listening to his beloved forces radio station.

Em eventually got Emmet ready for the trip to the zoo, and just after ten thirty, Mikey, Jessie, and Jade arrived with their kids. They were brought into the kitchen and while they made their coffees, she went into Fran with Emmet.

'Are ya off, love?'

'We're leaving in a few. But I thought... well, Fariq will be gettin' ready to pray in about an hour and a half so...'

'How do ya know?' he interrupts.

She walks over, picks up the remote control and changes the channel.

'It's the Islam channel. Now he would've done Fajr Adhaan before dawn this morning, and the next prayer is Zuhr Adhaan just after twelve. So he'll probably start his ablutions about ten or fifteen minutes before.'

Fran is staring at her perplexed.

She scrolls through and highlights, Call to Prayer, and the penny drops.

'That's the second one,' she switches Emmet onto her other arm, scrolls again and stops at Asr Adhann after three. 'That's the third one. What time are they finished at?'

'I don't rightly know.'

She begins scrolling again. 'Well, the fourth prayer is Maghrib Adhaan and that's just after six.'

'How do ya know all this, love?'

Just then, there is a tap on the door and she looks to find Jade there.

'Sorry to interrupt, but we have a situation,' she nods towards the kitchen.

'Go ahead.'

'Copy!' Jade says, and walks away.

Fran looks back at Em. 'What situation?'

'Dirty nappy, so she's bringing Mina up to my room to change her.'

'Ohh,' he narrows his eyes, his trademark trying to remember technique, as he has forgotten what he asked her.

'Look, Da, while you're doin' that, I'm gonna put mutton chops in his buggy. Say goodbye to Grandad!'

Emmet looks at Fran and there is nothing.

447

'Emmet, say byee!'

'Gnnng!'

'Bye, son.'

She leaves and returns about two minutes later. 'So, did ya remember?'

'I did. How do ya know all this?'

'Da, ya know the stuff I'm into, and sometimes they're the storyline. That's how I learned the greeting and a few other words. Then I found the Islam channel ages ago, and one thing leads to another.'

'So, do ya know much Muslim?'

'It's Arabic, Da!' she thinks. 'Nah, about fourtyish... maybe fifty words.'

Fran has an idea. He gets her to write down the times of the prayers and some words and their meanings. She explains that about ten or fifteen minutes before he prays, he will wash his hands, arms, face and feet.

'Before every prayer?'

'Every prayer, Da.'

'Why?'

'To be clean before his god, Allah.'

'So how will he do that?'

'Well, Da... I was thinkin' that before Zuhr Adh... midday prayer, that maybe ya could go out about twelve and offer him the bathroom to use.'

His eyes widen. 'That's a great idea, Em!'

'Here's a better one...' she purposely does not continue.

448

He sits looking at her for seconds. 'Well… what is it?'

'As I've shown ya, the prayers are on telly.'

Clink! Another penny drops.

'Ya mean, bring him in here when the prayers are on so he can pray with them?'

'Dad, you're a genius! Plus… he'll have some privacy.'

'No my girl, you're the genius!' he stands and hugs her.

She comes back in just before they leave. 'So, you're straight with everything?'

He reads off the times of the prayers and the times for Fariq to get ready.

'Well that's it, I'm outta here!' she kisses his forehead and then the four mothers and four buggies leave for their day out at the zoo.

CHAPTER SIXTY-FOUR

A few minutes before noon, and Fran is clock watching to make sure he times it right, he goes out back and walks up to the ever increasing pile of earth around the JCB. As he passes Pauli and Matt, he gives them each a pat on the shoulder, then wipes his hand on his tracksuit bottoms. He nods his head while thinking, bejasus, them lads are sweatin' like a couple of pigs.

Fariq has just emptied another barrow load and is walking towards him. They stop, and after a brief chat, Fariq whistles and gives a hand signal to Jack, then walks down the garden and out through the gap where the fence used to be. The machine falls silent and Jack climbs down from the cab and follows in the same direction. Fran walks over to Matt and Pauli.

'Dad, what did ya say to him?!' Pauli asks, sweat dripping off his face.

Fran recounts what Em told him and a wave of relief come over the two.

'Jesus, Fran, we thought ya sacked him!'

'No Matt, just givin' the lad a bit of privacy.'

'Dad, I'm impressed.'

'Me, too.' Matt adds.

When Fariq and Jack reappear through the gap, both are carrying bags, but Fariq has a mat under his arm. Jack walks a few feet onto the grass and sits down, and Fariq stops at the kitchen door.

'Aywah Inshaa'allah!' Fran says, with his arm outstretched towards the door while reading the words on his hand.

Fariq nods, smiles and enters the house.

'You speak Arabic, Fran?' Jack asks, opening a flask and pouring into a cup lid.

'No, me daughter told me a couple of words this morning,' he walks closer and starts sniffing while staring down at the cup. 'Is that a beef drink?'

'You want? Get a cup. My beef drink, is your beef drink. Inshaa'allah.'

The two grin and Fran heads for the kitchen.

Matt turns to Pauli. 'I think older men are mad,' he whispers.

'We're not mad, son,' Jack says, looking up at one, then the other. 'Maybe a little eccentric, but not mad,' he takes a sup.

Fran comes out with a cup and sits on the grass beside Jack, who fills it and the two start chatting.

'Do yous want tea?'

Fran looks around at Pauli. 'We're grand, son. But listen, if you or Matt want a slash or… well, go behind the shed because the bathroom is in use.'

'I didn't actually want a piss, but… now that ya mention it.' Matt says, and walks towards the shed.

Fran and Jack are talking about the Premiership and Pauli is standing there feeling like a spare part, so he heads to the kitchen.

On entering, he smells the lamb. 'Oh shit!' he runs to the cooker and checks it. He doesn't know how, but it looks alright and it smells beautiful. He picks off a bit to taste. 'Oh yumster!' he takes another piece, then goes to the kettle, puts it on and just as he takes out two cups, Matt enters. 'I thought you needed a wee?'

'So did I, but I don't. It must've been the power of persuasion or suggestion or something like that. Your da should've been one of those psychic dudes.'

What Matt has just said has gone straight through Pauli's ears and back out. All he is thinking about is Lucy, and wonders what she is doing this very second. He cannot wait to see her on Monday. The lamb comes in second. When the tea is made, they go back out and stand looking down at the older two.

'Lads, now lads, yous are making me feel uncomfortable,' Jack says, looking up at them. 'Sit down and give gravity less work to do.'

They look at each other and comply. They soon get involved in the discussion about the Premiership, and who may win and who might get relegated. Not too long after, Fariq comes out with a bag and sits between Matt and Jack.

'Thanks, Fran.'

'You're welcome,' he gets up. 'Right, I'll be back in a minute.'

Nearly four minutes later, he walks out with a tray and places it on the grass in the middle of their circle. On it are slices of lamb, slices of hard cheese, buttered sliced loaf and a bowl of Rita's most recently acquired coleslaw.

Fariq joins his hands across his chest. 'Ohh, Mister O'Neill, you are spoiling us!' Nobody expected that and they laugh. Then Jack takes a prepacked shop bought sandwich, in a hard triangular plastic wrapper, from his bag and holds it up.

'What will I do with this now?'

As Matt begins to reach for it, Pauli looks at him and he stops.

Fariq points at a group of starlings on the fence. 'Give it to those birds because they look hungry.'

He takes it from the plastic container and tosses it onto the grass beneath them. Fariq then takes a square plastic ice cream container, with raspberry ripple wrote on it, from his bag and opens it. 'Feel free.' Matt and Pauli simultaneously move forward and stare down at what looks like liquidised porridge, but a few days old. Jack is straight in with some sliced loaf, followed by Fran. Fariq takes out a large packet of pittas, a dozen eggs in a box, and another smaller plastic container which has quartered raw onions inside. Jack is first in again and starts tapping his egg against the side of the tray. Matt and Pauli glance at each other and grin. But no... the egg does not splatter. Instead, it cracks and Jack peels it. Fariq is next, then Fran.

'They're not raw?' Matt asks.

Fariq looks him in the eye for some seconds and his face is expressionless. 'I am a Muslim... not the KGB.'

Matt stares back and is on the point of apologising, when he notices Jack's face trying to hold back a smile, then Fariq laughs loudly. The rest follow and Matt joins in with relief. While he is laughing at what he does not think is all that funny a sentence, he decides that he will use it anyway when they go back to college, and maybe get a few laughs. Then he remembers that he isn't a Muslim.

Fariq explains that the substance in the ice cream container is hummus and Matt and Pauli snigger at the name. When they are finished, he proceeds to show how it should be eaten in order to get the "ultimate hummus experience."

He rips some pitta, scoops up some hummus and adds some quartered egg and onion and eats. Fran brought out five forks and a spoon for the coleslaw but it is left untouched. Only one fork was used to quarter each of their eggs.

This is a new experience for Matt and Pauli. The two picking at this and that with their hands while sitting in the baking sun, chatting with three older men.

One, which both, unknowing to the other, are planning to try out with the girls. Without the older men, of course. And barbecues don't count. But would the girls even like this hummus stuff? And if they were to take out some hard boiled eggs and raw onions, would the girls run for the hills? Pauli knows that Matt has enough problems with his insides already, and it could probably be this that will leave him sleeping outdoors after Becka's warning. He will wait and see if it has an adverse effect on him first before going any further with the idea.

Matt is wondering how far Becka could drag him by his ankles?

They learn from Fariq, that he was born in Birmingham. His mother was Iranian and his dad was Irish. He was fourteen when the three moved to Ireland.

Sean, his dad, had never been too concerned in which direction Fariq's religious beliefs went, and had never even mentioned baptism when he was born. So his mother, Nuriyah, brought him up in the way of Islam. Sean had tried to learn him some Irish to balance out the Arabic, but this resulted in three words that were used regularly in the home and in no way Gaelic. Fuck, shite and bollox.

He had been diagnosed with bowel cancer in England, and that was when he decided that they would move to Ireland. They rented a house near his parents in Nobber, County Meath, and fourteen months later, he died.

Nuriyah planned to stay there with Fariq, but Sean's mother, Maire, was a very difficult women. On a night out in the local GAA club, months before he died, she found out that Fariq had never been baptised and was a Muslim.

With her going to mass twice a day, and then raising the volume on the radio to maximum, for the Angelus at midday and at six every evening, this was hard for her to keep bottled up without saying anything, so she didn't. When it started, it was "Would ye not get the little lad christened? Sean was, and it done him the world of good" and other such statements. But Nuriyah could not understand this, as Sean had been a complete bastard. He drank as if his life depended on it, and what he gave her for food and the keep of the house, he may well have gave her nothing. Twenty-five pounds a week cannot feed a family of three, pay bills, rent, provide clothes and other bits and pieces in between. The television was an intermittent luxury as was the electricity and heat. Any clothes washing had to be done in the bath, which made her hands nearly raw from wringing them.

In the winter, she brought Fariq between friends who were still talking to her, while their husbands were at work, and there they would get heat and food.

On the days when she could not visit them, there was always the library. Pick a book, sit down and no one bothers you. You may not have food but at least you are warm for a few hours.

Then it came back to the fact that Sean was now dead. In fourteen years, he had never once mentioned anything concerning religion, and never asked about when her and Fariq would go to the Mosque or when Fariq would pray at home. She is pretty sure that he never even knew about Ramadan, or noticed them not eating until night came. But with him being in the pub, how could he notice?

She didn't budge on the baptism thing. And after no movement, Maire's actions became more aggressive, and she began coming to the house with six or seven of her old women friends every day. The topic of conversation was always about Fariq's religion. He would have to change to Catholicism to be accepted in school and for later life, concerning employment. Nuriyah knew that their argument was a weak one and their reasons were only for themselves.

One person against that many, especially in one's own home and on a daily basis, is not a pleasant experience and is one that she decided that she could not put up with anymore. So after a six-minute phonecall to her cousin in Dublin, a plan was put into action. Within two days, Nuriyah and Fariq were cruising to Dublin on board a Bus Eireann coach. They arrived at Bus Aras and were met by her cousin Asimah and her husband Aajan. The four walked to Rialto in the rain, stopping on the way to pick up the ingredients for the evening meal before going to Asimah's house. It was there that Fariq met his two long lost cousins, roommates and best friends. The witch in Nobber was mentioned occasionally, but was referred to as "Majda" and never seen again.

It was Jack who mentioned that there was work to be done, so they broke up. As he was picking up the shovel, he called to Fran who was walking to the house with Fariq beside him, both bringing the food back into the kitchen.

'You know we do a second lunch?!'

'I know, threeish!'

At five to three, Fran comes out and gets Fariq's attention. The machine is knocked off as Fran strolls up to it, and only then does he realise how much progress has been made. Fariq goes into the house.

'Well, how about tea or coffee until he comes back?'

'Dad, are you mad?! I'm going to sit in the fridge!' Pauli says, walking away.

'Me, too!' Matt walks a few steps and stops. 'Well... not really,' he stands looking around at the sky for seconds before following Pauli inside.

Minutes later, they come out with a bottle of cola each for themselves and tea for the seniors. After sitting back in their previous positions, the conversation starts up again. But this time the topic is the Champions League and then to the soon oncoming food. Matt and Pauli have agreed that the hummus stuff is quite nice, once you get past the sight of it. Jack tells them that he won't eat without Fariq being there. So even if he is starving, he will hold on until the prayers are finished. The smell of the lamb has the boys looking at each other. It is only a few hours since they have eaten and they were full to the brim, but now they are starving again.

Matt keeps glancing at the door, and wills Fariq to appear at any moment so as they can start on the food. While Pauli's belly is also waiting to be fed, his mind is miles away up north, and he is thinking about Lucy and her sweet little butt. When Fariq does come out, he has his tubs of food with him and the lads find themselves licking their lips. Fran's up, in and back out in seconds with the tray, but this time there is no coleslaw to be seen. While they are eating, Fariq tells a joke about Paddy Englishman, Paddy

Irishman and Paddy Muslimman, and this makes it difficult for them to eat while laughing.

They start back working minutes after four and end up calling it a day just under two hours later before Maghrib Athann. While Fariq is in the sitting room, they have a cup of tea in the back garden. When the two leave, Fran, Matt and Pauli go back up and stand at the edge of the pit and look into it again.

'I'm no expert on construction or excavation, but I think this will definitely be done by tomorrow evening.'

'Matty, I think you're right.'

Fran nods his head in agreement.

'Well, I'm gonna have a shower.'

'And I'm gonna split to me gaff and have one, too.'

'I'll drop around in about an hour,' Pauli says, walking away with Matt.

'Pauli, come 'ere.'

When he walks back, Fran holds out twenty euro. 'It's not much, but yous lads worked hard today, and with it being Saturday well, that's to get a box of beer.'

Pauli smiles and nearly takes Fran's hand from his wrist while taking the money. 'Thanks Dad!'

'Yeah Fran, fair play!' Matt adds.

The two turn and walk away and they have perked right up. Fran can hear them talking excitedly as they near the house. 'Ok, now here's a change of plan. I'll be in yours in half an hour, then we'll hit the supermarket and decide what to get.'

'I don't give a fuck once it has alcohol in it! AND I'll have the console nicely ticking over for when we get back.'

'Ohh, I forgot! We're almost at the queen alien's lair. Now we have to get that ugly mother tonight, deal?'

'And get her good, deal!' Matt agrees, as their voices get fainter.

Fran smiles but then he hears the front door bang. 'Shit, she's home.'

'Pauli, let me go first, I need a wee!'

'Ma, don't bleedin' broadcast it to the whole road!'

Minutes later, she walks into the kitchen, grabs a bottle from the fridge and stands at the back door. 'Fran!' she yells, and looks around the garden but there is no sight of him and no reply. 'Fran... I know that you're out there somewhere, I can smell ye. Show yourself!'

He slowly raises his head from the pit. 'Oh... hello love, you're home?!'

CHAPTER SIXTY-FIVE

Rita is opening up today so she left at ten to seven. Fran was just about to get a second can when he saw Jack pull up at 08:22.

Minutes later, Fariq knocks and is brought into the kitchen to find Jack sitting at the table, just after finishing a fry and he is on his second cup of tea.

'As salaam alaikum,' he says, lifting his cup.

'Wa alaikum salaam.'

They go on to talk in Arabic for nearly a minute. Fran is left looking between the two. When they seem as if they are finished, he goes with what he knows.

'As salaam alaikum.'

'Wa alaikum salaam.' Fariq says.

'Sorry, Fran. I just said hello, how are you? And Fariq said the same, and we had a little chat. We do this every morning as I'm trying to learn Arabic.'

'Oh good on ya then! Sounds like you're getting there.'

'Trying.' Jack says, and takes another sup of tea.

Fran looks at Fariq. 'Fancy a bit of breakfast?'

Fariq raises his nose slightly and sniffs while moving his head slowly from side to side. He stares at the rasher rinds on Jack's plate and narrows his eyes.

'There is a smell of law enforcement in this kitchen.'

The two laugh.

Fran nods towards the kettle. 'Help yourself, Fariq.'

He puts his bag on a chair and takes out his glass and places it on the table. He then takes out a rectangular shaped item wrapped in cloth, kisses it, and places it gently on the table beside the glass. He searches the bag before removing a pouch and holds it up with a sigh of relief. 'Tea!'

'Dozed off after Fajr Adhaan, eh Far?'

'A hard day's work and all that,' he says, with a grin and picks up the glass and makes his tea. Then he sits facing Jack and takes a sup.

Bang!

The three look at the ceiling.

'Ya little swine! No ya don't, come back... ya can't get away. I'll get ya... Aagh! Come outta there right now or I'll get the brush! Get out!'

Fariq and Jack look at Fran, who forces a smile.

'The grandson is awake,' he looks back at the ceiling. 'And so is his mother.'

'So that bang was the little fella falling out of the bed?' Jack asks. Fran nods.

'Does that happen often? I mean, that was some impact.'

Fran exhales. 'Most mornings. He's... the alarm clock. Actually, he doesn't quite fall out of a bed...'

Fariq and Jack look at each other, then back at Fran, and by his face, they know that this is going to be good.

'He sort of... launches himself out of his cot in the direction of the floor.'

'So this happens every morning? Your grandson throws himself out of a cot and onto a floor?'

'Yeah Fariq pretty much.'

'I think he needs help. Would you not bring him to see a psychiatrist or somebody like that?'

Fran has just learned that Fariq says it as it is. There is no beating around the bush with this lad.

'Fran, what Fariq meant... he didn't.'

'But I did, Jack. That boy needs help before he damages himself.'

Jack looks up at the ceiling, then out the window.

'No, he's right, it's ok. He shouldn't be diving onto the floor, it's way too dangerous. We all agree about that. But he's a bit young for the other thing at the moment.'

'How long has he been doing this?' Fariq asks.

Fran puts his hand to his chin and thinks. 'About two months.'

'He could be hungry?' Jack suggests, looking back around.

'Probably.'

'How old is the boy?' Fariq asks.

'Eh... nine months, Tuesday week.'

They quickly look at each other, then back at Fran.

'So… this boy that's throwing… launching himself from his cot… is nine months old? And has been doing it for two months?!'

Fran nods again. 'Yeah,' he replies, in almost a whisper.

The door opens and Pauli walks in. 'Morning, Dad, Jack, salaam alaikum, Fariq.'

They return his greeting.

He gets some bread and puts it in the toaster and preps two cups for tea.

'Matt's gonna be here in a few minutes,' he goes to the fridge and takes out what is left of the fried food. 'How's everyone for breakfast?'

'All eaten, son.'

He divides the food onto two plates and puts one in the microwave. He covers it with a plate, then places the other plate of food on top and covers that as well. When the toast pops up, he removes it and puts more in. As he is buttering the first four, the doorbell rings.

'I've got it, son.'

He starts the microwave and seconds later, Matt walks in.

'Salaam alaikum,' he says, to Fariq, who replies, 'And a good mornin' to ya all. Hey P, food ready and all? You're on the ball today, boyo!'

While they are eating their breakfast, the door opens and Em walks in. 'Yaaargh!' she screams, and runs into the sitting room.

'That's the daughter,' Fran says, and follows her. When he goes into the room, she is on the couch shaking. 'What's wrong, Em?'

'Da, I didn't know there was anyone else in there. I thought it was just yous three. And look at me, I'm in me pyjamas! And they're me summer ones!'

'Em, relax! What do ya want?'

'Just two biscuits and a yogurt for Emmet.'

'Ok love, I'll get them. You wait here.'

He goes to the kitchen, gets what she wants and returns to the room.

'Thanks, Da. Jasus, I'm sick!'

'Don't be, ya were too fast, nobody seen ya.'

She walks out and creeps to the closed over kitchen door. 'Marhab! as salaam alaikum!' she says, and runs up the stairs.

'Shukran! wa alaikum salaam!' Fariq says, and takes a sip of tea. 'It's like living back in Rialto again.'

The four laugh and in the process, Matt spits some food onto the table. This only makes things worse. He eventually picks it up and sticks it in his mouth. He looks at Pauli. 'There are loads of hungry people yadda yadda yadda!'

Pauli shakes his head and looks at the other three who are chuckling.

'That happens a bit around here.' Fran says.

'Not just here,' Matt says, and Pauli kicks him. 'Ouch! What was that for?!' he asks, rubbing his shin.

'Oh, I'm sorry! I thought that was the leg of the table,' he says, with a pretend concerned look on his face. When the three start talking again, he leans closer and whispers. 'Don't say anything about what happened in the garage.'

'I wasn't going to! That really hurt, P.'

'Sorry, Matt.'

CHAPTER SIXTY-SIX

Fran watched from the kitchen window for a while once the work had started, then retired to his inner sanctum with a fresh can of beer. Em came back down once she heard the engine start, but she still checked with Fran that the coast was clear before going near the kitchen.

'All ya have to do is look out your window, love.'

'No way! My blind is stayin' shut!' she says, going out the door. She returns with Emmet's high chair and a bowl of cereal, then runs up and gets him.

'Any plans today, love?'

'Me and the girls are goin' over to Newbridge.'

'Your mam told me about last weekend.'

'Well, if she's there, she'll be blanked by us. It'll be a normal day with normal people and a picnic for the kids... and us as well, of course,' she adds, while looking at him. 'So, how did it go yesterday with the prayers and stuff?'

'Like clockwork. He was really thankful, especially about the live prayers. He said that he does that at home, so it made him feel... at home. Even the boys are greetin' him in Arabic. They felt left out so they annoyed me to teach them that bit. I tell ya, him and Jack have wicked sense of humours.'

'Well, at least it went ok,' she places a spoonful of cereal into Emmet's mouth.

'Yeah Em, and all because of you. We wouldn't have had a clue about anything, ya done good, me girl.'

'Thanks Da. I just didn't want yous to make a show of yourselves, or the house.'

'Now that, we would have excelled at.'

Just before noon, Fran changes from the radio to the Islam channel and goes to the kitchen. He opens the oven door and stares at the leg of lamb. He is pretty sure that there wasn't this much left on it after putting it away, even after his sly sandwich last night when they were all in bed. There had been a fair bit on the leg, but then again, it was a bleeding big leg.

'Ah well, there'll be loads for the two lunches,' he says, to himself as he takes it out and prepares to slice. It is seconds later when Fariq tips on the glass and opens the door slightly. 'Go ahead, Fariq. I'm just slicing up the last of our tasty little woolly friend's leg.'

Fariq chuckles, gets his bag and goes upstairs.

Fran sticks his head out the door. 'Jack, I was wonder—'

'Grab your cup. I brought a bigger flask, so there's loads.'

'Good on ya!'

He comes out with a cup and two 2 litre bottles of cola for the boys. When Fariq reappears, lunch gets underway. It is a similar affair to yesterday with football coming up again. Matt and Pauli are enjoying themselves with the humorous banter and the relaxed atmosphere. Then it was back to work.

After Asr Athaan, second lunch began when Fariq came out. Fran watched Matt and Pauli devour the food, and they even gave the hummus a good thrashing after getting Fariq's approval. When he brought the tray back inside, there were a few slices of bread left on a plate. He took the lamb from the oven and sliced off a bit. Even though he had just eaten with them, he wanted another sandwich. He gave it a good spread of mustard and brown sauce, took a cool can from the fridge and went into the sitting room. The channel was changed from Islam to the radio, and he was just in time for the daily competition which was just over ten minutes away from starting. He is determined to win another goody bag, but he really wants another T-shirt. He sent his answer by text and once his name, among other correct entries was mentioned over the air, he went back out and took a wander up the garden to see how things were progressing. The lads were flying, and he hadn't realised how flying they were until he got to the pit. Nine feet down is a long way down, especially when you are afraid of heights. Matt and Pauli had to escort him back inside.

He is still recovering while listening to the radio with another can, when his phone rings. He checks the caller I.D out of habit even though the only people that have his number are the family. 'Oh Crap!' he swallows before he answers. 'Hello love, things quiet, are they?'

'Dead as a doorknob, not a feckin' sinner. Did Em go to Newbridge?'

'Yeah, she went for the picnic.'

'Good! I hope that little dirtbird doesn't show her tramps head, because from what Em told me, Mikey was a pubic hair away from putting it through a tree.'

He looks around the room but says nothing.

'Fran?'

'Yes, love?'

'Are ye listening to me, or did ye hold the phone up in the air while watchin' the sports news again?'

'No, love, I'd never do that! And the radio's on.'

'Well now I know ye are talkin' complete shite! Because ye told me that ye done it one night when ye were locked drunk. Remember the night ye got into the bed and fell straight back out of it again?'

'No, I don't actually! So I can't say that I believe ya.'

Shite Fran, what are ya doin'? He wonders as he holds the phone out in front of him and stares at it.

Her voice changes tone. 'Fran, is everything alright back there?'

'Yes, love,' he holds the phone up in the air this time while he swallows before returning it to his ear. 'Love everything's perfect.'

'Perfect? What's that supposed to mean? Fran, I'll be back soon, what's wrong?'

'Nothin', Re. Everything's pretty pretty... pretty—'

'Pretty what?! Francis, O'Neill, I'm asking ye this minute what's wrong? And I don't want, everything's pretty pretty pretty pretty, because obviously it's not if ye keep using the same word in a sentence. Now tell me!'

He swallows hard.

'I heard that, what's wrong?'

He tries to compose himself.

'Fran?!'

'Love… remember yesterday when ya got home from work?'

'Of course I do, I was there! And?'

'Well, ya know the way I was sort of checkin' out the pit?'

'Ye mean hiding in it, ye wuss! Go on, keep talking.'

'Let's just say that it's changed a little bit.'

'How little?'

'Re I'll put it this way. When ya come home today, and if I got in it to hide from ya, well… I'd need a ladder to get out.'

'What? It's that deep?'

'Actually Re, I'd need a ladder to get in.'

A while later, he hears the JCB at the side of the house. 'Well… that's it,' he says, getting up and going out back. Jack is walking between Pauli and Matt, who is pushing the wheelbarrow which he insisted on doing.

'Matt, leave it out of sight. We've to come back in the morning for the digger and that goes in the bucket.'

Matt parks it neatly, a few feet from the backdoor, just as Fariq comes through the gap and stops beside them. 'Fran, can I go up?'

'Of course, go ahead.' He goes inside and Fran asks who fancies a cuppa. The three put up their hands and head into the kitchen. When Fariq returns, they go out back and all remain silent. There is an awkwardness between the five as they stand there.

Fran breaks the silence. 'So Jack, breakfast in the mornin' or will ya have time?'

He nods. 'I can do a breakfast, Fran. Yeah that will be nice.'

Fran looks at Fariq.

'Let's just say that I'll have a few teas.'

Fran smiles. 'The kettle is yours.'

'Shukran.'

'What does that mean?' Matt asks.

'Thank you.' Fran answers.

'Till tomorrow, lads.' Fariq says.

'Yeah, bright and early.' Jack adds, and the two turn and head towards the gap.

'Fariq!' Pauli shouts, and runs in the backdoor. When he comes out, he goes to him and gives him his bag.

The three watch them drive away and they don't feel all that great.

Fran is the first to speak. 'What time are you lads in tomorrow?'

'We're not going in.' Pauli answers.

'Damn straight!' Matt adds, crossing his arms.

'What? Why?'

'Because we're going to finish this, we've decided, Dad.'

'What about your girls? They'll be expecting yous to stay with them?'

'We're goin' to stay with them but we'll get the train up later. We've already told them.' Matt answers.

'Dad, we're staying and that's it. First to give you a hand, and second to say goodbye to Fariq and Jack.'

'And secondly,' Matt looks at Pauli. 'Should I jump in here?'

'Go on, but it's thirdly.'

'Mister... Fran, me and P have had a great weekend here doing manual labour—'

'Hard labour!' Pauli interrupts.

'Yeah, hard labour, and we find that hard to say, the manual part, never mind doin' it. But we—'

'I know lads, I did, too. And I'm gonna miss them as well.'

Matt's eyes start to well up, so he turns. 'Just goin' the john,' he croakes.

Pauli turns. 'Just going to check to... see, make sure.'

'Go ahead, son.' Fran says, and watches as he walks towards the pit.

He needs his own space too so he goes into the sitting room.

After a few minutes, Matt comes down and goes out the back. It is not long before Rita's car pulls into the garden. Fran peeks out and sits back down.

'Shit,' he decides to stay and face the wrath. 'Now this is it.'

'Heya love! I brought home a couple of chops for your dinner,' she says, as she walks by the room into the kitchen.

With him being a grown man and with his past, he should be long gone beyond the point of shaking with fear. But right now, that is exactly what he is doing, and his face is contorted while he waits for the scream. Instead, she walks in, gives him a peck on the cheek while putting a can on his table, and then sits on the couch with a bottle of beer. He glances at her while she watches the TV, or pretends to, and her face seems normal. She looks at him, smiles, then looks back at the TV as she takes a sup from her bottle. This is one of those times when he thinks of sayings like…"You can't teach an old dog new tricks." Or "Leopards can't change their spots." But the one that he is thinking of at this very moment is bang on the money. "You will never understand a woman."

He decides to chance it. 'Hello, love.'

'What's with those two standing at that massive big hole in the garden?' she asks, switching channels.

'Ya know what? I'll go find out,' he says, getting up and swiftly leaves the room. When he gets close to them, he stops a few feet behind.

'That's a new one, Dad. Ya got it off Ma, yet we didn't hear her Banshee voice screaming our business all over the bleeding county,' he turns and faces Fran. 'What did she do, give you the old... hiss through the teeth version, did she?'

He walks closer and takes Pauli's hand and places 30 euro in it, then does the same to Matt. 'That's for today's work and for another few beers and… maybe a takeout or something,' he turns and starts back towards the house.

'Dad!'

He stops and looks around.

'Shukran!' they say in unison, while grinning.

CHAPTER SIXTY-SEVEN

Fran is in his chair with a can the next morning watching the sports news at 07:03. The only difference between this morning and previous mornings is that Matt and Pauli are also there. Matt arrived at 06:37, just to be "on time for it."

The two are on their second cup of tea.

Fran thought, and still does think, that both of them look bollox tired, and they should. Hard manual labour is something that neither of them has experienced before, especially two days on the trot.

Rita walked her arse in just before seven and done a double take when she saw them. "What are ye both doing up so early?"

Fran explained and she was not at all happy with them taking a day off college. But then thought, the more hands to the shovel, and hopefully that hole will be just a dark patch by the time she gets home. She knows about the Monday to Thursday thing, but so far hasn't been given the reasoning behind it yet.

She comes in with tea in one hand and a piece of lamb in the other. She takes a bite and then a sup from her cup and the three stare at her.

'Jasus, Fran, that halal lamb is lovely. I think I'll get Sophie to pick me up another leg for the Sunday lunch. What do ye think?'

Fran is trying to keep a straight face. 'I think lamb is lamb.'

While chewing, she looks down at him. 'Lamb is lamb? What does that mean?' She looks at the boys and giggles while nodding her head at Fran.

Sleepiness has suddenly vanished, and both sit up and wait for Fran to put Rita and her giggling chewing mouth in her place. He clears his throat and explains that halal is only the method of killing the lamb, and could not alter the flavour as… lamb is lamb.

'He's right, Mam.' Pauli says, and Matt nods his head in agreement.

There is no more giggling and not even a smile, as she eats the rest of it while looking at Fran. 'Well… will I get some for Sunday or what?!'

'Yeah love, that sounds lovely.'

'Eh, will I be here to eat it?'

She looks at Matt. 'Matt, if ye weren't here, it would be like trying to drink from something that doesn't have a handle.'

Fran holds up his can. 'Ya mean somethin' like this?' he takes a quick sup and smiles at her, then does his double wink.

Matt and Pauli try to laugh quietly as she looks at her watchless wrist, then walks towards the door. 'I'm going up to get ready for work.'

When she comes down, she enters the room and stops inside the door. 'So yous are staying up there tonight?'

'We're getting the train up later and Becka and Lucy are going to meet us at the station. We'll be there for a few days.' Pauli says.

'Right Franner, just ye and Em for grub then. Fancy anything?'

'Nah love, I'm grand for tonight. I'll probably have a couple of chips.'

She looks around at the three depressed faces, and decides to have her next tea in the kitchen where there is a bit of an atmosphere, and leaves the room. Jasus, what the hell happened here over the weekend, she wonders as she puts the kettle on.

The three had been watching goals scored over the weekend, again and again. At 07:43, according to the clock on the TV, Fariq and Jack walk into the garden and the three look at each other. There is a soft knock on the door and they go out and Fran opens it.

'Good morning, lads.' Jack says.

Pauli and Matt smile meekly and nod.

'Ok Fran, just thought that we'd give you the heads up. Your container is a few minutes away and the crane is behind it, and that's why we're walking. We left my car at the entrance to the estate, as Fariq will be driving the JCB back to John's place. One thing, what end do you want the containers doors facing?'

'Eh away from the house ya know, towards the shed.'

'Grand, I'll just ring the driver,' he turns and after a bit of chatting on the phone, hangs up and turns back around. 'Sorted. We should have asked you that before.'

'Right so, come in and have some tea and that bit of breakfast.'

When they enter the kitchen, it is empty. Fran walks to the backdoor and looks around the garden but Rita is nowhere to be seen. Then he hears the front door opening and closing and footsteps going up the stairs.

He nukes the breakfast he made earlier, but fries the eggs there and then and serves it up to Jack with tea and toast. Fariq does his own thing concerning his tea, and the boys are all tea'd out. Within minutes, the sound of a truck gets louder. As the backdoor is already open, the five go out and round the side of the house and wait. It is here that Fran gets the first sight of his container as he watches it drive past, and then reverse around the corner. Matt and Pauli had helped with the work over the last few days, but only after seeing it roll by do they believe that it is actually going to happen. Seconds later, the sound of something else is heard coming up the road.

Matt looks at Pauli. 'I don't think that's the milkman.'

Fariq and Jack look at each other and grin.

'Lamb of Jasus!' Fran exclaims, on seeing the crane drive by and go around the corner as well. 'Where are they going?'

'It will be much easier to lift the container and place it from the side, because it's only going over the wall a few feet.' Fariq explains.

'And it'll be quicker. You're lucky that you have a corner house because this makes it much easier. Right, we'll be back in a few minutes. We just have to organise the lifting of this thing with the other lads.'

The two walk out of the garden and around the corner.

Rita opens the front door. 'Fran, I'm going to go now. I sort of... ye know, don't want to be here for this,' he walks over to her and they go inside. 'This is weird.'

'I know, love. Even I don't believe it's happening.'

'Well look, I'm gonna go before it starts. Are ye sure ye don't want me to bring ye back something for your tea, because I'm getting goujons for the Em's?'

'Oh, in that case, goujons sound good with a few chips and some potato salad, but no coleslaw.'

'O'Neill, you're a bleedin' headwrecker,' she picks up her bag and keys and gives him a kiss on the lips. 'See ye later, honey.'

'Later Re,' he watches her close the door. After standing looking at it for a few seconds, he walks over and opens it. 'Rita!'

She is standing at the opened car door. 'Ye want coleslaw?'

He walks to her and stares into her eyes and now she looks nervous. He kisses her, but this one is a much more passionate affair. Nearly half a minute passes before they seperate and she is shaking as she smiles at him.

'Get a room!' a voice shouts from nowhere.

She keeps looking at him with that smile.

'I'll see you later, baby.'

This snaps her out of it and she giggles nervously. 'This estate… they're all mad.'

He looks to his right at the front end of a JCB and the back end of a crane, then back at her. 'They're mad?!' they stand there laughing, but soon he is standing there alone watching her drive away. 'Things are going to change around here, and I mean big style!' he says, still looking up the road but her car is long gone.

It is nearly twenty minutes later when Pauli runs into the room wearing a high visiblity vest. 'Dad, they're just about to start, come on.'

When the two come out the backdoor, they stand next to Matt, who is also wearing a yellow vest. The crane is lifting the container. Jack and Fariq are in the garden wearing vests as well and both are holding two-way radios.

Fariq is positioned at the top of the garden beside the shed, near where he dumped the earth. Jack is standing near the centre of the pit, on the furthest side from the crane. The driver of the truck is standing on the wall at the opposite end of the garden from Fariq, and he is also vested and holding a radio.

When the container comes over the wall, it has straps looped through holes on the bottom of each corner. The truck driver drops from the wall and takes hold of the one swinging nearest him. Fariq grabs the one nearest the shed and Matt runs up and takes the other at Fariq's end. Pauli takes the one nearest him and he and Matt grin and wave to each other. Jack has been talking through his radio to the crane operator all this time. The container begins lowering slowly and the four move around, pulling here and there as they try to position it. When it is a few feet above the hole, it stops. Fariq begins removing his strap from the hole at the corner and Matt does the same. At the far end, the truck driver and Pauli are removing there ones as well.

Fran has been watching all of this closely and is very impressed with the boys. When the straps are removed, the container slowly starts to lower again, but this time the four are pushing their corners to line it up for its descent.

Then suddenly, it is landed. The hooks are released from the holes at the top and then the crane boom raises and retracts over the wall. Within a few minutes, it drives off following the truck. The five stand looking down at the container.

'Well, there you go, Fran. One new sitting room. Ok Far, you drive or me?'

'You drive, I'll shovel.'

Jack walks away and the three look at Fariq.

'Well yous didn't think we'd let yous try to cover this baby on your own?'

Jack moved the excavated earth from the gap at the side of the house to cover most of the container, while the three helped with their shovels. A few feet at the end where the doors are was left uncovered. That part would need a lot of TLC and that would be Fran's department. They stayed for another tea before leaving. When all the goodbyes were said, Fariq drove off in the JCB with Jack sitting inside, on the way to get his car at the entrance to the estate. The three go back and stand looking at the rectangular mess of earth.

'A bit of raking and some grass seeds and in a few weeks, you'll never notice a thing.'

'Yeah that's true, Matt.' Fran says, scratching his head.

It is then that Pauli realises that they can still make it to college. They have twenty-three minutes to get showered, dressed and to the station.

'I'll never make it, P.'

'You will if you shower here!'

'What about me clothes? These are sweaty and stinking!'

'Matt, we're the same build, grab something upstairs.'

'Right, let's do it! At least that way, we see the girls sooner. Who goes first?'

'You snooze, you lose, pal!' Pauli says, running for the backdoor.

Matt runs after him. 'Ok, I'll sort me clothes out then.'

'And I think I'll have a sausage and bacon sarnie with a brew!' Fran says, with a smile while turning towards the house.

They make it to the station four minutes before the train.

'We were lucky there, pal!'

Pauli is so excited at the thoughts of seeing Lucy sooner than he expected, and of tonight and the next few days and nights, that he finds it hard to speak. So he nods at Matt and shakes a little.

CHAPTER SIXTY-EIGHT

When they walk into class, the girls stare at them for a moment before smiling and coming over. 'Well, hello there handsome! I thought you told me that you had to help your dad today?' Lucy asks, taking his hand.

'Wasn't as much to do as we thought.'

Matt and Becka aren't as restrained and jump into a hug and start kissing.

Mister Collon enters the room. 'Well well, at least we know who found love in this class,' some of the students laugh half-heartedly at his comment. 'Ok class, now that we are all here, I have to tell yous that I had a chat with Miss McCabe this morning when she came in to collect her items. She asked me to say a "big high" and to say that "she really misses the gang" as she put it.'

Most students look towards the closed door, expecting it to open and for her to show herself with a smile at any second, but instead Mister Collon grabs there attention with a clearing of his throat and a cough and they look back at him.

'So there, I've relayed her message. Unfortunately, she could not stay and tell yous this herself, as she had a hospital appointment about,' he glances at his watch. 'Just over nine minutes ago,' there are a few "Ahhs" from students while looking back at the door. 'But during our little chat,' all heads turn back to him. 'She did mention a few things that she has given yous to prepare for in the coming weeks. She gave me a list of these projects and one in particular caught my eye immediately,' he pauses and they all stand looking at him and wait for him to finish. 'And... I have decided to give it a shot today! Miss McCabe was also kind enough to give me the music associated with said projects,' he pauses and looks around the class and notices that the students look a cross between bored and annoyed at his stopping and starting. 'Ok, so can anybody guess?' he looks around again and now most are either looking at the ceiling or exhaling loudly, or both. 'No? Well before I tell yous, I would like Misters Wolfe and O'Neill to join me centre stage.'

'Oh shit!' Matt mutters, under his breath.

'I think I know what it is.' Lucy whispers to Becka.

When they walk over to Mister Collon, he takes out a coin and looks from Matt to Pauli and back. 'Ok... heads or tales?'

They say nothing.

'Come on, pick!'

Again they remain silent.'Ok, I'll pick. Mister Wolfe, you are heads,' he looks at Pauli.

'I get it, I'm tails.'

'Why did you not say so sooner?'

After a quick glance at each of them, he flips the coin into the air, catches it and places it on the back of his hand.

'Hold on, hold on. What's this in aid of?' Pauli asks, before the coin's uncovered.

Mister Collon looks across at the table which has some plastic bags, his own bag and the portable sound system on it. 'That!'

Matt looks at the table. 'What?'

'That!' he repeats. 'The winner gets that piece of brown cloth.'

Giggling starts around the class.

'Good luck, P.'

'You too, Matt.'

'Alright, one… two… three!' he removes his hand to show heads. 'Congratulations, Mister Wolfe. YOU have just one a piece of cloth!'

Matt closes his eyes as it dawns on him. 'Oh no!'

Pauli cannot help but smile as he has also just realised what is going to happen.

Mister Collon claps his hands twice. 'Ok, who wants to be the two Mexicans?'

Other than Matt, Pauli and Mister Collon, all but two people do not raise their hands in the class, and they are Becka and Lucy. Out of the rest, the two gay lads are picked and are each given their line, if it could be called that.

The remaining students are divided into two groups and each group is given their word to say. There will be a five-minute prep and then they will go for it.

After Mister Collon appoints himself bartender, he gives Pauli and Matt word sheets just to refresh. Becka and Lucy decide not to approach them until just before the beginning. When the lads put down their pages, the girls make their move over to them before it starts.

'Kick his butt, Matt!' Becka says, just before kissing him.

Lucy kisses Pauli while patting his bum. 'Kick his further, O'Neill!'

'Ready to go in thirty!' Mister Collon announces, and the girls make their way back to their group. Matt and Pauli are standing in front of him when he calls out ten. It passes quickly because suddenly there is the sound of piano music. The two begin to sing and dance. Both have obviously practiced it as they are doing it almost identical to the DVD Miss McCabe had shown the class months before. Then it comes to the part when Matt ties the cloth around Pauli's head and the class laugh. There is a similar reaction when he jumps onto Matt's back. When they point at one of the gay lads, he shouts his line. Then at the other who does the same. Becka and Lucy's group are next to be pointed at by the two and deliver their word with gusto. The other group is next and they are determined to outdo Becka and Lucy's group, which they fail miserably at, as someone screeches loudly instead of shouting. Immediately, the two turn behind and face Mister Collon who flawlessly delivers his three words to the closing line of the song, and does so in an almost perfect voice and facial expression. Matt and Pauli then walk to the table and stand either side of it as the song ends. The class clap and cheer, and Lucy and Becka provide ear splitting whistles as Matt and Pauli take bows and blow kisses around the room. Mister Collon cannot help but to get involved as well and copies what the boys are doing. Only after things have quietened down, does he point at the two gay lads. 'Justin and Mike, who wants the cloth?'

He reassures everyone that they will get a go, and after the first performance, the rest of the students are really looking forward to it. Lucy and Becka partner back up with the two as Mike and Justin get their five to read over the words.

'I think that was a 50-50 butt kicking.' Becka says.

'I have to agree, but our group was better at the shouting of our one word.'

The two giggle as Mister Collon walks by on his way to the table.

'Wolfe, O'Neill that will take some beating. Well done!'

'Shit! Was that a compliment?' Matt whispers, looking around at the three.

'I think it was.' Becka says, almost disbelievingly.

'Yes it was Matt, for you AND Pauli!' he clarifies, without turning.

Lucy takes his hand and leads him away a few steps from Becka and Matt.

'You just keep amazing me. Dancing, singing.'

'I amaze you?!' he shakes his head. 'You don't have to do anything to make me feel like that about you, Lu.'

She kisses him. 'I can't wait to get you into my bed later.'

'Sounds like I have something to worry about.'

She grins. 'Don't worry, O'Neill... I won't bite.'